DESIRE'S AWAKENING

In the heavy silence, she turned her back on him and walked to the door. When her hand was on the knob, she heard his voice, and she realized that every nerve in her body had been hoping to hear it.

"Ravenna."

She heard him approach, and turned to find him staring at her. For a moment she, too, simply stared. All her senses became aware of him—his handsomeness, the rhythm of his breathing, the masculine scent of him.

"Ravenna," he murmured, then pulled her into his arms.

He was no longer her employer, but simply a man cradling a woman. And so they both forgot themselves as his lips claimed hers. It was her first kiss, something so magical that it blocked out all sight and sound and anything but itself. Her whole body became soft and open to him. She felt a kind of passion that young girls read about, the passion that leads to ravishment, then regret. What power was there! Suddenly she understood how a heroine could risk everything for a moment like this . . .

Secrets of the Heart

Joan Lord Matthews

Zebra Books
Kensington Publishing Corp.
http://www.zebrabooks.com

ZEBRA BOOKS are published by

Kensington Publishing Corp.
850 Third Avenue
New York, NY 10022

Zebra and the Z logo Reg. U.S. Pat. & TM Off.

First Printing: February, 1998
10 9 8 7 6 5 4 3 2 1

Printed in the United States of America

For my beautiful daughter, Lauren
who was welcomed into the world
on June 4, 1992
by a midwife's loving hands

Book I

Village of Taplow, Berkshire, England

One

December 21, 1843

The hour before dawn is well known to mystics, madmen, and midwives. Called the uhta *by our Saxon forebears, it is said to be the darkest hour—when spirits are the most active, when the greatest number of souls depart, and when the most babies are born. It is a time of pain and truth, when the soul's troubles—the* uht-caeren—*cannot be ignored. And yet it is said that God most often hears our prayers in that hour, and the mind is most receptive to the secrets of the heart . . .*

As Midwife Ravenna Marisse walked home during the *uhta* of the shortest day of 1843, she felt too tired to control her troubled thoughts.

She'd been awake, and cold, for the previous three days. Leaky cottage roofs had given her little protection as she'd helped two village women push their newborns into the world. The final, predawn birth—Maggie Warren's sixth— was not a happy event for anyone concerned, including the baby, who protested bitterly as he was pulled out of heaven and into man's hellish realm of poverty, disease, and too many mouths to feed. Before she left, Ravenna slipped Matt

Warren a packet of herbs for his wife, to be brewed into a tea and taken every morning.

Hopefully, they would put off Maggie's seventh child for a while.

Ravenna—or Raven, as her late father had often called her—walked home alone, with only his well-worn medical bag for company. The village paths were largely deserted, yet she'd refused escort from the eldest Warren boy. She carried no money, and besides, none of the cottagers would lay a hand on her.

The prospect of her own bed and an adequate fire kept Raven's quivering limbs upright. After a good rest, she'd heat up a bath. Unfortunately, there was no simple means to cleanse away the images that plagued her mind.

She'd spent a day and a night with young Jinny Shewan, letting the girl dig her nails into Ravenna's own cold-numbed wrists. Being the girl's first, the baby was slow and stubborn and ripped her mother up, which required all the stitching skills Raven's father had taught her. Jinny screamed and cursed as the barbaric hooped mending needle moved in and out of her torn flesh. Her burly husband had to hold her down, biting back his own empathetic cries.

If only Raven's father had been there, to encourage her, and remind her of her mission. *Ignore the pain,* he'd command. For the pain a doctor inflicts wards off the much greater suffering meted out by indifferent Nature.

When Raven got home, she was seeing black spots before her eyes. Her head throbbed. Her fingers were stiff as clothespins. After doffing her bloody apron and somehow managing to build a good fire, she sank into her father's massive armchair—one of the few items to have escaped the auctioneer's block—and wondered yet again if she'd done the right thing by coming to this place. In London, she could have married, a young medical student perhaps, with whom she could work side by side until the children came. After all, she was only twenty—not yet consigned to her spinning wheel.

And yet she was not ready to love another man, not ready to live with anyone again. How could she endure another complicated, tormented male mind like her father's? How could she share another life of sleeplessness, of suicidal dedication, perhaps only to be ruined by the thoughtless act of an equally thoughtless lord, who cared not a whit for the welfare of others, but only for his own pleasures.

Her father's career as a surgeon had come to an end when he was run down by a young viscount, who was far too drunk to have been driving his own gig. Though his life was spared, her father's right hand was crushed beyond mending and had to be amputated at the wrist. It was at a crucial time in his career—he and a young colleague, a Dr. Robert Liston, had been experimenting with an exciting new substance—diethyl ether—which could induce what they called *anaesthesia,* "insensibility." With it, man could conquer pain, and silence forever the screams that accompanied every stroke of the surgeon's knife.

Ether would assure Liston's place in history—and send Raven's father to his grave, for he began inhaling the stuff himself, to deaden the pain of a broken life.

As Raven drifted off to sleep that dark December morning, relishing the feel of the fire's heat upon her toes, she saw once more her father's face—the wild look in his eyes, the unshaven jaw, the scum around his lips. In those last days, he'd become repulsive to her. The ether made him violent while it was taking effect, and the furniture that hadn't been sold was either slashed or smashed with his one good hand. Their entire flat reeked of ether and vomit, and when the vapors finally killed him, Ravenna was happy to move.

On her meager salary as a doctor's assistant, she could not afford the rents in London, so Raven chose a far humbler place—the village of Taplow, where the air was clean, the Thames was nearby, and the people were in dire need of medical care. She'd set herself up as a midwife but gradually became a wise woman of sorts for the village, dispensing herbs and mixing medicines. The one doctor in the area was not like her father—the man required payment—but Raven needed little to sustain herself. She grew vegetables, kept chickens, and was amply supplied with milk by the Warrens, who kept a cow and whose five—now six—children were always in need of some kind of physic.

A firm knocking startled Raven out of her reverie.

She kept her eyes closed, hoping the caller would go away. She knew of no third woman near her time, and whoever it was could simply come back in the evening with his sniffles or banged thumb.

The knocking persisted.

Go away, her weary mind said, and she slipped back into sleep.

"Be anyone home?" an unfamiliar voice called, and the knocking intensified.

"Who is it?" Ravenna croaked hoarsely.

"Miss, be you there?"

Raven struggled to get to her feet, but utter exhaustion had set in, a kind of living rigor mortis. Her brief taste of sleep had left her feeling much worse than before.

"Mistress?" the voice repeated. "Be Midwife Ravenna Marisse within?"

"Come in, the door isn't bolted," she said, somewhat thankful she'd been too tired to change into a sleeping gown.

A well-dressed, aging manservant entered the cottage, bowing and shuffling and looking ill at ease.

She turned her head to face him, but still could not rise from the chair.

"Yes?" she asked. "I am Ravenna Marisse. I don't believe I know you."

"Beggin' your pardon, miss. My name is John Travers,

over from the big house." Lowering his eyes, he gave an awkward bow.

"Forgive me, John Travers, for not greeting you properly, but I haven't had a wink of sleep since—I can't even remember."

The man fidgeted with his hands.

"Beggin' your pardon again, but they at the big house, they do ask that you come with me. Mistress Anne, she . . . be . . ."

Ravenna had seen this before, the male embarrassment over the process of giving birth.

"When did the pains start?" she asked.

"Well, I'm not sure, but Mistress Anne, she took to her bed several days ago. The doctor sent for you, miss."

"The doctor?" Raven asked, a bit startled. "Dr. Longacre?"

The man nodded.

This was a surprise, since Longacre disapproved of her—she practiced witchcraft, not medicine.

"Mistress Anne . . she be a frail little thing, and it being her first, that is, the first to come to its time . . ."

Ravenna blinked her eyes a few times, trying to keep them open, then rose unsteadily to her feet.

"I'm afraid I don't have a horse."

"I've brought the gig, miss. 'Tis a bit cold, but she's fast. Mister Charles can race her—"

"That will be fine, John Travers," Ravenna said, though she should have taken this statement as an omen.

The viscount had been racing his gig through London when he ran her father down.

But she did not heed her instincts or her body's craving for sleep. Instead, she bundled herself up in her cloak, which felt damp and uninviting, picked up her medical bag, regretfully doused the fire, and followed the man unsteadily out the door.

She was not prepared for her reentry into the bitter cold.

"Let me help you," John Travers said, swinging into the gig, then pulling her up beside him. He was still strong and may have been handsome before too much sun and hard work had etched deep lines into his face.

Ravenna huddled next to him on the hard seat, suddenly craving the company of this human being who had no pressing medical need.

"So Mistress Anne has lost a child before?" Raven asked after they had settled into their journey.

"She's been with child several times," the man answered. "But never come to her time. Just like the others, Mistress Clarity . . . and Mistress Justine. It's the—the—"

"Oh, yes, I know," Raven said, a spate of rumors tumbling into her head. "I've heard talk in the village. It's regarded as some sort of curse—on the whole family, isn't it?"

" 'Tis not something they at the big house do talk about," the man said with great seriousness. "But 'tis true enough."

The big house. Harlixton Hall. With four strong sons still in residence, and all of their wives barren.

Well, the curse is about to be broken, Raven thought, *if I have any say in it.*

"We all do miss the sounds of children," Travers said. And he told her of the stillbirths, the miscarriages, the wife who died, and the one who fled.

As Travers rambled on, calling all the "Misters" and "Mistresses" by their Christian names, Raven noted that he mentioned five wives, a spate of dead infants, but only three sons.

"And the fourth son?" she asked. "What is his part in this?"

"Mister Garreth?" the man replied a bit ominously. "He's the eldest, and must needs take a wife. But there's never been a young lady to turn his head, miss. He's as cold as his mother, my Lady Philippa—that is, after she married that vicar. 'Afore that, ah, she was a charmer, so full of life she was. I knew her since she was a girl. It was that vicar what did something to her, closed her up like her father 'afore her and her son after her. 'Twas the vicar what put a curse on the family, on his own children. But God willing, you'll help Mistress Anne defeat it."

Raven settled back into her seat, wondering what her life would have been like had she married or been sired by a good workingman like her present company. Would she be happy sharing her thoughts with a simple, honest mind, a man who believed in curses and probably ghosts as well? Would she have missed the crazed discourse with tortured geniuses that was commonplace in her father's house? Those questions would remain unanswered as she leaned into the comfort of her escort's sleeve, not knowing—or caring—what lay ahead.

Two

She must have fallen asleep, for Raven's next conscious image was of an enormous house, with more windows than she could count. The front portico was bigger than some cottages she'd visited, and jutting out on either side of the main house were two long, curving wings, each adorned with enough columns to rival the Parthenon.

Ravenna blinked a few times, wondering if by some miracle she was back in London, gazing at the Palace.

"Here we are, miss," John Travers said brightly, still sitting beside her and not at all minding that she remained huddled against him.

Her limbs were useless logs, her spirit weak and lazy, and she had neither the desire nor the energy to alight from her seat. A sorry soldier she was proving to be, not at all up to defeating a curse.

Fortunately she had some stimulating herbs in her bag, which she would try to take, hoping that no one would notice and think her an opium eater.

Travers swung from his perch, then helped her to descend from the gig. She was glad her father could not see her wobbly legs. He would have chided her weakness, saying, "What kind of doctor will you be, then, if you can't stay awake for three short days?" But good John Travers, ever tolerant of her distress, swung his strong arm around her, helping her limp toward the entrance to the north wing.

A wizened porter of some sort nodded from his tiny booth as they entered.

Travers escorted her into a long, winding hall, and they walked past pantries and kitchens and other rooms for servants. Undoubtedly the front door was reserved for the family's equals, while the entrance they'd used was for tradesmen and inferiors.

Eventually their journey led them to the front reception hall, whose vastness astounded Raven even if the dark, dour furnishings did not. Large Turkish rugs adorned the floor, and heavy velvet drapes covered the windows. Lined up along one wall was a collection of well-polished suits of armor, and Ravenna was amused by how small those legendary knights of the Round Table must have been. Another wall was taken up by an immense fireplace, which was flanked on either side by two life-size portraits—one of a stern older man seated at a simple writing desk, while the other was of a fetching young woman standing with her hands clasped behind her awkwardly arched back.

Travers noticed she was staring at the woman and motioned for her to have a closer look.

"Likely you're wondering why she be standing like that," he said. " 'Tis Lady Philippa, and it seems she was carrying her babe—young Master Garreth, that is—on her back. When the vicar—God have mercy on his unforgiving soul—saw the portrait, he declared it heathen and unseemly, and had the artist paint over the child. But it were too late to change the lady's pose."

Raven stared at the young woman's eyes. The girl seemed innocent enough, with the first blush of motherhood on her. What toil or torment had transformed her—as the gossips told it—into a haggard hermitesse who now lived somewhere in the upper floors?

"I wonder if she would see me," Raven mused aloud.

"She be sick," Travers answered, "and will see no one."

"Perhaps I could help her. I have—"

"No, miss," he stated firmly.

"But—"

"No," Travers said, "and speak no more of it." In his eyes was an unexpected hardness that brooked no disobedience. "But come," he continued, his kindliness returning, "Mistress Anne be upstairs."

Raven nodded, but resolved that she would see Lady Philippa before she left the house.

He turned her gently, then pointed toward a wide, intricately carved wooden staircase. When she had more energy, she would ask Travers its history and derivation, for it seemed more suitable to the extravagant yet mineral-poor French. The English, that is, the upper classes, generally chose marble or slate.

As she and John approached the stairs, Ravenna wondered where she would find the strength to ascend that intimidating column. She craved the stimulants in her bag.

Her strength came, as it had, from her companion, who still gripped her firmly and began pulling her up each step. She promised herself that, when she took her leave, she would examine more closely the garish wooden carvings of medieval figures protruding at regular intervals from the banister and the portraits of prior Harlixtons arranged in a zigzag fashion up the wall. But on this maiden ascent, she had not even the strength to look straight ahead.

Closing her eyes, she allowed her body to relax, relishing a few more moments of weakness before her work recommenced. Almost immediately she slipped into an ambulatory sleep, her legs climbing without direction from her mind. John's arm tightened around her waist as her head sagged heavily into his shoulder. Her rag-doll posture was so comfortable that for a moment she actually believed herself to be back in her own bed, just settling into a cozy rest.

It was in this stuporous state that she began to hear murmurings, deep, hushed tones, descending toward her. The tones became words, two distinct voices, young, male, educated. She cracked open her eyes and saw two vague figures coming down the stairs.

"Who's that?" one of the voices asked, and after a confused moment, Ravenna realized the question referred to her.

"John, what's the meaning of this?" a second, deeper voice asked.

Ravenna's eyes snapped wide open.

John Travers murmured in her ear, " 'Tis all right, miss," but were she not so exhausted, she would have been horribly embarrassed.

For another confused moment, nothing more was said, and she simply gaped at the two male figures. The shorter, fair-haired one had a slight, narrow build, and he sported a thin, unbecoming beard that looked as if the moths had gotten to it. He seemed distracted and impatient, looking beyond his servant's shoulder and down the stairs as if awaiting someone else. His companion, however—a tall, dark tower of a man—stared directly ahead. That is, he stared directly at Raven. There was a hardness in his eyes, and he seemed to be unmasking her, exposing her as a fraud.

"Here's Mister Garreth," John Travers said respectfully, "and his brother Mister Charles." Nodding in her direction, he told them, "This be Miss Ravenna Marisse, the—"

"My wife is upstairs," said the fair-haired man, turning his attention to her. "Please hurry." Ravenna recognized by the sound of his voice that it was he who had initially spoken.

"I'll do my best," she replied, wondering how these two men—different as David and Goliath—could be brothers.

Letting go of John's arm, she forced herself upward on her own power. As she passed her dark accuser, her arm brushed the sleeve of his jacket. She flinched, her inhaled breath catching in her throat.

"Your reputation precedes you," he murmured. "See that you live up to it."

She nodded, looking modestly toward the floor. But to her horror, her eyes became willful, and they tried to wander immodestly up the contours of his body. Even half-asleep, her nerves reacted to his presence. He was the handsomest, most intimidating man she had ever seen, and though she had thought herself indifferent to the male realm, at that moment she became drenched in an unreasoning, girlish desire to touch him. Her cheeks became hot as she struggled to keep her eyes cast down, away from the curve of his thigh, the tight cut of his trousers, the flair of his torso—

Abruptly she pulled away and took several rapid steps, focusing her attention on the landing above. She could no longer remain in this man's presence.

She was sure he mistook this for haughtiness, for as she proceeded up the stairs, she felt his gaze yet upon her, those dark eyes drawing her back.

It was a fleeting, chance encounter—one easily forgotten in the flurry of such a time. And yet much later, as she reflected on that moment, she realized that she was forever changed—the way the loss of virtue, accomplished in a mere moment, forever changes a woman. Garreth took something from her as she passed him on the stairs—was it her innocence? her independence? her solitude? She would never know for sure.

She knew only that, in meeting him, she had crossed a bridge into an unknown realm, and that for her, as she was soon to discover, there would be no going back.

Three

She was ushered into a bedchamber that was full of contrasts—both to her own simple life and to what she had just experienced in the dingy, dank cottages of the village women.

This room seemed as large as a hospital ward, and Raven thought, with some disdain, about how many women could have labored comfortably in such an immense chamber.

A pale young woman lay in the enormous four-poster bed, warmed not only by an ample quilt but by a roaring fire across the room. In fact, having just come out of the December cold, Raven thought the room stifling.

The furnishings were lavish as a king's, and she recalled at that odd moment the divine admonition to sell all that one had and give it to the poor. Certainly the poor of her times could have benefitted from the proceeds of such unnecessary splendor.

The woman in the bed, however, was no different from any other terrified mother-to-be. She had a panicked, lost-lamb look on her exhausted face—perhaps she was shocked that she could not fob this obligation off on the servants, that birth, unlike wealth, did not spare the rich from doing their own work.

She lay perfectly still as Raven approached her, then suddenly her eyes opened wide and she began to thrash and cry out hoarsely.

"Mistress Anne," said Dr. Longacre, whom Raven suddenly noticed for the first time, "you must bear down. Don't fight the work of your body. Help your baby to be born."

Standing next to the bed was another woman, with the same lost look as this Mistress Anne.

The pain subsided, and the woman fell back exhausted, closed her eyes, and blocked out the doctor and her opulent surroundings.

Clearly both the patient and the doctor had lost control of the situation.

Longacre turned to Raven finally and said, "My assistant tells me you are quite successful with stubborn cases."

He nodded toward a young man who was sorting through a selection of ghastly-looking medical instruments. If Anne had had the strength to notice them, she might have given birth out of sheer fright.

Raven looked farther around the room, noting the presence of several other maids standing uselessly in corners. After donning a clean surgical apron, she asked if she could be left alone with the patient and one other woman, a servant or a relative, someone Anne liked and trusted.

The doctor seemed caught between annoyance and relief—annoyance, Raven guessed, because she was ordering him out of his own sick chamber, and undoubtedly because she might take credit for breaking the Harlixton curse. But relief as well, since he had clearly run out of patience for the fragile china doll who was no match for a woman's work.

As soon as the room was cleared of all extraneous persons—including the crestfallen assistant—and Anne had finished screaming through another useless pain, Raven walked over to the bed very confidently and spoke with as much authority as she could muster.

"Anne," she stated, overlooking the shocked gasp of the maid who remained, that a midwife would call her mistress by such a familiar form of address. "Anne," she repeated, grasping Anne's right arm, "you must get up and walk."

A moan escaped the woman's lips, and she gave an exhausted shake of her head.

"Anne, you must," Raven insisted, and she practically pulled the girl to her feet. Immediately Anne's knees buckled and she collapsed against Raven's chest.

"Help me get her over to a chair," Raven shouted in the general direction of the maid, then together they half carried Anne to a comfortable-looking wing chair, where she collapsed again.

"Now," Raven said, turning to the maid, "what's your name?"

"Manda," the maid replied, making a slight curtsy.

"Manda, bring me my bag." When she had complied, Raven pulled out a small packet of herbs and bade her go make a strong tea with it. Raven looked at the hearth and noticed that a pot of water had already been suspended over the fire. Good, she thought, since Anne's lips were bruised black from dehydration. With unsteady hands, she took out a pinch of *ma huang*—a stimulating herb used in the Orient—and placed it under Mistress Anne's tongue; Raven was too tired now to be sensible and take some herself. Anne's eyes opened briefly and she tried to spit it out.

"Leave it in, Anne," Raven commanded, and when the maid gasped again, Raven turned and said, "This is not a social gathering. A person in pain responds better to their Christian name."

Then she urged Anne to get up again, and again dragged her to her feet.

Soon she had Anne walking around, coaxing the girl to lean into her and push downward during the pains. Miraculously Anne began to comply, perhaps because the stimulant was doing its job.

"Now Anne," Raven said, "I know that you are a lady, and that all this must be terribly frightening."

Anne murmured something weakly that indicated her agreement.

"Birth is messy—as well as frightening—for everyone, including the Queen, and it will require you to forget your station in life for a while. After you have your baby in your arms, we'll clean you both up, you'll be every bit a lady again, and what we went through will be our secret." She looked out into the room and Manda's curly head bobbed in compliance. "Your husband will never know what you endured to give birth to your baby—except that you showed great courage, as much as a soldier in battle. Do you understand?"

Anne took a shallow, trembling breath, then nodded tentatively.

Leading Anne back to the bed, Raven bade her to recline, saying that she had delivered hundreds of women and that Anne must not fear her hands. Then gently Raven reached under the wrinkled nightdress to examine her patient. Anne flinched at this contact.

"When did the doctor last examine you?" Raven asked, annoyance creasing her brow.

"Well . . ." Anne licked her lips. "Not since . . . I—I can't remember." Which was as Raven had thought. He, too, had treated Anne like a lady, to the point where he was forgetting his duty to her as a patient.

As Raven examined Mistress Anne, she felt dismay. Anne's body was nowhere near ready to expel the child. In fact, Raven had some doubt as to whether the girl was capable of doing so. There was a certain intrinsic deformity of the female organs, some immaturity perhaps, and something else, some overall problem that could not be defined. Bending her head, Raven listened to the baby's heartbeat and found it to be slow and erratic. She began fearing the child would not survive the hazards of birth, or if it did, its mother might not.

The curse on this family would not be broken so easily.

"Where's the tea?" Raven asked sharply, and within a

moment a steaming cup was offered to her by Manda's trembling hands.

"Drink this," she commanded, handing it to Anne, "and when you've finished, I want you to drink another cup. And here . . . come here and sit on the floor—"

"The floor?" both the lady and her maid asked in unison.

"Yes, the floor, like a peasant tailor. And when a pain comes, I want you to put the soles of your feet together and press."

At that, Anne struggled to smile. "Well, Manda," she said with something approaching mirth in her voice, " 'tis only what your mother and my own endured to give life to us both. Though I doubt if either was asked to behave like a savage to do so."

"Yes, ma'am . . . I mean, no, ma'am," Manda replied nervously, curtsying for want of a better thing to do.

Presently Raven had Anne drinking, sitting, and pressing, and for over an hour, Anne seemed to endure the pain fairly well. In odd moments, the midwife allowed her mind to wander from her patient back to the young men on the stairs.

One of them had done this to her, opened her thighs and buried his seed deep within her.

The other man . . . Raven shuddered involuntarily as an image of him flashed in her mind, the heat of passion drenching his brow, his eyes closed, his body convulsing—

"Help me!" Anne shrieked suddenly, breaking into Raven's thoughts. "It's getting worse . . . I—I can't stand it!"

But her voice was strong, if hoarse, and Raven knew the girl was making progress.

"I'm going to examine you again," said Raven, helping Anne to her feet and leading her back to the bed.

Anne averted her eyes when Raven probed inside her.

"I have good news," Raven said finally as she withdrew her hand. "The birth is imminent."

"God bless you, ma'am," Manda exclaimed, and clapped her pudgy hands together.

"Now I need something heavy," Raven instructed the little maid. "An object too heavy for a woman to pick up. Ask several of the footmen to bring something made of iron—an anvil or something similar. Bring it to this room."

"An anvil, miss?" Manda said meekly. "I don't know as we have an—"

"I don't care what it is," Ravenna said impatiently. "Something too heavy for you or I to pick up."

Thinking the midwife a bit touched in the head—and indeed Raven was so tired, she felt the room swaying every time she rose to her feet—Manda nevertheless curtsied and went off in search of an anvil-like object.

"Now Anne, listen to me," Raven said. "As I've told you, your baby is ready to be born. He doesn't know he is about to be part of a wealthy family in a civilized country. As far as he knows, he could be a Stone Age barbarian, a medieval peasant, or the son of King Alfred the Great. He expects you to help him into the world the way every mother has always done. So it is time to forget utterly that you are a lady and become a handmaiden of Nature. When the next pain comes, I want you to close your eyes and push your baby. Here, I'll prop you up and you push with your feet against me."

Awkwardly, Anne got into the position Raven wanted.

"And I want you to grunt . . ."

"Grunt?" Anne gasped, as if the very word were indecent.

"Yes, and pant, and pretend you're a bargeman lifting a heavy load. Remember, your husband will never know. And enough of girlish screams. They serve no purpose."

When the next pain came, Anne let out an anemic moan and pushed feebly against the midwife.

"No, no, that won't help," Raven snapped. "Let me show you"—and she let out a lusty groan that startled Mistress Anne.

Just then there came a knock on the door, and a soft masculine voice called out, "We're come with the, uh, we've come with the broken bell from the steeple. It's mighty heavy, miss. Will that do?"

A bell, Raven thought. Not exactly what she had in mind, but it would have to suffice.

"Anne, lie down," Raven said, helping her patient back into bed and covering her quickly. "Remember, no one will know what is transpiring in this room."

Two awkward, embarrassed footmen entered the room hesitantly, trying not to look toward the bed. They were carrying a hastily cleaned-off steeple bell with an obvious crack down the side.

"Where d'you want it, miss?" one of them asked.

Studying it, Raven said, "Lay it on its side in the center of the floor."

Thinking she had bats in her own belfry, they complied, then bowed awkwardly and made a hasty retreat.

Anne, to her surprise, was actually smiling at their embarrassment.

"Now, Anne," Raven said, uncovering her once more and helping her to her feet, "we're going to walk over to the bell, and squat—"

"Squat?" Again she spoke with distaste, at such an unladylike word.

"Yes." Leading Anne over to the bell, Raven sat on her haunches, pulling her skirts aside so Anne could see her bent knees. "When the next pain comes, I want you to grasp the sides of the bell and try to lift it . . . Of course, you won't be able to, but strain as if your child's life depended on it. And all the while grunt and groan. You're a savage for the next hour, remember. Not a fine lady in her civilized house, but something even finer, I promise you."

When the next pain came, Anne did exactly as she was told. Raven got alongside her, and she grunted and panted as well, remembering how the old Indian woman had demonstrated to her father using a large pot full of earth. The hag told him how the savages in America gave birth easily compared to the suffering and agony of England's civilized wives. The woman had been sold into slavery as a young girl, but this piece of chattel had had more medical wisdom than the royal surgeon himself.

Light was just appearing across the dull winter horizon when the squalls of a baby boy filled the room. A child of the *uhta,* whose newborn will to live had apparently defeated the forces of death at work during that hour and in that family.

A smile broke out on Anne's lips as Raven handed the bundled-up infant into her waiting arms.

"I did it," Anne whispered, gazing in awe at the tiny creature fashioned of her own flesh.

Raven smiled back at her, suppressing the personal longing she always felt after handing a baby into another woman's waiting arms.

"He's perfect, Mistress Anne," Ravenna said, inclining her head in deference to her patient and the child.

That slight gesture made Raven's temples throb. Her former exhaustion was rapidly returning. Her hands shook as she clamped and cut the cord and delivered the afterbirth.

As eager as she was to return home, however, there was still work to do. She probed the woman's abdomen, noting that the womb remained flaccid, that her body had not begun to stanch the inner bleeding. Ignoring Anne's startled cries, she pushed firmly on the pelvic area, coaxing the womb to retract, for Anne was losing a lot of blood. She also bade Manda to begin mopping up the spreading stain.

"Do you have to do this now?" Anne asked testily, and Raven knew she was hurting her. "I want my husband. Can't you leave me alone?"

"No," Raven retorted, remembering her father's admonitions. *Distance yourself from the pain, or you will never help the patient.*

Manda let out a small cry as she examined her blood-drenched towel and ran to get another one.

"I'm all right," Anne insisted. "And he is perfect, isn't he? My own little perfect—oh!" she moaned in response to Raven's probing. "Everything is fine now. Stop that at once!"

"I'm sorry, Mistress Anne, but I have to continue. Please forgive me."

"Where's Ch-Charles?" she asked, starting to slur her words.

For a quick moment, Raven assessed the situation. With her knowledge, she could save this patient, unless—and she shuddered at the thought—unless Anne could not be saved.

"Mistress Anne," she said loudly, but this time the girl ignored her, focusing instead on the baby.

"Perfect," Anne murmured.

"Anne," Ravenna fairly shouted into her face. "You must stand up." Then over her shoulder. she cried, "Manda, help me"

The little maid rushed over, picked up the baby and placed it gently in the cradle by the side of the bed, then helped her lift Anne up. The relaxed body undulated precariously, her arms and legs swaying like reeds in a strong wind. She was much worse than Raven had thought.

"Anne," she ordered. "Stay awake."

Once more they had her walking about, while Raven prayed that the exercise and the downward pull of gravity would help contract the womb. It was what the old Indian had told her.

But Anne's body wasn't responding. Her blood was staining a crooked trail upon the rug. Her mass became heavier as she steadily lost consciousness. The baby was squalling, protesting his lack of maternal contact.

"Anne!" Raven shouted, then she slapped her patient soundly on the cheek just as the doctor and the anxious husband burst through the door.

"Is it—" Charles began happily, then stopped in his tracks and looked at Raven quizzically.

"Quickly, sir," she shouted at him. "Help me keep your wife on her feet. She's hemorrhaging."

"On her feet?" the man asked in bewilderment.

"Are you mad?" the doctor cried. "Get her back in bed at once."

"Is the baby all right?" the husband asked.

"I think so, sir," she said. "I haven't had the time . . . Now please help me."

"You're dismissed," the doctor said. "What you propose will kill her."

"Help me," she said to Charles.

The husband looked helplessly from face to face.

"Decide, sir," the doctor said.

"Your wife is dying," Raven said.

"Under your care," the doctor added with an edge of cruel triumph.

Anne let out a sigh, then collapsed completely in Manda's arms.

"Lord a-mercy," Manda gasped.

"Decide, sir," the doctor insisted, as if the major issue were political rather than medical.

"Help her!" Charles cried to both of them.

"She's f-fainted," Raven said, so exhausted she, too, was slurring her words, yet her ears were too numb to hear how badly she must have sounded. Too tired to say anything more, she simply began pulling Mistress Anne toward the largest chair. The Indian woman had told her to avoid the supine position at all costs.

Charles lunged over to her side and slung his wife's slack form into his arms.

"Where do you want her?" he asked.

"In the chair," she replied, pointing. "And Manda, quickly, get my bag." When she had it in her hands, she pulled out several packets of herbs, tore off the paper coverings, and quickly mixed their contents.

"What's all that?" the doctor asked mockingly. "More witchcraft?"

"It's her only chance—" she began, but he cut her off.

"Leave," he ordered.

"But sir—"

"You're dismissed."

This time it was her turn to look helplessly toward Charles, who said, "Don't be too hasty, Longacre. After all, my son lives, thanks to—"

Without waiting for permission, Raven opened Anne's slack jaw and pushed the herbal compound under her tongue. Then she pressed roughly on Anne's abdomen once more. She did not respond at all, and Raven cried, "Quickly, sir, press down."

Charles did as she had bidden him, and together they pressed and massaged, working well like practiced partners. For a moment Ravenna got swept up in the excitement of the challenge, feeling close to this slight young man.

"Call her name, sir," Raven urged him.

"Anne . . ." Charles said softly.

"No, much louder. Shout! Rouse her if you can."

"Anne!" he cried, his voice almost breaking as he got no response.

"Anne!" Ravenna called. *"Anne, your son awaits you!"*

But all their good work could not make up for a hopeless condition. Neither she nor Charles could stop the bleeding, even though she used every technique the old woman had taught her. Within an hour, while the tardy sun shone brilliantly and mockingly into the windows, Mistress Anne of Harlixton Hall was dead.

The husband said little when it was over, but Raven took his silence to indicate a paralysis of conflicting emotions. After all, the child was alive. Manda wept softly in the corner while the doctor examined the infant, trying to distance himself from the blanched and bloody corpse in the chair. Raven doffed yet another stained apron, then stuffed it back into her bag.

When Longacre was done with his exam, he thanked and dismissed her in a single command.

This time she was willing to go, for exhaustion and defeat were twin daggers piercing her heart. Losing Anne was a tremendous setback for Ravenna, and she recalled the agony etched in her father's face whenever a patient died on him. Carefully she thought over all the interventions she had performed, trying to find a flaw in her own actions. As she walked out the door, she ached for a mentor.

She was the first to leave that room of great contrasts—of darkness then dawn, birth then death, hope then grief—but rather than being the one to alert the family, she thought to make her way through the unknowing household and escape the aftermath.

Alone in the hall, she wondered whether John Travers was about and who would take her home, since she was now in no condition to walk the long distance to the village.

She wavered at the edge of the stairs, fighting tears, trying to rally her strength to descend. Then she saw him again, the dark one, the cold son who had once ridden playfully on his mother's back. He was standing at the foot of the staircase, as if waiting for her. A thin smile had molded his lips. Clearly he had heard the good news—and for the moment had been spared the bad.

Something, some understanding, passed between them, and it compelled her to begin her long descent. There was something approaching kindness in his eyes; perhaps he wanted to thank her, for she had given her best effort.

She started to smile, then her head became leaden. The air around her crystallized, then shattered. A buzzing pierced her ears as she pitched forward. The last thing she remembered before falling was the startled look on Garreth's face as he bolted up the stairs.

Four

When she awoke, she was unsure whether it was in the middle of a dream, for she had no recognition of her surroundings.

She was in a luxurious bed, and as she gazed around, Ravenna saw a roaring fire cheering up a massive room. Her body was clothed in a soft mauve gown, cut from silk finer than any she'd ever seen.

Sitting up, dumbfounded, she was greeted by the relieved eyes of a young girl.

"Oh miss, you gave us such a fright, fainting like that."

It all came back to her in a painful flash.

Flinching, Raven turned her eyes toward the wall, ashamed to look at the girl. Not only had she let the girl's mistress die, but had not stayed on her feet long enough to accept responsibility for her failure.

"We know you done all you could for Mistress Anne," the girl said with genuine warmth, "but 'twas God's will that she be taken from us. His ways are not for the likes of us to judge."

Turning her eyes back, Ravenna thanked the girl with a thin smile. Then once more she longed to have a simpler mind, like John Travers's or this young woman's, for they believed absolutely in their simple maxims, and in the goodness of their God.

The slender maid was dressed in mourning, and studying her face, Ravenna detected a thin rim of red under her eyes.

Raven laid her head back against the sumptuous satin-covered pillow and felt dismal.

"Did I actually faint?" she asked somewhat rhetorically. "I remember being thoroughly exhausted."

"Mister Travers told us in the staff hall that you hadn't a wink o' sleep—'Not a wink,' he said—in almost a week."

Smiling, Raven said, "Three days it was. Though it felt like a week. But tell me. I had just left Mistress Anne's room . . . then . . ." Her voice wavered, and she found she could not continue.

The little maid got a gleam in her eye, as if she were about to convey a rare piece of gossip.

"Oh, miss, you fainted dead away on the stairs, and Mister Garreth, he ran up and caught you 'afore you could fall too far. You've a nasty bump above your eye as it is."

Raven reached up and confirmed with a wince that the girl was right.

"Go on," she said.

"I didn't see what happened, because I was just goin' into the baby's room, and . . ." She paused, perhaps reliving the moment she had first seen Anne in death.

"It hurts. I know," Raven said. "Anne should have lived."

"And with Mr. Charles . . . oh, miss, he is ever so grateful to you, even though . . ." The little maid bit her lower lip.

"Is he proud of his son?"

The girl beamed. "Oh, is he ever! The little one's the first child to make it through the bloody curse. And he's the heir, at least till Mister Garreth takes a bride, which won't be a'tall likely, given that no young lady in all of England has ever pleased him."

"I've heard that before."

"And his mother bein' sick for so long, he's had no one

tossin' eligible misses under 'is nose, if you know what I mean."

"I do." Raven smiled, thinking that she had been in a similar predicament, with no mother to prod her into taking a husband. "He seems handsome enough," she added. "Are the local ladies trying to catch his fancy?"

"Oh, are they ever, miss. And titled ladies too, what with his mother being Lady Philippa Harlixton and all."

"Do you ever see her? Lady Philippa, I mean. Do you think she would see me?"

"Oh, no, miss," the girl said with the same finality that Travers had had in his voice. "She do see no one."

"Not even Dr. Longacre?"

"I dunno, ma'am. 'Tis not for the likes of me to ask."

Raven became more determined than ever that she would see Lady Philippa, to determine whether she could help her.

"And did you know her husband?"

"The vicar? Oh, no, miss. I've only been in service these three years. He was gone long 'afore that."

Raven knew a little about the peerage, that a lord's daughter did not lose her title when she married beneath her station, but her children took on the rank of their father. That would make Garreth, for all his family's apparent wealth, an untitled gentleman.

Yet the idea of titles struck her as being useless, or worse, medieval. America, in that regard, seemed much more sensible, with their rather outrageous assertion that all men are created equal.

"But tell me," Raven said, "how did I get the bump on my head if Mister Garreth was there to rescue me?"

"It seems you did fall straight down, on your forehead, and did flip over once 'afore he caught you. You could've broken your neck, Mister Travers said. And Mister Garreth, he seemed that concerned, not wanting you to come to any harm after you helped birth his nephew."

"Well, I feel fine now," Raven said. "How long have I slept?"

" 'Tis after midnight, miss. You slept right through dinner and into a new day."

Embarrassment darkened Raven's cheeks.

The maid went over and pulled a curtain. "See? 'Tis black as the Devil's heart outside."

"And how did I get into this room? And into this beautiful gown?"

"Mister Garreth carried you himself. 'Tis the finest guest room in the house, miss. The windows overlook the gardens, and there's a grand view o' the Thames."

Raven's cheeks became a deeper crimson as she imagined herself in the arms of the dark son, the one whom no girl on earth could please.

"We, uh, washed your clothes for you, what with the mess from the birthing and all."

"Thank you . . . what is your name?"

"Becky, miss."

"You shouldn't have done that, Becky. I can wash my own clothes."

Unfortunately, the maid took this as an insult, for she said, "If you're not pleased with—"

"Oh, no, not at all," Raven interrupted. "It's just that, well, I'm a working person, like yourself. I am not used to all this wealth, nor do I quite approve of it."

"Well, miss, 'tis the way of the world, isn't it?"

"This world anyway."

She smiled. "Yes, miss. That it is."

Raven lay back in her otherworldly bed for a moment, feeling quite abashed and confused. What was she to do next? It was hours before she could break her fast, even though she was truly famished. She glanced around the room but did not see her clothes. A wicked part of her wondered whether Garreth had stayed to watch her limp form being stripped of its bloody things and re-dressed in adornments more suitable to a mistress than a midwife. Perhaps he would yet return, send away the little maid, then make passionate love to her till dawn.

Raven smiled to herself, for she knew little of the details of passionate lovemaking. Her experience lay with what came after—the screams during labor, the cursing, the vows that "If 'e ever come near me again, the cur, I'll kill 'im." Not exactly what one read in novels of the heart.

"My clothes," she began, "where are—"

She was interrupted by a soft knocking. Becky rose, trotted over to the door, then asked who it was without offering the caller admittance.

"It's Charles, Becky," came the voice through the door.

"Miss?" she inquired, looking over her shoulder.

"It's all right," Raven reassured her, though she was scarcely ready to face him. "Come in," she called out, and Becky stood aside.

Then the door opened, and Charles, the husband, no, the newly made widower, walked in.

"Miss Marisse," he said formally, inclining his head as he approached the bed, then seated himself in an adjacent servant's chair. "I am greatly in your debt."

She knew he meant well, but she felt mocked by his polite statement. She would have preferred a genuine show of outrage, accusation, and grief.

"Sir," she said, clearing her throat. "For as long as I live, I will regret not having the skill to save your wife."

The young man's face clouded. "Perhaps she was doomed from the day she married me. I presume the village gossips have acquainted you with the details of our 'curse'?"

"I do not believe in such things," she answered quickly.

"Nor I," he replied. "Yet I don't think either my wife or my child stood a chance before you came."

Then he gave her a look of such gratefulness that she forgot her embarrassment—indeed, she forgot her grief—

and smiled warmly at him. He returned her gesture with a sincere smile of his own.

He did not attract her particularly—not like his dark brother anyway—but as he continued smiling, she thought she saw a gradual transformation of the contours of his face. The salutation in his eyes was no longer of greeting or gratefulness, but carried a hint of lust.

"Who will care for your son now?" she asked, perhaps more businesslike than she had intended.

"Nothing in that regard will change," he answered. "The head nurse, nursery maid, and so forth, are already in residence. It was decided beforehand that my son would live here, owing to the pitiful conditions in the village, and that the wet nurse would be brought in—"

"Who is to suckle the child?" she interrupted.

"A girl," he said, shrugging. "You know better than I of such matters. A Rosy, I think."

"Rosy Thorne," Raven said. "I attended the birth of her son not a fortnight ago."

"Indeed," he replied with a degree of indifference. Perhaps such information was akin to gossip in his mind.

"Is she here now?"

"I assume so, yes. The housekeeper handles all such arrangements."

It was on the tip of her tongue to warn him about such "arrangements"—that the villagers carried with them a host of ailments—but with the mother cold and ready for her grave, little Master Harlixton really had no choice.

"May I see the child?" Raven asked, hoping to give Rosy some basic advice on cleanliness.

"Of course. I'll send the housekeeper to you." With that, he rose and walked toward the door, turning back one final time and inclining his head before he left.

"Poor man," Raven said. "Caught between joy for his son and grief for his wife."

Becky licked her lips, glanced toward the door as if it

had ears, then confided, "Don't feel too sorry for that one, miss. He's slipped between the sheets with many more ladies than his wife. He never truly loved her, and that's a fact. 'Twas an heir he was after, and it looks like you gave him one. He'll be that grateful to you."

Then she gave Raven a strange, knowing look.

Not certain how to respond, Raven settled back into her guest's bed and closed her eyes.

"You'll sleep now," she heard Becky say, then the girl added, "I'll go see if I can get you some tea and biscuits, to tide you over till morning."

The last thing Ravenna heard before she fell asleep again was the sound of the maid softly opening and closing the door.

Five

When Raven awoke, for the second time in her borrowed bed, her dress and underthings had been returned to her. A pot of cold tea and a plate of biscuits sat beside them. She wondered whether the maids had commented on the absence of a corset, since that had been an issue among the matrons of London whenever she and her father had attended a formal social gathering. Yet in this rural place she was, of course, considered one of the serving class, not a lady who aspired to a fashion plate's figure.

It was simply that she knew about female anatomy and the dangers of compressing the internal organs. It was no wonder that many an upper-class lady died giving birth.

It took her only a few minutes to wash and dress herself, then she sat in the chair vacated by the good little Becky and wondered how she could gracefully take her leave.

Rising to her feet, Raven walked over and opened the door, only to find that another maid was bringing a tray down the hall. When the girl saw her peeking around the door, she gave a slight grimace of disapproval, so Raven quickly retreated into the room but remained standing as the girl, who looked as young as Becky, brought in something hot and heavenly.

"Becky's asleep now, miss, but she had Cook make you something special-like, before the rest of the house is up. It's only tea and muffins, but they're ever so good. And

Mister Garreth, he asked that you break your fast with the rest of the family."

"That's very thoughtful of him," Raven began, "but I'm afraid I must take my leave as quickly as possible. Someone in the village may need me."

"Yes, miss," she said, planting the tray on an ornate writing table. "But Mister Garreth, and Mister Charles as well, I believe, asked specifically that you join the rest of the family for a meal before you go. They usually breakfast late, around ten, after the sun has risen."

Annoyance coursed through Raven's mind. Despite the lateness of sunrise during England's harsh northern winters, the working people were up early and hard at their labors in the dark, while these idle folk lolled around in bed for most of the morning. She was sure that she'd quickly learn to despise the place, even if its master had the most exquisite features she'd ever seen on a man.

Perhaps it really was time to go to America, to learn medicine from the savages and consider all people her peers. Perhaps among the native Americans, she would learn more about preventing the blood loss that had led to Anne's death.

Despite her mood, Ravenna ate her light breakfast with gusto. It was normal for her to be hungry after a long birth—"Raven-ous," her father would tease her—saying she'd been named for her appetite as well as her black hair.

"These are delicious," she said to the maid, yet another young girl whose wages probably kept her family going. "And what is your name?" she asked between bites.

" 'Tis Prudence, ma'am. I be the sister of Doris, wife of Geoffrey, the cobbler. You did save her life, I believe, when she had the twins."

Raven smiled in appreciation. In that instance her intervention had worked, and she needed to be reminded of it.

"And how are the little boys?" she asked.

"Oh, they're a handful, they are," said Prudence, smiling.

"I see them every time I go into the village. You can't tell 'em apart, except by the cut what Timmy got on his knee. I sometimes have to roll up the breeches to tell which boy it is."

"Are they walking yet?"

"That they are. Walkin' and gettin' into the worst sorts of mischief."

Raven bade the girl share her breakfast, but she refused, saying she had eaten her fill in the kitchen, which was probably a gentle falsehood. Secretly grateful, though, Raven finished the whole plate and hankered for more.

Maybe she would join the family in the breakfast room after all.

"How will I know when it's time to go down?" she asked finally.

"I'll stay with you awhile," Prudence said, "then Manda will come and get you."

The house was beginning to resemble a way station, with all the comings and goings. The life of the rich seemed complicated in and of itself, though without any purpose other than to sustain itself.

And yet there was something not quite so rich, something not quite right about the place, Raven thought. There were servants, yes, and the place was spotless, but the furnishings were dour and out of fashion. The drapes and bed curtains could have used some renewing. It reminded her of the rooms she and her father had kept in his final days. Their housekeeper, then finally she alone, kept the place clean and tidy, but age and the natural forces of decay had been clearly visible there—as here.

There was no disguising a dying house.

In fact, there was something not quite right about the entire family, most of whom she was soon to meet. At that early time, she could not put her finger on it, and indeed she would not know for quite some time. She noted only the strangeness of four grown sons, three of them married, living in the same house with their reclusive, invalid mother, who allegedly lived like an unquiet spirit on the upper floors.

"Might I find John Travers up and about?" Raven asked after she'd licked her plate clean and drunk every drop of tea.

"I should think so. He's usually the first one up."

"I was wondering if he could offer me a ride home," she explained. "It was he who brought me here"—she had to think for a moment—"yesterday morning."

"I'll go ask him, though I wouldn't expect breakfast to be over till midday. Mistress Justine and Mistress Clarity—I 'spect they'll want to know all about the fashions in London."

"From me?" Raven asked, laughing. "And how would I know?"

"Why, the whole village knows how you did come from London itself to help us. The ladies in this house will 'spect that—"

"I know little of their world. I spent most of my time helping my father and his colleagues attend the poor, who had as many diseases as your rich ladies have dresses, I suspect."

She was surprised at the bitterness in her own voice, and she feared little Prudence was taken aback as well.

"Don't judge 'em like that," the maid said. "They, too, 've had their share of pain."

Of course, Raven thought. Some of the stillborn children were obviously theirs. How ironic it was that wealth and fertility seemed hardly connected, that the poor and starving of the world never seemed to lose their ability to breed. And yet these pampered misses could not produce a single child and live to raise it.

Raven's thoughts turned again to Garreth, strong and vital and intimidating. He did not seem to belong in this house any more than she did.

Would he escape the "curse" when it was his turn to sire an heir?

She shuddered inwardly at that thought, for already she was imagining herself with him—in his bed—when he did so.

Six

Breakfast proved to be a lavish affair, with more food than some families saw in a week. Everything looked irresistible to Raven—since she was still "Raven-ous"—and she was grateful yet again for her lack of a corset.

As Raven walked nervously toward the breakfast room, she prepared herself for seeing Garreth again. Like a shy miss, she practiced looking nonchalant and in control of her emotions. But as she approached the ornate, mirrored room, her composure crumbled when she realized the breakfast conversation was about herself.

". . . And she took one look at our handsome brother," a girlish voice was saying, "and fainted dead away on the stairs." This was followed by laughter in various pitches.

Raven paused just out of sight, her cheeks growing pink from embarrassment.

"So shall we marry him off? It's time he settled down."

"Don't be absurd, Jussie," a male voice scolded. "A midwife, for God's sake."

"And why not? She's not a common nurse, Heath. She could hardly have learned to attend *women* as a camp follower in France."

"Yet she's hardly the type of person . . . a midwife who *faints*—"

"She was ill, I believe," said a tenor voice, which Raven

recognized as Charles's, "but she rose from her bed to attend us. I'll be forever in her debt."

"Well, brother"—the woman's voice—"will *you* have her, then?"

Raven made her entrance at that moment and cut off further speculation as to her health or life history.

As she walked through the doorway, five pairs of eyes turned in her direction. Again, embarrassment stained her cheeks, and were she not so hungry, she may have turned around and fled.

"Ah," said Charles, rising from his chair. "Here's Ravenna now." He motioned for her to approach and stand beside him. "I hope you are refreshed after your well-deserved rest," he added, pulling out a chair next to him and helping her be seated.

The other pairs of eyes were still upon her, none of which she recognized. Though everyone was dressed in black, the mood in the room was far from somber.

Without asking, a footman appeared at her side and poured a cup of tea.

"I am quite refreshed, thank you," she replied, trying to smile but feeling horribly ill at ease. After all, she was the person who had let their sister die, even though they seemed to have quite forgotten the poor woman.

"I'm Justine," one of the women blurted out, and Raven recognized hers as the voice who was so intrigued by her unceremonious fall down the stairs.

Raven nodded.

"And here is Clarity. She's married to this boor." Playfully Justine poked the man at her side, who had arisen immediately upon Raven's entrance into the room and was reseating himself. Upon hearing this mention of himself, he restraightened reflexively.

"St. Clair Pembroke, at your service," he said, inclining his head. Awkwardly he remained standing, and Raven si-

lently mused that this son of the upper classes was as uncertain about etiquette as she was at that moment.

"Garreth is already out and about," Justine chattered on.
"You won't see him, I'm afraid, since he's always attending
to this and that on the estate. So you'll have to settle for
Charles." And incredibly, she winked at the midwife.

It was on the tip of Raven's tongue to ask Justine whether,
if she died in childbirth, she would want her husband flirt-
ing with the midwife who'd lost her. Raven said nothing,
however, merely smiled politely, then turned to the final
man standing and cued him with her eye.

"Heath Pembroke," he said, nodding.

Inclining her head in return, she said softly, "Please be
seated."

Five pairs of eyes regarded her curiously. In an instant,
she felt like an out-of-place fool. Who was she to be acting
like the mistress of the house?

Fortunately, the footman reappeared with a large bowl of
exotic fresh fruits, undoubtedly grown in a forcing garden,
and a steaming plate loaded high with eggs and sausages
and more of the cook's heavenly biscuits. Vowing that she
would behave like a lady, Raven tried to control the actions
of her fork, but once her plate had been filled, she found
herself eating much faster than would have been considered
decorous. No one seemed to notice as they chattered on
about plans for a lavish christening party. Anne's death was
totally ignored.

Yet, as she regarded the two women, Raven began per-
ceiving some of the complex feelings each must have been
harboring in her mind. The look of longing was apparent
on Justine's face despite the gaiety of her conversation. Had
she been the mother of the most recent stillborn child? Was
she the replacement for the other wife who died or the one
who ran away? Was she now thinking of the children she'd
conceived and lost?

Ravenna had seen envy even among chickens. When

Hera, one of her hens, had had a brood of chicks while the other, Cressida, remained barren, Raven could see sorrow in poor Cressida's ignorant bird face, the emptiness while her sister proudly bustled her chicks across the yard. All during that spring, Cressida pecked aimlessly in the yard, and finally died as the autumn approached. The need to nurture transcended all lines and barriers, it seemed, even between man and fowl. Despite what the Church taught, she felt that even her hen had had a soul, and that soul was grieving. How much more must these two women be feeling?

"We haven't had a party in a saint's age," said Clarity. "Miss Marisse, I do hope you can attend."

There was a slight pause in the conversation, as if the invitation had been a gaffe of some sort.

It was Charles who filled the void. "Of course, Miss Marisse, you must come. Anne would not want you or any of us to mourn, but to rejoice. She gave us an heir."

"Thank you," Raven said slowly. "I would be proud to attend. And I do believe that Anne found great—how shall I describe it?—great satisfaction in her final moments. The last word she said was 'perfect.' "

Her comment did not have the effect she'd anticipated, for no one nodded or agreed, just looked from one to another inscrutably. She had no chance to ponder their lack of response, however, for Manda entered the room and approached the table, saying, "Beggin' your pardon, miss, but Rosy's been asking for you. She says the baby—"

"What about the baby?" Charles demanded, springing to his feet as all eyes focused immediately on the little maid.

" 'Tis nothing to alarm yourself, sir," the maid said, curtsying. "But Rosy would like Miss Ravenna to take a peek at young Master Andrew. He feels, well, hot-like."

All the eyes shifted, en masse, toward the midwife.

"I'll go to her right now," Ravenna said, and rose, looking longingly at the unfinished sausages on her plate.

She had not acknowledged to anyone—perhaps even herself—that the baby did not look right. She had assumed the doctor would make his own assessment, yet she would also understand if he kept this intelligence to himself, given the mother was not even buried in her grave. She prayed that Rosy would give the little one the strength to survive, rather than the fever that would kill him.

As Ravenna walked with the maid through the main hall, visions of that first dark morning came back to her. The carved wooden staircase still loomed ahead of her and she found herself getting a touch seasick from some unconscious memory of falling. Again, her body shuddered, thinking of Garreth rushing up to catch her, then carrying her up to the guest room. She thanked God that little Justine hadn't seen the actual event. She would have turned it into a romantic novel by now.

As they walked up the stairs, Raven's eyes darted to the figures carved into the banister.

"These be some of the lords and ladies that once did live in the house," Manda said, trying to hurry and yet obviously proud of her knowledge. "This be the Duke of Buck'n'ham from the time of Charles I. And this be his son, the second duke, and this"—she giggled a bit—"this be the Countess of Shrewsbury. She eloped with the second duke, though she was already married. And her husband—the Earl of something—followed her, but her lover up and killed him."

Ravenna stared hard at the wooden representation of the countess, and wondered what she had looked like in childbirth.

"And see above you," Manda said, and they both raised their eyes. Raven hadn't noticed before, but the ceiling above the upper stairs was decorated with an impressive fresco of four children.

"That litter belonged to the countess herself—they be her four children dressed up as the four seasons. One of the older staff could tell you the names and titles, but they be too long for me."

The depictions were lovely, with the children's faces painted to represent the various times of the year. There were two boys and two girls, with pink or blue flushing their cheeks, depending on their sex and the season they represented.

That was long before the Harlixton curse.

As the two women climbed, their eyes instinctively remaining fixed on the ceiling, Ravenna again heard the deep human tones from the first night. She looked back over her shoulder and saw him, Garreth, the dark one. He was standing just inside the front door, handing his gloves and crop to the butler. He turned to go toward the breakfast room, then without provocation looked up and saw her staring at him. She tried, somewhat halfheartedly, to avert her eyes, but he held her face steady, his gaze as powerful as two hands placed against her cheeks.

Never before entering this house had Ravenna so doubted her ability to control her behavior, but she found that, in Garreth's presence, she was no longer her father's daughter. Only when he turned to go, after a nod in her direction, did she become Ravenna Marisse again, and not some gawking serving girl, ready to throw herself at her new master's feet.

Seven

The baby was burning with fever.

There was fever in the village, and the tough ones survived it, but this motherless weakling, solitary heir to a cursed family and their fortune, might not have the means to fight.

"How long has he been feverish?" Ravenna asked Rosy.

"Since the wee hours of the morning," the girl answered, coughing like a chimney sweep, then hawking up a chunk of phlegm. "But I was that afraid to call you, being you were ill and all."

The girl was sitting in a sumptuous rocker in the overdecorated nursery, trying to nurse the baby, who was doing his best to comply but without much success.

Glancing around, Raven spotted the water ewer and walked over to wash her hands. That was something her father had insisted on, convinced, like young Monsieur Pasteur, that it reduced the incidence of sepsis, although his colleagues laughed at him, claiming him to be womanish in his belief.

When Raven returned, she took the baby from his nurse's arms and sat with him in a nearby wingchair.

His condition was worse than she'd thought. His breathing was labored, and his skin had a blue-purple tint to it. It would be dangerous to experiment with herbs and medications on a newborn, but they were his only chance.

Turning to the maid who'd served as her escort, Raven said, "Please, Manda, go fetch my medical bag. I assume it's in the room where I slept last night."

"Right away, miss," she said, then rushed out the door.

Turning back to Rosy, Raven asked, "And how is your child? Danny, is it?"

"Danny," she said, nodding. "Oh, he's a wonder. I do so miss him. Mistress Anne, well, she said I could bring him to live here in a week or so. I'm"—her face clouded over—"not sure now what is to happen."

"Who's nursing him now, in the interim?" she asked.

"The what, miss?"

"Who is caring for him during the next several weeks?"

"Why, Mum, of course."

Then Raven recalled that the mother had recently had a baby of her own, but it being her twelfth—or was it thirteenth?—the forty-year-old woman had had no need of a midwife's services.

Rosy added, her eyes twinkling, "Mum learned how to do two at once with the twins. 'Tis no trouble, she says."

Raven thought again of America, making an odd analogy in her mind. All men were created equal, but women obviously were not. Their status was meted out not by laws or governments but by something far more capricious and cruel. In the realm of women, Rosy and her mother were queens, lavished by nature's gifts, whereas the Pembrokes were beggars, the have-nots from whom even what they had might soon be taken.

When Manda returned, she brought Charles with her.

He gave the midwife a bleak, helpless look, then asked, "Will my son live?"

It was on the tip of her tongue to be truthful to him, to tell him her doubts, when the door opened again and Garreth entered.

He said not a word to announce himself, but Raven felt his presence surround her like a cloak. As he approached, she knew that she would go to any length to save the child, so that Garreth would think well of her.

"Your baby will live," she said with determination, as if her own life depended on it.

First she worked at lowering the fever. The two men stayed to watch while she cooled the baby's skin with a mixture of tepid water and wine. She measured out a number of herbs—using instinct rather than sound empirical knowledge to determine what to use—then dipped her finger in the brew that Manda made for her and coaxed the baby to suck off the drops. He was a difficult patient, if one can so characterize a newborn, for he did not have the fierce will to survive she often saw among the poor, even the newborn poor.

Ravenna found herself getting angry and impatient with him, commanding him on some elemental level to fight for his life. Throughout the day and into the night, they all stayed with him. Food was brought to them, and dishes removed, but in a strange alliance, they became like a medical team trying to save a life. Charles pitched in like an orderly, while Garreth hovered like the chief surgeon, silently judging. At one point in the early evening Garreth approached and stood behind Ravenna, watching over her shoulder as she swabbed down the baby's arms and legs with surgical spirits.

Despite the other noises in the room, her ears could suddenly hear nothing except the rhythm of his breathing. The steady intake and exhalation of breath reminded her that he was only a human being, but his presence disturbed her like some supernatural force. He did not touch her, yet her skin reacted as if prickled by a thousand sharp needles. How she longed simply to lean back into him, to feel his hands around her shoulders, her head against his chest. She had been around few men except her father and the weak-limbed, ill-groomed geniuses he consorted with. She'd had little experience with raw male power.

When Garreth finally moved away, she struggled to regain herself. She dared not look at him.

It was well after midnight when the baby's fever began to abate. Raven sent the men out of the room, then tucked Rosy and the baby in bed, ordering her to nurse him as often as he could tolerate it.

When she left the room and descended the stairs, they were waiting for her—David and Goliath, as unalike as ice and fire—and both arose as she reached the front hall, this time on her feet.

"I believe the child will survive," she said, not waiting to be addressed.

Charles gave out a heavy sigh of relief, though it was not his approval that she sought. Timidly, she turned her attention toward Garreth, breathlessly awaiting a word of approval, like a young student receiving a final grade.

Charles also turned his eyes, and she could tell that he, too, approached Garreth as a student would a master.

Garreth inclined his head toward her, murmured a word of thanks, then said, "It's late. Please be our guest again tonight."

"Thank you, sir," she said.

"Yes," said Charles eagerly, taking her arm. "I'll ask Cook to prepare us something before we retire. I'm famished." As Garreth turned to go, Charles called, "Will you join us?"

Garreth pondered this offer while Charles and Ravenna waited, each hoping for a different answer.

"No," Garreth said, and both she and Charles sighed, again for different reasons.

As Charles escorted her away, Ravenna glanced over her shoulder to catch a final glimpse of Garreth.

But he had disappeared from view, having left the main hall on his way to the south wing, which she had yet to visit.

The hall was still and silent. Not even the dust was

stirring. Yet she felt an indelible impression in the room, as if Garreth had carved a permanent pathway through the air.

Eight

She awoke early the next morning, during the dark winter *uht* time, and having nothing to read, no chores to perform, Ravenna grew impatient for the sun to rise so she could be on her way. Like a stallion confined in a tight stall, she paced and sputtered in her room, large and lavish though it was, and ached for release.

When the first light diluted the dark sky, she donned her cloak and left the house, determined that if she could not find John Travers, she would simply walk home.

She was not worried about her chickens, since she knew the eldest Warren boy would notice her absence and tend to her chores, but she was growing concerned that the longer she remained amid the splendor of upper-class existence, the more it would seduce her.

The more Garreth would seduce her.

She saw no one as she left the house by the northern exit—even the porter was absent—and after a futile search for John Travers, she commenced the long walk home.

The hardened earth of the driveway crunched under her feet as she covered about a quarter mile, looking back periodically to see if anyone had joined her on the road. Each time her eyes returned to the road ahead, disappointed that she was the sole traveler.

As she reached the turn in the drive, which, once taken, would put the house out of view, she stopped. Though thoroughly rested, she found that her feet simply refused to move. She tried to force herself forward, as one cajoles an intransigent mule. Her body remained in its place. Did she really want to leave? And do so in this sneak-thief fashion? The leaden feeling in her legs was giving her an answer. Something was anchoring her to this land, drawing her back to the house.

If she left, perhaps John Travers would one day soon be dispatched to retrieve her. Baby Andrew was still not well and needed constant care.

But that was not soon enough. Her heart knew what it wanted, even though her mind was not ready to admit to it.

She turned back, and with feet now light as gauze, she retraced her steps.

Approaching, she began to feel foolish. What was her excuse for being out? And for coming back so soon?

She decided she would explore the sculpture gardens at the back of the mansion, then amble slowly toward the Thames, which had been visible from her guest room window.

By the time she returned from her walk, she could join the family for its late breakfast.

Frozen twigs crackled under her feet, and she wondered what this immense yard would look like in the summer. There were carved evergreens along each carefully etched path, their needles sparse and frozen now but green nevertheless. The paths, when viewed from the house, created an orderly geometric design, and she saw triangular places where flowers might appear in spring. John Travers had told her that Harlixton had many lovely gardens to explore, at least one in every direction of the compass.

She kept the Thames always in her sight—if she simply wandered along its bank, she would eventually find London, as distant as that dark, dirty city seemed to her amid this Berkshire countryside.

Approaching the actual edge of the river was harder than

she'd thought, however, for the cultivation stopped short of what should have been a proper shore. Thick overgrowth lined the bank, protecting the foot traveler from getting too close to the river itself. The river was frozen solid here—an unusual occurrence in London—and she was bound and determined to run her hand along the smooth surface of the ice.

Raising her hood for protection, she cautiously drew aside a curtain of winter-stripped branches. She imagined that this kind of trespass would have been impossible in summer. Several twigs snapped in protest. But not feeling the same sort of respect for the trees that she would have had they been lush with leaves, she shoved more of the branches aside. Quickly she grew impatient with these dead-looking things that impeded her progress. Touch the ice she would.

She took a tentative step into the thicket, then another. And another. Soon she was in the midst of hostile bushes, feeling like the prince in the fairy story who must hack his way through the evil forest to get to his lady love. Except that the princess in this case was an indifferent river, which was content to exist whether anyone approached it or not.

She took another step, then gasped as a sharp twig grazed her winter-chapped cheek, drawing blood.

The cold compounded the sting, and she winced in pain as she touched the injured spot. She pondered for a moment as to whether she should retreat. In turning her head, however, another branch lanced her forehead, this time making her feel a touch of panic. She was stuck.

Pulling her hood down farther over her forehead, Raven bent over and slowly retraced her steps. She was ready to admit defeat. But the trees seemed to have rewoven themselves into a seamless mesh, and she could not find a suitable exit point. She felt as if she had just pushed her way through a hostile mob that was refusing absolutely to let her retrace her steps. Finally she decided to get on her hands and knees and crawl her way out.

This strategy worked better, and with her face near the ground, she crept like an animal back to safety. Progress was slow, with her cloak impeding her almost as much as the thicket, but she focused only on one inch at a time—one inch, then another, then another, her face tucked under her hood for protection.

Relief flooded through her as she flopped out of the thicket and onto the open path. At last she was free. But she gasped as her head bumped into something dark and solid. She looked up awkwardly, her hood falling off her head.

Garreth, master of Harlixton Hall, stood in her path, staring down at her with knit brows.

"Oh, good heavens!" she cried, jumping to her feet, only to get her cloak caught under her heel.

Instantly his arm snaked out and grabbed hers as she teetered sideways. For the second time, he had saved her from falling.

"There is a path leading to the riverbank, Miss Marisse," he said, pulling her upright. "I assume that was your destination."

She nodded, her cheeks flushing and adding to the sting of the multiple cuts on her face.

He motioned farther along the river, holding her by the elbow as if she would fall without his support.

"Thank you, sir," she said.

"Let me show you."

"Thank you," she repeated, breathing heavily in spite of herself.

As they fell in step together, his grasp slid naturally downward so that he became her escort rather than her rescuer.

"I saw you through the library window," he said after a period of silence, "and wanted to warn you about the river edge. The gardeners often speak of cutting away all the natural growth, but I have thus far resisted them. The river deserves some protection from all this"—he waved his hand disdainfully backward in the direction of the sculpture garden—"human intrusion."

"You do not like the gardens, then?"

"Good Lord no," Garreth replied quickly. "They were the handiwork of my grandfather's gardeners. Unfortunately, the damage would take years to undo."

"How would you have these grounds, sir?"

He thought for a moment, then replied, "To be honest, I'm not sure. It would not do to have a wild American forest adjoining our home, and yet I can't abide by the sculpted trees. There are things given to us by Nature that I feel should not be tampered with. A tree should grow as it wills, not as we will it."

Ravenna smiled inwardly, for it was the sort of statement her father often made.

"Though the gardens are very beautiful," she said, "I find I must agree with you. I often long to be away from civilization. Perhaps I shall go to America one day, and see for myself their immense, untamed forests."

"Is it a personal interest of yours—America, that is?"

"I guess you could say that. Yes."

"I, too, am intrigued by a country that is new," he said. "Full of possibilities and challenges. A chance to build, to start again. I should like that."

As they walked, Raven's girlish imagination built on Garreth's comments. Her mind conjured up an image of the rugged American terrain, teeming with life and natural vitality. From that, she quickly imagined them living together in a log-built cabin in America. Garreth would till the fields while she'd attend the settler women, who grew up strong and sturdy from hard work and simple living. A good, honest life, with children working at their side, black-haired as the sultans of Persia.

Children. For the second time, she imagined having Garreth's children, being held in Garreth's powerful arms while he made love to her and gave her the greatest gift a man could give a woman. Imperceptibly her breathing quickened as she focused on the sensation of his arm brushing against hers, trying to imagine it bare and warm under a handwoven blanket.

"The path is right up there," he said, but she hardly heard him. Her mind was still in America, in a rough-hewn bed with Garreth pulling off her homespun flannel nightgown and making love to her everywhere.

He paused, but she kept going, like a sleepwalker, till he gently pulled her back.

"This path was carved over the years by people like yourself, wishing to get a closer look at the river."

She went ahead of him then, walking right up to the river's edge and touching the ice with her fingertips.

"This must be a wonderful spot in summer," she said, turning her head and smiling at him.

"Oh, it is," he said. "The river was my favorite place to explore as a boy. I used to come here and pretend I was hunting big game. It's very easy to transport oneself anywhere when one is young . . . Just as you were somewhere many miles away just now."

He joined her at the edge of the river, and despite the loud whooshing of the wind, she thought she could detect an acceleration of his breathing. The sounds of nature seemed to fade suddenly as her mind focused only on his breathing, and the strong arm that was lightly touching her cloak.

Turning toward him, she looked up and tried to imagine him as a boy, the face not quite so angular, the skin soft with youth, before the emergence of a beard.

He returned her gaze, but there remained that enigmatic look in his eyes, not unlike her father's haunted guise.

Staring up at him quickly embarrassed her, and she tried

to look away, but his eyes held hers. The feel of his gloved hand still resting on her arm was as powerful as pain. He had her full attention now, and every part of her was waiting for him to proceed.

"You've scratched yourself," he said finally.

She reached up to touch her blush-stained cheek. "On the branches. It was silly of me to try to go that way."

"Quite. Please be more careful in future."

"I shall. Thank you."

A single gesture, a small signal of assent, would have sent her into his arms. But he simply stared at her face, like a doctor, assessing the injuries.

Then he reached out with his free hand and touched one of her wounds.

She kept waiting, perhaps hoping for his expression to change, as Charles's had, into one of desire.

He lowered his hand and turned to go.

Ravenna stepped back, feeling the sting of being undesired.

"I—I must go and—and check on the baby," she said, not meaning it. Andrew was the last thing on her mind.

"I'll escort you to breakfast," Garreth said.

They walked back without words or physical contact. Their arms hung unnaturally at their sides. But Raven listened again to his breathing, to the sounds of his body, and she thought she could hear the strong thumping of an unquiet heart.

Nine

Ravenna stayed for Anne's funeral, which was followed, incredibly, by little Andrew's christening. Initially appalled by the juxtaposition of those two sacraments, she soon obtained some comfort from the random infant noises that interrupted the vicar's eulogy, reminding everyone that a part of Anne still lived.

Ravenna borrowed a black bombazine and crepe dress from Justine, an attractive, girlish thing that, alas, fit only over the corset Justine had provided her as well. Struggling to breathe and cursing her sex for silently enduring such a contraption, Ravenna nevertheless blushed when Garreth eyed her figure, obviously approving.

She returned to Harlixton Hall with the family, but this time only to fetch her clothes and rejoin John Travers in the carriage. Having no further excuse for delay, she'd finally had a word with him and he had readily agreed to escort her home.

Quietly she packed her medical bag, changed into her own loose-fitting dress, and said a silent good-bye and thanks to her bedroom of several nights. As she descended the stairs, saying farewell to the intricate carvings, she imagined again the moment of her fall and Garreth's strong arms as he scooped her up and carried her to safety.

Travers was waiting for her atop the family coach, which sported the Harlixton crest on the door.

"Well now, miss," Travers said as he helped her up the step, "you've brought good fortune to this house. An heir to carry on. The noises of a child. I'll miss you, that I will."

"And I you," she said, then stepped in and seated herself.

It was a bleak day, with the gray sky matching her somber mood. Had it been any other afternoon, she would have enjoyed watching the scenery pass by, but on this occasion, she was preoccupied by her own dismal inner landscape.

She'd not felt envious or deprived when she first embarked on her journey to Harlixton. Now, in less than a week, a pall had fallen over her life. She dreaded what lay ahead, wanted to run away, crouch and hide. Nothing would ever be the same for her again—she'd been touched, no, *seized* by something far too strong for her. She had tasted the fruit of life's forbidden knowledge, and like Eve, she'd suddenly noticed her own nakedness.

Staring out the window, she studied the contours of Garreth's land. They passed through wooded areas, followed by fields, orchards, several rows of cottages, woods again, a frozen pond. It seemed almost wicked for one family to own so much land, and she used that thought to put distance between Garreth and herself. Yet the cottages on his land looked much more opulent and well tended than the squalid huts in the village. The thatching on all of them seemed lush and uniformly new. Garreth was a good steward to his lands, and that thought, alas, drew her closer to him once more.

She tried instead to think about practical things, lighting the fire in her cottage, borrowing something from the Warrens for dinner. Hopefully Matt Warren had not let the roof cave in during her absence.

But she was not to see her roof that day, nor the next, nor the next, for they had scarcely driven through the wrought iron entrance to Harlixton grounds, when a lone rider came galloping up to the side of the coach. She hid the relief she felt when she recognized Charles, breathing heavily as he reined in his horse.

"Ravenna," he cried, then coughed as he gulped in the chilly air. "Andrew's taken a turn for the worse. It must have been the strain of today's events. You must come back."

"Has the fever returned, Charles?" she said with the appropriate apprehension in her voice.

"Yes. And he is having trouble breathing again. Come, ride back with me." Then he shouted, "John, Ravenna is returning with me."

During the ride back, she closed her eyes, and clinging to the rough masculine cloak as she struggled to remain seated behind Charles, she imagined another cloak, another rider, another masculine form, but one with broad shoulders and back and hair black as midnight.

Thin, anemic Charles was taking her back to him.

Ten

The baby had pertussis. That was the only conclusion she could make after hearing the tiny child's racked and tortured breathing. Ravenna hadn't recognized it at first, because newborns don't display the classic symptoms right away. But now, as she heard him *cough cough cough,* then gasp, then *whoop,* then stop breathing as he frantically tried to clear his windpipe, the diagnosis was clear.

In eighteen-year-old Rosy, the illness was a trifle; in Andrew, it could be a death sentence. Indeed, the whooping cough killed a handful of village children every year.

Regrettably, Ravenna advised Charles to dismiss the girl, since Andrew would now be vulnerable to any other ailment she contracted during her visits to the village.

One bout of influenza could kill him.

Secretly, she was also relieved that Rosy could now return to her own child, where she belonged. Raven gave the girl several packets of disease-fighting herbs to brew into tea and give to her own child. She would also do what she could to help her family make up for the lost wages.

And of course, she was relieved that circumstances would now permit her to see Garreth regularly, since Andrew's convalescence would be lengthy, requiring ongoing medical care.

After preparing an antispasmodic decoction to be dripped into little Andrew's mouth and leaving strict orders that he was never to be left alone, she quit the nursery and descended the stairs, in search of Charles.

While she was crossing the main hall, saluting Lady Philippa's likeness, Wyngate the butler accosted her.

"Miss," he began, in a manner as starched as his collar, "Mr. Pembroke would like a word with you."

He escorted her across the hall, then into the mysterious south wing. After knocking gently on one of the many doors in a long, white hallway, Wyngate entered, announced her, then ushered her into the room. Garreth was seated at a desk, but he rose immediately upon her admittance.

"Miss Marisse," he said politely, then motioned toward a wing chair facing the desk.

The room resembled the library at the back of the house, with floor-to-ceiling shelves against one wall, but there was also a cozy, enclosed feeling to the place.

Garreth's study.

She tried to appear calm, but she felt her cheeks redden. She was as nervous and thrilled as a schoolgirl having a private interview with her favorite master.

After collecting his thoughts, Garreth began, "Miss Marisse, on behalf of our entire family, I wish to thank you for your service."

She looked away, then back at him timidly. "I only wish I'd had more experience with the, uh, with the medical circumstances that led to Anne's, I mean, to your sister-in-law's death. I—I only wish my father had been here."

"Your father . . ."

"Was a surgeon."

Garreth pondered this, then nodded. "Ah, yes. I see. I wondered where I had heard your name before. He was Sir Richmond Marisse, wasn't he, just recently knighted by the Queen."

"Yes. For his work with the destitute in London. They contract diseases medical science has never even heard of, let alone treated."

Garreth looked at her thoughtfully, then said, "Your father, ah, died shortly afterward, I'd also heard."

"Yes," she replied, commanding her feelings to stay put.

"I offer you my condolences."

"Thank you, sir. He was a—a great man."

"And you are continuing his work, it seems, tending to the poor and powerless."

"I do what I can, though I could hardly take his place."

"And your path crosses Longacre's frequently, I take it?"

"Not at all. I was quite surprised when he sent for me."

"I can imagine it was quite a humbling experience for him to defer to a young woman, hardly more than a girl."

She straightened, not knowing if that was a compliment or an insult.

"Yes, sir," she said for want of anything better.

"Your reputation, I'm sure, will be greatly embellished by the birth of my nephew. The breaking of the Harlixton curse, and so forth."

"I do not believe in curses."

"Nor I. Nevertheless, we have had a series of misfortunes in this family, as you know. My mother was apparently the last to have made her peace with Nature. Whereas my brothers and I, well, it seems we're a pack of Henry the Eighths."

"Hopefully, your nephew will usher in a whole dynasty of Harlixtons," she said matter-of-factly, though she was surprised that he would discuss such an indelicate subject with an unmarried woman, midwife or no.

"Pembrokes, actually," he replied, heedless of her embarrassment. "My mother was born Lady Philippa Harlixton, but my father was vicar of the Reading parish, an untitled gentleman by the name of Pembroke."

"To the Pembrokes, then," Raven said, smiling, then she noticed that suddenly Garreth's eyes were far away, as if the mention of his father had touched on some unbidden and perhaps painful memory. Feeling embarrassed by the silence, she said hesitantly, "You said 'was.' Is he . . ." She hesitated.

"You and I are of a kind, it seems. Both without a father."

"Oh," she whispered, looking down at her hands. "I'm sorry. I . . . I know how you feel."

His eyes remained out of focus, and as she watched him, she forgot about his musculature and his magnetic face and stared for a moment at his eyes. Haunted eyes. Was the loss of his father as devastating to him as hers was for her? But as she studied him, she saw something else, something quite unrelated to grief. She recalled that same haunted look in her father's eyes, the private, unquenchable torment. So this pampered son of the aristocracy had his own demons.

She stood up.

"I thank you for providing me with a sumptuous room and for not blaming me for your sister-in-law's death. Your nephew is not well, but I will instruct one of your staff in preparing a suitable infant formula for him. I advise strongly against having anyone from the village nurse or attend to him. If you wish, I will visit him daily—wearing a cloth over my mouth."

"A cloth . . ." Garreth repeated, still preoccupied with his own thoughts.

"Yes. It was my father's idea. Actually, he once conferred with a young French chemist, a Monsieur Louis Pasteur, who is convinced that disease is spread by—"

Garreth's eyes snapped into focus. "Please sit down," he said. "I wish to discuss the matter of payment for your services to—"

"There's no need—"

Then the door burst open, and she was interrupted as Charles cried, "Ravenna, you're not leaving."

"But sir—"

"Promise me you will stay at least until Andrew is out of danger."

"Sir," she said, "the child has pertussis, and needs continual care. But one of the maids, someone who lives here, can be trained—"

"Garreth, she must stay."

During the course of their interview, Garreth had neither asked her to stay nor sent her packing. Thus she and Charles again turned toward him, this time as if he were the judge and they the petitioners.

"Ravenna," Garreth said, and her nerves reacted to his use of her Christian name, "you are welcome to stay until the boy is well again."

Her heart heaved a sigh of relief, yet she found herself saying dispassionately, "I'll be honest with you. The child is not strong. It's possible . . ." She hesitated.

"Yes, go on," Charles said, his frightened eyes scrutinizing her face as family members often do when they feel a doctor is hiding something from them.

"It's possible that he might be sickly throughout his youth. I would not presume to say. He appears to have a weak constitution. Something not quite right."

"No!" Charles protested.

"But sir—"

"It's not true! And even so, aren't there medicines, treatments—"

"Sir—"

"Charles . . ." Garreth said with warning in his voice.

Again, both she and Charles were silenced.

"What she is saying, dear brother," Garreth continued, "is that little Andrew is the latest victim of the Harlixton curse." There was irony, almost sarcasm, in his voice.

"As I told you before," Ravenna said quickly, "I do not believe in curses."

"Yet the boy is not like those hale and hearty infants you frequently deliver in the village." This was from Charles.

She mulled over this statement, wondering if the irony in it was also intentional.

"Hearty at birth, yes," she replied. "But by their first

birthday, they are often full of worms and lice, their skin a mass of sores from infections or scorbutus. Your son will escape their fate at least, but he will need God's help to survive his own."

Charles stared at her for a long moment as a panoply of emotions washed over his face.

"You, too, will help him do that," Charles said finally.

Before she could reply, they heard a knocking on the door, then Wyngate entered, carrying a tray.

"Sir," the butler said to Garreth, then nodded toward Charles, then Raven.

"Wyngate, Miss Marisse has agreed to stay with us indefinitely. Prepare a suite for her, one that overlooks the gardens."

"Very good, sir." Then he nodded toward her again, spun on his heel, and departed.

"The back rooms all have a good view of the Thames," Garreth said.

"I . . ." she began slowly, not knowing how to say that she had not agreed to stay. Then she looked into his face again, recognizing that she would use any pretense to see that face on a regular basis. But could she turn her back on the village women who needed her—who had no one else?

"Sir," she said to Garreth. "A lot of people depend on me in the village."

"I do not intend to make you a prisoner here. You are free to come and go and care for them as you will."

Garreth had her attention now, but out of the corner of her eye, she saw that Charles had reacted to Garreth's use of the singular pronoun, as if Garreth were excluding him from the conversation.

She shook her head. "But if they need immediate attention, they won't come. Not up to a rich man's door."

Again Charles reacted to the singular, and she regretted her use of it.

Garreth pondered her reply for a moment. "You must have your own door, then. On Harlixton land."

"Sir?"

"Your own consulting room. Let the villagers come directly to you."

"And if a woman should go into labor before dawn . . ."

"There is an old cottage that once housed the gate-keeper's family. It's on the very edge of our land. Set up an infirmary there while continuing to live here, in the house, as our guest. Why not? That way a groundsman can come up to the house, inform you if anyone requires your services in the middle of the night. They need never go up to, as you say, a rich man's door."

It was an awkward arrangement, one that would require the villagers to journey a ways to obtain her help. Yet in her own infirmary, she could control the conditions under which she worked. A baby could be born without his two-year-old sister coughing into his face as he struggled to take his first breath.

"It is a generous offer, sir," she said, then turned toward Charles and nodded, to include him in the discourse. "Yet I must refuse, as it is too burdensome to the women I attend. My work is in the village. It is I who must go there."

"You can't," Charles cried. "If you leave, my son will die."

That last statement was spoken with great passion, as if she were listening not to an educated English gentleman but to a superstitious peasant who's convinced that his cow can be cured only by a certain Gypsy's incantations.

"We've waited a long time for an heir," Garreth said. "I would not wish to lose him."

Raven left Garreth's study fearing this new change in her life, yet realizing that she would have stayed without any coaxing at all.

Eleven

Ravenna would still seek out John Travers that afternoon, but only to return to her cottage to fetch her meager belongings. Since the rent was paid until spring, she would offer the place to the Warrens, provided they look after the chickens, tend to the roof, and see that the moths didn't eat up her father's chair. The older children could perhaps bunk there at night, feeling as if they had their own secret castle.

Walking along the winding corridor toward the side entrance, she spotted Travers in the servants hall. After she acquainted him with her change in status, he nodded and smiled brightly.

" 'Tis a good thing, that," he said. "We sorely need your care for the wee master."

As he went to fetch the coach, she stood in the front drive, studying the immense house in which she would soon live. There were basically three stories aboveground, and the windows, though long and impressive, diminished in grandeur the higher one looked. She examined each window in turn, looking for some sign of life on the topmost floor, wondering where the aging Lady Philippa had set up her hermitage.

Suddenly, she heard a vaguely familiar cracked voice. She turned, and a quite familiar, dreaded face from her past came into view. Surprised, she averted her eyes, as if what she could no longer see would no longer exist.

"Well, if it ain't the midwife 'erself," the voice called out. "And what be ye doin' 'ere? Bringin' more bloody bastards into th' world?"

Cholly Makepiece. The one man in the county who could possibly wish her ill.

"I could ask the same of you, Cholly."

"Why, you—"

"What you're doing here, I mean."

He straightened up to his full, enormous height, well over six feet, though obviously her breeding gave her stature in his eyes. "I be employed by Mister Charles, twice a week. You remember that, missy. Remember to watch yer backside on Tuesdays and Thursdays."

Ravenna had taken in his only daughter—who was fifteen, unmarried, and pregnant—after he'd beaten her severely so that she'd lose the baby, then thrown her out of his house when she hadn't. The girl had stayed with Ravenna until the baby came.

Cholly had punched the girl repeatedly in the stomach to get her to miscarry—he'd not have a bastard as his first grandchild. But she had given birth to a fine son, had kept the child, and was now in service with a friend of Ravenna's father.

Cholly had blamed Ravenna and her witchcraft for saving the child, when actually he simply did not know enough about female anatomy. He should have aimed lower, since the womb had not yet ascended into the abdominal cavity.

But Raven had not been content simply to rescue the daughter. She brought charges against Cholly—of brutality and attempted murder. The local authorities had laughed at her—a father could surely beat his ruined daughter if he chose—but the chief magistrate was a humane man who'd known Sir Richmond well. He sentenced Cholly to six months imprisonment at hard labor and thus made a ruling unprecedented in the local justice system.

Meeting Cholly again was an afterclap Ravenna had never considered.

"Your daughter deserved a chance," Ravenna said.

"She deserved to be 'orsewhipped. Just like you, uppity miss. I gave 'er everything I could, and she done this to me. And you and your witch's brew brought the dead babe back to life."

It was a delusion of his, that somehow he had killed the baby but Raven had used some magic potion to raise him from the dead.

"Mind your backside," he called as she walked past him toward the northern entrance so she could wait by the porter's office.

She would bring him to Garreth's notice and have the man dismissed. How dare he threaten her.

But if she cost him his job, he would come after her for sure. No, she would try, instead, to stand clear of him.

And lock her door on Tuesdays and Thursdays.

Twelve

True to his word, Garreth provided Raven with a consulting clinic on the edge of Harlixton land. He gave her full use of the cottage he'd spoken of that was just inside the main gate. Bailey, the gatekeeper, and his wife had used it while they were raising their family. But now that the children were grown and poor Mrs. Bailey was dead from the chicken pox, Mr. Bailey had requested smaller premises in which to reside.

He got his smaller cottage and Raven got her clinic.

Initially, she had trouble convincing the village women to come to the place, since a clinic was a rather novel idea to them. Particularly strange was her invitation that they give birth outside their own homes, even though their cottages were dank, dark, and crowded. So, too, did fear of the curse initially keep them away—perhaps the barrenness of the Harlixton wives would strike them as well. But after Pamela Tewkes was delivered of her baby girl in the clinic, with Justine assisting, her effusive praise—"An' I didn' even 'ave to wash the bedding!"—gave the other women confidence. Soon women were traveling to her from the neighboring villages, from Burnham and Cookham and even from the next county. Since Raven was well tended to as a member of the Harlixton household, she charged only a token fee, and then only if a woman could clearly afford it.

Looking back, she often mused that those first months after her clinic opened were some of the happiest of her life. She didn't see Garreth often, but as winter slipped gradually into spring, her vocation consumed most of her energy. Like a man, she buried herself in work, hoping to hold her heart at bay. She didn't even allow herself to dream, for after all, she could hardly expect Garreth, pampered son of the aristocracy, to work at her side, dirtying his hands in the twin mess of birth and poverty.

Despite the long hours she spent in her clinic, and even though Master Andrew seemed to be contracting one illness after another and required her frequent attention, she found she still had a lot of time on her hands to think and to write. She reflected on all the interventions she'd performed to save Anne's life, and although she had tried everything that modern and traditional medicine had to offer, she felt the need to consult with someone possessing more experience. Thus in her spare time she composed a letter to Herr Doktor Wolfgang Grunewald, an acquaintance of her father's who practiced in Berlin. It took her several weeks of polishing and revising until she felt satisfied that she had faithfully recounted the facts of the case. And then she added her final suspicions—that the woman herself had some constitutional weakness, as did her baby. She finally asked him for any advice on improving the survival chances of her little foster son.

When she finally had signed and sealed and given the letter to John Travers to post, she felt a great sense of accomplishment. Several months later, she received a succinct but useful reply. Herr Doktor Grunewald had evaluated the interventions she'd employed, then suggested several continental techniques she'd had no knowledge of. He also recommended a tonic of certain mineral salts to be drunk throughout pregnancy, to fortify the blood.

Still, the case of Anne Pembroke continued to haunt her. Sometimes she reworked the outcome in her mind so that

Anne survived, fell instantly in love with her adorable son and heir, and they lived happily ever after.

That fairy tale gave her pleasure even when she was only half aware that her mind had wandered over to it. Then reality would tap her on the shoulder, and Anne would be dead once more. She had not saved Anne, but she would save the next woman. Indeed, she became obsessed with saving "the next woman," as if that would somehow give meaning to Anne's death.

Because the clinic was situated at the entrance to Harlixton land, it was necessary for her to get a ride or an escort up to the main hall at the end of the day. The driveway was, after all, several miles long through woods and fields, and outside the protection of the villagers or the household staff, she feared animals, poachers, and of course, Cholly Makepiece. Several times she spent the night alone, sleeping fitfully on the examining couch, with only the nearby gatekeeper as her protector, though most nights Charles came to collect her on his enormous roan. Closing her eyes, she would sink into his cloak, imagining it was Garreth's broad back she rested upon.

Oftentimes Charles would draw her out of her fancies, asking about her work, about aspects of Andrew's care, about drugs and medicines and the plants used by savage healers. She doubted he had any real interest in herbs, yet he let her ramble on, nodding and asking polite, well-placed questions. That he was courting her became an unspoken truth between them, but she used the fact of Anne's recent death to put a barrier around herself.

It was on one of their unhurried evening rides that she let slip the fact that Cholly Makepiece had threatened her.

Charles frowned and set his jaw in an angry scowl. "Why didn't you tell me this earlier? Although he's a good carpenter and I should hate to lose him, I'll have the man thrown off if you'd like."

"Oh, no, don't do that," she countered quickly, explaining that a dismissal would make the man even more dangerous.

Charles turned his head around and said, "You have nothing to fear, my—that is, you're almost part of my family. Makepiece wouldn't dare harm you."

"I hope not. Though obviously family ties do not deter him."

"Ravenna," Charles said, and he reached back to grasp her hand for an instant, "as long as you live under my roof, you are under my protection. No harm will come to you."

She smiled at the boasting in that lordly statement, which could not have been made had they not been alone.

"I believe you," she said, wishing it were true. "But sometimes when I am by myself in the clinic, I think I see shadows, feel I am being watched."

"I'll talk to him," Charles said, then held up his hand to ward off her objections. "A friendly chat. Trust me. I know how to handle him."

Early next morning, she glanced out her window and saw Charles and Cholly having a heated discussion on one of the garden paths. Cholly was waving his arms angrily, then he lunged at Charles, who quickly jumped back out of his way and glared indignantly at the hired man. Finally Cholly stormed off.

After breakfast, as she was crossing the drive to see if she could catch a ride with John Travers to the clinic, Cholly stepped out of the carriage house and blocked her way.

"Watch who ye be talkin' to, missy," he warned her with a sneer. "Else harm might come to ye."

As if to emphasize his threat, he took a step toward her.

"Is there any problem here?" a voice asked curtly, and they both turned to see Charles with a threatening look on his face.

"Well now," Cholly replied, the sneer still in his voice, "that depends on you, don' it?"

"Remember what I said, Makepiece," said Charles imperiously. "If you—"

"I'll handle this, Charles," a deeper, richer voice declared, and now it was three heads who turned as Garreth walked toward them from the stables, his tight-fitting riding breeches showing off the outline of his powerful thighs.

In an instant Charles had been demoted from rescuer to younger brother. The resentment shone clearly in his eyes.

"Stay away from Miss Marisse, Cholly," Garreth said before she could protest that he wasn't bothering her.

"I only wanted to—"

"Leave her alone. And I'll have none of your insolence."

How she regretted Garreth's appearance at that moment, for as he walked away, the two remaining pairs of male eyes looked at her resentfully.

Afterward, she had John Travers drive her into the village, where she hired the second Warren boy—sixteen-year-old Nigel, who had dreams of becoming a pugilist—as a guard for the clinic. Initially, the presence of a male deterred some of the older women, while it spurred business among the girls, who got to glimpse Nigel flex his muscles a time or two as he helped her tend to the immediate grounds.

Cholly kept his distance from then on, but sometimes in the early evening, when all other human sounds had ceased, Ravenna imagined heavy breathing at the window, and she wondered whether the rhythmic noises she sometimes heard were really Cholly's heavy boots shuffling up to her door.

Thirteen

She was making tinctures in her clinic late one evening when Raven heard quick, light footsteps running up to the cottage. Assuming it was Charles coming to coax her home, she walked over to the door. On her face she affixed a smile that was halfway between what she would want to give to Garreth and what she should properly grant to his younger brother.

As her fingers closed around the doorknob, she realized with a start that the noise had ceased suddenly, no sound of anyone stamping the dirt from his feet, no knocking or general noises to make himself known. Her heart beat faster, for she was alone and vulnerable. Cholly hadn't bothered her since that initial warning, but Nigel—anticipating her brother-in-law's arrival—had just left, and Mr. Bailey was off on holiday. She pressed her ear against the door and listened.

Her heartbeat was louder than any noises she could hear from outside.

Tentatively, she opened the door and stepped out several paces. "Hello?" she called, glancing around and listening.

Someone was breathing heavily in the darkness, and she jumped at the sound. It took her one panic-stricken moment to realize the noise was coming from herself.

"Oh, Ravenna," she sighed, smiling at her own silliness. Charles was overdue, and as she walked back into the cottage, she almost relished seeing him again, riding safely behind him back to the house.

Hurriedly, she put away her herbs and tinctures, doffed her apron, and wrapped herself in her shawl. If Charles did not come in a minute, she would walk home, too afraid on this night to stay alone.

As she waited near the door, rocking impatiently on her heels, she started to feel warm. *Thermogenesis,* she laughed to herself, the body heating itself up in response to fear.

She laced and relaced her fingers, remembering her father when he was waiting for some chemical reaction to occur before he could proceed to the next step—how he would curse and sputter at the waste of a few minutes.

Lord, she felt warm. Even her cheeks felt flushed.

Then, out the window, she detected an unnatural tawny hue developing in the sky, as if dawn were breaking. And the air was becoming thick and warm. She coughed, then her brain snapped to attention.

Fire.

She could hear it now, the unmistakable popping sound of flames. Quickly, she looked around to see what she could grab before she bolted out of the place. The only thing she valued was her father's medical bag, yet not finding it with a single sweep of her eyes, she instinctively rushed to the door and turned the knob. Her head was already feeling heavy from stress, her body uncoordinated.

The door wouldn't budge.

Assuming fear had weakened her, she pulled harder.

Nothing.

Her face was uncomfortably hot, as in Brighton on a particularly humid day, and the air was becoming more and more unbreathable.

She looked around, spotted her water pitcher, and took a few precious seconds to douse a kerchief with the cool liquid and hold the cloth over her face.

Rushing back to the door, she began pulling frantically at

the knob, panting and calling for help at the same time, though the chance of someone passing was remote at that hour. Being miles away, the big house certainly had no view of this tiny cottage even if it was burning brightly against the night sky.

In response, something went *whoosh* and suddenly there was fire burning *inside* the cottage.

"Help me!" she screamed, although she should not have wasted her breath. Then unable to stop myself, she shrieked, "Garreth! Please come!"

She could hear nothing besides the hungry licking of flames. The cottage would be consumed within minutes.

The air was almost too hot to breathe, and she thought longingly of the fresh, crisp night just outside the walls. Oh, never would she complain of the cold again.

The door refused to open, but she hadn't tried the window. How stupid not to have abandoned the door after her initial attempt.

Looking around, she finally spotted her father's bag, then grabbed it, and, like a discus thrower, wound up and heaved it at the window.

The hot glass yielded slightly but did not break.

She hit it again, and again it gave a little but stayed intact.

Something harder was required. The ironic part of her thought back suddenly of Andrew's birth and how the two footmen had brought in the cracked bell. How she wished for those two youths now. A steeple bell would surely shatter one thin window.

She glanced around, then spotted her examining stool. Picking it up, she used all her remaining strength to heave it at the window.

This time the glass cracked, and she hit at the crack again and again, as if the window itself were fire and she was beating out the flames. Soon she had smashed open a hole wide enough to crawl through.

She set the stool down, then stood on it, her skin crawling

at the thought of climbing through broken glass. Again the window seemed like the fire itself, the hole a ring of flames such as savage tigers were forced to leap through at the circus.

Yet she could survive multiple cuts. She could not survive much longer in the smoke. Rallying her courage, she gingerly grasped the jagged base of the hole, hoping her skirt would protect her legs. A huge gust of flame swept through the cottage, setting her dress and hair on fire. Appalled, she clutched on to the splintered glass as if it were a life raft and threw herself through the hole, hitting the spring-softened earth with a blessed thud.

For several moments, she just lay there, her heart pounding so furiously it filled her ears to the bursting point with aroused blood. Her hands were bleeding, her face throbbed, but she was no longer aflame and she'd broken no bones. The heat was still unbearable, so somehow she got to her feet and staggered ten yards away. Then she sat down in a stupor, watching her clinic become an immense bonfire, shooting its flames high into the night sky, then finally collapse on itself and turn to sparks, like ten thousand disturbed fireflies.

How quickly the fire diminished after the walls came down. At her distance, the heat soon became perversely pleasant. Her skin had not burned, and she was starting to shiver. Getting to her feet, she noticed a large black lump lying a short distance from the ashes. Approaching it, she recognized her father's medical bag with the clasp open and some of the contents spilling out. Later on, she thought and rethought over all her actions during the fire but did not remember throwing the bag out the window.

Yet she, or someone else, had. As she retrieved it and then collapsed back to the ground, she wondered whether her father had been with her, his spirit guiding her, giving her courage, then rescuing that material piece of himself so she could continue his work.

Sifting through some of the spillage, she found a bottle of salve to put on her hands and soothe her chapped face.

How she longed for John Travers at that moment. Or Charles. She didn't have the courage to long for Garreth, who had rescued her on two other occasions.

But nobody came. In a daze, she stumbled through the darkness back to the house. When she finally made it through the servants door, the porter gasped then grabbed her, shouting for Manda and Becky. They were like angels of mercy, and she felt like a newborn babe in arms as they lay her on a couch in the servants hall and ran for some younger male assistance.

Neither Garreth nor Charles was at home, but Heath, the youngest son, came dashing down the hall, then seemed to fall apart at the sight of a female body in semi-charred attire. "G-get Frederick," he stuttered, clearly nonplussed. "And send for the doctor."

"I'm all right," Ravenna insisted, then lay back, her head pounding.

And she *was* all right, her wounds superficial. But even in her stupor, she thought back to the sound of footsteps. Someone wanted to kill her. Did Cholly hate her that much?

But no, she felt he had another motive in mind.

He wanted simply to close her clinic, to send young women like his daughter back to their cramped, vermin-infested cottages.

In that respect, he would surely succeed.

Since she owned no land, and had given up her own cottage to the Warrens, she had nowhere to rebuild. Although she needed his protection, she could hardly ask Garreth to further risk his property for her.

She had no choice but to attend to her patients in their own cottages again.

And leave Garreth's household forever.

Fourteen

According to the late Sir Richmond Marisse, Ravenna's esteemed father, one of the characteristics of a good friend is that, when it is time to go, he lets you leave.

In that regard, Harlixton Hall was not Ravenna's good friend. For as much as she tried to quit the place, some unbidden tie kept holding her back.

It took her several days to prepare a new, and this time adamant, resignation speech for Garreth. Yet *this* time the thought of leaving was much more painful to her. She felt all caught up in the family's problems, unable to detach her mind or get her bearings. As she crossed the main hall and walked toward Garreth's study, saluting the portrait of Lady Philippa as usual, it seemed as if she were leaving home for the unknown, and not the reverse.

You have to go, her inner voice warned, reminding her that there was something sinister about the entire family, or rather, the entire house in which she'd been destined to live for a while.

There was indeed some curse, some family secret, which she could not fathom. Some inner sickness or disturbance that was affecting everyone, including herself.

She had been experiencing a slight irregularity of the heart rhythm of late, nothing to be alarmed about except that for her age and gender it was most uncommon.

Her father had also experienced it—so it must have had

some inherited component. But he was a graying, broken man when it started, long gone in his vapors, not a fresh young woman hardly on the threshold of adulthood. No, it was not any Marisse curse that was finally catching up with her, but some dark secret in the Pembroke heart that was striking her own.

Yet she, like her father, was feeling an acute sense of failure, and in this area, the feeling was completely Marissian. She had let a woman die for lack of medical experience, her clinic was a charred ruin, and even little Andrew appeared to be failing despite her care.

So what kind of doctor will you be, then? her inner father sneered. *You can't even save a child.*

A shudder of helplessness coursed through her at that stern voice. As she approached Garreth's door, she felt the knot of her existence loosen. Her thoughts became frayed threads. She wanted to run away, but even her legs became slack. Where could she go? Home? Did she even have a home anymore?

The Warrens had undoubtedly overrun her cottage like rabbits, and indeed she began thinking of her cottage as the Warrens' warren, but perhaps they would grant her her own little bed once more.

And the idea of company, now that she had experienced a house full of people, was not unpleasant to her.

She paused in front of Garreth's closed door, taking several calming breaths, which restored her resolve. She would tell him that she was badly needed elsewhere, that she did not have the temperament of a nursemaid, and that she would repay him for the cottage she had destroyed through her own carelessness—for she had told him simply that a lamp had fallen on some tinctures and set the place afire. If she told him it had been destroyed by an arsonist, he might insist she remain for her own protection.

As she raised her hand to knock, she heard a muffled sound coming from the room. She listened again and heard heavy footsteps, not steps actually, but a kind of staggering gait, as if someone were drunk and about to fall.

It was unbecoming for a grown woman to spy, but if someone within were in need, then she should enter without waiting.

Bending down, she peered through the keyhole.

At first she saw nothing. The room appeared unoccupied. Then a figure came into view. It was Garreth himself, and he was holding his long, graceful fingers up to his eyes, as if he were covering his face in shame.

She watched carefully, since he was restraining himself even in the privacy of his own quarters. Then, with a muffled sigh, he lowered his hands and she caught a glimpse of the eyes.

They were her father's . . . and the pain in them seemed unbearable.

His face with streaked with tears.

Despite herself, she scanned the room as best she could for evidence of a bottle, a decanter, a snifter, but it was difficult to see the length of the desk. Suddenly Garreth emitted a soft, hoarse sob, as if something had broken out of his control.

He moved unsteadily toward the wing chair and out of her field of vision, but she could hear the sobbing coming fast now. She listened for any words but heard only the guttural sounds of grief.

There was no shame in tears, her father had always said to injured soldiers who bit down on rags to stanch their screams. Some of the best broke down quickly, and she had grown to respect that. Tears were the body's natural way of cleansing out poisons, and it took courage to weep.

She looked again, but Garreth was moving farther away from the door, perhaps to look out the window.

Her impulse was to go in and comfort him, but she feared that he would be mortified. To have thus broken down in front of a servant, who was neither his confidant nor his butler at that.

Her heart fluttered at that thought. Yes, she'd been really nothing more than a servant in his house, and he as distant to her as to all the others.

He came back into her field of vision, this time carrying a snifter half full of brandy.

Her blood turned cold at the sight.

Her sympathy for what he must be suffering evaporated in an instant.

The tears of a drunken man are as worthy as his piss.

She blushed at the vulgarity of that statement, but another image of her father returned, with the stench of ether and sweat tainting the purity of his tears.

She turned away, telling her fluttering heart that she had best stay away from Mr. Garreth Pembroke, that she had buried one man with a bottle of poison at his side and could not give her affections to another.

Muffled sobs could be heard in the room, and despite the fact that footsteps approached and thus she would soon be discovered and humiliated, she bent down again . . .

. . . just in time to hear Garreth shake his head and whisper, "Forgive me."

The footsteps were growing louder, and Raven jumped up. She would not allow herself to be branded a spy. Quickly looking around for a suitable hiding place, she spotted a large pedestal upon which was an even larger Grecian urn. Would the combined height conceal her? With no time to ponder this question, she dove behind the pottery and crouched low on the floor.

Instantly, she regretted this move, for to be discovered hiding behind a pot would be far more humiliating than to have been encountered outside the study door. She felt close to tears herself while she waited for Wyngate, or even Charles, to spot her and demand she come out with an explanation.

The footsteps, however, stopped short of her hiding place. Peeking around the pedestal, she saw a servant she'd never met stop in front of a door she'd never seen open. The maid was carrying a draped tray, undoubtedly with lunch underneath the napkin. Out of her apron pocket she pulled a key, turned it in the lock, then entered and closed the door behind herself.

Raven was at some distance, but she thought she heard the sound of footsteps ascending a staircase.

Jumping out from her hiding place, relief flooding her as she was once more alone and uncompromised, she walked quickly to the unknown door and tugged at the knob.

Of course it had been relocked.

Perhaps she would seek out John Travers to ask him what lay on the other side.

But there was no need. The secret of the locked door was as apparent as if the servant had shouted out her destination.

Lady Philippa's hermitage lay at the other side of that door. Ravenna was sure of it.

So once again she found she could not leave that house, that family.

Lady Philippa, she vowed the next time she passed her portrait. *I will find you before I go. And in doing so, I will uncover what secrets lie concealed in your heart—and in the hearts of those you love.*

Fifteen

Word of Sarah Henson's death did not reach Ravenna till the day the villagers buried her in the churchyard. No one blamed the midwife for not being there to save her, but the consensus among the gossips was that if she *had* been there . . .

Raven took the news quite hard, for Sarah, like Anne, had died of postpartum hemorrhage. Sarah had, therefore, been the "next woman," whom Raven might have saved in order to redeem herself.

Why had no one sent for her? The answer to that question was obvious, and as she had feared: In the eyes of the villagers, she was now an outsider. Who would dare call for her at midnight to attend a routine birth, despite Ravenna's insistence that the cottagers do exactly that?

Sarah's death was a painful warning to her. Like Aeneas, she was being told by the gods to stop pursuing an impossible love, lest it destroy her.

Garreth, as fate would have it, was holed up in his study on the afternoon she chose yet again to announce her resignation. *As God is my witness,* she vowed as she stood in front of his door, *by evening I will be gone from this house.*

She knocked on the study door and heard Garreth's deep voice grant her admittance.

When she entered, a smile flickered across his lips.

"Miss Marisse," he said with the proper courtesy, then stood and waited for her to approach his desk.

"Sir."

She took several steps toward him, but stopped, feeling once more the embarrassment he always evoked in her.

"My nephew is much improved, and Charles says that it is entirely owing to your care."

"Thank you, sir."

"And the staff has never been healthier, thanks to your medicines and ministrations."

"Thank you, sir."

"I hope you have plans for rebuilding your infirmary. I quite forgive you for burning it to the ground, though I hope you will be more careful in future."

"Yes, sir."

"Don't work so hard, or so late at night that you can't contain a simple lamp fire."

"No, sir." She felt as awkward as a child called on the carpet. "I'll be more vigilant, even though . . ."

He waited for her to finish. When she did not, he prompted her. " 'Even though' . . . you were about to say . . ."

She was about to say that she was feeling increasingly unwell, had become prone to dizzy spells, to lapses in concentration. It had something to do with his house, or with her residence there.

But of course she did not make such bold accusations. She simply said, "Nothing of importance, sir."

Sensing her discomfort, he said, "But please, do sit down." Then he motioned for her to sit in the wing chair facing his desk. After she was seated, he came around the desk and leaned casually against one corner. She was not expecting such informality from him, or such proximity.

He waited patiently for her to state her business, and she looked down at her hands, her carefully prepared speech having fled her mind. Finally she wet her lips and began.

"Several days ago, sir, a young woman in the village died for lack of medical care."

"Was there no doctor for her?" She glanced up and saw genuine concern in Garreth's eyes.

"No."

"Where was Longacre?"

"He only sees patients who can pay him."

"Is that true?"

"Do you doubt me?" she retorted, feeling inappropriately defensive. Perhaps it was her mind's way of putting up a barrier between Garreth and her heart.

He stared hard into her eyes, and her anger melted. She was simply no match for him.

"Would you like me to speak to him about this?"

She thought for a moment, then said, "No, sir."

"Would you like me to help her family in some way?"

"No . . ."

"No?"

"I mean, yes, of course—I mean . . . Sir," she said, trying to maintain her composure. "The woman bled to death after the birth of her baby . . . like Anne. I know more now . . . I should have been there. I believe I could have saved her."

He pondered her words for a moment, and as she watched his face, she sensed that he was feeling genuine grief. Finally he said, "This is one of the common hazards of childbearing, I take it."

"Yes. Particularly among the poor and undernourished."

"How can you be so certain you could have helped her, then?" His statement was intended to be of comfort to her, but she took it as a challenge.

"Sir, if I'd been called—"

"Yet why weren't you? I told you this is not a prison. You are free to come and go as you please."

"But I cannot. That is, they cannot. The villagers . . ." She stood up and retreated several steps from the desk.

"I've come to you this afternoon to say that I simply must return to my former way of life, my own cottage, to—"

"I don't understand."

"I don't belong here," she said, shaking her head.

"And why is that?"

She found herself losing her train of thought. For an instant, Garreth reminded her of her father, who was always able to unsettle her mind with only a sentence or two.

"I just explained to you—"

"You have explained nothing to me, Miss Marisse, except that you have some fanciful notion of yourself as a savior of the poor and destitute."

"Sir," she said, rallying her anger. "The poor and destitute, as you say, have no one else. As pitiful and unskilled as I am, it is my duty to help them."

"Is it? And what about my family?"

"Sir, your nephew—"

"You will not leave here."

She looked at him in amazement. It was not for him to decide. "Sir, I am not . . . that is, Andrew does not need me anymore. I mean, he does not need *me* . . ."

"Tell Charles that," Garreth quipped.

"What I'm trying to say is—"

"Please sit down, Miss Marisse," he said, motioning again to the wing chair.

"Thank you, but I prefer to stand."

He stared at her thoughtfully, then said, "I see that you indeed blame yourself for the young woman's death."

Lowering her eyes, she nodded dismally. "Yes. Yes, I do. As I do for Anne's death."

"Do you believe, then, that you can control everything? Even life and death itself?"

"No, sir," she replied with honesty. "But I've reviewed Anne's case over and over in my mind, and I wrote to a colleague of my father's, an eminent physician in Berlin, and he told me that I . . ."

She stopped speaking, because Garreth's eyes were suddenly far away. His mind was clearly not on what she was saying. Her cheeks grew red with embarrassment—after all, what did he care about her preoccupations, her guilt?

"I'll go now," she whispered, and when he still said nothing, she added, "I'll explain my decision to Charles."

In the heavy silence, she turned her back on him and walked to the door. When her hand was on the knob, she heard his voice, and she realized that every nerve in her body had been hoping to hear it.

"Ravenna."

She closed her eyes, sensing she could not leave, sensing there was something unfinished between them, something unrelated to Charles or Andrew or her position in the household.

She heard him approach her, then finally felt his presence hovering behind her back, his breath upon her hair. She turned and found him staring at her.

For a moment she, too, simply stared. All her senses became aware of him—his handsomeness, the rhythm of his breathing, the masculine scent of him.

"Ravenna," he murmured, then pulled her into his arms.

There was something inevitable about what was to happen next. He was no longer her employer, but simply a man cradling a woman. And so they both forgot themselves as his lips claimed hers. It was her first kiss, something so magical that it blocked out all sight and sound and anything but itself. Her whole body became soft and open to him. She wanted him to touch her everywhere, to toss her up into his arms and carry her off to a plump feather bed and kiss her and kiss her until her sorrow withered and fell off like an old skin.

She sighed, and he deepened the kiss, coaxing her lips open and pressing his teeth against hers. It was such a moment of beauty in her stark world that she wanted to weep, but she closed her eyes tightly against tears, fearing the embarrassment they would cause her.

His lips broke from hers, and he crushed her to his chest. She could feel his heart beating rapidly, and so powerfully she feared it would crack his ribs. She had never been in such intimate contact with a man, and she wanted to stay pinned to Garreth's chest, listening to his heartbeat, forever.

"Sir," she whispered, but he hushed her and tightened his grip.

"Garreth," she began again, then his hands and lips were all over her as a frenzy overtook him. He thrust his hands roughly in her hair, pulling away the ribbon she always used to tie it back and grabbing fistfuls of curls as he pressed her face against his. It was a kind of passion that young girls read about, the passion that leads to ravishment, then regret. What power was there! Suddenly she understood how a heroine could risk everything for a moment like this.

But she had little to risk. She was a virgin, yes, but did not intend to use her virginity as a bargaining tool to acquire a husband. She had a calling; she did not need a husband.

Yet this . . . this moment was something she had not reckoned on. When it was over, she would certainly be dismissed and sent on her way—which was what she wanted anyway. But the memory would be hers always.

Giving in to a newly found desire, Ravenna wrapped her arms around Garreth's neck and drew him closer to her. How quickly her body had learned to respond to him . . . how right and natural it seemed.

"Garreth," she whispered dreamily.

This time the sound of his name had a chilling, sobering effect on him. Abruptly he released her and turned away. The cold air of the room shocked her face after losing the heavy warmth of his breathing.

"Forgive me," he said, adjusting the sleeves of his shirt. "As you see, there are some things that cannot be controlled."

A humiliating moment of silence ensued, broken only by the unschooled counterpoint of their rapid breathing.

"I'll . . ." she said tentatively, smoothing out her skirt. "I'll go now."

He nodded, exhaling as he did so, then replied, "I'll inform my family of your wish to leave us."

She tiptoed—again—toward the door, tears threatening to spill down her face and humiliate her.

"Take this," he called out behind her, and she turned and saw the knotted ribbon in his hand. "Tie back your hair."

She stood gaping at him, knowing that if she returned to his side, she would never leave him. She would beg him to let her stay. At that moment, the course of her life depended on which direction she walked, toward him or away.

If only she had the resolve of a man. Once decided, a man's course of action became etched into his mind. But she was forever like a curtain in the wind—flapping and waving in every direction at once, never of her own choosing.

"Take it, Ravenna," he repeated, holding the ribbon at arm's length.

She looked backward toward the door. "Sir, I—"

"Take it," he growled. "And forgive me for my indiscretion."

A single tear decided her fate. For after one had escaped the vise grip of her will, a torrent fell down her face. She cried for Sarah, and her father, for the frustration of loving Garreth, and the loneliness of so many years. And she found herself walking blindly toward him, falling into his open arms, allowing him to kiss her forehead in a chaste, comforting salute.

He wrapped her in a shawl and sat with her a long while, not coaxing her to talk or explain herself. Servants knocked at the door to inquire about pouring the tea or tending to the fire or drawing the drapes, but Garreth sent them away.

Undoubtedly, it was all over the servants hall that something suspicious was transpiring in the study.

Finally he began asking questions about her father, her life in London, her work in the village.

"It was unfair of me to take you from your work," he said when his curiosity had apparently been satisfied. "It was selfish and wrong. You are free to go back to your villagers."

"Thank you," she said, even though she felt a rush of cold air chill her heart. She tried to rise, but his arm remained firmly around her shoulder.

"Only answer me this question," he continued. "Would you give up your work—for me?"

She stared deeply into his eyes then, afraid of what he would say next. There was no pride or distance in his face now, only a strange, perhaps desperate humility, as if he were a servant and she his mistress.

"For you?" she repeated stupidly.

"To become"—and then she sensed he choked out the words—"my wife?"

A dozen images flashed through her mind just then—of Anne's face, beatific and trusting as Ravenna let her die; of little Manda as she told her of Sarah's death; of her father grimly sawing off a leg while she assisted him, forcing down her own terror; of her father in his last days, the spirit already dead while the body hastened to join it.

"Yes," she whispered, and Garreth turned her face up to his and kissed her again.

Book II

Harlixton Hall

Sixteen

June 12, 1844

The marriage of Ravenna Marisse to Garreth Pembroke was a simple affair, as there were no mothers or elder female relations on hand to complicate it. Only the family and the servants were in official attendance at the church, though many of the bride's patients from the village showed up as well, to indicate perhaps that they felt no betrayal on her part and to wish the newlyweds happiness in their married life.

Garreth was clearly uncomfortable in his high starched collar and grim marriage suit, but no more uncomfortable than the bride in Justine's muslin and silk wedding dress, complete with a hot, unnecessary white silk shawl and an inhuman, asphyxiatingly tight corset. Would that she had been born into an age when women were released from such chambers of torture and ill health.

Half the county, it seemed, attended the wedding breakfast, which offered tables overflowing with hot rolls and meat pies, ham and tongue and roast turkey, oranges and raspberries and a pineapple from the forcing garden, and a ridiculously large wedding cake with white and yellow marzipan icing. The bride tasted little of it, since she could hardly breathe. After all the guests had left, and she was in her own clothes again, she crept down to the kitchen and begged Cook for samples of everything she had missed.

When evening came, the bride retired early, in advance of her new husband. She had refused the assistance of a maid, since the slightest wink or smirk would have mortified her. Wandering alone through Garreth's suite made Raven realize how apprehensive she was about fulfilling her wifely duties.

In a year's time, would she like lying in his bed, with him snoring and perhaps smelling of wine and stomach vapors while she tried valiantly to sleep with a huge pregnant belly?

She felt her middle expand with just the imagining of it, and she had to press against her fine silk nightrail—a gift outright, not a loan, from Justine—to make sure her belly was still firm.

The room had a sparse, masculine air about it. The furnishings were in various shades of brown and beige, the objects utilitarian—a comb, a shaving mug and brush, a razor, a strop, cuff links, a plain jewel box. She looked down at her wedding ring—the only piece of jewelry that was truly hers. She had a small box for it, a gift from the carpenter's son. Perhaps she should buy a bigger one; the wife of a wealthy man would certainly have more things to add.

She picked up the shaving mug, then dropped it quickly as she heard her husband's footsteps on the hall carpet.

Feeling out of place and exposed, she looked around for concealment, then dove into the confines of his bed—clearly the least safe shelter in the room.

Holding the summer counterpane high against her face, she tried to quell her fears by remembering the sensation of being in Garreth's arms, of being overwhelmed by his power, and—

The door opened and her husband entered the chamber

wordlessly. If he saw her, he did not acknowledge her presence.

She felt panic-stricken, ridiculous—should she have remained fully dressed? Having no mother or married aunt to advise her on these things, she had simply decided that it would be less embarrassing to present herself in her nightclothes to avoid the awkwardness of undressing.

How was it supposed to be between a newlywed man and wife? She had never thought to ask her father, even if it had been appropriate for an unmarried daughter to ask her male parent.

Garreth walked over to a wooden stand and removed his coat, then waistcoat and cravat, and draped them neatly over the pommel. It could have been any other night, it seemed. But did his manservant generally help him disrobe? Again, she had no knowledge of the ways of the rich.

Deftly he pulled the somewhat wrinkled holland shirt out of his trousers and unbuttoned it, removing the cuff links and placing them next to others in a porcelain bowl by the dressing table. Holding her breath, she watched him shrug out of his shirt, the powerful muscles of his shoulders and arms appearing in outline beneath his form-fitting undershirt.

She had only felt those strong shoulders, never seen the skin, and she embarrassed herself by gawking at the fine masculine curves.

He turned to face her, and she shyly studied the contours of his chest, the ebony curls, the well-toned muscles. He saw that his bride was watching him, and the shadow of a smile curved his lips as he reached down and removed his shoes.

With his head bent, she was able to study once more the powerful muscles of his back, the broad splay of his shoulders, and again she imagined being held by those arms, forgetting that in a few moments that would indeed be what would happen.

He straightened and again caught her studying him. She blushed instantly. There were many things she wanted to say, but couldn't think of anything significant or worthwhile enough to break the silence.

He walked over to an armchair, sat, and removed his stockings and garters. As he arose, he unfastened the top buttons of his trousers. Raven closed her eyes, thinking she could not bear to see him become naked. But remove his trousers he did, then he walked over to the whale oil lamp and turned it completely off.

"There," he whispered finally. "Will darkness be a suitable covering for you?"

There was a full moon, however, and even without a lamp, she saw him clearly in the silver glow. It had not been her place to draw the curtains, and with the servants banished, the heavy drapes had stayed wide open.

He sat on the edge of the bed, removed his smallclothes, then turned and nestled naked under the counterpane. It was the first time she had ever been in a bed with another human being.

She closed her eyes and tried to sink into pure sensation—this was her wedding night—a rite of passage from maidenhood to womanhood and hopefully motherhood. She was making a journey that almost every other woman throughout time had made before her. *There never was virgin got till virginity was first lost . . .* Who had said that? Someone in a play by Shakespeare.

She imagined the little girl she might someday hold in her arms, the little virgin who would emerge from the sacrifice of her own virginity, a girl not unlike the dozens she had delivered into the world. Yet hers would be swaddled in a blanket of fine wool, not a bundle of rags. Her daughter would wear a starched white christening gown and be her father's pride . . .

Garreth touched her shoulder, and she lurched away from him, not quite ready to face the responsibility ahead of her.

"Ravenna," he said softly, and she sighed with relief that he had spoken with tenderness.

But saying no more, he turned her body toward him, cradled her face in his hands, and kissed her, a gentle, moist kiss of respect.

He was her husband now, and she need not restrain herself, so she tried to ease into his kiss, reaching her arms up and curving them around his neck. He beckoned her lips apart with his tongue, and she opened herself to him, feeling him begin a moist probing of her teeth, her own tongue, her interior space.

His hands reached up and gently unpinned the heavy coil of her hair until it fell sloppily around her head and shoulders. How she had envied the girls of pure English blood their silky tresses, while she with her Eastern ancestry was fated to carry the mane of barbarians.

"You have beautiful hair," Garreth said, and she found herself laughing, feeling suddenly at ease with a subject that had plagued her so much as a child.

"It's not human hair," she quipped.

Looking at her quizzically, he replied, "It's lovely. So black."

"But so coarse, and . . . unladylike. My father used to say that when God was distributing hair to all the families at the beginning of time, he ran out when he got to the Marisses. 'Come, bring us some animal hair,' he commanded, and this is what we got."

Garreth made no further reply to her silly chatter, but simply ran his hands through the heavy curls, and she giggled nervously when his fingers got snagged in them.

"See, I told you," she said. "Not the hair of a human."

He released her for a moment, then sat up, his back leaning against a pillow. It seemed, incredibly, as if he was deciding whether or not to continue.

"Garreth?" she inquired. "Is there—something the matter?"

He turned his head and looked at her. A hard, unexplained stare was on his face. Her girlish excitement disappeared abruptly as she saw that she was sharing the bed not with Garreth Pembroke, but with some distant shadow of himself.

Again, she wondered hopelessly whether all men were ruled by ghosts and demons or whether it was simply her ill fate to have been first sired by and now married to such a one. The prospect of sharing her life once more with a man's Furies abruptly overwhelmed her. She looked away, terrified she would burst into tears.

For a moment, they lay in their separate worlds, their bodies barely touching, like two halves of an unfastened coat. In response to her question, Garreth said without looking at her, "Forgive me. Perhaps I should not have married you."

His words could not have been more ill chosen. She recalled his blubbering tears in the library, and those same words—*forgive me*—and her chest began to heave.

"Oh, Christ," he grumbled in disgust. "Don't start that."

"You—you—" she said, then tried to mumble an apology.

"Ravenna, I can't understand a word you're saying."

She sniffled like a hurt child who was trying to be brave. "I'm sorry. I can understand why you wouldn't . . . want me."

Abruptly, he snapped out of his trance. Turning, he cried, "Not want you!" Then he pulled her hard against the length of him, and before she could catch her breath, his lips claimed hers.

Closing her eyes, she felt as if all will were being stripped from her. Whatever powers directed Garreth's life had turned their forces upon her. Suddenly, his lips left hers, and with a single fluid movement, Garreth had her gown up and over her head. Impatiently he tossed the wadded silk off the bed and thrust the remaining tangle of bedclothes away from her body. Seeing her thus stripped had a civilizing effect on him, and the fear that undoubtedly showed in her eyes calmed him down.

A part of her needed urgently to be covered up, to be protected from Garreth's intrusive maleness. Having no gown or sheet, she reached out to Garreth himself, and he threw himself on top of her like a heavy quilt.

"Not want you!" he whispered again, then he entwined his legs tightly around hers while his hands sought her breasts, pressing and squeezing them like plush toys in the hands of a greedy child.

Bending his head down, he suckled first one then the other nipple, this time with a gentleman's practiced lips, knowing just where to caress her with just the right pressure. She wondered where he had received his "practice," if no other woman had ever turned his head. A year from now, when she was fat and used and safely his, perhaps he would tell her.

Gradually she was melting, forgetting about everything but the moment, her head listing to one side while she closed her eyes, unable to silence the sigh that escaped her lips.

He kissed her nipples without mercy as they became alert, straining peaks, begging for more. But his lips moved on, kissing her belly, her hips, moving lower. She felt the soft curls of his head and chest warming her skin.

For a moment, he lay still against her, head against her belly, legs folded over hers. It was if he was simply enjoying a moment of peace between them—flesh pressing flesh, two naked beings discovering the secrets within each other. Ravenna felt the peace within him, and shared it. Growing ever bolder, she reached down to pull his shoulders up to hers, to feel his face against hers. He responded quickly, remolding his body anew, pressing his lips once more upon hers.

This time his hand moved down her body, tracing the same path abandoned by his lips until it reached that shy,

untested part of hers. For an instant, her thighs tightened—a
virgin's reflex—but then her muscles relaxed. In the next
instant, she found herself craving his touch more than anything she had ever wanted before.

Seeking the small nub of sensitive flesh that no one had
ever touched, Garreth found and massaged it, and Raven's
legs went rigid, then limp with the sensation. Her body was
a kettle of water and he fire, heating her up relentlessly
against her will or control. Her mind became diffuse, unable
to think, as her body became focused on Garreth's hand,
on the swelling center of her body.

She was sighing in rhythm to his caresses now, wanting
the warmth never to subside, wanting the rest of her life to
consist of this torrent of sensation. And she felt again what
she had sensed in Garreth's study—that this was a moment
worth giving up everything for.

Gradually, the caressing of his hands and lips ceased. She
opened her eyes and saw that he had straddled her body,
his arms holding himself up at a distance over her so she
could see his face. She opened her eyes wide for him, giving him her full attention. *It's time,* his eyes said, and she
understood. It was time for both of them to decide, to
choose and be chosen, for their choice would be irrevocable.

Yes, she told him with her eyes.

And then he brought his body very close to hers, gripped
her hand in his powerful fingers, and guided it down to the
rigid, swollen organ that would join them forever. All her
knowledge of anatomy and procreation had not prepared
her for the massiveness of an erect male. She wondered
whether she was feeling what every maiden since the beginning of time must have felt—a fear of being too small,
too fragile, too afraid to go on. But as he drew her fingers
down the shaft, shuddering as the fingertips touched and
explored him, Ravenna marveled at how smooth the skin
was, how rounded the point of entry, as if made to woo
rather than conquer.

This iron rod covered in velvet, which forever separated man from woman, would soon make them one. Sometimes when she handed a naked babe into its mother's eager arms, she would marvel at the tiny sex organs, wondering what children this little one would someday bear or sire. Though God had ordained women to be the lesser sex, still she would feel a kind of awe when looking at the sex of a tiny girl—the shy, protected part that would stay hidden behind a secret veil until a man said *Now, it's time* and she said *Yes.*

But this was no time to daydream. Impulsively, she wriggled her fingers away from Garreth's grasp and began an independent exploration of him, holding the shaft, feeling the prominent veins, the delicate organs underneath, the soft intervening hair. He flipped over and lay on his back, allowing her fingers better access. She traced his hips, his thighs, every part of him. He closed his eyes, and it was Garreth's turn to sigh.

The feeling of intimacy was delicious. She bent her head down and gently kissed his lips.

"Forgive me if I hurt you," he said, turning her on her back and easing himself over her.

Again, it was an unfortunate choice of words, for her body went rigid at the hearing of them.

So the demons would intrude even now.

"Ravenna?" he whispered, trying to interpret the new rift that was developing between them.

She closed her eyes, trying to regain the harmony that had existed just a moment before. But Garreth misinterpreted her closed face as a closing of her heart.

"Oh, Christ," he spat out again. "Well . . . perhaps I'm rushing you. Rest now. I'm a patient man." Then he rolled over on his side, putting at least a foot of mattress between them. "Good night, Ravenna."

For several moments, Ravenna simply stared at the broad back that was turned toward her. She had been alone with her husband less than an hour, and already she felt inadequate to the task of being married to him. Would everything in their life together become this difficult? She studied the ebb and flow of his shoulders and lungs, fearing that he would fall asleep and hence abandon her on her wedding night. The faceless wall of flesh barred her from seeing his expression, but his posture alone was a statement of rejection.

Despite his words, he didn't really want her.

No, she resolved in her mind. She would not allow the rift between them to grow into a chasm. Clearly, he wanted her. The demons were her enemies, the demons were keeping her from her beloved Garreth. Tentatively, she placed her fingers on his back. From the slight shudder her touch elicited, she knew her husband was not asleep, and not unaware of her.

Growing bolder, she inched her body closer to his, pressing first her cheek, then her breasts, then her entire length against his. He did not move, but she knew that he was coming back to her, that the Garreth she loved was coming back to her, that they were sinking into each other again, feeling a harmony of spirits that would merge into a single song.

"My love," she whispered into the soft hair behind his ear, feeling bolder than she had dared to feel since she'd first met him on the stairs. "My love," she soothed him, the heat of her own breath on his skin.

Wordlessly, he rolled on his stomach, sighing as he moved to reassure her that he welcomed her touch and wanted more of it. Drunk now with her own sense of power and rightness, she began to massage his back, touching and kneading the taut muscles, bending down to place a trail of kisses along his spine.

"My love," she repeated yet again.

Then it was her turn to tell him that it was time, her turn to take command. Tugging gently at his arm, she rolled his body over so that he was facing her. A flame of desire licked at the center of her body as she saw the soft, drunken expression on his face.

Opening his eyes, he reached out to her, their arms and legs merging like dreamy images around and into each other. At the core of her molten, dream body, Ravenna felt the hardness of her husband pushing into her, craving admittance.

Both of them felt the thin membrane of resistance.

The fear Ravenna should have felt was so remote, so far away. She nestled her cheek once more against her husband's neck.

She felt another push, more insistent this time.

Opening her eyes, Ravenna saw apprehension clouding Garreth's face. He was afraid of hurting her.

But she was beyond hurt, too warm, too deliciously aflame to register pain. Instinctively, she opened her thighs a bit wider and arched up to meet his first thrust.

The shock of their joining hit her like a fist. She felt a trickle of something warm carve a tiny path down her thigh.

Then there was pain, and heat, and power, much stronger than she'd imagined. *Oh, silly maiden!* she chided herself. *Did you not know? Did you not suppose?* Suddenly, she was being scorched from within, her inner space becoming a pillar of fire. She would not survive this, she thought, as she felt the essence of herself slip away. She became Leda or Daphne or a dozen other mythic maidens impaled by a male god. Her body tried to push him away. Her feet dug into the mattress as her muscles sought to expel him.

But gradually, miraculously, the pain subsided. The hot hurt became a healing warmth. The rhythm of his presence inside her became like a hand administering a soothing balm. She found she could move with him, fall into his rhythm as if it were familiar. She felt open, opened and relaxed and unafraid. A terrifying bridge had been crossed; she was now on the other side of a great divide.

She opened her eyes and studied Garreth's straining face, the concentration creasing his brow. It was fascinating to watch him, to see the beads of sweat on his face and shoulders, to feel responsible for having this effect on another human being. Closing her eyes again, she found herself sinking, the borders and boundaries of her life becoming diffuse and indistinct. She felt as close to Garreth as she had to any other person—closer, for now there seemed to be no demarcation separating herself from him. She was becoming Garreth, moving as he moved, breathing as he breathed. They were like two dancers who had performed so long together that they moved like a single artist.

Their breathing accelerated as some ever-increasing force grabbed hold of both of them. They clung to one another as the force propelled them upward, out of their bodies. They were no longer Garreth and Ravenna, but air and fire.

Then the force exploded and hurled them in every direction. Garreth cried out and clutched Raven's shoulders as they fell. They crashed headlong into a soft shore, where they lay gasping, waiting for all the fragments to descend.

No longer air and fire, but warm earth and cool water.

As they lay there, collecting their thoughts, settling into sleep, Raven sensed somehow that while Garreth had become once more a separate being, she had not.

For she knew at that moment that she was carrying Garreth's child.

Seventeen

There were bad signs.

Ravenna had scarcely revealed to Garreth that she was with child when she realized that she would not carry it to term. Although she said daily prayers that her child would be born and would live to carry on his father's name, her medical knowledge was sufficient to diagnose an impending miscarriage.

Garreth knew nothing of her premonitions, yet he tried to keep their secret from the rest of the family. Childbearing, as John Travers had warned Ravenna that cold morning in December, was a terrifying subject among the Pembrokes. A wife who was with child had the mark of death upon her brow as surely as she carried a potential new life within her womb.

Despite their determination to confine the news within the walls of their bedchamber, the rest of the family soon found out. Maids, laundresses in particular, had a way of deducing such news by the absence of certain items from the wash. In that way, Sadie told Manda, who told Justine, who came right out and asked her sister-in-law.

"Yes, it's true," Ravenna confirmed, but said nothing more. Justine hugged her tightly, then kissed her cheek. Perhaps Justine was wondering whether in nine months' time she'd be burying her sister-in-law in the churchyard next to Anne.

"Dear sister," Justine said. "You're strong. You'll survive."

She invited Raven into her bedroom, where she treated her to a private showing of her own loose-fitting garments.

"You may borrow them all, if you're not superstitious," Justine said.

Bluntly, Raven asked her how many children she had lost. Justine said, "Three," and her eyes immediately teared up. Soon she was sobbing while Raven held her in her arms as if she were a patient. And like a doctor, Raven asked her to describe what happened, to recall any unusual signs or feelings.

Justine listed a host of them.

Her story kept Raven awake that night, for she recognized in Justine's case a pattern, one that was not dissimilar to her own condition.

Raven spent the rest of the night fighting sleep, as if by some conscious vigilance she could ward off Death when he came to claim her child. She heard his footsteps all around her, though of course, they were the noises of the house, creaks and groans, perhaps the footsteps of a servant summoned to fetch a late-night soporific.

Owing to her delicate condition, Raven's senses were heightened. She saw, heard, and felt more than she ever had before. Perhaps that was why her heart, strained already by fear as well as by the great love she felt for her husband, was becoming more and more arrhythmic. The flips and flops were increasing in intensity and duration. Perhaps Death intended to take away her life as well as her child's.

She slept only fitfully the next night, and the next, and many of the succeeding nights. The ragged beating of her heart, the noises, and a general feeling of doom kept waking her up. Sometimes, to pass a long, lonely hour while she waited for sleep to return, she propped herself up in bed and simply stared at her husband. Even in sleep, he radiated a power and beauty that suffused her with life-giving energy, that rallied her own strength. She would fight whatever this thing was that stood in the way of their happiness. *I will live,* she vowed, and *bear Garreth a child with sturdy legs and hair black as a Gypsy's.*

They were well into the summer, with its compensatory long days and short nights, when Ravenna started hearing patterns in the noises of the night. There was some sort of thumping, hollow and rhythmic, coming from the upper rooms. The sound of a crutch or peg leg limping across the floorboards. She hadn't heard it before her marriage because her guest chamber was on the other side of the house.

Soon she was straining to listen to the thumping. Perhaps it was a branch hitting the outer wall of the house. But no, it was definitely coming from *inside* the house.

Lady Philippa, perhaps exercising with a cane or crutch.

Night after night Ravenna heard it, until she could instantly pick it out from other noises, the way a mother can pick out the sound of her baby crying in a distant room.

One night she would leave her husband's bed and let the rhythm lead her to Lady Philippa herself.

Why she was so determined to find the older woman, she was not sure. Simple curiosity was a large part of it. She wanted to see this person who had once been young, who had given birth to her husband, who had carried him playfully on her back. She also had a stubborn, perhaps arrogant notion that she could cure her mother-in-law of whatever it was that was slowly killing her.

Unless Lady Philippa, like the men in Raven's life, had her own demons, for which there was no cure.

Every night, Garreth made tender love to her—she'd assured him it would not hurt the baby—then dropped off into a heavy sleep, cradling her in his arms or with one arm thrown protectively around her shoulder. But as his breathing became even and automatic, she would wriggle out of his grasp and seek her own portion of the massive four-poster, huddling her arms and legs up to her body as she waited for the dawn, enduring the cramps, the sickness, the fragmented, irregular beating of her heart.

And every night she would hear the thumping, like an unquiet spirit.

Eventually, she would fall into a restless sleep, usually during the predawn *uht* time, only to be awakened by the early sunshine—feeling exhausted and queasy. Sometimes Garreth would be at her side; often he would be already up and about.

Though she dearly loved her husband, Raven felt lost and despondent. Once her pregnancy became known, Garreth forbade her from tending anyone in the village—he would not have the mother of his child falling ill from fever, even though it was not the season.

So she spent her days with Justine and Clarity, sharing their pleasant, useless activities, to ease the tension of waiting. Indeed, there always seemed something planned that would fill up the day—a social call to a neighbor, courtesy calls to the cottagers on the estate, receiving and entertaining the neighbors who'd received and entertained them. Each of these activities required a different gown and accessories, which filled up more time in the dressing and undressing.

Like everything else in the household, Garreth seemed insulated from this uselessness. He worked from dawn to dinner, sharing his responsibilities with no one—not his brothers, not his wife. Tentatively, Raven asked Mrs. Oakes, the housekeeper, if she might participate in the managing of the household, but the woman invariably answered, " 'Tis all arranged, ma'am," then would speak no further of it.

Ravenna's closest friend in the family remained Charles, who still probed her mind when they took tea together.

"You'd make a good surgeon," she told him more than once, for his mind was sharp and his interest in medicine keen.

Usually he'd laugh, shrugging off her praise. Sometimes

he would just stare at her sadly, for reasons she could not fathom.

Except she knew that he shared what she was feeling—the apprehension, the dread. Sometimes, as they conversed, Ravenna saw a look of resignation in Charles's eyes, as if he had already accepted that she would be dead in a year's time. Indeed, the malaise of the big house was affecting her the way it had everyone else.

Once again, only Garreth seemed immune, and that became a part of the Harlixton secret she sought to uncover.

It was during the predawn hour one morning in August when she heard a scream, distant yet piercing, like the scream of a dying man, or a woman at the moment her child is born.

Having just fallen into an uneasy sleep, Ravenna bolted upright, her head pounding in protest, her heart jumping into her throat. As she pressed a hand against her chest, she listened for the sound again.

Nothing.

Garreth stirred, then shifted in bed.

She listened for the thumping.

Still nothing, though the birds were beginning their daily cacophony.

Craving her husband's protection, she opened his arm like a favorite doll's and slid into his embrace.

Even in sleep, he wrapped his arms around her, and the sliver of a smile warmed his face.

"Garreth," she whispered. "How I love you."

His eyes still closed, he turned on his side and his lips instinctively found hers. The kiss they shared had nothing of the frenzy of lovemaking. His lips were warm and calming and protective. She opened herself to him, lips and tongue and inner space merging into one.

Her nerves, the cells of her skin, the outer and inner boundaries of her body, all craved his touch. Without shame, she slid her cotton gown up over her head, then reached over and took away Garreth's thin shirt. Their bodies, like their lips, sought and found one another. They seemed a perfect match as they clung together, curve against curve, like the pieces of a well-crafted puzzle.

"How I love you," she whispered again as she felt the rigid male part of him slide into her body. There was no fear, no resistance now—only a sense of awe—as her body hugged him in a welcoming embrace.

Early light peaked through the parting in their heavy curtains. Her heart, for the moment, beat steady as a clock.

As Garreth held her tightly, the rhythm of his lovemaking strong and sure, she felt as safe as a baby being rocked to sleep in her father's arms. In the light of dawn, her nighttime fears seemed groundless. Had she really heard a scream disturb the peace of the upper floors? Had she really felt the imminence of her own death as her heart coughed and fluttered, threatening to stall like a tiny sailboat that has lost its wind?

Her mind froze at this train of thought, for she was falling victim to something even more terrifying than the Harlixton curse.

She had acquired her own demons.

Eighteen

By some miracle, weeks, then months, passed and still her baby lived inside her. Ravenna's spirits brightened considerably, and she began to fall into Garreth's happiness and confidence in the survival of his son.

"Of course it will be a son," he said to her over and over as he felt her belly for signs of his impending heir.

One morning in early September, as Ravenna brushed out her hair, Garreth burst through their chamber door and announced that they were to have a picnic along the path leading to the Thames. He had instructed Cook to prepare a basket of nourishing foods, and although her body had hardly changed in shape and function, he grabbed the pillows off the bed and announced that he would make a soft nest for her, to ease the burden of her condition.

He was in high spirits, a Garreth she rarely saw.

"My darling," he said, as he picked up her brush and continued to do the work of a maid, "how lovely you are." Pulling her heavy mane of hair aside, he bent his head and kissed the back of her neck.

Closing her eyes, she sank into a pool of pure sensation as his lips tasted every part of her neck.

"How soft . . ." he murmured. Setting the brush down, he wrapped his arms around her from behind her chair. They looked at their reflection in the mirror in front of them, and she felt awed once more that this powerful man was her husband, that he had chosen her to be his mate, to bear his child.

Still staring, she watched as his hands grasped the neck of her loose-fitting gown and pulled the fabric down off her shoulders, exposing her breasts, which were plump and sensitive owing to her condition. The nipples had already started to swell and darken, and she watched breathlessly as Garreth's long fingers stroked them, pitilessly, until desire coursed through the rest of her body.

Abruptly, Garreth jerked her to her feet, swooped her in his arms, and carried her to their freshly made bed. Her gown had become a tangle around her waist, and as he laid her gently on the bed, he pulled it off her body. She noticed his eyes darting briefly down to her still-flat belly. She could always notice the interest in his eyes—it was intensely fascinating to everyone, at least the first time, to see a pregnant woman's waist expand without heed to fashion, following an ancient pattern that knew nothing of corsets or the hour-glass figure.

She bit her lip, for she was unable to assure him that his son was quite safe and thriving inside her.

For a moment, Garreth's passion cooled as he sat down on the edge of the bed and laid his hand on her stomach.

"You are afraid, I think," he said.

She nodded. "Now that it's finally my turn."

Garreth laughed. "I never knew you to be vain or faint-hearted. You will be as beautiful to me when you are as stout as a bear as you are to me now. More beautiful still when you carry our son in your arms."

"Garreth," she said, as he continued to smile. "Do you remember when you rode upon your mother's back?"

"No, of course not," he said playfully. "I was too young."

Sitting up, her curiosity apparent on her face, she asked, "Do you think Lady Philippa remembers? Might I ask her? Might I see her sometime and—"

"No," he said, standing abruptly. The playfulness was gone.

"But Garreth, maybe she can be helped."

"Her welfare doesn't concern you, Ravenna."

"But if I might—"

"Leave this alone," he warned her.

"Why, Garreth? If she can be treated—"

"By you?" he retorted, the contempt of a stranger suddenly in his voice. To her dismay, a barrier had once more been raised between them.

"Yes," she replied, lifting her chin in defiance. "What harm can it do?"

At that, he laughed. "You should have asked yourself that before you attended my sister-in-law."

Raven was too shocked to respond. His words had hurt as surely as a slap across the face.

They went ahead with their picnic, but it was a tense, solemn affair. When they returned, Cholly Makepiece was lurking in the shadows at the back of the house, and Raven thought she heard him hiss at her as she passed. Garreth excused himself as they entered the parlor, and craving company, she sought out her in-laws, finally finding Charles, with whom she took tea alone.

That night her heart condition worsened. Her heart fluttered like a bird beating its wings against a trapper's cage. She wondered whether Garreth would find her dead in the morning. But the light of day found her quite alive, and as Garreth washed and dressed and bade her a courteous good morning, she began hatching her plan.

She would find the key to Lady Philippa's sanctum, break in, and by interviewing her, discover the secret of her son's unhappiness.

Nineteen

On one of her frequent walks through the wooded areas of the Harlixton estate, Ravenna came across a small patch of *Dioscorea villosa,* whose roots the savages in America used to prevent miscarriages. Again her source of this information was the old Indian slave woman, and feeling that this was somehow a sign that her baby might yet be spared, she ran back to the house to get some digging tools and her father's medical bag, which contained bottles and spirits for storage and preservation.

Returning to the precious plants, which were quite rare in England, she knelt on the ground and began to dig. All the while she wondered what Cook would say when she asked to have use of her stove and the largest pot in the kitchen for several hours.

As she was carefully extracting one well-formed tuber from the ground, Raven noticed out of the corner of one eye a slight female figure hurrying down the drive. Glancing in her direction, she recognized the maid who'd taken food to Lady Philippa.

Another sign.

Jumping to her feet and quickly gathering her belongings, Raven shouted, "Hello! Hello, there! Wait for me, please!"

If the girl heard her, she paid no heed, and she quickened her pace, for she was running from Ravenna quickly. Owing to the many bends in the drive, the girl would soon disap-

pear from Raven's view, whereupon she could sprint far
ahead if she chose.

"Miss!" Ravenna cried again. "Miss, please wait!" But
the girl hurried on.

Impulsively, Ravenna left her tools and bag and broke
into a run, but her skirts, her erratic heart, and of course,
her condition made her no match for the lithe figure ahead.

"Stop!" she called out, holding her skirts high as her
feet pounded against the ground. "Oh, please—"

A dagger-sharp pain in her abdomen cut off her words.

It was Raven who stopped then, immediately, and collapsed to the ground, rolling on to her left side to take any
pressure off the womb. She hardly dared to breathe.

Oh, dear God. Was this the beginning? she wondered,
feeling paralyzed with indecision. Should she lie perfectly
still, hoping the episode was mere overexertion, which
would pass without harm?

Should she get back to the house as quickly as possible
to prepare her decoction of Indian root?

Or should she simply do nothing and defer to Nature's
will?

The pain subsided, and though she heaved a sigh of relief,
she feared its return. A regular pattern of pain, though in-
frequent at first, would signal her child's death.

Five minutes or so passed. Then another five. The pain
did not return. Encouraged, she sought to rise to her feet,
only to find that she was afraid to do so. She waited five
more minutes. Then another five.

"Miss Ravenna!" she heard a high voice cry from some
distance.

Raising her head in embarrassment, she saw a young girl
running toward her up the drive.

"Oh, miss!" the girl said between pants as she ran closer.
"Thank God I found you!"

Sheepishly, Ravenna got to her feet. The girl, in her agitated state, did not seem to have noticed the oddity of some-one lying on the ground.

"You are—"

"Robin," the girl gasped. "It's me sister, Emma. Her time is come, and—"

"Emma? Daughter of—your father is the blacksmith?"

The girl nodded, and Raven felt a stab of guilt. She had not even known Emma was with child.

"The baby, it simply won't come. Please help her, for 'twill split her right open."

"How long has—"

"Since Sunday night," she said, her breathing becoming more regular.

It was now Wednesday morning.

"And how long have the pains been bad?"

"Oh, they seem awful every time. Emma screamed most of yesterday, but now she just moans a great deal. She do hardly recognize anyone."

Emma was a small, fragile girl with narrow hipbones. Not suited for childbearing. Raven had never met her beau, but if he was some burly brute, she might never survive the birthing of his husky offspring.

"Is she bleeding?"

"Uh-huh."

"A lot?"

"Yes."

The look of alarm must have been apparent on her face, for little Robin's own face blanched and she quickly asked, "Why? Is my sister dying?"

"I don't know," Ravenna said truthfully. "But heavy bleeding of any sort is not normal."

"Please come."

To attend a woman who might be beyond saving was something she hadn't anticipated for that day. For one thing, she would be violating Garreth's strict order forbidding her from working, particularly among the villagers. For another, she had her own child to think about. She needed to get back to the house.

"I'm not sure I can help."

The girl seemed close to tears. "Oh, *please* come," she cried. "Emma might die!"

Again Ravenna felt the paralysis of indecision, the tug-of-war between two opposing forces that caused a stalemate.

"I—I need to get back to the house," she mumbled.

"Oh, *please*," the girl said again, this time weeping openly.

Sir Richmond's medical bag was at hand. Garreth was away for the day. Emma may have been beyond saving, but . . .

Perhaps Ravenna's own child was beyond saving as well, and a decoction of the finest herbs would not spare his life.

"I'd like to come, Robin, truly I would," she said. "But my husband forbids me to work among the villagers, and besides, it's too far for me to walk. I'm expecting my own child."

Robin's face lit up at her announcement. "Oh, ma'am! I'm that happy for you! May he be born safe and sound."

"Thank you," she said. She was beginning to waver.

"But as for it being too far," she said with a conspiratorial note in her voice, "I d'know Rex, who works in your stables. He'll saddle us a horse for sure."

"You know Rex?"

"That I do," she girl said, and she blushed. "He'll do anything for me. You stay put. I'll get him to saddle us a horse."

"Oh, no, you can't," Raven said quickly. "He's under strict orders—"

"He'll listen to me," the girl said with both confidence and defiance in her voice. "Or I'll have his head."

"Ah," Ravenna said, smiling. "He must be your intended." That would explain why Robin had had the courage to come up the drive while others shied away.

"Yes, ma'am," she said, returning her smile. "Now, you just wait here."

Raven retrieved her medical bag, left the digging tools by a familiar tree, then waited dutifully at the side of the road as Robin sprinted to the house. Although she'd taken no oath that compelled her to offer her services, she felt a strong moral obligation to help, one that transcended even her love and fear of her husband.

Presently, she heard the steady sound of galloping hooves. Rex, with Emma clinging to his back, was astride her favorite mare, Galatea, who was also the gentlest in Garreth's stable.

"Ma'am," he said, jumping off the horse, then approaching her awkwardly.

"Rex," she said, "thank you for your assistance."

"If Mister Garreth—if your husband finds out, ma'am, he'll have my head."

"And if you did say no," Robin called from the back of the horse, *"I'd"*a had your head, Rex Pomerance. Now, stand aside."

"Here, Mistress Ravenna," he said, motioning that he intended to assist her in climbing into the saddle.

"Thanks, Rex," she said, as he boosted her in front of Robin. "My husband is a reasonable man," she said hopefully. "He will understand."

She had observed only one cesarean section in her short career, and Raven shuddered at the thought of having to perform one. Yet after they'd arrived at the blacksmith's cottage and she'd examined his daughter, she realized that surgery was the only thing that would save the girl.

Ravenna had watched a fair amount of cutting and stitching; she knew that it was a question of logic and careful thinking as one proceeded, keeping track of where one was going, as on a branching path where the way back is uncertain and hence the landmarks must be carefully noted.

Kneeling down so the exhausted, half-dead, laboring woman could hear her better, Raven said, "Emma."

She murmured something unintelligible.

"Emma," she continued. "I'm going to help you." To Ross, the woman's father, she whispered, "The baby is too large. It can't pass through."

" 'Twas what killed their mother," he replied, his voice unsteady. "She barely survived the birth of the girls. The son she bore me were too big; he died and took her with him."

Straightening, Ravenna said, "Your daughter's only chance is through surgery."

"Holy Mother of God. She'll not survive . . ."

"Maybe not. And I—I am not a skilled surgeon." She had an impulse to ride the distance to Longacre's home and beg him to come with her.

There wasn't time, even if there'd been a chance he would come.

"But she'll die if she don't try."

The blacksmith's second wife, who'd been sitting in a rocking chair weeping softly, stood up. "I know you to be an honest woman," she said. "Do what you can to save her. I love the girl like she was my own."

"I need some boiling water," Raven said. "A bowl at first, then as much as you can provide me."

The woman nodded, then went quickly to the hearth.

Ravenna opened her medical bag, pulling out the chart and the thin needles her father had obtained from Dr. Wo, a Chinese surgeon who'd bought passage on a trading ship and had sailed to London in search of a better life. The needles were used to practice the ancient art of *chen chiu,* which apparently deadened pain as effectively as ether.

She had not had much experience with the needles, but the doctor had allowed her to practice on him, teaching her where to insert the slender wires in his forehead, then encouraging her to cut him with a knife while he claimed he felt no pain. She had no choice but to try them on Emma, since in her condition an anaesthetic dose of whiskey might kill her.

Ravenna prayed to whatever Chinese gods there were to assist her in placing the needles correctly.

"I am going to insert these needles in your daughter's forehead," she said to the blacksmith. "I know that seems strange to you, but it is a technique used in the Orient for centuries. If placed correctly, the needles will help deaden the pain. Now, I need as many sheets and towels as you have—clean ones—and three strong men besides yourself. I want you all to wash your hands and faces."

Using the diagrams Dr. Wo had given to Sir Richmond, Raven carefully inserted the needles in Emma's forehead. The drawings were hard to follow, since the writing was in Chinese and the pictures were not well executed, but she studied them carefully and remembered where she had placed them in Dr. Wo.

And again she prayed.

The smith returned with three young men, neighborhood lads, she guessed, and all of them filthy.

"Wash!" she commanded, and seeing their dirty shirts, added, "and put on some clean clothes!"

The smith was quite prosperous as far as the villagers were concerned, but he had only two shirts besides the one he wore. He and another man changed; the remaining two dutifully stripped off their shirts and went bare-chested.

After they had all washed, complaining about the heat of the water, she bade them each to hold down a leg or a shoulder.

If Dr. Wo's needles didn't work, she would need their strength to immobilize poor Emma.

"Now, Robin," she said, "you wash your hands, too, then

I want you to hold this sheet against your sister's neck. Up high, like this, so that she can't see what's going on."

"Aye," said the chalk-white girl, then she complied.

The sheet had a way of dehumanizing Emma, since all Ravenna could see now was a body—a faceless torso, belly, and legs.

Exposing the abdomen, she carefully swabbed it off with hot water and a tincture of antiseptic herbs.

She felt for the outline of the womb, which seemed full to bursting, then she felt for the position of the baby. A little foot kicked her in indignation, and she grinned.

"The baby's alive," she announced, then heard a round of relieved, approving comments.

Carefully, Ravenna thrust her surgical tools in the fire, then wiped them off with the boiling water.

Praying once more to both the Christian and the Chinese dieties, she located the top of the womb and carefully made the first cut.

Emma murmured softly, but more out of surprise than agony, and her arms and legs remained still.

Raven's relief at that moment was indescribable.

Feeling heartened, she tried to pretend that she was her father. The Chinese doctor had taught her about joining with one's master, of losing one's apprentice self and absorbing the master's skill. Thinking of her father's sure hands, and the sense of mission that had gotten him through the roughest cases, Ravenna carefully cut through the abdominal wall. Emma seemed at peace and free of pain.

Raven calmed every nerve in her body, thought only of her father, not of Ravenna, of the unsure, inexperienced girl, but of the surgeon, the doctor, the skilled and confident healer. . . .

A transformation began—she could sense it. Her hand became steady as she opened the womb and reached the baby. It was a miraculous moment, like that of an explorer discovering a new land.

Gently, she reached in and lifted out the baby. As she had suspected, the head had been stuck in the pelvic girdle and she had to pull gently to disengage it. The baby emerged with an angry circular welt around the top of his head, but no worse than a firstborn emerging from the tight confines of an untried birth canal. Almost immediately he began to howl out his protest against leaving such a warm nest.

"It's a fine boy," Ravenna said loudly, reaching for a towel to wrap him in. Cheers and laughter filled the house.

She clamped and severed the cord, a bit more hastily than she would for a normal birth, since she had more decisions to make, about delivering the afterbirth and quickly sewing up the poor girl.

"Here, Grandfather," she said to the smith. "Admire your new grandson."

Without a word, he reached for the wrapped bundle. She could see tears in his eyes.

Mentally asking her father how next to proceed, she gently tugged on the afterbirth, hoping that this unnatural act would not cause a hemorrhage. In her weakened state, Emma would not survive it.

She peeked over the sheet and saw that the smith was offering the child to his exhausted daughter.

The girl crooked open an eye and smiled, though not quite aware of what had happened.

Then, lulled as she was by the success of the operation, Ravenna was not prepared for what happened next. When reaching for the child, the new mother accidentally brushed her forehead, dislodging the needles that had been carefully inserted into her skin.

Almost immediately, she tilted her head down in shock and began to screech, clawing at the sheet against her neck and trying to thrash her way out of the bed.

"Hold her!" Raven commanded, but for an instant her burly helpers were as stunned as she was.

"Oh, please, hold her!" she screamed. "I must finish this, or she'll bleed to death."

Clumsily, they complied. Raven yanked on the afterbirth with more force than was medically wise, but she simply had to begin sewing the girl up.

Raven had to block out the screams, distance herself from the pain, though in her weakened and emotionally heightened state, she was finding it impossible. Her connection to her father, like a cut cord, seemed irrevocably severed, and she was but a pulp of useless arms and legs and indecisions.

Should she try to reinsert the needles? Emma might bleed to death before she finished. What to do next? How to proceed? She couldn't think, couldn't take charge.

"Hold her steady! I'll be finished soon. The worst is over," she lied.

But the stitching had to be done carefully, since Emma was young and would want more children after the horror of this one's birth had faded into oblivion.

The girl was sinking, thank God, into shock, and she began to tremble violently. "Hold her!" Raven warned the fainting men. She had watched her father sew up the stump after many an amputation, and it was always like this—the screams, the shock, the trembling, then blessed sleep.

Emma's body stopped shaking, and Raven could proceed. But Sir Richmond had forsaken her; she was again Ravenna Marisse, who had stitched only skin.

How could she sew up organs—human flesh! *Human flesh.* She felt a distinct tightening of her own abdomen.

What had seemed so orderly with her father guiding her now seemed a mass of meat and blood. She couldn't get her bearings. *I can't do this. I can't.*

Yet, upon losing her father, she became her mother, what she'd heard of her—stern, unforgiving, the descendant of Puritans. *You must do this, my girl,* she ordered. Raven tried to get her flaccid hands to obey.

The pain in her abdomen relaxed.

Preparing the silk, she took a tentative stitch to close the womb. Fortunately, the girl was now so unconscious that this new violation of her body went unremarked. Encouraged, Raven stitched as rapidly as she could. At times the body twitched, and she found herself shouting "Hold her!" much louder than was necessary in the close quarters.

The four burly men obeyed like servants, too weak to protest or disobey.

The tightening in Ravenna's abdomen returned, this time a bit stronger.

She finished sewing up the womb, amazed that she could perceive it shrinking, contracting of its own accord now that the baby was safely out.

Fortunately, the smith's wife had taken the baby outside into the warm day, removing it from the horror within.

Once the womb was properly repaired, Raven felt encouraged. With luck, Emma would bear a houseful of children.

She could handle the rest, she thought, swabbing off the blood and carefully stitching up the abdominal wall, then, at last, the outer skin.

When it was over, and she examined her work, she felt totally drained of her own life's blood. She had done well, but she would never have made a surgeon. This would never become routine to her.

The contraction of her abdomen relaxed again, and it took her a moment to realize that she had had a half-dozen or so since the stitching began.

She would not think about that now. She could not.

Emma was still unconscious, but Raven studied her meridian map and inserted new needles, not sure to what purpose but hoping they might ease the postoperative pain.

Then she left strict orders with Robin that *no* one was to dislodge them for at least two days.

Summoning the smith's wife, Raven bade her allow the child to suckle at his mother's breast. It would help heal his welts, make him feel safe, and speed Emma's recovery. Even with his mother in a reposing state, the little baby latched on like a veteran and suckled contentedly while his grandmother held him.

As Raven was cleaning up to go, the new mother herself opened an eye. It was not clear if she could see anything, but Raven thought she saw her smile.

Ravenna felt another tightening in her belly.

"I must go now," she said, packing up her bag.

"But your dress," exclaimed Mistress Smith. "It's soaked with blood."

"I'm used to it," she said half-truthfully.

"Here, let me give you one of mine," she offered. "I'll wash yours and send it 'round with Robin."

"Oh, no, I—"

"I insist. It's a trifle after you saved our Emma's life— and the child."

Actually, it was quite an offer, since the woman probably had only two dresses to her name.

"I do appreciate your kindness," Raven said, since going home in a bloody gown would surely scream out her disobedience.

As she disrobed in as much privacy as could be provided for her amid a gaggle of grown men, she felt her abdomen harden again, this time like a rock and quite painfully. She needed to take her leave quickly and get home, so that what had happened in this honest cottage would not be held responsible for what was now, she was sure, about to happen next.

"It's a lovely dress," Ravenna said after she'd changed. And she meant it. Though the material was plain, she could see that the seams had been stitched and mended with great care. *Not unlike my own stitching,* she thought, suddenly feeling overcome by what she had just been through.

"We must repay you somehow," the smith's wife replied. "We have money. Tell us your fee."

"Don't worry—" Raven began, then her voice broke. Saying nothing more, she fled from the cottage as her tears fell like a summer shower.

Another pain hit her as she struggled to get into the saddle. One of her assistants, the burliest of the bunch, came quickly out of the cottage and helped her mount.

"Thank ye, ma'am," he said, "for saving my son's life."

She nodded, too distraught to reply as she turned Galatea toward home.

The gown she was wearing was way too large, but she felt comfortable in it. The pain in her belly was getting worse, but her mind could focus only on the dress. How it suited her, how great a gift it had been. The gown of a lady, no matter how well fashioned, would never fit her, never suit who she was. As she raced home while struggling to stay in the saddle, she told herself yet again that she would never become Garreth's wife, in the real sense. Like the gowns she wore at his expense, the life she was expected to lead at Harlixton Hall would never really fit.

Suddenly, she felt a sharp pain, which almost unseated her, then a gentle pop, and warm liquid oozed from her body. Her first thought was that she would ruin the beautiful gown she wore.

"Forgive me," she told the smith's wife as if she were beside her. "It's such a lovely dress."

The cramps were strong and constant now. She found it difficult to ride. It was too late to go home anyway. She would not make it into the house and up to her chamber.

"Oh," she moaned aloud, wincing at the pain, then wincing at the thought, of the poor girl she'd just attended who had endured several *days* of this pain.

"Forgive me," she wailed as the pain redoubled.

She stopped her horse, then dropped clumsily to her feet. The back of her borrowed dress was brightly stained.

As she led the horse toward a stout tree, her tears flowing freely as her blood, Ravenna grieved for the dress. She sat down heavily, supporting her back against the tree. When Garreth found her, all she could say as he hoisted her up was, "Forgive me . . . please . . . it's such a lovely dress . . ."

Twenty

As on that previous occasion, Garreth carried her up the great wooden staircase and installed her in the guest room.

It was not the thrilling, romantic moment Ravenna had imagined the earlier event to be.

Just as Garreth wordlessly left the room, Manda rushed in to attend her. Master and maid collided in the doorway, and as Manda curtsied and gasped, they collided twice more while she struggled to get out of his way.

"Sorry, sir, sorry, truly I—"

"It's all right, Manda," Garreth said with cold exasperation, then disappeared into the hall.

Presently Becky arrived and announced, "We're to dress you, mistress." But instead of a satin gown, they clothed her in serviceable cotton, and they placed a small mountain of rags and towels underneath her hips.

Manda was unusually quiet, though it was clear she had a lot she wanted to say. When Becky left with a bundle of bloody clothing, Raven broke the uneasy silence.

"Manda," she said, trying to appear calm, "I know what has happened. I know I've lost the baby."

"Oh, mistress, I'm ever so sorry—"

Raven held up her hand the way her father had when he wanted silence.

But this did not stop the poor girl, and Ravenna thought

ironically that even in this she did not have her father's command.

"Oh, miss," the maid cried on. "I prayed that you would be spared. I think we all prayed. We thought you'd be different."

"Oh," Ravenna said with understanding. "So the household thinks it's the curse."

Manda nodded, her tears falling afresh. " 'Tis so unfair."

"But this can happen to any woman."

The maid wiped her eyes with her skirt. "That's not how Mister Garreth do see it."

"Manda," she said, sitting up in bed, embarrassed that the servants had to contend with her bloody rags. "Do you think he's dreadfully angry?"

"Well"—Manda looked conspiratorially around the room—"he went half crazed when he found out you'd gone to the village. He was shouting at Rex and Mister Travers, saying you were killing his son." She looked at her mistress wretchedly. "Then, when he found you bleeding like that, and near to death—"

"Manda," Ravenna broke in, almost in annoyance, "a miscarriage is not a life-threatening occurrence . . . as frightening as it may look. I'll be up and about in no time."

"No, mistress. Your husband gave us strict orders that you were to be confined to this room until the doctor pronounced you fit. And then you were to stay around the grounds. He was near to dismissing Rex—"

"Oh, no, but it was at my insistence—"

"I know, mistress, and it was Rex who did come clean right away when you did not return. So Mister Garreth is excusing him with just a stern warning."

"Well, thank goodness for that."

"Yes, mistress."

"But tell me, does my husband know *why* I went to the village, and what happened there?"

"He knows. The word spread quickly about the village

how you did save poor Emma's life. The smith has been singing your praises. 'Tis a miracle that Mistress Ravenna was brought to us,' he said."

Her remark rallied Raven's spirits, and her lips curved into a smile. She needed to remember that Emma's child had been spared.

"Do you wish anything to eat?" Manda asked hopefully.

"Well, now that you mention the subject, I am quite starving. Do you suppose Cook could make me some of her muffins?"

Manda giggled. "I'm sure she'd be delighted. And some tea?"

"Oh, that sounds heavenly," Raven said, leaning back against the pillows. Then she recalled something and her body shot upright.

"Manda," she said, remembering the bundle that Becky had left with, "the dress I was wearing . . ."

"Becky'll take good care of it. She and Hannah are friends."

But Raven was not reassured. "Can you fetch her?" she asked anxiously.

"Well, if you—"

"Please, Manda. Run and get her. Hurry."

After Manda had rushed out the door, the wait seemed interminable. She imagined Hannah's dress aflame with the household refuse. Some evil voice told her it would not survive the curse, as her clinic had not survived.

When Becky entered the room, her face told her everything.

"The dress," Ravenna said dully.

"Oh, ma'am . . ." she began, twisting her apron and shuffling her feet. "Your husband . . ."

"What did he do?"

"He was angry, ma'am, you must excuse him."

"What did he do?" she fairly shouted.

"He, well . . ."

"Tell me!"

"He—he ripped the dress right out of my hands, tore it in two, and said to burn it. I'm ever so sorry, ma'am, since I know 'twas Hannah's." She turned to go. "I'll be back with your meal."

As Becky tiptoed out the door, Raven watched her hips sway in her dress. Once again Ravenna could tell when a dress suited its wearer, as common as the clothing was.

Ravenna would have the Pembroke dressmaker turn out something simple but elegant, something a smith's wife could be proud of but not too embarrassed to wear.

Yet how could she replace something that had been given in love? How dare her husband have it destroyed . . .

In his eyes, though, she had destroyed something that he had given to her in love—his child, doomed though it was from the start.

She felt a strong urgency to find him, beg his forgiveness, tell him that they were young, that she would conceive again.

She arose unsteadily, feeling sticky and unclean. When Manda returned, she would ask for a bath, then put on her own gown and find her beloved husband.

Twenty-one

After she had bathed and dressed in fresh clothes and filled herself to bursting with muffins and scalding hot tea, Ravenna felt strong enough to seek Garreth out.

Unfortunately, Manda refused to let her leave the room.

" 'Tis doctor's orders, as well as your husband's," she lectured her mistress.

"My husband, where is he?" Ravenna asked as Manda escorted her back to bed, motioned for her to get in, then pulled the covers high up to her chin.

"I dunno, ma'am," she said, "but I'll ask Wyngate to send him here if you like."

"Please do that," Ravenna said, resolving to escape her room the minute Manda left her alone.

But she was not left alone. Manda rang for Polly, who was told to inform Trevor, a footman, that Wyngate was to inform Mister Garreth that Mistress Ravenna wished to speak to him.

Having never run a household and feeling shy about asserting herself in this one, she could not command all these people to step aside and let her pass, but she was sorely tempted.

She was no longer a new bride, but still no one consulted her on the menus, the running of the house, and so forth. She was treated with respect but not like the mistress. She seemed more like one of the children, as, when she thought about it, did the other sons and their wives. Someone was making decisions—Wyngate or Mrs. Oakes—though she doubted Garreth gave them free rein. Perhaps Lady Philippa was still of sound mind, and it was her decisions, made in absentia, that controlled Harlixton Hall, while the next generation frolicked aimlessly through their lives. Was even Garreth expected to defer to her? Did that mean that he saw her regularly? Would Ravenna have the courage to ask, when the mere mention of his mother's name caused Garreth to turn away from his wife?

She spent the rest of the day in her guest room, feeling like a guest, an unwelcome one at that. As every day, servants knocked, entered, provided whatever service they were bound to perform, then left. Each time a knock on the door came, Ravenna's nerves snapped to attention. Every time the visitor wasn't Garreth, she felt both disappointment and relief.

Justine dined with her in her prison cell, which was what she had dubbed her room by the end of the day.

"Is he very angry?" Raven asked her sister-in-law bluntly after they had set their dishes aside.

Justine sighed and thought for a moment, as if trying to find the words to soften bad news.

"I wish I could say otherwise, but I'm afraid he's in the blackest mood I've ever seen him in. He blames you—"

"I know. I should not have left the house."

Justine looked away for a moment. "Well, there is that. But even he recognizes that another woman's life was at stake. You could hardly refuse to help her."

"There's more, then?"

She glanced at Raven skeptically. "Of course," she said, then reiterated what Manda had said. "Don't you see? He's angry because he thought, well, we all thought, that somehow, because you'd saved Andrew, you were different from the rest of us. You were stronger—that you'd prevail against the, against this *thing*—and your presence would save the rest of us. It's not fair really, but Garreth thought—"

A strong knock on the door and the sound of the knob rotating caused both women to turn their heads. Without waiting for admittance, Garreth planted himself squarely just inside the room. "Ravenna," he stated.

"I'll go now," Justine whispered, standing, then walking briskly toward the door.

"Justine," Garreth said perfunctorily as she swept past him.

"Brother," she replied, nodding, then disappeared through the door.

In that brief moment when Garreth's attention had turned away from his wife, she became reacquainted with his physical form, the sharp angles, the tense mouth and jaw, his male beauty. Any fear she'd had of him was replaced by a fundamental longing. She needed his protection, needed to be enfolded in his arms, to be soothed and rocked and reassured. Closing her eyes, she lay her head back into the pillows, already anticipating his touch.

"Well, Ravenna," he said, and her eyes snapped open. Her instant of longing had made her vulnerable. She was not prepared to face the frost in his tone.

"Garreth, what can I say—"

"There is nothing to say, is there? You've made your loyalties perfectly clear." He took a step toward her. "And they are not with your husband, nor with your duties as a wife and future mother of our children."

"Garreth!"

"Don't expect my sympathy for what you've just suffered. It was your choice. Is it not true that you'd been having pains—that instead of taking immediately to your bed, you chose to ride to the village, soak yourself in another woman's blood, and save her child at the expense of your own? *Is it not true?*"

"No," she said defensively.

"No?" His right eyebrow rose derisively. "This is idle gossip that half the villagers are reporting?"

"Well, it's . . ." Ravenna looked down at her hands and tried to compose herself. "Well, it's partly true. I . . . was already having pains, but—"

"There is nothing more to say, then. You made your choice."

"No!" She attempted to stand up, but he was at her side in an instant, his hands pressing against her shoulders.

"Longacre's orders are that you're to stay in bed."

"But he's wrong," she retorted. "After a miscarriage, it's healthier to be on one's feet. It helps the body—"

"This is your medical recommendation?"

"Yes."

"And was it also your medical recommendation that staying on your feet and performing surgery would help your child?"

"Well, no . . . but . . ." She looked into his eyes, trying to read what Garreth was really feeling.

"But what? I await your defense."

"Garreth . . ." she began, licking her dehydrated lips as if to make the words come easier.

But she couldn't tell him—couldn't admit that their child had been doomed from the start, which meant perhaps they themselves were doomed to die without issue.

His expression seemed as quizzical as it was angry. But as she studied his eyes, they began dueling with hers, as if trying to force a confession from her. She was no match for his eyes, or any part of him, and she felt herself disintegrating under his gaze. Opening her arms, she welcomed him to her breast, to ask his forgiveness the only way she knew how.

"Hold me," she whispered, wanting to share with him the grief, which was still raw and fresh, unwashed by the cleansing power of time. "Our child . . ." Then she broke into inelegant sobs.

His arms remained at his sides, his eyes clear and un-forgiving.

"I can't help you, Ravenna," he said without emotion.

Her empty arms fell to her lap. There were a dozen things he could have said—he could even have pretended to comfort her, as one offers polite words of sympathy at the funeral of a distant relation. But to thus reject her was inhuman, and she better understood his reputation for heartlessness.

"Hold me," she repeated, turning her head away and hiding her eyes in the bedclothes as she waited for his response.

She heard his boots clicking on the floorboards as he walked toward the door, opened it, then left the room, closing the door behind him.

In the moment of quiet that ensued, she took a deep breath and found her spirits strangely rallying. Perhaps it was the relief of actually being alone, of being unburdened by the weight of anyone else's presence. Garreth had rejected her, yes, but he, too, was a burden—his moods and demons like parasites on her soul.

Jumping out of the bed, she ran as best she could toward the door. She was prepared to burst out of the room, if only to escape her prison cell. Then she stopped in her tracks as she heard a sound. She listened, and heard it again.

It was coming from Garreth, and it was unmistakable, like a knife plunged into the heart.

On the other side of her door, Garreth was weeping.

Twenty-two

Within a week Ravenna had recovered and, upon her own initiative, returned to Garreth's bed. But as much as their bodies both desired contact, they slept without touching, this time like the two halves of a coat grown way too small for the wearer.

She thought constantly about leaving, returning to her cottage full of Warren offspring and resuming her medical practice. And leave she would, but only after she had resolved the unfinished business she had with the Harlixton household—and that was to see Lady Philippa, to learn her secrets.

Night after night the sounds kept awakening her: *Thump, swish swish, thump, swish swish . . .*

Night after night she would resolve to find Lady Philippa, only to shy away from the task, as if she were seeking out the great goddess, whose face, so the story goes, no one can look upon and live.

But one night, when she could no longer listen to the sound without taking some action, Ravenna rose from her marriage bed, donned her robe, then tiptoed toward the door.

On his side of the mattress, Garreth slept fitfully, his arm flung over his eyes in an attempt to block out God knows what.

Gingerly Raven turned the knob, then slid around the door into the cooler air of the hall.

By now, she knew every tattletale squeak in the floorboards, and she inched her way noiselessly down the corridor, knowing which spots to avoid, which to trust. She was in her own home now, yet she felt as illegitimate as the day she had entered to attend her poor, doomed sister-in-law.

She had similarly learned the secrets of the great wooden stairs, and she crept down them with the skill of a seasoned burglar.

Embers were slowly dying in the great fireplace, and she wondered if she and Garreth would ever live as master and mistress in this house, without a gaggle of brothers and sisters-in-law, or if they would ever spend half the night curled up snugly on the great sofa, watching the fire give off its warmth and waning light.

No one would be up at this hour, but she didn't relax until she reached the south wing.

The hallway in the south wing was unlit, and she hadn't thought to take a lamp. Chiding herself for her growing carelessness, she entered Garreth's study and lit one of his. She should have hurried away, but instead she lingered, running her fingers across his desk and around the curved back of his chair. Letters were neatly stacked under a paperweight; pen, inkwell, and blotter were lined up like soldiers of varying heights. She needed to look, to examine the evidence of his daytime presence in the room. Despite their estrangement, Ravenna still loved her husband, loved the things he touched, the things he owned. She could have stayed there all night but forced herself to go, fearing Garreth might awaken and come looking for her.

When she reached the door where the unnamed servant had entered, Ravenna's heart skipped a beat. Instinctively she coughed to relax the chest muscles, then recoiled at the noise she'd made.

Her heart fluttered again, and she felt the dread tightening in her chest.

She would have to travel to London soon, to visit Madame Liu Soo Ling and see what remedies she could offer.

Without much hope, Ravenna tried the door. To her amazement, it was unlocked. Quickly she pushed it open and entered, breathing in shallow puffs to quell the growing irregularity of her heartbeat.

The key was on the other side of the doorknob, and she grabbed it triumphantly. The servant on night duty had apparently grown lax and deserved a reprimand.

The door opened up to a black hallway, which was barely illuminated by her lamp, and a column of wooden steps.

The air smelled of must and lack of circulation. Ravenna collected herself before she began to climb the narrow staircase, not knowing which board would sound an alarm to awaken the sentinels.

But then, making a quick decision, she quickly retraced her steps, locked the door from the inside, and tucked the key safely in her pocket. Reflecting back on that evening, she would not understand the reasoning for this move, but it was a decision that would haunt her for many weeks afterward.

The stairway seemed to lead directly toward heaven, or to a realm as yet uncharted by mortals. Her heartbeat was settling into a rapid, nervous rhythm, though it had regained its regularity.

The slow climb seemed interminable, then she arrived at a narrow landing, about the length and width of a tall man. A hallway led in three directions, with closed doors blocking her path.

Just then she heard the familiar thumping, loud and distinct now, as if right above her. Startled, she loosened her grasp on the lamp and it fell, splashing hot oil on her legs.

Oh, God, God, God, she cursed silently as her light waned, then vanished, and she was left standing in an unseen puddle of oil and glass. She pondered her options at that moment. Clean it up and risk cutting her fingers? Leave it there and risk setting foot in it when she retraced her steps?

She bent over and very gingerly felt for the pieces of glass, gasping when she almost lost her balance and fell directly into the mess.

She had no cloth to assist her, and finally tore out the lining of one of the pockets in her robe, then wiped the dangerous puddle to one side of the landing.

Unfortunately, she not could tell if she had gotten all the pieces, and when she straightened up, she let out a strangled cry as a dagger-sharp piece of glass pierced the bottom of her right foot, which was hardly protected by the thin slippers she wore.

Although her footfall was light, the glass managed to go deep into her heel. Perhaps she would have to stitch up the cut.

While again cursing her carelessness, she adopted the businesslike demeanor of a doctor and simply pulled the glass straight out. A brief gush of tears burst unbidden from her eyes in response to the pain. Her fingers probed the wound while she empathized with every writhing soldier who had been thus tortured by her father.

It was a puncture all right. She would not bleed to death, but she needed her sewing silk.

It was a sign to retreat. She had no business being there, and this was the goddess's warning to stay away.

Tearing out the remaining pocket from her robe, she bound her foot as best she could and stood up.

Turning back the way she'd come, she felt her heart flutter again. She took several calming breaths, crept past the broken lamp, then began her retreat.

But the unknown beckoned her like a Siren, and curiosity forced her to turn around again toward her original goal. It had become a chronic failing of hers since entering Harlixton Hall, this continual changing of direction, resolving to go to one place, then ending up in another.

The thumping was centered above her, so she tiptoed toward the middle door and opened it. Another dark stairway loomed ahead.

Her heel was throbbing, but she could put weight on the ball well enough. If she was lucky, it wouldn't become infected by the microbes on the dusty floor. Were she mistress of this portion of the house, she'd dismiss the whole cleaning staff at once.

The thumping grew louder and traveled back and forth above her head. Apparently, the peg-legged prisoner was pacing the floor.

Again she got to a landing, and with her good foot, she explored the dimensions of the floor. With her outstretched hands as eyes, she again located three closed doors.

She was reminded of the children's stories in which the hero comes to a set of doors—behind which there are a lady, a tiger, and a . . .

She'd forgotten what else.

The thumping was quite distinct now, on this floor and to the right.

Tiptoeing, her heart thumping in a rhythm to match the irregular sounds in the air, she opened the right-hand door.

The corridor was similarly dark, and disappointed, she inched along, favoring her right foot and trailing her fingers on the wall.

She felt hand-painted wallpaper, peeling and eaten in places, and elaborate carved moldings that may still have been beautiful despite the nicks and splinters.

Her fingers hit upon the frame of a doorway. Groping for the knob, she grasped it and pulled.

Locked.

She continued feeling her way along the corridor.

Perhaps it was her imagination, but she thought she saw a faint glow ahead, only a line on the floor.

Heartened, she coaxed her feet to go a little faster.

The line grew more distinct, as did the thumping.

Whoever was making the ghostly sounds was definitely ahead of her.

The line grew brighter still, and she could begin to make out a door, yes, and the knob.

She felt like Plato's cave dweller coming out into the light.

Grasping the doorknob, she began to turn it, then she hesitated.

Should she knock? Was it her place simply to barge in to another's private chamber? How would Garreth react if he found out?

Her hand held the knob as she decided what to do. She could still turn back, leaving this hallway and its secrets undisturbed.

But that would never satisfy her. Exhaling, she turned the knob. The thumping within suddenly stopped.

"Lady Philippa?" she called out tentatively.

There was no reply.

"Lady Philippa?" she repeated. "May I come—"

"No," a harsh voice whispered, but it was *behind* her. Gasping, she started to turn as a strong arm seized her around the neck and pulled her backward.

She tried to scream, but a hand clamped roughly over her mouth.

"Silence," the voice hissed, "or I break your bloody neck."

For a moment, she felt indignation rather than fear. After all, she was mistress of the house and could say and do as she pleased.

Yet this was a sinister realm that recognized neither privilege nor position, like the space under one's childhood bed, where the household monsters dwelled.

The arm dragged her backward while she grabbed at the stiff, unwelcome cuff under her chin. She had no idea whether the man intended to hurt her or simply remove her, but his strength was cutting off her ability to breathe.

Only one man among the servants had such strength.

"Cholly," she gasped. "Let go. I can't—"

"Shut up," the voice whispered with all the effect of a loudly barked command.

"Cholly, is that—"

Abruptly, the arm let go, then spun her around and slapped her viciously on the cheek.

"Enough," the voice warned, "or I'll teach you not to meddle in things what don't concern you."

He used the diction of a servant, yet the accent—what she could tell of it from the toneless whispers—was educated. And the build was wrong—the voice came at her just above her eyes, whereas Cholly towered over her. Perhaps there were more servants whom she did not know, who shared the secrets of the upper rooms. "I'll go now," she offered. "I'm so—"

Her assailant slapped her again.

"You're not going nowhere," he murmured.

Holding her under the arms, he dragged her down the corridor, toward the landing. At first she thought he meant to shove her down the stairs. Instead he opened one of the other doors, his hand finding the knob easily as if he could see in the dark, with the intention of pulling her through.

However, his grasp loosened slightly as he navigated both of them, like some clumsy four-legged beast, through the doorway. Sensing her chance, she kicked backward, and her heel made contact with his shin.

"Bitch, I'll teach you to—"

She kicked him again, then slammed her elbow backward into his belly. He wasn't really hurt, but he was distracted long enough for her to wriggle around in his grasp. Then, swallowing her revulsion for what she was about to do, she raised her foot and kicked him in the place where no woman should kick a man.

This time he howled audibly and cried, "You slut," but his speech was throatier than she remembered Cholly's being. Perhaps pain had altered the tone of his voice.

Turning, she lurched down the stairs, no longer heeding the pain from her wound.

The door to the first landing, she had thankfully left open, and she prayed she would be able to dodge the pool of glass and oil.

She prayed equally that he wouldn't.

Reaching the landing, she found she could jump over it, and she regained her balance, rather clumsily but on her feet, on the lower staircase.

Smiling with the prospect of victory, she plunged down the stairs, ever aware of her pursuer's progress.

He reached the landing, then she heard a cry and a heavy thud.

"Damn you," the voice croaked, and she heard the crunch of glass and further curses. "Ow . . . Christ . . . you slut. I'll get you for this."

She pushed her feet to descend faster, confident that once she had reached the safety of the outer hallway, her attacker would not pursue her and thereby unmask himself.

Reaching the bottom step, she groped around, found the door leading to the outer hallway, then tapped under the doorknob with the key until she located the keyhole. She pushed the key into the tiny opening, but to her horror, the key somehow missed its mark and fell, unseen, to the floor.

For several erratic heartbeats, she remained motionless in disbelief. Then she threw herself on the floor, feeling around frantically for the slight protrusion of metal that would grant her her freedom.

"Damn," the voice cried again, then she heard his footsteps, albeit a little uneven, approaching fast.

The key . . . where was it? Where . . . where . . . then she felt it, and exulting, she grasped it in her hand just as a body lunged at her, throwing, then pinning her, to the floor. She felt his breath on her neck.

Angrily, her attacker pulled her hair back, then slammed her face down on the hard wooden boards. Pain shot through her cheek to the bone.

Catching her breath, she cried, "Who are you?" but he responded by slamming her cheek down on the floor again. This fresh pain upon already assaulted tissues brought tears to her eyes.

She lay motionless in a sloppy heap, her tears coming freely now. Ravenna Marisse, midwife and would-be surgeon, who was so familiar with physical pain, was a baby when it came to enduring it herself.

A childish side of her resolved never to move again, to simply wait until her father came to rescue her.

The man bent over her, turning her head this way and that. In this posture, he seemed familiar, but he reminded her of Garreth, not Cholly or any of the servants. The blows must have rattled her senses.

His fingers then trailed down her neck and around toward her breasts. There was blood dripping from one of his hands, and a few drops tickled her skin.

"No," she croaked, then huddled tightly into herself like an animal playing dead.

"Curse you," the man whispered, then sat back on his haunches to assess the injury to his hand.

Impulsively, Ravenna jumped to her feet, the key still clutched in her fist.

"Here now . . ." the man warned.

Ravenna turned toward him and kicked, hitting something pliable like a thigh.

The man grunted as she spun around and struggled to find the keyhole. Her attacker grasped at her, finally grabbing her arm and pulling it back. She resisted with all her strength, gasping in an unladylike fashion as her arm bent farther and farther, the key still clutched in her stubborn fingers.

But he was so obviously stronger, stronger than any Pembroke, indeed stronger even than Cholly, and her arm moved relentlessly backward against her will.

Then, to the surprise of both of them, her arm let out a loud crack.

She screamed even before the pain exploded inside her like an incendiary device.

Her attacker let go, perhaps as appalled as she was.

The key fell from her useless, dangling fingers, and she crumbled to the floor on top of it, thinking of her father and the horror he must have endured.

It's only broken, she told herself over and over in her mind. *Not like Papa . . . not like him.*

The pain was sickening, but before she could scream again, a sharp blow, merciful as a guillotine, put her to sleep.

Twenty-three

Ravenna heard someone call her name, and she struggled to respond but was lost in a maelstrom of semiconsciousness, her body whirling around in the dark vortex leading toward the bottom of the sea.

"Ravenna . . . Ravenna . . ." the voice kept repeating. "For God's sake, get Longacre. Have Travers ride and fetch the doctor."

The voice had a familiar ring to it. Where had she heard it before?

"Mister Charles? What's happened?" a girlish voice asked from a higher place. Ravenna heard a gasp, then a tumble of words, which came closer as someone's feet flew down the stairs.

"I'm not sure," said the first voice. "But I think her arm is broken. Apparently she fell."

"Oh, no . . . my poor mistress."

"Here, take this, and get rid of it," a voice ordered with great authority. *Charles, is that you?* Raven struggled to open her eyes as some sort of vessel—a flask? a lamp?—was whisked from her side and waved in the air. "Tell no one."

"Of course, sir."

"Especially not her husband."

"No, sir."

"Becky?" Raven murmured, then she heard a much

deeper voice booming as if from heaven. "Good Lord, Ravenna! Can you hear me?"

She struggled to respond, to whisper her husband's name and reassure him that she was all right, but she was too tired, too far away, and the whirlpool that held her in its grasp was too powerful.

"Tell me what happened . . ." the voice said, then she heard murmurings, unintelligible.

". . . this is how it begins . . ."

". . . how it was with Mother . . ."

"No . . ."

"I'm sorry . . . she has all the signs . . ."

Good-bye, Garreth . . . she thought, hoping that he would receive the message before the sea swallowed her up. There was something bitter in her mouth. She tried to spit it out but it clung to her teeth and tongue. *What is it? What is it? Get away. Get away.*

For what seemed like an eternity, all she saw were vague images. Sketchy memories of people staring at her . . . of pain and her body's involuntary response to it. She dreamed of her father, the specter she could never be free of, her husband who no longer wanted her. Even her mother came, beckoning to her to join her in a place inhabited by the spirits of disappointed wives and lovers. There was something in her mouth, bitter, metallic. Perhaps it was the coin the Greeks put in the mouths of their dead to pay Charon for safe passage across the River Styx.

Finally it was pain that brought her back to the living, the pain that reminded her that she was not dead yet, nor was she being released from this life to reside in a different realm.

A fire burned out of control in her arm, and when she finally regained a more permanent consciousness, it was the pain that kept her eyes focused.

Justine and Charles were sitting at her bedside.

"How long . . ." she mumbled, running her tongue over her lower lip.

"Well, sister," Charles said. "I see you've joined us once again."

"Ravenna," said Justine, rising and showing genuine concern in her face.

"What happened to—" Then it all came back to her, and she shuddered as she remembered the dark corridor, the attacker, the struggle, and finally—"

"You've broken your arm," said Charles. "Longacre set it for you in your absence."

"You fell on the stairs," Justine chimed in.

"No, I . . ." Then she looked from one face to the other. She didn't know how much any of the members of the household knew about the hidden wing, so she kept her counsel.

"I would say that old French staircase is quite unlucky for you," Charles quipped.

"Oh, so it *is* French?" she said, unable to focus on the topic of the moment. "I thought so. But you must believe me, I didn't—"

"You were not yourself," Justine said gently.

"I—can't quite remember."

"It must be the grief of losing the baby." Justine took her hand. "I know what you are feeling."

Raven bit her lip, then nodded vaguely.

"You'll have another child. We all will."

Raven looked around the room. The guest room. So once again she had been banished from her husband's bed.

"And Garreth?" she asked hopefully.

"He'll be in London for a while. Business that could not wait, even for this. But he gave us strict orders to look after you. And this time you are not to get up."

Ravenna's head was pounding along with her arm; her foot was throbbing as well, and upon drawing back the bedclothes, she discovered that her puncture wound had been hastily mended. How like a man, she thought with disdain as she studied Longacre's large, uneven stitches.

All in all, she felt an overwhelming sense of uselessness. Injured in hand and foot, banished and imprisoned by her husband, she could now no longer return to her former life no matter how much she wished it.

What was it about this house that drew her into it like a drowning pool, that made her more incapable of leaving the harder she tried to escape?

"Are you hungry, dear sister?" Justine asked.

"I'm . . . more thirsty," she whispered.

"Of course." Justine went over the bureau to pour her a glass of water. "I'll have Cook prepare a pot of tea. Do you have any herbs to put in it? To help heal a broken bone?"

As Justine was fussing at the bureau, Raven turned her attention to Charles and said as clearly as she could, "What did you find next to me at the bottom of the stairs?"

He glanced away briefly.

"I don't know what you mean."

"The—thing you gave Becky to destroy."

"Sister, you never regained consciousness until we carried you to this room. It must have been a dream."

"But I saw it. Something—white—or glass." The image came more into focus, but it was still so hard to remember.

Charles looked at her squarely. "I did no such thing. Remember that, Ravenna. It was only a dream."

She struggled with her memories. She had taken a lamp, hadn't she?

But the vessel on the stairs . . . where had she seen it? It was . . . a . . . a decanter . . . from Garreth's study.

"It was a bottle of spirits you saw," she said.

"No, sister," Charles corrected her, but there was an edge in his voice that belied his reply.

So the household thought she'd been drinking when she fell down the stairs!

"Someone planted it there," she insisted. "I did not have a bottle."

"And I agree with you. There was *no* bottle."

Justine returned, but Raven held up her hand in refusal of the glass of water offered to her.

"I must sleep," she murmured, turning her head away from both of them.

"Of course," Justine said, but as Raven closed her eyes, she felt Justine staring at her—both of them staring at her—as if they were in collusion with her attacker.

As if they, like the house, wished her ill.

Twenty-four

For almost a week, solitude and pain were Raven's only real companions by day, insomnia her only bed partner. Charles continued to take tea with her, though she'd become a fainting lady, it seemed, growing seasick at the sight of nourishment and hence sending Charles away after less than an hour. Garreth had not returned from London, or if he had, preferred to remain hidden from her view.

Every day she limped up to the nursery to visit little Andrew, but even he seemed to have no further need of her, since his pertussis had abated and he was plumping up like a Yorkshire pudding just out of the oven.

Every night she huddled in her guest's bed, overly aware of the stiff cast around her arm and the dismal shroud around her heart.

Exactly a week after her accident, Garreth returned to her. She was lying in bed, intently studying the night noises like a music student analyzing a Bach counterpoint, when the door opened, then closed.

His body was a mass of blacks and grays as he stood just inside the door. She couldn't see the expression on his face, but she didn't care. Out of her control, her breathing accelerated and tears collected in her eyes. Damn him for having that effect on her.

Sitting up in bed, she reached over to light the lamp, to

have a better look at whom she would be facing—husband? lover? accuser? stranger?

"Don't," he said quietly, then walked over to the edge of the bed.

Instantly, she withdrew her hand, as if she'd been slapped.

As he approached, she saw that he was wearing only a holland shirt and trousers. The hair on his chest was visible at the neck. He came closer still, and she saw that he was not angry, nor was a mask of indifference pulled over his face. He seemed calm and familiar, as if this were any night and he were any man preparing to bed down with his wife.

The shirt was half open, and as Garreth undid the remaining buttons and stripped to the waist, Ravenna tried to calm her breathing. Sitting on the bed, Garreth removed his shoes and stockings, trousers and smallclothes.

She made room for him as wordlessly he slipped under the quilt. For a moment they both sat up in bed, their arms touching, and she felt silly relief that it was her other arm that had the cast on it. Then he shifted his body toward her and took her in his arms, pulling her down and under him. Before she closed her eyes, she took one last look at his face for rage or malice. Finding none, she relaxed and let all the sensations of Garreth's presence wash over her.

His lips found hers, and suddenly they were kissing like young lovers who couldn't get enough of each other. She clung to him clumsily, fearing that her cast might irritate the skin on his back, but he seemed oblivious of her injury. Kissing her harder with a mounting frenzy, he soon had her nightgown in his fist, preparing to tug it off her shoulders.

It was then that he took a serious look at her cast, since it stood in the way of a fluid stripping of her body. Growling in irritation, he grasped the center of the gown with both hands and ripped it apart, then tore the sleeve around her injured arm, until he could pull off the shreds and toss them on the floor.

She managed only a squeak of protest as his hands attacked her breasts, kneading the flesh roughly with the palms of his hands, then rubbing both nipples between merciless fingers until she gasped at the sensation. She threw her head back and forgot about everything but Garreth's hands, Garreth's presence, the power he had over her.

The male part of him was rock-hard, she could feel it pressing against her thigh, but Garreth seemed in no hurry to seek his own release. Instead his hands and lips became explorers, probing her body, seeking out the sensitive places. She felt diffuse pleasure everywhere, though the warmth moved inward, toward the center of her body, where it grew in heat and strength. Her body craved him like an opiate; she felt like an addict begging for a drug.

His fingers moved down her belly, hips, thighs, down to the secret center. She sighed shamelessly as he touched her, using his hands as instruments of pleasure and mastery. She lost all decorum as he touched her; she was his slave, his harlot, his chattel.

She forgot who she was and all her upbringing; she fell into the same frenzy Garreth was feeling. Using her good hand, she stroked his chest, pressing and testing the taut flesh, moving down toward the slim waist and flat abdomen, finally finding the part of him her own body craved. With too much boldness, it seemed, she wrapped her fingers around the hard column, marveling yet again at the smoothness of the skin, the contours so well suited to her own. Garreth's eyes snapped into focus as he felt her hand upon him, and she could sense the struggle going on in his mind. Soon it was she who had the power, and Garreth puffed and gasped as she stroked and probed him.

Then a need to possess her seemed to rally in his body, and he pulled her hand away from him. A virgin no longer, she knew exactly how to turn, how to open herself to him. Swiftly he entered her, and she clasped him tightly with her legs as he moved, pushing into the center of her, giving her the best part of himself. Tension built inside her; she was straining, panting, spinning, thrashing.

"I love you," she whispered, hoping he heard her through the heavy sounds that filled the air. Her body shook and convulsed as she gripped him with her arms, legs, the inside of her body. Then a harsh cry escaped his lips as his own release came. They gripped each other, both of them now frightened slaves to a power beyond them.

When it was over, when she felt his wetness inside her, bringing with it the possibility of new life, another child, she sensed that they had started fresh, that they could put behind them the child they'd lost and think about the brace of offspring to come.

It was this comforting thought that was lulling her into a peaceful sleep when she heard Garreth whisper in the darkness, "Don't."

She turned toward him.

"Don't," he repeated. "Don't love me." Then he turned away, pulling the quilt over his shoulder.

When she awoke the next morning, alone, her feeling of doom returned. Garreth had set off for London again, giving strict orders that she was not to leave the grounds. Would she ever leave? she wondered. Would she ever feel whole again outside the circle of Garreth's arms? A shooting pain in her own arm gave her an answer, but it was not the one she sought.

Twenty-five

Ravenna's arm stubbornly refused to heal. Every time Longacre came to replace the bandages, the skin remained bruised, the bone soft, the fingers numb and inflexible. Like her father before her, she spent her days pacing, wasting energy that could have been used in service to others if she'd had two hands instead of one.

And after their one magical night of reconciliation, Garreth kept his distance from her. She began to doubt whether she had any future at all.

Thoughts of dying began to preoccupy her waking hours as well as her dreams.

Justine and Clarity grew tired of her company and sought friendship elsewhere. On Labour Day, Clarity announced her pregnancy, eagerly took the herbs Ravenna gave her, then miscarried by the equinox. No one blamed Ravenna— at least not to her face—but she grieved nonetheless for this new failure.

As for Raven herself, her monthly courses came and went, each time Nature's cruel reminder that a baby had been lost, that her husband was a stranger to her.

Her solace, as summer slipped into autumn, was her daily walk down by the river. The fall foliage was a riot of colors, and the back gardens were still pretty, despite their seasonal waning. The natural world was slowly dying, and its fate matched Raven's mood. Would that she could die like a maple leaf and return in spring, with another chance to live.

The autumn breeze was crisp and clean as she wandered down to the edge of the river one October afternoon, this time heedless of the scratches and cuts as she pushed her way though the uncultivated bushes. The foliage was still dense from a summer of growing, but she didn't care. She couldn't bring herself to use the footpath to the river. Instead, she would pry her way through the thick curtain and get to the water's edge, using her broken arm as a hacking tool and shield.

But the effort proved too much for her; everything suddenly seemed too much for her. She did not want to live anymore, and the river seemed inviting, its cold, pitiless waves beckoning her like Death's icy fingers.

How if she simply slipped and fell off the edge . . .

That was impossible. She would have to fight her way to the water.

But she could do it. It would mean some preliminary pain, but the frigid water would bathe her cuts as it chilled the life out of her.

To kill herself seemed a whim of the moment, foolish but irresistible, like buying a honey cake with one's last penny. After all, she had nothing to live for—Garreth didn't want her, she couldn't work, she would never have his child.

Pushing her way through the remaining branches, she let her feet have a will of their own, and without further thought, she simply walked off the slim shelf of earth and into the Thames.

The water was so cold that her instantly numbed flesh began to feel warm.

It was inviting, never to have to struggle again, to have her broken, irregular heartbeat simply freeze into silence.

She lay on her back as if she were getting comfortable in bed while the swift current carried her away from Harlixton Hall. She would, at last, escape its hold on her . . .

Despite her cast, she found she could swim a little on her back, and so she did, feeling quite warm and numb now, the water rocking her like an immense hammock. She kicked her legs as much as her skirts would allow. Soon she became weightless, forgetting even the drag of the splints on her injured arm.

From a long way off she heard shouting, someone calling her name, but it was too far away. Perhaps it was her father calling her to his side. Yes, that was it, her father. In her mind she saw him waving, his hand once more intact, his face composed.

The current dunked her under and she could no longer breathe. But she found she didn't need to breathe. She became a baby *in utero,* swimming happily in a world without air.

Nothing could hurt her now. She was in her mother's womb. A branch of weed caught her around the waist and she welcomed it, thinking it a cord, attaching her firmly to her mother for sustenance. *Mother, I love you . . . I return to you . . .*

Then rough hands gripped her head and jerked her upward. Her face hit the air and the shock caused her to cough and gasp. She tried to speak, but no sound emerged.

So this is what it's like to be born. No wonder newborns cry.

"Easy, now, I've got you," a voice gasped.

She was dragged by the shoulders away from her mother's embrace, pulled through the rough thicket, and flung on the hard ground.

By then she had coughed up enough water to be able to speak, but she found herself screaming instead.

"Shh . . ." the voice said soothingly. "You're safe now."

Her eyes focused, her mind began to work again, and she realized what she had done. She had almost died. Almost lost Garreth forever, and the child they would conceive.

Looking away in shame, she alternately coughed and wept.

"You would have drowned, Ravenna," the voice said, this time more sternly. "Never, *ever* go that close to the river again."

It was Charles, but he spoke with an authority she rarely saw in him.

There was enormous concern in his eyes. And she saw that he, too, was dripping wet and starting to shiver. Saving her had strained his limited physical resources.

"Don't . . . tell . . ." she stammered.

"No. Garreth will never know. But you must get back to the house quickly before you catch your death."

"And you, Charles." She tried to sit. "I think I'm—"

"Lie still a moment."

She sat up anyway when she realized that he was in as dreadful a shape as she was.

"I can walk, Charles. Please, let's hurry. You're shivering as well."

"I'm fine. My concern is only for you."

For a moment they just looked at each other, one pair of eyes searching another. Charles had saved Ravenna's life, and that event had joined them in an indefinable way. Cupping her face with his trembling hands, Charles bent his lips to hers and kissed her.

Neither had the energy left to resist the other. The kiss was something, as even Garreth would acknowledge, that could not be controlled. Yet after Charles released her, his head sagged and she found she had to cling to him, to keep him from falling.

After a short rest, both of them got up, then limped and stumbled back to the house. She was amazed at Charles's ongoing weakness; she resolved to suggest a tonic for him. As they entered the side door, the porter rushed to their assistance, barking orders to the maids to fetch them towels and build up the fire. Soon they were sipping hot tea in the servants hall, bundled up in blankets next to the fire while servants were dispatched to get them each a suit of dry clothing.

Somehow the servants knew that no one in the family was to hear of what had happened.

They knew, too, that the staff would inflate a simple rescue into an epic of mythopoeic proportions by nightfall.

And Garreth would somehow hear of it, though from the gossips, since she trusted that Charles would keep her secret safe.

After changing clothes, Charles left the servants area abruptly, without even saying "Good afternoon."

"Charles . . ." she called as he disappeared down the hallway. "Thank you." She wasn't sure, however, if she meant it.

That night he did not appear for dinner, having come down with a chill.

She excused myself early and slipped Frederick a packet of herbs for a restorative tea.

Frederick said, "Of course, madam," then gave her a knowing wink.

After dinner Ravenna lay on her guest's bed and imagined Garreth bursting through the door, demanding to know what was going on between Charles and herself. Then to punish her, he would rip every stitch of clothing from her body, run his fingers cruelly over every inch of her flesh, squeezing her breasts with his pitiless hands, then ramming his raging body into her.

In that act of violence and anger, a child would be conceived, and he would be a more perfect specimen of his father, a Galahad who would bring purity back to Lancelot's fallen family.

But Garreth did not come to her, and she found herself dwelling on a dismal future of empty arms . . . a waist always firm and slim enough to fit into a wretched corset . . . breasts that never sagged heavily with milk . . . a body that faded from time rather than use.

She could always go back to—

No, she could never go back to a life without Garreth. He had possessed her like a demon, controlled her like a curse.

Holding a pillow tightly like a child, she rocked back and forth until she fell asleep.

Twenty-six

For the following week, she became Charles's personal nurse, for he was having a hard time recovering from their ordeal. Ravenna didn't mind, however, for nursing was a worthy task, and she couldn't help growing fond of her brother-in-law.

His questions about medicine persisted, particularly the things she administered to him. Sometimes, to lighten their mood, his questions turned silly. "Are there herbs to make one smarter?" he asked.

"Yes," she answered truthfully.

"Live longer?"

"Perhaps."

"Become handsomer?"

She laughed and replied, "You surely have no need of that one," wishing to cheer him up.

He did not take it with the lightheartedness she'd hoped for. "Do you really mean it?" he asked with genuine hope and expectation in his eyes.

She blushed. "Forgive me, Charles. I should not have flirted with you."

"Why not?" he asked.

"Because I'm married, of course."

"Are you?" he retorted, and she regretted the course their conversation was taking.

"Charles—"

"It seems to me, sister, that we are of a kind—widower and widow. Perhaps you will—"

"No," she interrupted him, rising.

He sobered at once. "Please don't go. I promise not to offend you again. It's just that . . . oh, Ravenna, besides the birth of my son, meeting you has been the only good thing to have happened to me in a long while."

"Charles, don't," she said wretchedly.

"And after today, I shan't mention this again—if I can help it. But Ravenna . . . I love you." He held up his hand. "Don't worry, sister. Your virtue is safe. It's only that once more my elder brother"—he said the words with distaste— "has gotten there ahead of me, has taken then misused the thing that I wanted, that I would have taken better care of."

"No, Charles," she pleaded with him.

"He doesn't love you."

"No!"

"You see how he neglects you."

"Stop!"

He paused for a moment. "All right," he agreed. "But let us always remain friends. And please remain a friend to my son, since . . ."

She was not sure how he would have finished that sentence, but in her mind she finished it for him: . . . *since you may never have a son of your own.*

"I have to go now." She turned her back to him, then lost her balance, commanding her body to stay upright as her mind became heavy with an inner fog.

"What is it?" Charles asked with alarm.

"I'm not sure," she said, rubbing her temples. "A dizziness. I've had it often lately."

Charles stretched, kicking the counterpane off his legs so that she could see he wore nothing but his nightshirt.

"I see," he said, then pointing to her cast, he added, "You and I *are* of a kind, and you know it. The curse has gotten to you, too."

Abruptly she put her hurt arm behind her back.

"I'm leaving, Charles," she said, walking toward the door.

"Only *Garreth* is immune to it," he called out. "He'll outlive you, sister! He'll outlive us all."

That remark caused her to stop in her tracks. Turning, she asked with the dispassion of a scientist, "Do you have any idea why?"

Her tone caught him off guard. Thinking for a moment, he replied, "No, I really don't. Except that since childhood, Garreth was always the strongest of us. He never gets sick, while we . . . well, as you see." He pointed to his bed.

"I was never sick as a child either," she said, "and yet after coming to this house . . ." She told him about her heart, how the erratic rhythm was keeping her awake. About how she expected her arm to go putrid with every passing day. "Every time Longacre removes the bandages, I expect to see a mass of . . ."

She returned to the bed and sat down. Charles took her good hand. She didn't withdraw it.

"Is there anyone who can help you? A friend of your father's perhaps?"

"There's a Madame Liu Soo Ling, in London. She practices an art called *chen chiu,* a mode of healing and pain relief using tiny needles."

"Let us go to her, then," Charles said brightly.

"Us?"

"Yes, you and I and your maid and whatever chaperones you deem necessary."

"And Garreth?" Given his explosive nature, he might regard this innocent venture as an elopement.

He smirked. "Servants are a special breed of human being, with roving eyes and wagging tongues. What better protector than a servant, who is sure to spread any indiscretion to the far corners of the country upon our return?

Garreth will hear nothing amiss, because there will be nothing to tell."

She thought for a moment, then said, "Very well. I will have to write to Madame Liu and relate to her my symptoms."

He stood. "And we can stay with Aunt Edith."

A relieved smile brightened Raven's face. "You have an aunt in London? Why, *she* will serve as our chaperone."

"She's not a blood relative. Rather, a friend of our mother's family. But she'll have us, I'm sure."

"Thank you, Charles," she said, squeezing his hand. He gave her a look full of wanting, and she did not look away.

He and she *were* of a kind—fated, it seemed, never to have the thing they wanted most.

Book III

London

Twenty-seven

Ravenna anticipated her trip to London with more hopefulness than perhaps was seemly. For indeed she tempted the Fates, and the Fates punished her in kind.

She had vowed, when she'd first left the urban smoke and soot behind for the fresh air of Taplow village, that she would never return, never cross into the city limits, with their own brand of poverty and despair. She had left her father behind—so she'd thought anyway—and city folk even more unfortunate than the villagers, who in their rural poverty could at least walk the countryside and see the riches that Nature provides without cost or favor of rank.

In returning to London, however, Ravenna had to face not only the ghosts from her own past but others even more potent and frightening—whose existence she had only fathomed before her departure.

Since Garreth was reputedly in London, Raven's heart hoped, of course, that she would somehow cross his path, as troubling a situation as that would prove for her brother-in-law. For although the subject of jealousy had never come up between her husband and herself, envy was the trait that gave Charles's life its negative inspiration. He was jealous of everything that was Garreth's—Garreth's robust health, his stature, the order of his birth, and now, it seemed, his wife.

As the morning of their departure grew nearer, Raven's

wardrobe seemed to grow all out of proportion for a three-day journey. Manda had been tacitly instructed—by Charles, Ravenna assumed—to dip into Anne's closet whenever her own proved wanting. Anne had been as extravagant as her two sisters-in-law, and thus Raven had a whole shop's worth of clothing to choose from. During the early days of her marriage, the gowns appeared in her room singly—she needed a dress for a formal dinner, then one in which to receive the Countess of Something when she came to a garden party. And in the beginning, Manda was discreet about whence the gowns had originated.

Now with the trip to London imminent, the maid actually escorted Ravenna into Anne's dressing room, threw open the closet doors as if she were the dressmaker herself, and commanded, "Choose! Nine or ten should be enough, says Mister Charles."

Nine or ten? Ravenna asked herself, then dutifully pointed to the requisite variety, including a morning dress of green and pink striped and figured silk, an afternoon dress of blue corded silk with embroidered lace-edged flounces, a dinner gown of cream-colored Levantine, and a mauve traveling dress of gored crinoline with a matching cape.

It was up to Manda to supply the multitude of accompaniments—the shifts, chemises, shawls, gloves, reticules, and idiotic flowered, fruited, veiled, and beribboned bonnets that fashion dictated Ravenna wear along with each gown. Fortunately, Anne's foot was of a size with Raven's, so she was spared a visit from the bootmaker preferred by the Pembroke wives.

They left Harlixton Hall on the morning of October fourth, a crisp, clear day that was too cool for summer, too warm for fall. Undoubtedly London would be much hotter, Raven thought, much less pleasant. Manda sat with them in the coach; Frederick joined the driver on top, since the two men were distant cousins. This was Manda's first trip outside Berkshire, and Raven allowed herself to fall into the maid's enthusiasm, longing as she often did for a simple mind, which could find great meaning and pleasure in simple things.

Manda kept her nose pressed against the glass like a puppy longing for an outdoor run, and every time they came upon even the slightest evidence of civilization during their half-day journey, she'd exclaim, "Oh, ma'am, I b'lieve we're there!"

Charles tolerated the chatter well; in fact, Raven thought he rather enjoyed it, since, like his sister-in-law, he could be distracted from his own concerns.

When they finally arrived at the outskirts of Westminster, Manda's eyes were as wide as Columbus's must have been when he landed in the New World. She had never seen so many buildings before. They entered the city limits along the Kensington road, which led directly into the fashionable areas of the city, past St. James's Park and Square, the Royal Gardens, down Pall Mall, past Charing Cross, and finally along the Strand. Even the driver could hear the little maid's squeals of delight, and with Charles's permission, the man took them on a roundabout tour, across Fleet Street and into the older, original eastern part of the city, past the old London walls, and then—on Raven's insistence—into Cheapside. It was there that Manda's face grew somber. Perhaps she had expected that everyone lived in Piccadilly; instead, she saw firsthand the other side—the dirt, the homeless children staring with vacant eyes into the street. Manda smelled the stench of human and animal waste. Even her beloved Thames was not spared, for down by the docks lived some of London's worst cases, and the crystal-clear river that flowed next to her Berkshire home was an ugly brown-gray in the city.

"Oh, ma'am," Manda said, holding her shawl up to her nose, "how do people live here?"

Raven smiled. "I used to wonder that myself."

However, they quickly turned around, passing St. Paul's and back to the more fashionable areas of the city. Aunt Edith had a town house in Lincoln's Inn Fields. By the time they reached their destination, Manda's eyes were once more as round and bright as moons.

"Oh, ma'am," she cried, " 'tis every bit as splendid as Mr. Wyngate said."

How easy it is to forget what we've just seen. With that thought, Raven felt a lump rise in her throat, for her father—who'd had every motive and opportunity—had never forgotten.

Aunt Edith's door flew open as they alighted from the coach, and a large woman, who proved to be Aunt Edith herself, rushed out to greet them with the ebullience of a schoolgirl.

"My dear," she said, opening her arms and beckoning Raven to rest her head against a soft, enormous bosom. And Raven did so, feeling instantly accepted, comforted, even loved.

"Aunt Edith," she sighed, following Charles's strict order that she was to call her nothing else.

After allowing Raven to nestle against her for what seemed like an excessive amount of time, Aunt Edith held her at arm's length, then exclaimed, "Well, Garreth has certainly found himself a beauty."

Charles had his back turned, but Ravenna could tell by the way he hunched his shoulders that this innocent comment had hurt him.

"Thank you, Aunt," she replied, realizing, to her horror, that her wayward tears were once more rallying. After all, she had had almost no mothering in her life, and the touch and voice of a sympathetic older woman were almost more than she could stand. To distract herself, she motioned for Manda to approach, not at all sure whether it was etiquette to introduce one's maid to the lady of the house. But as she opened her mouth, Aunt Edith spoke again.

"I knew your father, Ravenna," she said. "He and I worked together on several charitable projects."

That remark sent Raven over the edge. Soon she was blubbering incoherently while Aunt Edith patted her hand and said, "There, there. Go ahead. It will do you good to cry."

"I—I don't know what comes over me lately. It—it seems I am always close to tears."

Aunt Edith looked at her curiously, then asked, "My dear, you don't suppose you are—" Then she stopped herself. "No, forgive me. It's too soon after . . ."

That comment prompted fresh tears, and Ravenna did not think to ask how Aunt Edith knew this sad fact of her existence. Had Charles been so specific in his letter?

As Frederick supervised the unloading of the luggage, a large, friendly dog bounded out of the house, barking and circling them.

"This is Beowulf," Aunt Edith said, "so named for his great brute strength. But he will be your devoted slave if you take him for a walk and play fetch with a stick."

Raven bent over and attempted to hug the beast. In return, she got a slobbery kiss on the nose and two paw prints on her borrowed dress.

"Get down at once," Aunt Edith commanded, but Raven laughed, allowing herself to be licked by the dog's coarse tongue. Straightening up, she said, "Well, I feel much better. Do you think Beowulf would like a walk right away?"

"As you see," Aunt Edith replied, pointing at the dog, who, despite his bulk, was leaping in the air like a weight-lifter turned acrobat. "Charles!" she called out through the open doorway. When he returned, she announced, "Ravenna and Beowulf would like a walk in the Fields. Please have them home before tea."

"Yes, Aunt," Charles said dutifully, and Raven smiled at him, though a slight chill passed through her body. After

all, Lincoln's Inn Fields was not as fashionable as S
James's—it would be quite deserted in the northern area:

"I'll just freshen up a bit," Ravenna said, then accepte
the escort of a shy little maid.

Up in her room—alas, another ornate guest room—R:
venna riffled through the new clothes she'd brought, tryin
to find a suitable garment. Finally she selected a loose-fi
ting, pink flowered muslin day dress, which Anne migh
have worn in early pregnancy, then rapidly re-dressed her
self, tossing her infernal corset on the floor and wearin
only a cotton shift under her gown.

Manda was just coming in to unpack as Ravenna rushe
out the door, her pounding heart full of impossible expec
tations.

"Sorry about the mess," Ravenna called as she raced pas
the maid.

Manda looked at her wonderingly as Raven skipped dow:
the stairs.

Twenty-eight

Lincoln's Inn Fields proved to be a lovely expanse, dense and wooded like the original land must have been. Ravenna had visited there only twice before, as it was a bit removed from her father's rooms along the Strand.

Both she and Beowulf felt a refreshing sense of freedom when they left the city streets; only Charles seemed uncomfortable, already exhausted from a few moments' exertion.

Ravenna found a large stick and, with her good arm, tossed it far in front of them. Utterly delighted, Beowulf galloped ahead, retrieved the stick, then proudly brought it back and lay it at Ravenna's feet like a priceless offering.

Soon they had quite a game going. She was grateful for the exertion, since her body, like Charles's, had begun deteriorating from lack of proper exercise.

She became bolder in her throws, purposely tossing the stick high up in the air, or behind bushes, to give the eager dog more of a challenge. She could get much better distance the higher she threw it, so up in the air it went, often disappearing into the flora.

It was after her best throw yet that the dog vanished for some minutes.

Ravenna grew anxious as they waited. "Do you think he got lost?" she asked Charles.

"Oh, no," he said, laughing. "This is quite near his home, after all."

A silence fell between them, then Charles took her good hand. She felt a tightening in her stomach.

"Charles, we might be seen," she complained, trying unsuccessfully to release her hand. Looking around, however, she noted that they had strayed quite a bit from the main paths and no one was in view.

"Does that matter?" he retorted. "We're related, after all. You and I are both Pembrokes."

He gripped her fingers with an amazing strength, unexpected from one who had gasped for breath during a simple walk.

They continued on for a while in silence. The dog had not returned. Despite the increasing sounds of nature that greeted them as they went deeper into the wood, Ravenna grew ever more aware of the human sounds next to her—the heavier breathing, the swish of woolen coat-sleeves, the crunching of boots upon dried twigs.

Charles was not at all like Garreth, yet he was a man— and hence his male sounds reminded her of what she had lost.

They came to a portion of soggy earth, where a natural spring had apparently been backed up by an accumulation of debris. It offered a perfect excuse for Charles to grasp her arm and assist her.

His gesture proved awkward, however, since her other, useless hand was incapable of hiking up her skirts.

"Charles," she said gently, "I—I need my hand," but he didn't understand and maintained a firm grip. Suddenly, her legs became twisted in her skirts and down she fell into the puddle of mud.

"Ravenna, good Lord!" Charles shouted, hauling her to her feet.

"It's my own clumsiness," she said, trying to wrestle her arm free from his grasp.

Instead, he threw his other arm under her and picked her up.

"Charles," she protested, but he ignored her, and there seemed a faraway look in his eyes, a dazed expression she'd seen on other members of the family. Once again she was surprised by his sudden strength.

"Charles, please," she insisted, struggling in his arms.

He walked her over to a dry patch of earth, then set her down none too gently.

"Charles," she repeated, quickly trying to get to her feet.

But this time he pushed her down, then dropped to his knees beside her.

"Don't fight me, Ravenna," he whispered.

"Charles, for God's sake," she cried, but he took no heed of her.

"Dearest," he murmured.

"Charles, I'll scream," she warned, but she doubted he even heard her. Besides, she would not have had the courage to do something as impulsive and indelicate as scream.

"I won't hurt you," he soothed her.

"Let me go," she pleaded as he lowered his lips to kiss her.

Her mind was repulsed in every corner, and yet there was something unmistakably Pembrokian about him, and for an instant her body wavered on the brink of an impersonal response. Charles took this for assent and sighed happily as he opened his mouth to force entrance into hers.

"Dearest," he murmured again. "I've wanted you ever since I first saw you on the stairs. Perhaps it was destiny that Anne should die, so that you could assume her—"

"Charles!" Her eyebrows rose in horror.

"She didn't excite me," he said while she turned her face firmly to one side to elude his lips.

"Please let me go."

"Never," he said, then he cupped her face with his hands while his nails dug painfully into her cheeks.

"Let her go," a low voice growled, and out of the corner

of one eye she saw Garreth, a stick in his hand, Beowulf panting obediently beside him.

But Charles had not heard his brother's threatening words. Or if he had, he paid them no mind. Still in his daze, he sought to maul Ravenna's lips.

"Charles! Let me go!" she screamed, energized by the sound of her husband's voice.

"There's no need to pretend, my dear," Charles said, loud enough for Garreth to hear. "We love each other. You must tell him so."

"No!" Ravenna cried, then the weight of her brother-in-law's body was hauled off her. She watched as Garreth wound back his fist.

"No!" she cried again, but this time out of reflex. She felt a normal human dread of seeing another person injured.

Garreth's head turned with a snap.

"Do I hear concern in your voice?" he snarled.

She leapt to her feet. "Please, Garreth," she said. "Your brother is—not himself."

Garreth stared from her to Charles, then back to her and again to Charles, who was rapidly sobering up.

Finally, Garreth released his brother and said with contempt, "Get out of my sight." Then as Charles moved away from them, Garreth called out, "Touch my wife again and I'll kill you both."

Charles glanced over his shoulder and gave Ravenna a clear-eyed look that was full of mutiny. He had been demoted from brave seducer to younger brother, and once again his wounded spirit was flooded with thoughts of vengeance.

Nevertheless he slunk away, back toward the entry gates.

When Charles was out of sight, Garreth turned to Raven and spat out, "You would do better to have a stout gamekeeper between your thighs than a Pembroke. We're cursed, my dear, and well you know it."

For a strained moment they simply stared at each other.

Then Ravenna's shoulders were heaving, her ever-present tears pouring from her eyes. Even when Garreth was in a despicable mood, she wanted him. Even his contempt was preferable to his absence. Immediately he was at her side, gripping her shoulders with hard, punishing hands.

"Oh, Garreth," she whimpered as he pushed her back down to the hard ground, to resume, it seemed, what his brother had left unfinished.

Her tears flowed freely as he covered her body with his long length. Another couple strolled into their view, she heard a gasp, then a girlish giggle, then retreating footsteps, but she didn't care.

Garreth, the man she loved, the man who was destroying her bit by bit, was close to her again, and her body shook in anticipation of being touched by him.

"Garreth, Garreth." She closed her eyes and felt the wetness on her lashes. "Don't leave me again. Please don't hate me for what happened."

She had intended these words to refer to the miscarriage, but he took them to mean something else, perhaps some dalliance with Charles that he'd concocted in his mind, for Garreth raised his hand as if to strike her. She flinched, anticipating a blow. But Garreth held back. His arm remained suspended in midair while he balled his fingers into a tight, frustrated fist.

The dog circled them at a distance, sensing they did not wish to be disturbed and hence not pressing them for another game of fetch.

Ravenna would have covered her face, but Garreth's weight had pinned down her one good arm.

Coming close to striking her seemed to have released something in Garreth, for he became quiet, looking down at her with something that approached tragedy.

"I have ruined you," he said, and when she shook her head in protest, he silenced her with two firm hands on either side of her face.

"No . . ." she insisted.

"Don't say anything more. It's too late."

"No," she repeated, offering him, by the look in her eye, everything that she possessed.

He wavered then, like a schoolboy on his first tryst. It was she who pulled his lips to hers as best she could, she who opened her mouth to taste the inside of his. Then she was kissing every part of his face—cheeks, temples, the soft hair above his ear. He was her life, her drug, and she would gladly be destroyed by him as payment for being near him.

"Stop it," he said weakly, but she couldn't stop, would never stop loving and wanting him, never stop fighting to rescue him from whatever demons held him in thrall.

"Come back to me, Garreth," she murmured, clutching a fistful of his hair with her one good hand.

Then he was kissing her in a frenzy of his own, with pent-up desire bursting out of him. His kisses were brutal; his teeth split open her lips until she tasted blood. She cursed her useless arm, for she wanted to reach up and tear his clothes off him, every piece that separated his flesh from hers.

It was starting to rain, and she hoped for a downpour that would drive away prying eyes and give them an excuse for their ruined clothes.

She fumbled with the buttons of his shirt, pulling at the fabric like a hungry infant who is all desire and no skill. Garreth saw this and sought to help her, ripping the shirt open with a single tug of his hand, then pulling out the tails, kissing her as he threw off his coat and cravat and shirt.

Despite the haste in his fingers, he unfastened her bodice without tearing it, rolling her over to gain access to the buttons, then rolling her back as he tugged the fabric off her shoulders. She winced as he put pressure on her injured arm, but a voice inside her said *Don't stop. Don't ever stop.*

She took one last look at his perfect body, now stripped to the waist, before the rain began to fall in earnest, drenching his hair and face and cascading down his powerful shoulders. She smiled as she closed her eyes against the large droplets splashing down on her face.

In such weather, no one would be around to disturb them.

Despite the protection of Garreth's body, the rain pelted her chest, gluing the thin shift to her skin. The cotton turned translucent, and her nipples, hardened by the cold and her desire, poked up against the fabric. Garreth's hands were on them in an instant, playing with them between his fingers. She moaned as sensation shot through her body, and he tugged the shift down from her shoulders, burying his face against her naked breast.

His hungry mouth sucked hard on one nipple while his fingers grabbed and toyed with the other. She gasped and the rain poured into her mouth. Surrounded by mud, suffused with lust, she felt no longer human, but primal as the dog, who was sitting under a tree waiting for them to finish.

She kicked at her skirt, wanting to be rid of it, wanting nothing between them. With her good hand she grabbed at the material and tried to wrench it down. Garreth lifted his head, saw her struggles, then he helped her, pulling off the rest of her clothing—dress, petticoat, stockings, shoes—in a single soggy mass.

Her nakedness only intensified her desire for him, and she opened her thighs, arching her back and beckoning his body to join with hers.

She trailed the fingers of her good hand down his chest, across the firm abdomen, and finally into the waistband of his trousers. He responded by ripping open the remaining fasteners and stripping off the rest of his clothing.

Garreth's hard length was pressed against the hollows of her body, and she could feel the swollen male part of him between her thighs. She wanted him so much, could hardly stand the longing, and she reached down to guide him into her.

"Please . . ." she entreated him. "Let's begin again. We'll have another child . . ."

But once more, it was like all the other times when she'd said or done the wrong thing. Garreth jolted as if struck, then pushed her fingers away roughly and stood up, his broad chest heaving from anger and perhaps frustration.

"Garreth!" she fairly screamed at him. "For God's sake, what is it? What's *wrong?* Am I never to be forgiven for having lost your child?"

His shoulders lurched at that comment, again as if she'd struck him, then he exhaled wearily.

She rolled over on her side, aware now of the twigs and thorns that hectored her skin. The rain had stopped, and the dog trotted over and sniffed at her.

How could the man she loved so much bring her such grief?

She felt a shadow on her face and looked up. He was standing next to her curled-up body, his height and mass exaggerated by her fetal posture.

"You are unwell," he said. "The servants' tongues are full of stories, Ravenna. The frequent tears, the headaches, dizzy spells, a heart that doesn't beat properly, an arm that doesn't heal. Isn't it clear to you now? You should not have married me."

Raven curled her arms and legs closer to her vital organs.

Reaching out and grasping her good left wrist, he pulled her to her feet. After hurriedly covering himself, he helped her into her dress. The end of the rain would mean the return of prying eyes.

When they arrived at Aunt Edith's door, they were informed that Charles had left for Berkshire. Garreth bade her gather her things and her maid and accompany him to Harlixton House, in the more fashionable Leicester Square, where he'd been staying for the previous fortnight. He'd already had a guest room prepared, in anticipation of her visit.

Twenty-nine

Ravenna awoke very early the next morning, dressed, and sat by herself in her guest's room, which had the elaborate trappings of every other guest's room she'd stayed in since leaving her own modest cottage.

She curled up in the window seat for quite a while, watching the tradesmen go about their early-morning business, the maids out doing the shopping, the carriages transporting gentlefolk in their pursuit of pleasure. Indeed, the rest of the world, everyone but herself, seemed to have a purpose and destination.

Her arm was throbbing, and she rubbed the weak hand, making a feeble fist and exercising the atrophied finger muscles.

Manda entered the room with a tea tray and was about to pour her mistress a cup, when Ravenna heard the front door open and close, then saw Garreth walking briskly down the street, away from Leicester Square toward Holburn.

Leaping up, Raven announced, "I'm going out!"

"Out, ma'am?" Manda exclaimed.

"Yes. It's—a perfect morning for a walk."

"Should I come with you, then?"

"No, don't trouble yourself," she said, dashing out the door and into the hall. "I'll be back soon."

Once out in the street, Ravenna hurried after Garreth as

he turned onto Holburn. He was walking east, toward the rougher sections of the city. Perhaps she would soon discover why Garreth spent so much time in London.

Holburn was a long, curving road spanning most of the Westminster section of the city; its semicircular shape mimicked almost exactly the curve of the Thames to the south. Garreth seemed to be walking the entire length of the road, covering several miles at a brisk pace, while Raven struggled to keep up with him, cursing her long skirt and tight lady's shoes. Finally, he turned into Snow Hill, then along Newgate Street, into Cheapside and the poorer wards of the city.

It was unusual for a well-dressed gentleman to be alone and on foot in this area; even more so for a gentlewoman. As Raven passed the stock market, with its ripe smells of cattle and manure, then went up Poultry Lane, she felt the eyes of the rough brokers and traders upon her, assessing her like the livestock and other commodities they sold. With Garreth still in view, she felt no real danger, but when he finally turned away from the stockyards and onto Lombard Street, she felt alone and vulnerable, and hurried to get closer to him.

The streets were dark and dirty, the air much harder to breathe because of the fires set by the homeless for warmth, cooking, and sometimes as a focal point for conversation. Garreth walked along Lombard Street until he stopped in front of a three-story house, apparently a rooming house, climbed the stoop, and knocked on the front door. Seeing this, Raven darted across the street and secreted herself behind an enormous pile of garbage, holding her shawl up to her nose to elude the smell.

After a short interval, a woman opened the door. Despite her simple attire, she looked pretty—she was fair and slight and her cheekbones were angular and patrician, like Charles's. Her hair was wrapped in a modest bun at the neck, and she carried a set of keys at her waist.

When she saw Garreth, her face broke into a warm smile and she welcomed him in with a large sweep of her hand. Feeling more curious than jealous, Raven wondered whether this woman was the object of his clandestine visit or merely the landlady who housed Garreth's *chère-amie* within her walls.

Yet this location, this rooming house, made no sense. If Garreth was keeping a lover, wouldn't he provide her with a decent place to live in more respectable environs?

That word, *lover,* brought color to Raven's face. It would explain Garreth's frequent absences, the long period of bachelorhood before their marriage—and of course, his gentlemanly experience. Had he forsworn his mistress after he took a wife, only to return when the wife proved an unsuitable mate? Or had he maintained this liaison throughout his married life, having chosen Ravenna only in a failed attempt to breed an heir.

He had never confessed any love for her. Could it be that his affections belonged to this fetching chatelaine while he'd sought merely to fulfill his obligations with his wife? After all, Ravenna—with her herbs and her medical knowledge and her arrogance—would have seemed the perfect choice for defeating the Pembroke curse, his best hope for siring a living heir and keeping it alive.

The front door opened again and a girl of ten or so skipped down the stoop. The fingers of her right hand were clenched into a fist, and Raven suspected they concealed a penny or two of grocery money. Since this was not the safest neighborhood for a young female alone, Raven hurried across the street and hailed her.

"Young lady," she called out. The girl slowed down and looked at her without fear in her eyes.

"Ma'am," she answered, giving a quick, shallow curtsy.

"Is it safe for you to be on the street alone?" Raven said, falling in step with her.

"Quite safe, ma'am," she said. "I've lived on this street all my life. No one would hurt me."

She spoke the Queen's English, using a respectable accent. With a change of clothing, she could have blended quite easily with the children of Hanover Square.

"Was that your mother who came to the door before you?"

"Yes, ma'am." Again she did a quick curtsy without missing a step.

"And your . . ." Raven found she could not ask this question directly, so she instead inquired, "What is your name?"

"Peg."

"That's a lovely name."

"Thank you, ma'am. What's yours?"

Without thinking, she answered, "Ravenna," then prayed the girl would not think to pass this conversation on to her mother.

" 'Tis pretty as well. It sounds like the name of King Arthur's sister or something."

Raven laughed at that. "My mother came from Armenian and Persian stock; I hardly think she'd heard of King Arthur when she named me."

"You must have her hair," Peg commented.

"Yes. My father was fair actually. Like yourself."

"My father is dark," Peg said with a touch of pride in her voice. "Like *you.*"

Raven's heart began skipping beats, and she suddenly felt hot. She needed Madame Liu's cardiac preparation. "And does he live . . ." She stumbled, again not knowing how to phrase her question.

"He lives in a big house far away," Peg said proudly, not at all embarrassed by that revelation.

"And his name?"

"Pembroke," the girl said.

Raven stopped dead in her tracks and looked at her. Garreth's child. So the curse applied only to wives.

"And . . . do you have any brothers?"

"Oh, no, ma'am. There's only me."

Garreth's child—the lasting product of a liaison obviously begun in adolescence—but not his heir. An illegitimate girl stood little chance of inheriting.

"How much farther do you go?" Ravenna asked.

"To the butcher's, just ahead."

"Will you be quite safe, Peg? I must turn off now."

"Oh, quite safe, ma'am. Thank you, ma'am."

She curtsied again, and Raven smiled. "Good-bye, Peg," she said, and turned down Gracechurch Street, heading south toward the Thames. She'd traveled almost half the length of London on foot that morning. If she'd gone much farther, she'd have reached the Tower itself.

Madame Liu lived on Lower Thames Street, scarcely a block away from the rough dock area. But she, like Ravenna, was quite safe in her own environment, for she, like her pupil, was respected as a healer. Raven would visit her, then attempt to hire a hackney to take her back to Harlixton House, where she would pack and prepare to leave.

After that, she knew not what she would do.

Thirty

"Ravenna!" Madame Liu greeted her warmly when she found her old pupil at the door. "Please come in, take tea, and tell me about your new life."

Again Ravenna felt the lump rise in her throat. Madame Liu, too, was old enough to be the good mother she so desperately needed.

The Chinese woman opened her arms and hugged Ravenna warmly, but Raven dared not collapse upon the modest bosom as she had on Aunt Edith's. To do so would have risked injuring the tiny Oriental.

Madame Liu smelled of flora and fresh earth, since she herself grew many of the herbs she sold.

Upon releasing Ravenna, she glanced at the injured arm, then lifted it up like a piece of drift wood.

"It won't heal," Raven said simply.

Lowering the arm back to Raven's side as if it had no control of its own, Madame Liu glanced into Raven's right eye, spreading the lids with thumb and index finger to get a better look.

"Your heart has been bothering you, too, I see."

"Yes."

"That's what killed you father in the end, you know."

Raven stared in surprise. "No, I didn't know that. I thought it was the—the pneumonia."

"Oh, it was that, too. And the lack of good food and

fresh air, and so on." She took Raven's good hand. "But in the end, it was the heart that gave out. It did not wish to continue beating."

"How do you know this, madam?"

She motioned to her own dark eyes. "I saw it in his eyes."

"You opened them . . ."

"On that last day, before the undertakers arrived."

Immediately the tears, Raven's naughty companions, sprang out of confinement.

Taking a deep breath, she said, "It's been well over a year. Almost two. And it still hurts."

"Ravenna, your father died because he no longer had the will to live. You English think the will is located in the mind. It is the mind that directs the poor body, you say, like a workhorse. But we Chinese, we know better. It is the heart that houses the will. When there is no will to live, the heart dies." She squeezed Raven's hand, with surprising strength for one so delicate-looking. "And so it is happening to you, I fear. You, too, are losing an inner battle."

"No," she protested weakly.

"Ravenna," Madame Liu said with a tone of concerned scolding. "Your eyes tell me something that your lips are afraid to say."

Then Raven nodded, took a deep breath, and told her everything—about Anne's death, little Andrew's health problems, the string of misfortunes in the Harlixton household, her own loss, her husband's inscrutable behavior.

"And still you love him," Madame Liu stated.

Raven wiped several last tears away from her cheek. The skin felt raw from so much wiping. "Yes," she said simply.

"And he loves you."

Raven shook her head. "I—I'm not sure." Then she smiled. "Could you perhaps provide me with a love potion, like the one Isolde gave to Tristan?"

Madame Liu smiled in return. "Perhaps." Then she stood. "Perhaps I could gave you something more useful."

"Yes?"

"This family, you say they are all . . ." She walked over to the shelves of dried herbs in labeled glass bottles.

"I'm not really sure what's wrong with them. Except that they are unwell. All of them, except my husband, and servants, of course. I dare not examine them, but I fear that I have contracted their disorder."

"Perhaps," Madame Liu said. "And perhaps not."

Standing on a cane stool, she reached for several bottles. With her slight stature, she resembled a child exploring the kitchen in her mother's absence. Then she moved the stool to another location, and another, each time taking down several bottles of herbs.

"There now," she said brightly. "I have several medicines for you, and for your husband. And several different ones for the members of your family. Don't tell them, of course. Ask the cook to slip them into the tea. Tell her they're magic herbs to fight the curse. If she's like any normal servant, she'll believe in such things and will help you."

"Can you tell me what they are?"

"No," Madame Liu said, and her answer surprised Ravenna.

"Madame, I'm not a simple peasant girl."

"Shh, shh, I know that. If they work, I'll tell you. If they don't . . . well, we'll try other things."

"I need something that will help my arm," she reminded her teacher.

Again Madame Liu looked at her with a gentle scold. "No, Ravenna, you need something to help your heart."

Raven took her first dose with the tea that Madame Liu gave her, trying to detect any flavor.

"I can't taste a thing," she protested.

"And neither will your family," Madame Liu replied, laughing.

It was late afternoon when they finally bade each other farewell. As Raven walked briskly westward, she noted with apprehension that the sun had already disappeared behind the buildings, an unfortunate consequence of being both in the city and in the waning days of the year.

She tried to project an air of confidence as she walked, but every passerby looked threatening. Her arm seemed more useless than ever. If someone accosted her, she would have little defense.

A man coughed behind her and she turned, scanning the faces, looking for an attacker.

"Give us a kiss," a sailor whispered as he walked by, intentionally brushing her arm as he passed.

She shouldn't have stayed that late, but she so craved sympathetic company that she felt an impulse never to return to her current life, her marriage. She could become Madame Liu's apprentice, learning medicine, as her father had, from the array of diseases that walked the London streets. The Church did not recognize divorce—even if one was married to Henry the Eighth—but she didn't care. She would never marry again, and as for Garreth's freedom, his need for an heir . . .

They were his problems. He didn't love her, just as Charles had never loved Anne.

Impulsively she turned and headed back toward Madame Liu's. It was too late to walk back half the length of London, no cabs could be hired in such a place, and for that brief moment, she found she had had enough of Garreth's demons. She felt sure her Chinese friend would take her in, at least for the night.

Feeling giddy with rebellion, Raven picked up her skirts with her good hand and hurried back toward Lower Thames Street. Although she was sure there would still be sunlight in the Taplow sky, here the streets were dark as pitch, and the lamplighters were slow to do their job in such a neighborhood.

The passersby had become ghostly gray masses. Ironically only the faces of the homeless were clear, made visible by the fires that served as hearth and home.

Ravenna felt chilly and quickened her pace. She had not dressed for the crisp weather of a fall evening. Madame Liu's fire, surrounded as it was by four walls, was a welcome prospect.

The streets became so dark that at first she did not see the two men emerging from Madame Liu's door. As Raven approached, however, she noted that the Oriental was not at the other side of the door, bidding them farewell as she would normal customers. In fact, they left the door open as they bolted down the stoop, each carrying a sack. That they could be thieves did not at first occur to her—despite their thieflike manner, Madame Liu had nothing of real value for a criminal.

When the men saw Ravenna, however, they hesitated, then one of them said something to the other and they began walking toward her. For a moment she simply watched them approach, then instinct told her to flee. She did not know them, and perhaps they meant her some harm.

They both wore heavy cloaks, strange at this time of year, and the extra weight and bulk slowed them down. Despite her skirt and her injured arm, she had the advantage.

But her feet were already tired, and her heels were rubbed raw from the miles of walking she'd already done. She didn't know how much longer she could keep up her pace.

She felt unreal, as if in a dream where shadow figures pursue one into a corner. She closed and opened her eyes several times, wishing this were a nightmare, hoping to find herself safely in bed, even if it was a guest's bed.

Her feet were suddenly on fire from the pain. Blisters had formed on her toes; her left heel was a mass of pulp. Surely if they were thieves, they would demand money; she would give them what she had, and they would disappear into the night. That seemed preferable to the agony of shoe leather rubbing against bone.

Once she'd made her decision to stop, her legs crumbled beneath her. Down she went into a heap on the street. As the men approached, she focused idly on the filth of the street: the wad of sputum next to her good hand, the puddle—undoubtedly urine—under her cheek. She prepared herself for an attack.

A hand reached down and hoisted her to her feet.

" 'Ere now, miss, I'd watch me step if I was you."

The hand released her, and the two men hurried away. Blinking, Raven watched their forms become wavering shadows, then vanish into the night.

Presently a police wagon rolled down the uneven street, and the kindly officer gave her a ride back to Leicester Square.

A pot of tea was waiting for her when she hobbled into her guest room. Gratefully, she sprawled out on the divan and sipped the warm brew, hoping it would soothe her, for she was feeling too exhausted and agitated to sleep. Several times she thought she heard Garreth's voice in the hallway. But she decided her mind was playing tricks on her, for she also thought she heard Charles talking in low tones on the street below her window.

When she had finished a second cup of tea, she rose to her feet to undress and prepare for bed. Then, without warning, her heartbeat went totally awry. Soon there was no rhythm at all, just a rapid series of uneven thumps and quivers. She clutched her chest as pain shot into her throat and out her eyes and ears.

She was hot, chilled, and dizzy. Her arms burned as pain radiated down each one to the fingertips.

"Garreth," she whispered then her heart seemed to stop, and she was plunged into a dream out of which she would not emerge for many nights.

Thirty-one

The events that followed passed in a blur, and long after they were over, Ravenna recalled only impressions of what had happened to her: a bumpiness of a carriage ride that sent shooting pains through her bad arm as she lay semistuporous on the seat; the sensation of hands touching her, some gentle, others rough; the hard arms of men carrying her; the soft hands of women spooning broth into her mouth and holding her head as she gagged from the strong flavor.

She received visitors—but like Macbeth, she saw ghosts, the mental images of everyone she had ever known. And she saw scenes and events, too: Dr. Liston when he dined with them and discussed with her father their beloved diethel ether; young Monsieur Pasteur describing his microbes; Her Majesty knighting her father for his services to the poor.

Ravenna tried to respond to the images, but she couldn't talk. Her lips had swollen to gigantic proportions and all she could manage was *"Ruh-ruh-ruh . . ."*

She was not even sure where she was: London? Harlixton? Sometimes she was back in their rooms on the Strand, and her father was proud and whole. Then without warning a carriage would mow him down, sometimes breaking right through the sitting room wall and into Papa's study. Other times she was in Garreth's bedchamber, waiting for him to come to her, but he never came. Only Charles came, or

Cholly, sneering as he approached her, telling her to mind herself on Wednesdays . . . or was it Thursdays?

She wanted only to sleep, but her heart kept fluttering, annoying her into consciousness. It had lost its regularity altogether, and it beat like random gunfire. Perhaps it would quiver, then stop.

She was aware of someone holding her head many times, spooning in a bitter broth. *Who are you,* she wanted to say but her lips didn't work. *"Ruh-ruh-ruh,"* she said over and over.

She vaguely remembered Garreth approaching her, looking into her eyes, then asking, "How long has she been like this?" But he was also the doctor, the same person with two identities, like a figure in a dream who is oneself and someone else as well. She thought he took her hand, and she struggled to squeeze his fingers, but the only thing she could do was murmur *"Ruh-ruh-ruh."*

The air grew colder, and the fire beside her burned hotter as time passed. She was not conscious of the change of season; awareness came later, in retrospect.

One day a man came to her. His face was streaked with red and blue, his voice resonating against the walls.

"Ravenna, you must wake up," the voice ordered her. But she didn't understand it at the time, and heard only *"Ruh-RUH-ruh, ruh ruh ruh RUH."* A rough hand grabbed the collar of her gown and pulled her skyward.

"Ravenna," the voice commanded. "Ravenna, wake up. Andrew is sick and needs your skill. Please, Ravenna, please wake up."

"Ruh . . . ruh . . ." she asked.

"Ravenna, it's Charles . . ." the image said, but she didn't believe him. Charles was at Harlixton . . . Charles had a wife. Lady Anne, wasn't that her name?

She heard someone crying, a young girl crying. *Don't cry,* her mind said, then her own tears blubbered forth. "Oh, ma'am, 'tis the curse," the girl said. "First Lady Philippa, then Mistress Madeleine, then Mistress Anne, and now you."

The mention of Lady Philippa perked up Raven's inner ears. *What about her?* she asked, while she heard *"Ruh-ruh-ruh"* escape her enormous lips. There were eyes, large, open eyes peering into hers, listening to her. "Ma'am?" she heard over and over. *"Ruh-ruh-ruh,"* she said in response.

She recalled gentle hands changing her clothes, pulling her into a sitting position while she flopped and sagged like a soldier who has lost the use of his arms and legs. " 'Tis the monthly flux," one voice whispered to another. "Get fresh linen," a voice said in response. They were speaking over her head, as if she were in a vegetative state. But her mind snapped to attention. They were speaking of her, of her failure as a wife, her lack of a husband, her empty womb. She felt noisy sobs pushing their way out of her throat. "There, there," somebody said while she wailed out her loss. "Do you think she's coming 'round?" another voice asked. "No," came the response. "Lady Philippa was like this in the beginning."

Raven's body convulsed as she thought of a life of barrenness. Lady Philippa had produced four sons; Raven had none.

"Ravenna," a high voice said sternly, and another one said, "Here now, when so familiar?" Raven struggled to open her eyes.

" 'Tis what she herself said," replied the first voice, "when attendin' Mistress Anne. 'Use the Christian name,' she said. 'Twill help the sick to hear you.' "

Raven tried to smile, tried to praise the voice.

"Ravenna, what is it? Can you hear me?"

"Ruh-ruh-ruh."

New sighs filled the room.

But there were other, more pleasant images: Garreth coming to her in a dream, pulling back the counterpane and quietly slipping into bed beside her. Garreth, her husband, wordlessly removing her sickgown and enfolding her body in his powerful arms, making gentle, healing love to her, soothing her swollen lips with a kiss. Then he released her from her body, and she floated out of bed, across the room, and through the closed door. Down the corridor and to the staircase she drifted, sliding down the steps without touching them, across the main hall, and to the south wing. *Lady Philippa,* she said, nodding at her picture. *Soon I will have a child, your grandchild, my lady, whom I'll carry on my back, as you once did your son.*

The doorway to the south tower opened to her like a gate to heaven and up she floated, protected from assault because she had no physical substance. Up she rose into the sinister realm of Harlixton Hall, the place where demons ruled the younger mortals, like puppeteers manipulating carved figures on strings.

She heard the ghostly noises again, *Thump swish swish,* beckoning her. The door at the end of the hall stood unlocked, inviting her to enter and share its secrets.

Weightless, she floated through the door and found another long hall, with closed doors on either side, leading into infinity. She opened several of the doors, discovering a series of bedchambers, none of them occupied.

More guest rooms. she thought, for all the wives who'd become guests, then become nothing . . .

For hours, or days, she opened doors and looked into vacant rooms. Finally, she spotted a strip of light coming from the door at the end of the hall. She heard the sounds that heralded the unquiet spirit: *thump swish swish.*

She turned the knob and found it locked. But undaunted, she simply floated through the door, into an enormous room, with a wall of windows that could have let in a blaze of light were it not for the thick drapes.

An immense four-poster stood against one wall.

The counterpane was a bit mussed. Something stirred in

the bed, and Ravenna recoiled, flailing her arms like a bird who seeks to steady himself in a brisk wind.

She floated a bit nearer and saw a frail, sleeping figure, barely able to make a dent in the mattress.

She had nothing to fear from this stick figure, and yet Ravenna trembled as she approached.

The sleeper seemed fantastical, some old hag from a fairy tale.

Open sores covered her face and arms. Her hair was nearly gone, as were her teeth. Her chest rattled with each breath.

Raven had seen these sores before; they were not the common wounds of the old and bedridden.

"Lady Philippa," she whispered.

The eyebrows fluttered.

"Lady Philippa," she repeated, then she was grabbed from behind. A man's cloak was thrown over her head, and she was back in her guest's bed, while someone held her head and poured broth into her mouth. The soup was scalding, and it smelled of rot. She tasted mandrake and cohosh and rotten grain.

"Ruh-ruh-ruh," she said, and her guardian replied, "There, there now. 'Tis orders, ma'am, to make you well."

"Orders, whose orders?" she demanded.

"There, now," the voice repeated. "Someday you'll be able to talk again."

The image of the hag stayed with Ravenna. She had seen those sores before. In Cheapside, with her father.

Her mind struggled to focus. For the first time in she didn't know how long, she began fighting to regain her senses. She fought the flood of images that fell unbidden out of her mind and pranced around the room.

Think, Ravenna, think, her father said, and there he was in the room, with Dr. Wo, the master of *chen chiu.*

Father, help me, she cried to him, then Dr. Wo said,

Merge with us. We will help you. We will become as one with you.

Then a veil of gauze fell from her inner eyes, and she analyzed her symptoms: the images, the swollen lips, the inability to talk.

I'm dying, she said, but her father said, *No.*

I saw the sores.

Look at your arms, he said, and she looked.

They're clean.

They talked about her symptoms, about the odor of the tea, and Dr. Wo told her to think of the two men with the bags in their hands. It was crazy, but the maids were giving her something—something to poison her mind.

The smell, her father said, and she thought of rot, of grain that's been left to spoil. *Think.*

Ravenna thought. She struggled to identify the smell. It was . . . it was . . . the smell of—

Ergot, she said triumphantly. *They're poisoning me with ergot.*

And dieffenbachia, and bloodroot, Dr. Wo added. *To make you dumb.*

And foxglove, she offered, *to destroy my heart.*

Yes, said the Asian. *And pennyroyal, which killed your child.*

His words sliced her like a knife.

No, she protested, thrashing her head from side to side.

Yes, he said.

Why? WHY?

Find the antidote, her father said, and together they talked. She needed his medical bag, but she couldn't get out of bed.

"Ruh-ruh-ruh," she cried. A maid jumped out of her chair and came running.

"Here now, ma'am," she scolded her, "you must get back in bed."

"Ruh-ruh-ruh," she pleaded, but the maid held her fast, calling out, "Becky, send for Mister Garreth!"

This time, with her father's help, she knew what she was doing, and she screamed.

"Becky!" the maid called out, then the door opened and a man and a woman charged into her room.

"Ravenna!" the man shouted, and she tried to focus her eyes on the face.

She could see him clearly: It was Charles, not Garreth.

"She needs some more broth," Charles said, and her mind froze.

"Are you sure, sir?" the maid asked. "It don't seem to be doin' much good."

"I know," he admitted. "But it's her only chance. Her physician in London—the Chinese woman—said this may pull her out of it."

"Ruh-ruh-ruh," she protested. There was something not right here.

"I don't know as I believe it," the girl persisted. "She does worse after we give it to her."

Charles is doing this to me, she said to her father, and he nodded. *What do I do about it?*

The antidote, Dr. Wo repeated.

Which?

Think, Ravenna, her father said.

Woodruff.

Maybe, said her father.

Skullcap.

Perhaps.

Ephedra, she said.

Maybe, he said.

Don't you know? she retorted.

My knowledge is limited to what you know. My wisdom is something you've always known but aren't aware of. Once you realize that, you will put me to rest.

Father, she said in exasperation. *This is not the time for riddles.*

The antidote, Ravenna. It's something you've always known.

Ephedra, she said, then she knew she was right.

When the maid came in with more broth, she clamped her teeth shut. The girl tried to force-feed her, and she spat out everything that was poured into her mouth.

"Beggin' your pardon, ma'am," she began, and Raven could tell she felt foolish, as if she were talking to a tombstone. "But Mister Charles, he insists that you have this medicine, that we're to give you nothin' else to drink."

"Ruh-ruh-ruh," Raven said, though she already felt her lips becoming competent again, her mind clearing. So Charles was doing this to her, but at the time she could not discern the reason—so obvious in retrospect—could not even ask the question why.

That night she had trouble sleeping, for the first time in days. She felt her brain becoming more and more lucid, her eyes clear again. The images of her father and Dr. Wo faded as the room—her guest room—reappeared as it always was, without a crowd of mental figments, inhabited by only a servant or two.

When she awoke the next morning, she had a ghastly headache and an intense thirst, but she felt sane. The ergot and dumb cane were leaving her body. She needed water, and she needed her medical bag.

In one corner of the room, a maid was slumped over in a rocker, obviously asleep. Ravenna did not recognize her and, in any event, was prepared to fight her if she could, to get a drink of water.

As quietly as possible, Ravenna drew back the counterpane and shifted her body until her weak, perpetually numb feet were on the floor. This simple movement made her feel faint, and she saw black spots before her eyes.

She felt, in sum, the way she had when she was first

summoned to Harlixton Hall on that fateful December morning. Perhaps, she would have been much better off had Maggie spent an extra hour in birthing her son; then John Travers would have found her cottage cold and empty.

Forcing herself to breathe deeply, Ravenna ventured to stand upright. Pain shot through her legs and lower back, and she crumbled back into a sitting position.

While barely out of girlhood, she was experiencing first-hand the sensation of being old. She would remember this morning when attending the aged and infirm.

She inhaled again, then attempted once more to stand. This time she was successful, and though the soles of her feet seemed on fire from the renewed circulation, she took her first step.

Her medical bag was on the dressing table across the room. Charles, despite his plot against her, had not thought to remove it. She took another step, bending at the waist to rest for a moment, then straightening and continuing.

She would retrieve the medical bag, return, and conceal it in the bedclothes. Then she would try to gulp some water from the pitcher before her keeper woke up.

She took another step. Then another. By the time she reached the dressing table, she had gained some confidence. Clasping the bag tightly to her chest, she pivoted awkwardly on one leg and tried to hurry back to the bed. Her keeper muttered something in her sleep, and Raven threw down first the bag then herself upon the mattress and waited, panting from the effort.

Her keeper shifted her position but did not open her eyes. Clumsily, Raven shoved the medical bag deep under the counterpane. When the maids came to change the sheets, she would throw a mock tantrum and frighten them away.

Feeling heartened, she repositioned the counterpane, then got once more to her feet. Her throat was dry as a discarded snake's skin, and if she didn't have water soon, dehydration would institute its own form of illucidity in her mind.

The water ewer was on a bureau at the far side of the room, near her keeper's chair. Her physical need made her bold as she walked unsteadily across the room. The ewer beckoned like an oasis.

The maid was still asleep as she attained her physical goal, but then she was confronted with the next step: lifting the pitcher and either drinking directly from it or pouring some into the bowl. In her weakened state, the pitcher seemed as heavy as the tower bell Frederick had brought in for Mistress Anne those many months ago.

Feeling like a weight lifter who is struggling to support a heavy iron, she grasped the sides of the pitcher with both hands and lifted it.

Controlling the round vessel as she poured from it seemed out of the question, so instead she simply upended the pitcher against her lips, hoping that some of the precious liquid would spill into her mouth.

"Here now," her keeper cried out, and startled, Raven dropped the pitcher to the floor, where it broke with a loud crash. Water and shards of china sprayed her legs.

"Get away," Ravenna hissed.

"Here, what's this?" the maid asked. "You can talk?" She took a step toward her.

"Stand back, I say."

Raven looked at her with eyes that, to the maid, glittered with madness. The girl took several quick steps toward the door, then Raven lunged at her like a predatory feline, holding tight as they both fell to the floor. Ravenna had no idea how to fight, even if she'd had the physical strength to do so. Instead she relied on an old trick used on the streets of London to immobilize an attacker: She simply pressed her thumb against the girl's windpipe till she stopped breathing. At first the girl gagged, trying to fight Ravenna. Then she quickly lost consciousness from the lack of air.

When Raven was quite sure the girl was asleep, she placed her gently on the floor, then turned toward the broken water pitcher. Most of the water had spilled out, but small puddles of it had formed in the various concave pieces of china spread around the floor. One after the other, Raven swallowed each puddle as at a Chinese tea-tasting, then downed the contents of a glass the maid had set aside for herself. Water had never tasted so delicious.

Retrieving her medical bag from its five-minute hiding place, Raven thrust her feet into some slippers and walked toward the door.

Dawn had barely broken in the east. If she was lucky, perhaps she could escape the confines of her room without being seen. If she was noticed, surely Garreth would be made aware of her flight and would protect her from his deranged brother.

But if Garreth were involved in this demented plan to drive her mad . . . well, in that case, she had nothing to live for anyway and would not fear her fate.

Thirty-two

She encountered no one as she traversed the long hallway and walked unsteadily down the great wooden staircase— her final descent, she thought—so unlike the first, when her future husband had caught her like a tossed-down bridal bouquet.

She dawdled only a moment in the front hallway, reac-quainting herself with the ridiculous suits of armor and moth-eaten tapestries, the imposing fireplace, and of course, the portrait of Lady Philippa *sans fils*.

She stared at the fresh young face for longer than she should have. *Ah, she was a charmer,* Travers had said. *So full of life, she was.*

As if she were still in a drug-induced dream, Ravenna's legs began walking toward the south wing. The door to the secret floors was locked, but she took her father's collection of skeletons out of the medical bag and eventually found one that fit the ancient mechanism.

Bright daylight shining through the open door made the stairs seem less sinister as she climbed them, though she felt an increasing sense of apprehension as the light faded incrementally with each stair she climbed.

And with every step, she winced, for her body anticipated a blow from behind, an attack that would cripple her arm for life.

She reached the first landing. She listened.

She could hear nothing, no thumping of a cane or stump.

She could go either right, left, or forward. As in her dream, she chose to go forward.

She walked through the door, again wincing as the hinges squeaked their protest.

She was in the corridor of doors, and she walked immediately to the door on the end. A servant was slumped over in a chair in the hallway, fast asleep. At his side was a crutch.

A crutch! Ravenna laughed to herself. For months, she'd tracked the ghost and demon noises of the house, only to discover that their source was a simple piece of wood.

Ravenna brushed past the guard, no longer afraid of anyone. Without knocking, she entered.

This scene, too, was as it had been in her dream—an enormous four-poster with a frail sleeping figure barely denting the mattress.

Had her father's spirit walked these halls, then conveyed his report in a vision? He had often talked of such possibilities—of the mentally deranged possessing great powers, contacting spirits, seeing around corners or into the future.

"Lady Philippa," she said, as she approached the bed.

The eyelids fluttered, trying to open.

Ravenna picked up the frail arm, pressing against the half-dead flesh as she searched for a pulse.

It was slow and uneven.

Lady Philippa was dying, clearly, yet had probably been like this for months. Perhaps years. She could have died in a moment, or lingered like that indefinitely.

Her face was a mass of open sores, sores Ravenna had seen in London, and in her dream.

She placed her head against the old woman's chest, feeling a strange sort of comfort there.

Even in her condition, Lady Philippa was a mother still.

The thin blue lips murmured something.

Looking up, Raven said, "Lady Philippa, it is you, isn't it?"

The lips murmured again. It sounded like *"Ruh-ruh-ruh."*
Lady Philippa was like that . . . in the beginning.
Ravenna had discovered the source of the Harlixton curse.

So the images of her father and Dr. Wo had been wrong. Ravenna may have been poisoned by herbs, but whatever Charles had done to her was a trifle in comparison to what marrying into the Harlixton household had done, and would do, to her. Perhaps Charles had sought to protect her, she thought wryly—kill her off to save her from something much worse than a drug-induced death.

The Harlixton curse was a disease that men and women gave to each other; the Church would call it just punishment for wantonness. Yet mothers passed it to their unborn children, who had a lifetime of problems—if they lived. The symptoms varied from victim to victim; sometimes they didn't emerge till adulthood. The third generation was always affected—either born dead or too weak to live long.

No wonder the Harlixton wives were barren.

As Ravenna was barren.

All of them would eventually become like this, growing ugly, sterile, disfigured, insane. No wonder Garreth had resisted marriage—no wonder he'd asked for his wife's forgiveness.

At the time of his accident, Raven's father had been working on a cure for this scourge of the poor and homeless. He'd tried *allium sativum* with some success. She would take it herself as soon as she got far away from here.

But first she would try to rouse Lady Philippa, to find out who had done this to her.

Reaching into her bag, Raven took out a large pinch of ephedra and pressed it between the woman's gum and upper lip. Another pinch she inserted under the tongue.

"Lady Philippa," she repeated, then ordered, "Philippa, wake up."

The eyelids fluttered again, then opened. Ephedra, when pressed against the gum, worked quickly.

Confused eyes looked at Raven.

"Philippa," Raven soothed, taking her arm and stroking the flaccid inner skin.

"You," the woman whispered. "Ravenna."

At the sound of her name, Ravenna lurched backward, almost pulling the old woman out of bed.

"How do you know my name?"

"Garreth . . ."

"Does he see you?" Raven asked. "Does he know that—that . . ."

At Raven's hesitation, the aged mouth curved into what Ravenna took to be a rudimentary smile.

"You must not . . . fear him," Lady Philippa said, then took several deep, agitated breaths.

The ephedra was affecting her heart, and she seemed startled by its rapid, strong beating.

In a moment, the stuff might kill her.

But then she was in a useless, vegetative state. It was better to send her on her way, thought Raven, despite the Church's admonitions against mercy killing.

"Lady Philippa," she said. "Whom must I not fear?"

Just then she heard some commotion in the hall, a shout of protest, and a thump as if someone were being thrown against a wall.

The door banged open and Garreth stormed into the room.

They stared at each other wordlessly, husband and wife, each accusing the other with eyes that knew only half-truths.

"Well, Ravenna."

"Garreth."

He took a step toward her, and instinctively she recoiled.

Even though he was her beloved Garreth, he was the one who had planted the seed deep inside her, not of their own miraculous child, but of sickness, decay, and death.

"So now you know," he said dismally.

"Yes," she replied. Again he reached out for her, and she jumped back as if he were a poisonous snake.

"Ravenna, for God's sake," he cried. "If you knew how much I fought against loving you . . ."

His words tore her apart. For months she had hoped for a confession of love, but not like this, not when it was too late.

"Can you ever forgive me?" he pleaded.

"No," she replied, shaking her head. "Not for this."

"My son," Lady Philippa murmured, and Garreth's head snapped in her direction.

"Mother!" he exclaimed. "I thought you would never speak again."

Raven approached him, then whispered against his shoulder, "I gave her something. She won't remain conscious for long."

"Come to me, Garreth," Lady Harlixton said, her limp arms rising an inch off the mattress in a gesture of welcome.

"Mother . . ." He sat on the edge of the bed and placed his cheek against her chest. The outlines of her small, flaccid breasts, more loose skin than anything else, were visible under her thin gown. Even in the midst of these discoveries, Raven's heart warmed at the evidence of the love that was shared by mother and son. Love that she would never experience with her own child.

"Garreth," Raven said, "maybe I can help you. Help your family, and myself as well. My father worked with—"

"No," Lady Philippa said, with more strength and conviction than seemed possible from her feeble body.

Just then Charles burst through the door, and Garreth rose immediately.

"Why did you bring her here?" Charles demanded, pointing at Raven. "Did you want to show her—what *she* will become?" To the amazement of everyone in the room—for by this time several servants had also congregated just inside the door—Charles laughed out loud.

Ravenna had meant to ask him why, why he would cause her so much suffering, but Raven understood now. Many things were becoming clear to her. The sickness was well established in her brother-in-law, was already affecting his mind.

"No," Lady Philippa said again, and lifted a shaky hand toward her. "Come here, daughter," she said to Raven. "You must not fear him."

The look in Lady Philippa's eyes conveyed tenderness and clarity. For a moment Ravenna could recognize the young woman in the portrait.

All eyes turned toward the hag in the bed, then toward the younger woman as she approached her mother-in-law.

Someone near the door let out a muffled sob, then a young girl's voice exclaimed, "She 'asn't spoken in weeks. 'Tis a miracle, it is."

"Well, Raven," Charles sneered, "you see now the pisspot into which you have fallen. Perhaps Anne was the lucky one, after all."

"Charles, everyone else, leave us," Lady Philippa commanded, with surprising matriarchal authority.

"But Mother," Charles protested like a whining second son.

"Leave us, Charles. I have something to say to my eldest son . . . and my daughter."

Charles scowled at Garreth, mumbled something under his breath, then reluctantly trailed behind the servants, humiliated once more. With luck, Raven resolved, she would never see him again. As soon as the morning was over, she would leave for London and seek out her father's colleagues, anyone who may have kept records of his work.

He himself had tossed most of his own notes into the fireplace during any of a long series of rages.

When the door was finally closed behind the retreating group, Lady Philippa beckoned Garreth and Ravenna to sit beside her.

"My time is nearly gone," the old woman began.

"Nonsense, Mother, you have years left to—"

"Silence, my son. You need not stand on polite ceremony. I know Death intimately; he has been my steadfast companion for years now. What I have to relate to you is not for the ears of my other children, at least not yet. When I am gone, you can decide for yourself what to do with this knowledge."

Garreth glanced at his wife with such an agonized expression that Raven knew she would forgive him, had forgiven him before he'd even asked. Her thoughts were only on his misfortune, on the waste of such a vibrant life.

Lady Philippa turned her head toward her son and said, "As I told your beautiful wife, she must not fear you. I can tell in her eyes that she knows about me, what manner of sickness I have. Isn't it true, Ravenna?"

Raven looked away, fighting back tears, then nodded.

"I am a pitiful sight, I agree. I am—disgusting to the eye."

"No!" both Garreth and Raven protested together.

"How you flatter me," she said, her withered lips pulling up into an uneven smile. "But the ugliness you see before you is my punishment. The Harlixton curse is mine, my daughter, given to me by my husband, may the Devil take his blackened soul into everlasting torment. He was the vicar of Reading on Sundays and the serpent in the Garden during the week. He tempted and seduced several innocent girls in other villages, after lying with a host of not-so-innocent wenches in London. One of them gave him this disease. He was diseased when he married me, and he brought this scourge to our marriage bed." She looked up and took Garreth's hand. Patting it gently, she said, "The vicar was a good man to kill, son. I'll not blame you for it."

Ravenna gasped in spite of herself as she watched Garreth's face go white.

"Mother, I . . . oh, Christ." He put his free hand up to his temple. "How did you know?"

"I know you better than anyone knows you," she answered, "except maybe your wife, though I suspect she knows very little about you. I could tell the change in you after the vicar's disappearance—your moodiness, your faraway eyes, the weight on your shoulders, and of course, your inability to look me in the eye. How I longed to tell you that it was all right, that we were well rid of him."

"But I didn't mean to kill him, Mother," Garreth said, his voice quavering. "You must believe that. I meant only— to confront him. To get him to stop—stop . . . hurting you. Oh, Mother, I could hear the sounds of him hitting you in your chamber, of your own muffled cries. It had to stop." He balled his hands into fists, and Raven sensed that he was feeling the rage again, an adolescent rage that drove him to become his mother's champion.

"If you knew that Garreth had, uh, had done this to his father, why didn't you tell him that you knew?" Raven asked, taking up the withered hand that Garreth had just released. "He's suffered a great deal, as you must know."

Lady Philippa smiled her uneven smile. "Ah, how wise you are, my daughter." Raven smiled in return at hearing that appellation. "Perhaps it may have spared my son much pain. But at the time I could not burden my innocent boy with these—these things. And how could I tell him I knew he had killed a man? The shame he carried inside was too great."

"But you must believe me, Mother," Garreth insisted. "I wanted only to talk to him. You see, I—I followed him to

London." Garreth's voice had risen in pitch, and Raven could tell that, in his mind, he had become that younger self. "I followed him to a house, in Cheapside, to another woman. But when I broke into the house, I found that she was not a whore, but a frightened girl, almost my own age. He had some hold over her, it seemed; he paid the rent for her and therefore felt he had the right to use her. I found myself defending both of you, Mother, against him. He pulled a pistol on me—the vicar carrying a weapon! He would have killed me—"

"That he would have," his mother said, nodding.

"But the girl, she helped me get the gun from him. Then when she told him to get out, to leave her alone, he attacked her, calling her a whore and damned before God. I tried to defend her with my fists, but he was too strong. I stopped him with the gun."

"You had to," Lady Harlixton said.

"I murdered my own father."

"No."

Garreth looked at her thoughtfully, then nodded his head. "Very well, then. A court would rule it justifiable, I'm sure. Killing in self-defense is not a crime. And yet I have to live with the memory, with knowing that I killed my own father."

"Except, my son, that he was not your father."

A door slammed far below them, and in the sudden stillness of the room, other distant household sounds could now be heard.

"Not my father?" Garreth said, incredulous. "Then who . . ."

"Your father is Alexander George Gordon, sixth—or is it seventh?—Earl of Henley. And you, if he chooses to acknowledge you, are his only heir."

"Mother!" Garreth cried. "What are you saying?"

"What I'm saying, Garreth," she began, then she turned

to Ravenna, "is that your wife is destined to be the next Countess of Henley."

"My lady," Raven said, "this means . . ." She was hoping for a miracle.

"It means that you are free to breed without the vicar's curse coming to haunt you and your children. I was already carrying you, Garreth, when my father married me off to that scoundrel. And he who'd sheathed himself inside many a whore's loins refused to touch me till my 'bloody bastard' was born. Said he wouldn't sup at a table bearing another man's scraps."

"Good God, Mother," Garreth cried.

"It was his hypocrisy that spared you, my son. Though I'm sorry to say, you were conceived outside the laws of God and man."

"I will not fault you for it, Mother."

"Thank you, Garreth. For I will tell you this . . .". And her face took on a radiance that softened her sores. "You were created out of a love that was as pure as any sanctified by the Church."

Raven squeezed her hand. "I know that to be true, my lady," she said.

"My Sandy—that was the name I called him—and I were to be married. We had pledged ourselves secretly to one another, even though I was sixteen and he barely of age. I promised to wait for him until he'd finished his studies at Cambridge. But we were so young and so much in love. We let our love lead us. My children, perhaps it is sinful of me to admit this, but we, we had to do what we did. It was something that could . . . not be controlled."

Garreth turned his head toward Ravenna, and they both smiled in private understanding.

"I'll not fault you, Mother," he said.

"Nor I," said Ravenna. "It is a trait you have passed on to your son. How well I know—and love him for it."

"When my father found out I was carrying Sandy's child,

he wouldn't let me see him or contact him. He felt I should be punished for my mortal sin, rather than redeemed by a hasty marriage. My father, you see, was a descendant of Cromwell and thus believed in stern retribution for one's sins, particularly sins of the flesh. The vicar was looking for a wife after his own had died of 'mysterious causes,' and my father made an agreement with him: my hand, my income, my body, in exchange for his silence. I was young and powerless; Sandy was far away and swept up in his new life. He never wrote to me, never came to visit during the holidays. He'd forgotten all about his country miss. When Sandy finally came to call, I was a married woman with a newborn son."

"So he never knew," Ravenna said.

"No. I'm sure he suspected, since the baby bore an uncanny resemblance to a portrait of himself as an infant. But he gave me only polite acknowledgment the one time I saw him, with my husband and father present, of course. We were never to meet again."

"How terrible for you," Raven whispered.

"How terrible for *him*. At least God blessed me with his son to love, a son who was spared the fate of my other children. But Sandy never married, and during those dark days, when I became an object to satisfy the vicar's . . . unchristian needs, I used to imagine him pining away out of love for me. It's foolish, I know—had he really, truly loved me, he would have come for me, don't you think? But I forgave him—any man should be forgiven his youthful indiscretions. Not like the vicar—him I do not forgive."

"I should have killed the hypocrite even sooner," Garreth murmured, clenching and unclenching his fists.

Lady Philippa nodded. "Perhaps that would have spared our family a lot of suffering. My other children were conceived out of hatred and turpitude; better that your brothers had never been born. But you, my son . . . my daughter . . . you must live. Get away from this place."

Garreth looked across the bed at his wife; his eyes were glittering with tears and love.

"We shall, Mother," he said.

"Bring me a sheet of paper, my ink, and seal," she said to him, pointing a shaky hand toward the writing table. "This foul-tasting substance your sorceress wife gave me will not last much longer."

Then, incredibly, she gave Raven a wink.

Sensing the urgency, Garreth ran to the desk and pulled open several drawers at once.

"Here they are, Mother," he said, rushing back to her side. A small escritoire was resting on the floor, dusty from disuse. Raven picked it up, wiped it off as best she could with the hem of her skirt, and arranged it over Lady Philippa's lap.

Then she and Garreth moved away, giving Lady Philippa some privacy.

The dying woman curved her stiff, deformed fingers around the pen and struggled to write. Raven's admiration for her grew with every passing moment. Someday medical science would find remedies for her affliction, she was sure, but Hippocrates himself couldn't cure this patient.

She resolved as well to write to Monsieur Pasteur for advice. Perhaps there was still a chance of saving Charles and his generation.

And of course, little Andrew.

"But Mother," Garreth began, "Ravenna lost our first child, like the others, and she was terribly ill, just like—"

"Ask Charles about that," Ravenna interrupted him. "And if he confesses what he did to me, ask him why."

When Lady Philippa had finished writing, she reached into the top of her nightdress and withdrew a necklace from between the sagging breasts.

"Help me, Ravenna," she said, and Raven bent over and unhooked the clasp.

She studied the cameo that was hanging on the chain; it

was a young Lady Philippa, like the portrait in the great hall.

"Sandy's gift to me when I turned sixteen, the year I conceived his child. Had we waited, I feel certain we would have been married."

That made her only about forty-five years old, Raven calculated. Yet she looked like a centenarian.

"In the eyes of God, you were married," Raven said gently. "The Church would only have echoed the vows you gave to each other."

"You are very kind, my daughter. Go and have a dozen children. Keep the best part of me alive."

She motioned for Garreth to help her seal the letter. Carefully she folded the single sheet of paper over the locket, then put them in an envelope. Using the flame from the lamp near the bed, Garreth melted wax and helped his mother affix the Harlixton seal.

"Take it," she said. "Take this to your father. He's been waiting for you for a long time. Perhaps he loves me still, though as the years passed, I realized that waiting for love that is never to be is as malicious a thing as a wasting disease. They both destroy you in the end."

"Mother, when we find him," Garreth said, "shall we bring him to you? I'm sure he will come."

Her eyes glazed over; she struggled to speak.

Garreth looked at Raven helplessly.

"I dare not give her any more right now," Raven said. "The strain on her heart could kill her."

Her lips were moving, as if she were using all of her remaining strength. "Take—the portrait with you. Let him remember me as I was, when you rode upon my—"

The corners of her mouth sagged, and her head lolled to one side. Saliva dribbled down her chin.

"Mother," Garreth said sharply, but her head fell onto her chest.

Raven felt for a pulse; it was still there, but fluttery and uneven. It was at that moment that she realized her own heart had been beating perfectly for several days.

"She's still alive. She could linger like this for weeks."

The expression on Garreth's face changed, and he pulled Ravenna against his chest, blocking out her view of everything else in the room. He held her so tight she could hardly breathe, then he cupped her face with his hands as his lips fell upon hers.

The kiss he gave her was full of welcoming, of homecoming and reunion. It was as if he were a soldier returning from the wars.

"My darling," he murmured when she'd been thoroughly kissed. "My life. I can hardly believe you've come back to me. That we can be together again."

"I never stopped loving you, Garreth. I never shall."

He clasped both her hands tightly. "We'll go to my father," he said. "Go and live with him. And we'll start anew, away from this place. And soon . . . we'll fill his house with grandchildren."

"Let's start tonight."

"Let's start right now."

He turned toward the bed a final time. "Mother, we'll see that you're cared for. You are still the mistress of your own house."

She didn't respond; her face was like a death mask. But out of the corner of one eye fell a single tear, which glistened like a star of hope as it caught the light.

Thirty-three

That afternoon, after tea, Garreth assembled the entire family in the drawing room.

Ravenna was not certain how much any of the individual players in this drama knew about the family, about Lady Philippa, about their own fate.

Except Charles, of course, who stood off to one corner like a sulking dog who had just been beaten repeatedly by his master's cane.

Ravenna stood at Garreth's side, which gave her a chance to peruse the Pembroke children with her newfound knowledge of their medical condition. Using a mental tablet, she scribbled down their symptoms in her head: first and foremost, the peculiar sallow complexion, then of course, the general languor and debility, the overall appearance of being unwell. Charles's strength at various times had surprised her, though she concluded that was a function of his developing madness—which often gave its victim remarkable powers. She felt certain now that it was he who had pursued her on the stairs, and had broken her wrist.

The pallid skin, so fashionably attractive on Clarity and Justine when compared to her dark, Mediterranean complexion, was the result of a secondary anemia. It was this anemia that had led to Anne's untimely death. If Raven could not cure her sisters-in-law, at least she could offer certain palliative measures.

"Thank you all for interrupting your daily activities," Garreth said, not without some irony, for they all led useless lives.

"All right, brother," Justine quipped. "Tell us what skeletons you've unearthed in the closet."

Ravenna cut short her gasp, wondering whether Justine was making a disrespectful remark about Lady Philippa. There was such a lack of knowledge or guile in her face, however, that Raven decided it was just a poor choice of words, that actually Justine knew very little. Charles did not have a loquacious personality, and she could see him wanting to conceal, rather than publish, his humiliation.

"I'll get right to the point. Ravenna and I are leaving Harlixton Hall. Forever."

Their collective gasps rose in the room like a cloud of dust.

"Garreth, old man . . ." This was from St. Clair.

"It has come to my attention that I stand to inherit certain properties in Buckinghamshire. Ravenna and I intend to make our home there." He looked toward the back of the room. "Charles."

Immediately, Charles stiffened, not sure what was to come next.

"Before I continue," Garreth said, "Ravenna would like to ask you a question."

She moved closer to him. To his credit, his eyes remained focused upon her as he waited for her rebuke.

"Well, Ravenna?" he demanded.

"It was you all along, wasn't it?"

"Yes," he admitted.

"Why?" she asked with equal simplicity.

"Isn't it obvious?" he said, and laughed. "My son stood to inherit the house, the land, everything, until my brother had the good fortune to marry you. I—I just couldn't let you give him a son. Can you understand that?"

"So all the questions, the discussions—"

"You handed me the murder weapon. You and your little Chinese friend."

"Charles—"

"It was I who helped you up right after we'd looted the witch's cupboard in London. I did a good impersonation of a city bloke, don't you think?" Then he laughed again, inappropriately. "And it was you who chose a partner for me! How do you think an idiot like Cholly Makepiece ever came into my employ? He and I had only one thing in common— our dislike for *you*."

"Charles—"

"A good carpenter indeed!" he snorted. "That imbecile couldn't do anything right—as you so astutely testified in court, and I quote from the transcript: 'His attack on his daughter failed owing to his ignorance of feminine anatomy. Had he but aimed the blows lower . . .' Oh, that was rich!"

"Charles," she said, "you *hired* him to—to—"

"To scare you off. To send you back to your own pitiful cottage. Garreth would never marry another after you." Then he turned to his older brother and scowled. "Yet it seems, Garreth, that once more you've won, haven't you? Your beautiful wife stood by you as she was threatened and attacked. And what's this now? Another inheritance? Isn't one fortune enough for you?"

"Charles," Garreth said with thinly veiled contempt, "I relinquish my claim to Harlixton Hall and the lands and all other holdings—to you, as your father's eldest son."

Again the gasps filled the room.

"Garreth," Justine cried, "what are you talking about— 'your' father?"

"I don't wish to discuss it now, Justine. Wait until we're safely gone, then ask Charles to fill your ears with the sad story of our unlucky family." Then, looking toward his brother again, he said, "It's all yours, Charles, and eventually your son's."

"Garreth," he said, shaking his head as if close to tears. "I—I don't know what to say."

"Just take it, man," he replied. "The estate, the position, it's what you've always wanted." He turned his head toward Ravenna. "I believe everyone deserves what he wants most in the world."

Then he took Ravenna's hand and kissed it.

Book IV

Riverside,
Henley on Thames,
Buckinghamshire, and
London

Thirty-four

November 1844

The gates to Riverside, the Earl of Henley's country seat, were even more impressive than the entrance to Harlixton land. Hosts of wrought iron angels greeted Garreth and Ravenna as they passed under the high arches; the gatekeeper's house was more like a lodge than a servant's dwelling.

Raven wondered whether her new father-in-law would let her establish a clinic on his enormous grounds.

The earl knew only that they intended to call, but not the nature of their visit. For Garreth, however, there was no turning back, and hence he'd brought everything he cared to take with him. The Harlixton papers and valuables he'd left with Charles.

They took the portrait of Lady Philippa; the other painting in the great hall was left behind. Even though Lord Harlixton was Garreth's grandfather, any man who could so ruin a young girl's life was no one to be remembered.

After much good-natured arguing over where to stow the luggage during their initial visit to Riverside, Raven had prevailed, and they had left their belongings at a nearby inn.

"Let our intentions be announced by our lips, not our parcels," she argued, and Garreth had finally relented.

The drive up to the house took nearly an hour. They passed several groups of neatly thatched cottages along the way. Men tending to a cow or some sheep and women fetching water or sweeping greeted them as they passed, and Raven thought, with anticipation, of all the babies she could deliver and the medicines she could dispense.

Perhaps she would become like Madame Liu, growing her own herbs. Indeed, as the future Countess of Henley, she could do anything she chose, and the Devil take convention.

She had learned from her experience at Harlixton Hall that life is short, and one must make the most of one's gifts.

"He may turn us away," she said, hoping that by voicing her fear, it would not come true. "Maybe we'll be relegated to one of those cottages and a garden plot."

"A keeper's cottage would not be unpleasant," Garreth responded, "as long as I could share it with you."

Garreth and Ravenna were like newlyweds returning from their honeymoon. They had left one life and were yet to begin another. And hence both of them felt a rootless, romantic freedom while they huddled together in the Harlixton coach.

Raven wanted to get to know her husband all over again, to probe the secret places, touch him where he wanted to be touched, linger over every part of him. They were nearing the end of their carriage ride, and she should have been ruled by discretion; yet his presence overpowered her like a love potion. Her fingers reached out to stroke and tug at his black hair; her lips touched lightly on his cheeks, his neck, the soft hair behind his ears; her body, having grown supple and reckless from desire, twisted and turned until it rested against the long length of him. It was the woman's place to be modest, to blush and say the driver might notice, but she had lost all girlish innocence.

"Mmmm," Garreth murmured as she parted the two halves of his woolen outer coat, loosened his neckcloth, then undid the top buttons of his shirt, exposing just enough of his chest so she could run her hand across it. She grew bolder, pressing and kneading the firm muscles, then planting moist, nibbling kisses on every inch of available skin.

Were they not both imprisoned in their respectable visiting costumes, and she in her corset, she would have stripped her husband—and herself—and begged him to join with her right then.

"If my father could only see me now," she quipped, quelling her breath with a hand pressed firmly between her breasts.

Garreth sat up straight, then looked her squarely in the eye. "But he can't, Ravenna," he stated with the authority of a schoolmaster. "He's gone. You have to let him go."

She nodded once, twice, then several more times in succession. "I have to let him go," she repeated. "I want to. I must."

Holding her arms outward, she welcomed Garreth into her embrace, hugging him with the fierceness of a lonely child. Her hands ran along his back, maddened by the barriers of coat and waistcoat and shirt and undershirt. He, in turn, trailed his fingers across her cloak-covered shoulders, her well-encased breasts, down along the corsetted torso and waist, and across the thick skirt and petticoats. Up his hands went again, reaching under her cloak, squeezing well-layered sleeves and trailing across the high, lace-trimmed neck of her dress. In a final act of desperation, he cupped her naked face between his hands and kissed her. If only his passion could ignite and burn the clothing off her.

"I feel like a lad on his first outing with an honorable maiden," Garreth complained. "Your virtue, my dear, is safe."

Raven settled back into her seat, accepting the fact that a corset had once more controlled her life. Garreth sighed as he redid the buttons of his shirt, reknotted the silk neckcloth, then simply draped his arm tightly around his wife's shoulder.

Their carriage turned a sharp left, and they came upon

a massive fountain, with water bubbling all around an enormous shell like a dozen natural springs. Inside the shell which must have been thirty feet across, Venus herself was emerging from the foam. Like the angels at the gate, it was a gaudy creation, perhaps something the French would have admired. Yet Raven took it as a good omen: Venus, goddess of love herself, dwelled within these grounds. Their love would flow freely here, away from the treacherous waters of their past.

The house was barely visible at the end of the driveway, the carriage was still a good mile away. Although it was November, seasonal flowers were still blooming on either side of the drive, and their yellows and oranges mingled with the tawny hues of the last autumn leaves.

"Isn't it beautiful?" Raven cried in delight as they passed all the colors. The autumn so far had been very mild, and the day both looked and felt like the one in October when she and Charles had embarked on their journey. Perhaps Nature had held up her progress toward winter to let Ravenna enjoy some of what she'd missed.

"Yes, it's splendid," Garreth said. "Though I suppose Harlixton is just as impressive to a stranger's eyes." He said this with a touch of longing, as if he had never bothered to look.

"The first time I came up your drive, it was on a dark winter morning, and I was drugged from exhaustion. I'm sure that had I first viewed Harlixton under these circumstances, I would have felt the same awe."

"That morning seems like a lifetime ago," he said.

"So it was."

Garreth took Raven's hand. "So it was."

Riverside was a veritable castle, with turrets and spires and a tower at every corner. Raven half expected to see watchmen in full medieval regalia walking along the parapeted roof, and wondered whether trumpeters would herald their approach.

As soon as their carriage stopped in front, the massive door opened and a tall, energetic butler emerged, followed by a maid and several footmen.

"Welcome to Riverside," the butler said, smiling like a kindly uncle as first Garreth then Ravenna alighted from the coach.

They had brought no servants with them, since they wanted to begin again afresh with people who did not know of their former lives.

Even the coach and driver would return to Harlixton as soon as Garreth said the word.

"Mrs. Pembroke, welcome to Riverside," the butler reiterated, bowing. "I am Boswell, at your service."

"Good afternoon, Boswell," she answered. "Are you any relation to the famous biographer?"

"Indeed I am, madam," he said, beaming. "We are cousins."

"Cousins?" she exclaimed, furrowing her brow.

"Across the generations, of course. His brother was my grandfather."

"I should love sometime to hear any stories you may have of Dr. Johnson that did not survive the editor's pen."

"Of course, madam. I should be honored," Boswell said, and she knew she had made an important ally in the house. "And might I show you my collection of manuscript pages?"

"Most certainly. It is I who would be honored."

As they were ushered into the house, Raven wondered how a man from a family of some celebrity could have ended up in service. But before they had crossed the enormous main hall into the drawing room, she had formulated her own answer: The original Boswell was undoubtedly like her father—devoted to great deeds rather than piling up great fortunes.

The interior of Riverside stood in stark contrast to Harlixton Hall. Riverside was stunning in its simplicity: The great hall was almost empty of furnishings. Instead, it was a wide open space that reminded one of a bright summer's afternoon. Every hue was a shade of milk or honey: cream-colored walls, light marble floors, drapes the color of wheat, even off-white furniture. Perhaps they had traversed the gates of heaven after all. Absent were the dark, dour furnishings of their former home—the suits of armor, the dark wood, the dismal tapestries, the slate fireplace.

The drawing room was all milk and honey as well, and the sun from the southern windows bounced off the crystal chandeliers, casting hundreds of dancing rainbows all over the room.

"I've never seen anything like this," Raven exclaimed.

"It was his lordship's own doing," Boswell said. "All the designs and furnishings were of his own choosing."

After making a quick circuit of the chamber, Raven settled herself into a cream-colored armchair while Garreth remained standing, the sealed letter from his mother in his right hand.

From a great distance, they heard the clicking of boots on marble, In spite of herself, Raven's heart rate accelerated—its rhythm was now regular as a clock, but anxiety was causing it to gallop like a racehorse.

She thought about jumping to her feet and grabbing Garreth's hand, then decided against it—this was a meeting between father and son.

Let them have their first moments unencumbered.

The walking grew louder, a crisp, youthful pace. The Earl of Henley, after all, was hardly an old man.

Will he accept us? she kept wondering as the clicking of boot heels grew steadily louder. Or Garreth, at least? *Will he trust us?* Would he accept Lady Philippa's letter as proof? Perhaps she'd exaggerated the earl's love for her, to quell her broken heart. Perhaps he'd stayed a bachelor by choice and hence would resent the appearance of children—and God forbid, grandchildren.

The footsteps seemed deafeningly close now, and Ravenna wished that time would stand still for a moment so she could further prepare her nerves. They were supplicants, after all, homeless and without resources. Garreth had taken a risk by renouncing his claim to the Harlixton fortune—and within the hour they might find themselves begging the Warrens to take them in.

A keeper's cottage would not be unpleasant . . . as long as I could share it with you . . . She had to remember that. No matter what happened, Garreth, reborn and free of his Furies, loved her with all his unburdened heart.

A shadow wavered in the hall as someone approached and prepared to turn and enter the room. Raven's heart was in her throat, and she took a painful breath.

Boswell moved quickly toward the doorway and announced, "The Earl of Henley."

A strapping, black-haired man with twinkling brown eyes walked briskly into the room. He paused just inside the door so they could all get a good look at one another.

Raven gasped as soon as she saw him, for he was the spit and image of her husband.

For a long moment, none of them said anything. The things that needed to be said would have to wait. Each man was viewing himself in the other—the father seeing what he once was, the son seeing what he would become. In an instant, each realized what had been missing in his own life, the lost piece the other man possessed.

Finally, it was Raven's wayward tears that once again decided the course of events. The existence of two Garreths in one room—one as husband, the other as father—overwhelmed her self-control, and the silence of the room was broken by a brief, choked sob.

Alexander Gordon, sixth Earl of Henley, opened his arms and said, "Son, I've waited a long time for this moment."

Raven sobbed again as Garreth walked toward his father, then threw his arms around the older man.

They held each other for longer than would be considered manly. But they were cut from the same cloth, neither caring for propriety.

Over and over, the earl said, "My boy . . . my son."

As she watched, Raven wondered why a man of such warmth had never married or produced a family of his own.

It was the housekeeper who ultimately interrupted their embrace by entering the room and offering tea and the most enormous selection of cakes and sandwiches Ravenna had ever seen on one tray.

Straightening up but leaving his arm loosely around Garreth's shoulders, the earl said, "Mrs. Kemp, my son is home at last."

"Welcome home, sir," the plump lady cried, with genuine warmth.

"But come now, my boy," the earl said, walking Garreth over to the tea tray. "Have a sampling of our cook's specialities. And you, my dear," he said, stretching his unoccupied right arm toward Ravenna. "Can you find it in your young heart to accept an aging rascal like me as your father?"

She nodded quickly, her unruly tears rendering her speechless, then sank against his lean body, feeling as safe and comfortable as a child in her own bed.

They formed an awkward tableau, a diverse collection of arms and legs clinging to and supporting one another, but Raven could have remained in their embrace forever.

Boswell and Mrs. Kemp bowed, unnoticed, then quit the room.

"How long have you known?" Garreth asked after a considerable interlude of silence.

The earl motioned for them both to be seated on a long white divan, then seated himself across from them in a cream-colored wing chair.

"Since the moment I laid eyes on you as an infant. And when I looked directly in your mother's eyes, and saw the agony that was written in them, I was sure." He was cold sober now, and even his eyes lost a portion of their sparkle. "She is—dead now?"

"I don't know," Garreth answered truthfully.

"She's dying, my lord," Raven interjected. "Yet she could linger for a while."

The earl looked at Raven thoughtfully. "Do you suppose, then, after all these years that she would still see me?"

Ravenna was tempted to say yes, but she held her tongue. "She wants you to remember her as she was. Her appearance is shocking, my lord."

"But I don't care!" the earl cried, practically springing to his feet. "I've loved her all these years."

"As she has loved you," Raven said.

The earl's eyes took on Garreth's faraway look, and Raven thought she saw a glimmer of tears pooling in them.

They sipped tea and nibbled cakes in the renewed silence, then Raven asked. "My lord—"

"Please, nothing so formal. I'm your father now, remember that, if you will have me, Ravenna. Though I admit I'll never take the place of Sir Richmond Marisse in your—"

"My lord! I mean—"

He smiled at her with great warmth. "Yes, I knew him, Ravenna. He came to me several times to sponsor certain charitable causes. I should be honored to be a father to his only child."

Ravenna was happier than she could ever remember, happier than a child at Christmas. In the short space of several days, she had gone from being orphan and scorned wife to becoming the beloved daughter of titled parents and the adored wife of the man she loved more than life itself. In time, she would ask her new father to sponsor the charitable cause that would make her life complete in every way—a new clinic. Let it never be said that all English gentlewomen lolled away their days in useless frivolity.

"My lord," she began, "that is, Father, if you knew that

Garreth was your son, why did you not seek him out, free him from that—"

"Ravenna . . ." Garreth warned her.

"It's all right, son," the earl reassured him. "I wish I could blame my crimes of omission on doddering old age, but I am hardly your senior. I was just eighteen when your mother and I conceived you. Had I not left for Cambridge, or had I been informed of her condition, I would have rushed home and married her on the spot. But I didn't know, you see. When I came home for Christmas, Wyngate told me that Philippa would not receive me."

"How terrible for you," Raven said.

"Yes. I wanted to kill the poor man for turning me away. I had written her dozens of letters—at least twice or thrice a week. When I received no response, I thought she was angry at me for having taken her virtue."

"She never got those letters," Garreth said. "She told us so herself, that she had written you often but never received a reply."

"She thought it was you who had abandoned her," Raven said.

"I had . . . never!" The earl looked away for a moment, pain clearly furrowing his brow. "I never received *her* letters. Undoubtedly they were never posted to me."

"Her father forced her to marry," Garreth said. "To save her reputation."

"Ah," the earl said, "we should have waited." He shook his head ruefully. "My sin has haunted all of us, I'm afraid. But you see, my children, we were so much in love, we simply could not hold back anything from each other. We . . . we had to . . . embrace each other as we did. I can tell by your faces that you understand."

Raven nodded, and Garreth said, "Yes, Father. We know."

"Then you will both forgive me for the circumstances that brought you, our only son, into being?"

"No," Raven said with firmness.

"No?" The earl cocked his brow, more out of curiosity than embarrassment or anger.

"There is nothing to forgive when you love someone so much."

"Ah," the earl said, nodding his head in gratitude and understanding.

Garreth said, "We brought you the portrait—the one that hung in the front hall."

"You have it?" the earl asked eagerly. "I've never actually seen it, you know, only heard about it from neighbors and guests, and heard, too, how the vicar had your likeness removed, Garreth." Then he added, "How unbecoming envy is in a vicar."

"The portrait is nevertheless quite lovely," Ravenna assured him.

"That is how I remember her—so lovely. Even that last time I saw her, when you were just born, Garreth, she was so much in love with you that, when she looked into your eyes, the misery in her own seemed momentarily to vanish. If I couldn't have her, at least she would have our child to love. And that appeased the ache in my heart—that at least we had made you."

"Ah," Raven said. "That explains something to me."

"What is that, my dear."

"She looks so happy in that portrait, though she had already been married to—to that blackguard for months. She told us herself that he wouldn't touch her as long as she was carrying your child, but if Garreth were—how old when you last saw her?"

"Only six months old, I believe. The portrait was nearing completion at the time."

"In that case, maybe the man's"—Raven struggled to think of an appropriate word—"degradation of Lady Philippa had not begun in earnest."

"Degradation?" the earl asked sharply.

"In time, Father," Garreth said, "we will talk of these things. They are not pleasant."

The earl covered his face with his hands. When he laid his hands back in his lap, tears were streaking his face.

"I must go to her," he said. "Ask her forgiveness. I don't care what she looks like—to me, she will always be the most beautiful woman in the world. . . . That is why I never married, particularly when I learned she had borne our child. I knew, Garreth, that we would meet someday, that we would announce to the world that you were my son and heir. Indeed, I feared siring a child within a legitimate marriage would pit brother against brother. I didn't want that for my family, or for you, the product of the one great love in my life."

Raven shook her head at the tragic waste of so many lives. "Why on earth would old Lord Harlixton prevent you from marrying his daughter? You're an earl, while the vicar was a . . . a—"

"A devil," Garreth interjected.

"Certainly he should have been attracted by your wealth, and what his grandchildren would inherit if Lady Philippa married you."

"If I had been there," the earl replied, "nothing would have stood in our way. But I heard no news of her until after she was married, so I'm not sure what transpired between the father and his daughter. I can only imagine, however, that Lord Harlixton, a descendant of Cromwell and a dour Puritan in heart and mind, thought to punish his daughter in some way. What better way than to chain her to a humorless man of God, who would make her rue her sins. And as for her wealth, I doubt Lord Harlixton cared much for acquiring more, since his own wealth was considerable, not only from the Harlixton inheritance, which came to him when a cousin died without issue, but also from his mother's side of the family, which had amassed an enormous fortune trading furs in the New World. Between the Harlixton fortune and my own considerable wealth, you, Garreth, will someday be one of the richest men in all of England."

"I am the richest man already, Father. I have you and Ravenna—what more could I ask for?"

"Our children, Garreth," Raven whispered.

"Ah," he said, smiling. "When our children are born, I will be the wealthiest man in all the known world. . . . But allow me to speak frankly, sir. I have . . . renounced my claim to Harlixton. Charles, my younger brother, has always wanted it for himself, and now for his son. He"—here Garreth clenched his teeth—"almost killed Ravenna to prevent us from producing an heir."

"Killed?" the earl cried. "Is he insane?"

"He might be," Raven answered truthfully. "He is suffering from . . ." She hesitated.

"Again, Father, we will tell you all about these things—in time. But suffice it to say that we come to you as poor relations, without a place to call our own. We are entirely at your mercy."

The earl stroked his chin as if in thought. "Well, then," he said seriously, "let's begin by . . . giving you a 'place.' In society, I mean. The name 'Pembroke,' for one thing, simply won't do."

"I quite agree," Garreth broke in. "Not an ounce of Pembroke blood flows in my veins."

"In my youth," the earl went on, "I adopted one of my father's lesser titles as my own. I was the Viscount Westbrook at Cambridge." Inclining his head first to Garreth, then to Ravenna, he asked, "My lord . . . my lady . . . does the name 'Westbrook' please you?"

"Ravenna?" Garreth inquired, grinning broadly.

"My lord, I defer to you," she said, grinning back.

"Westbrook it is. I thank you, Father."

Inwardly, Raven chided herself for being so delighted. The disdain of a lifetime had vanished in an instant. Yet it was not the title that pleased her so, but the man to whom it belonged.

"Ah, Garreth," the earl said wistfully. "How I wish I could have watched you grow to manhood. If only I had stayed home and lived the life of any other country gentleman. I could have married your mother, run my estates, raised a family, pursued the normal pleasures. Instead I took my studies at Cambridge seriously; I wanted to do something useful, you see, perhaps even make a name for myself. Even now I make up for my lack of family by throwing my doors open to the children of the cottagers. Perhaps you've noticed the bizarre way I have decorated my home—it's for the children. When everything is white, I can easily add red banners for Christmas, black for All Hallows' Eve, pink and lavender for Easter. And in the dark days of winter, we paint the ceiling of this room blue and draw trees and a great big sun on the walls."

"My goodness," Raven exclaimed, laughing.

"Boswell and Mrs. Kemp are quite accommodating about the messes the children and I make."

"Our own children will be blessed to have such a grandfather," Ravenna said. "My father took his degree at Cambridge, too. Did you perhaps know him there?"

The earl nodded. "Of course I knew of him. Victor Frankenstein, they called him. He was somewhat of an idol to me, for I wanted to be—"

Just then a sharp knocking on the door interrupted their conversation.

"Come in," the earl called, and Boswell entered, followed by two burly, ill-dressed men.

"Beggin' your pardon, my lord," one of the men said, clearly overwhelmed by the presence of nobility, "we apologize for the intrusion, but we be lookin' for one Garreth Pembroke of Harlixton Hall, county o' Berkshire."

Garreth stood up at once. "What's the meaning of this?"

The two men gaped at him until the spokesman managed to ask, "Be you Garreth Pembroke."

"State your business, man," Garreth said with contempt.

"No disrespect, sir," he said, bowing his head. "My lord, my lady." It was an ironic choice of words at that moment.

Suddenly the man was shoved aside as a third ruffian entered the room. Raven gasped when she recognized Cholly Makepiece.

Cholly gave them all a sneer, then said triumphantly, "That's 'im."

"Garreth Pembroke," the spokesman said with an unsteady voice, "as duly sworn deputies of the sheriff o' Buck'n'amshire, we arrest you in the name o' the Queen and Crown."

"What?" Ravenna cried, springing to her feet and grasping Garreth's arm.

"The charge is murder of one Edward Pembroke, late vicar of Reading. Please come with us, sir."

"He will not," the earl said, jumping to his feet as well and holding himself up to his full, imposing height. "Who set you up to this, Geoffrey? Go home and forget all this nonsense."

"It, uh," the man began, "it have nothin' to do with you, your lordship, but we, beggin' your pardon . . ."

"It's all right, Father," Garreth said. "I'll go with them. And clear my name." Then he grasped Raven's right hand and squeezed it hard. "They have no evidence," he whispered in her ear, then released her and walked toward his three accusers.

"Don't be too cocky, your highness," Cholly sneered, with mocking emphasis on the last two words. "They found the body—right where your lady friend said you did bury it. Perchance old Cholly'll see you hangin' high from—"

"Here now, mind yer tongue," the man called Geoffrey warned. As a local man, he clearly feared and respected the earl, while he undoubtedly had an intrinsic dislike for Cholly, a Berkshireman and outsider.

"My lord, I apologize for the—the . . but I be duly sworn . . ." Geoffrey bowed his head again.

"Very well. Be about your business, Geoff," the earl replied. "I'll speak to the sheriff myself." But he said this with some apprehension—murder was always a grave charge in civilized society.

"G'day, my lord," the poor man squeaked.

Panic coursed through Ravenna like venom from a snake bite. The earl rushed to her side to take Garreth's place.

Together they watched as the trio of thugs, like sinister incarnations of the three Fates, took from them the person they loved the most.

Thirty-five

There was hardly any snow on the ground as the Henley coach rumbled along the Kensington road into London, for a sojourn at Henley House, overlooking St. James's Square. Snuggled in her new fur-lined cloak, Raven leaned childlike against the broad arm of her father-in-law.

It was less than a year since she had huddled against another broad arm as John Travers drove her up the long drive toward an unimaginable fate.

So much had happened in that short year; yet there was so much left to resolve.

Garreth had been turned over to the London authorities and taken to the jail in Slough. Not even the earl's influence could get him released. Many people still remembered the vicar of Reading and his fiery sermons, and there seemed to be no mercy for the impudent young son who stood accused of his father's murder.

Raven never discovered how Cholly heard the confessions made in Lady Philippa's death chamber, but there were servants in the room before their mistress cleared them out. Charles himself could have remained behind and lurked like an interloper on the other side of the door.

Yet why would he want to ruin his brother, now that he had what *he* wanted most?

And Raven liked to think that even though Charles had tried to ruin her, he harbored no personal ill will toward her. Perhaps when all this was over, they would become cordial, even friends again.

The Slough prison was, fortunately, a rich man's house of detention, quite unlike the vermin-infested oubliettes reserved for the common man. Garreth was assigned his own quarters, including bedroom, sitting room, and water closet, and an adjoining room for a valet, who was allowed to come and go at scheduled intervals. She and the earl visited Garreth twice a week, and though imprisoned by strangers, Garreth was in higher spirits than she had ever seen him in Harlixton, when he was in prison of another sort.

Yet the charge of murder was real enough, as was the evidence. The Cheapside woman had led the sheriff to the decomposed body, which was buried in Upper Moor Fields. The ring of the Reading parish was still on its finger, and a watch with *ELP* engraved on it was found in the fragments of clothing.

The woman had sworn under oath that Garreth was the killer. He'd broken into her home and accused the vicar of adultery, when it was Garreth's own child she carried in her womb. Then he shot his father in a drunken rage and forced her to help him drag the body away.

If anyone inquired as to their business, they would say that they were getting their dead-drunk father some air, until they were way out of sight in the Fields.

It was a creditable story, but one Raven knew in her heart to be false. It was their intention—the earl's and her own— to seek out the woman and offer their protection, so that she could tell the truth without fear of reprisal from Cholly and his thugs.

First they made a stop at Madame Liu's, since she was also a party to Raven's fate. Raven would learn once and for all what Charles had given her.

When Madame Liu opened the door, Raven noticed at once the cast upon her forearm, so like the one she had discarded just days after moving into Riverside.

"My dear," Madame Liu cried when she saw Ravenna, and stretched out her good arm to offer half an embrace. "Come in! Come in! It is so good to see you again." As they walked into the modest home and Raven shrugged off her cloak, she exclaimed, "And without your cast! You will provide inspiration for me."

"Madame," Raven said after she had introduced her father-in-law and they had settled into the small sitting room, "let me make amends for your arm. It's my fault—"

"Your fault? But—"

"Those men who broke into your home—"

"You know about that? It was—most extraordinary."

"They were no ordinary thieves. I know this may sound bizarre to you, but one of them was probably my brother-in-law."

Madame Liu glanced quickly at the earl. Raising his hands in mock defense, he said, "Not *my* son, I assure you! Your attacker was from—another side of the family."

"I believe he was my brother-in-law," Raven continued, "for I'd been giving him lessons in the medicinal properties of herbs. I later discovered a book that he'd purchased in Oxford about folk healing. I doubt if he could have instructed a hired thief in what to steal from you."

"Indeed not. One of the men appeared quite knowledgeable in what to take, as if he were a healer himself. Although . . ."

"Although the specific plants he took were all dangerous if used improperly. Am I correct?"

Madame Liu pursed her lips. "Quite correct."

"You see, madame, he later used these medicinals in an attempt to drive me insane, and perhaps kill me."

"Kill you?" Madame Liu said with the same surprise the earl had shown. "But Ravenna, can this be? This is England—the nineteenth century! And in your own family?"

"They are no longer any family of mine. They are not even sane themselves."

And Ravenna told her of what had transpired in the past weeks, of her illness, of the Harlixton curse and Lady Philippa's condition.

"Could you describe the two men?" Raven asked.

"They wore hoods, which hung over and concealed their faces. But I remember their voices, the diction."

Then she offered two perfect impersonations, since she was a quick linguist and had even picked up five or six languages during her extended foreign travels. It was almost as if Charles and Cholly were in the room.

"And one was slight while the other one seemed to tower over him," the Oriental said.

"Yes," replied Raven. "Did they use any names?"

"None."

The earl interjected, "Why did you not just give them what they wanted? Why did you resist?"

"Oh, I didn't resist," Madame Liu assured them. "When I saw that they intended to rob me, I offered them my entire supply of medicinals. I assumed they would have no knowledge of how to use them, even though I was rather concerned, as you stated, Ravenna, that they selected things which can kill a person if used improperly."

"Ergot, for one," Raven said.

Madame Liu glanced quickly at her. "Yes. Good heavens, Ravenna, is that what he gave you?"

Raven nodded.

"And foxglove, which almost destroyed the rhythm of my heart."

"Oh, my dear, I'm so sorry."

But the earl persisted in his own point, which was a trait Raven respected in him. "If you did not resist your attackers, Madame Liu, then tell me, how did your arm come to be broken?"

She shuddered at his question, then he said quickly, "Forgive me. I should not have inquired."

"Please don't ask for forgiveness, my lord, for now that

you are here, Ravenna, perhaps you can clear something up for me."

"I'll try."

"After the men had helped themselves, the shorter one urged his partner to come along. Then the bigger man said"—and here she imitated Cholly perfectly—" 'I got me some unfinished business 'ere.' Then he seized my arm and pulled it behind my back. I was quite shocked, and even asked the shorter one to help me, since he seemed kinder and more reasonable than the other. But my captor said, ''Ere's one for Daisy, what should 'ave been dead.' And he twisted my wrist, savagely I might add, since the bone was broken in several places and has taken these many weeks to heal."

"Oh, God," Raven breathed, feeling the same sickness as when her own arm was broken. "It was Cholly, all right."

"Ravenna," the earl said with contempt written all over his face. "When we return, I'll have the man arrested. Was it he who attacked you as well?"

"To be honest, sir," Ravenna said, "I'm not sure. It was dark, so I couldn't see his face, but I sensed a man of slighter build."

"Perhaps it was your brother-in-law," Madame Liu offered. "For as I was clutching my broken arm, and whimpering quite pitifully, I might add, I heard the smaller man chide his partner harshly. 'That was a depraved act,' he said with contempt. 'Shape up at once.' But the bigger man said, 'Well, now, what's all this high-and-mighty? You 'ad your fun. Now it be my turn.' "

Ravenna pondered this a moment. "I think you are right. It probably was Charles himself. At the time, I marveled at the man's strength, totally beyond what Charles was normally capable of. But as you, Madame Liu—and my father— often told me, madness can give its sufferer extraordinary powers. It gave Charles the momentary strength to rescue me from the Thames."

"Rescue you?" the earl said.

Ravenna smiled. "Again, I will tell you yet another unpleasant story . . . in time. Now let us think of more pressing matters. Can we really demand to have Cholly arrested? I sense that I have nothing more to fear from Charles, but Cholly is another matter."

"We have the evidence certainly," the earl answered. "Both you and Madame Liu will be able to testify against him."

"Yes," Ravenna agreed. "And I hope he can be sent away permanently this time. You see," she explained, turning her attention to Madame Liu and trying to focus on the woman's face instead of her arm, "I had Cholly put in jail once, for beating his daughter, who was with child. Then I took her in until the baby came, and found a suitable position for her. Cholly never forgave me for that, since, Father, the jail that Cholly went to was quite different from the gentlemen's club that Garreth currently resides in."

"And his daughter's name was Daisy, wasn't it?" Madame Liu speculated.

"Yes," Raven responded. "I believe he sought to avenge himself upon you as well as on me, since we are both women of physic."

"And the unmarried daughter—Daisy—she is safe with her child?"

"Safe, yes, for she's in service in London, and Cholly doesn't know where. Sir Douglas Williams, a colleague of my father's, needed a housekeeper."

"I know of him," the earl said.

Turning back to her father-in-law, Raven said, "Might we call on him? Now that certain things have been made clear to me, I think I know who the baby's father was. There were problems with the baby, as with my nephew Andrew."

"Good Lord," the earl said. "You think it was the vicar's offspring?"

"Yes, I believe so. But I don't think Cholly knows. If he did, he might kill Garreth himself if given the opportunity."

"Certainly, we can call on him. I once met Sir Douglas at a professional gathering. Splendid man."

"Yes, he is. Patron of the orphanage at St. Giles in the Fields."

As they rose to depart, the earl shook his head and mused, "To think that one man, a churchman at that, could cause so much suffering to so many people."

"And still he rules us," Raven said angrily. "We must lay him to rest, or we will never be free to live our lives."

"We've all been ruled by the ghosts in our past, it seems," the earl said. "Your father, my beloved Philippa, the vicar. We would do well to put all their memories to rest, so that we can be free to live, and to love again."

Thirty-six

Ravenna and the Earl of Henley did not receive as warm a reception at the rooming house in Cheapside. In fact, the voices they heard from within all ceased after they had struck the door knocker; no one came to admit them.

Raven scribbled a note on her handkerchief and pushed it under the front door. She had no idea whether anyone read it—whether they could even read—but in any event, no one responded to her reassurance that they were Garreth's family come to help.

They had just reembarked into their coach, when a young girl came skipping down the road. It was the girl Ravenna had seen on the previous visit, and despite the cold and her bare legs, she seemed happy and animated.

Raven got out immediately and waited for the girl to approach. Upon noticing the coach, the girl stopped in her tracks and peered at it with wonder in her eyes, and maybe fear as well.

Other coaches and other strange, well-dressed personages had also visited her home, perhaps, and perhaps had done evil, hurtful things to those inside.

"Peg," Ravenna called, waving.

The girl peered at her, then said excitedly, "Ravenna!"

"Is your mother at home?"

"I b'lieve so, ma'am," she said. Then she skipped up the worn stoop and rapped sharply on the door.

To her surprise, no one let her in.

"Mum!" she called out. "It's Peg, Mum."

"Tell her that I must speak to her about—Garreth."

Peg turned around and stared at her. "Garreth?"

"I am his wife."

"Hmm," she mused. "You look more like his sister, with your hair all black-like." Turning back, she called out, " 'Tis Garreth's wife, Mum! She d'wish to speak to you."

The door opened a crack, then an arm grabbed the girl and pulled her into the house.

"Oh, please, wait!" Raven cried, rushing up the stoop in time to have the door slammed on her nose. "Please let us in!" she called, banging on the door.

"Let her go," the earl called from the step of the coach.

Rejoining him and letting him assist her into her seat, she said, "I worry about their safety. What if Cholly returns?"

"We'll come again tomorrow," the earl reassured her as they settled into the plush velvet and he beckoned her to lean her head against him. "Don't worry, we'll get them away from this place. You arrange it with them, and I'll see that it's done."

She took his hand and squeezed it, while he swung his other arm around and gripped her shoulders protectively.

"You've given me back my life, Father," she said.

"As you have mine, daughter."

They rode back to Henley House in silence, but both of them pondered the same thoughts.

Thirty-seven

The interior of Henley House was much like Riverside, with the same warm beige and honey colors and various shades of coffee with cream. Like Riverside, the earl's town house was frequently thrown open to groups of children—to the orphans of St. Giles, for instance. Workmen were already preparing for the earl's Christmas party, turning the ballroom into a candy house, complete with red and white stripes on the walls. The earl, of course, would dress up as Father Christmas.

Ravenna was settled into yet another guest room, this one elegantly simple in its furnishings. The windows overlooked the earl's private garden, so the curtains were flimsy, filmy things, intended merely to decorate, like the gauze worn by a dancer, rather than cover up, like the shrouds over the Harlixton windows.

At every juncture in her new life, Raven found herself comparing the deathlike atmosphere at Harlixton with the hopeful, rejuvenative air of those places graced by her dear father-in-law. She could understand perfectly how Lady Philippa could risk her reputation and her future by giving herself to him.

In her late-night fantasies, Raven imagined finding some miraculous cure for Lady Philippa's condition, then with the good lady restored to her previous beauty, Lord Alexander and his lady would live out their allotted years to-

gether at Riverside, bouncing their grandchildren on their
knees, making up for the lost years with more loving than
even newlyweds are blessed with. The fantasy would warm
Ravenna at night, for imagining them together made her
feel closer to Garreth, as if they were all connected somehow.

But in the morning, chilly reality would awaken her like
a January wind. Lady Philippa was either dead or dying,
her father-in-law was a bachelor, and Garreth was confined
in his new prison cell.

They were to dine with a Lord and Lady Thus-and-So
several days after their arrival. Having left the dead Anne's
dresses behind in the dying Harlixton Hall, Raven was at
a loss as to what to wear, except that she'd resigned herself
to her infernal corset. The future Countess of Henley could
hardly be presented in a simple shift—at least not the first
time. In a year, perhaps, she would set a new trend. She
imagined a multitude of things she would do once their
lives settled down, and one would be to write a treatise
citing the dangers of corsets and the beauty of the natural
female form. Perhaps her medical background, but particularly her new station in life, would afford her some influence over gentle ladies.

A light tapping on the door brought her out of her reverie,
and she recalled another occasion when light knocking was
like the hand of Fate, startling her out of one reality and
into quite another.

"My dear, are you awake?" her father-in-law's musical
voice called out.

"Yes, Father, but give me a moment. Though I am de-
cently encased in my corset, let me throw on a gown." In
the next moment she did just that, then called out, "Please
come in."

The Earl of Henley entered the room chuckling, for they
had already had a rollicking discussion of the evils of

whalebone stays—starting, of course, with the hazards to whales.

"How lovely you look this morning," Sandy said.

Ravenna looked down at her simple mauve day dress, tight-fitting over her stays, then remarked, "You hear that, corset? You've just received a compliment."

"Nonsense, it's the wearer who fills it with her charms."

"It is too early in the morning for idle flattery. Come, have some *ma huang* tea with me. It's still warm."

"Thank you," he said, sitting. "Is this another of your restorative tonics?"

"It's an old Chinese secret, actually," she said, pouring a cup and giving it to him. "It is said to prolong youth, and instill a sense of well-being. . . . Not that you lack in either regard."

Sandy smiled. "My dear, if you ever decide to leave the medical arts, I would recommend politics as a second career. My colleagues in Parliament could learn a few things from you." Then, tasting the warm liquid, he remarked, "The flavor is quite pleasant, not at all what I remember of the monstrous tonics from my youth."

"The medicinal flavor has been carefully disguised."

"Ah," he laughed. "Perhaps your craft is a bit like politics already." Then he said, more seriously, "Ravenna, I've—taken the liberty of inviting a few of your father's old friends over tonight."

She eyed him suspiciously. "How old?" She didn't know if she could face the ones who had known him in the end.

Sandy understood exactly what she was thinking. "Ravenna, nobody blames your father for what happened. None of them would have been able to go on in his condition—without a means to continue his livelihood, robbed of that one endeavor which gave his life its inspiration."

Ravenna looked away, determined that she would not cry. "No, I suppose not," she mumbled.

"That is why you must continue in his footsteps," the

earl urged her. "Meet with his friends. Make contacts in London. Enlist their help in opening your clinic at River-side."

She and the earl had talked about a clinic, and he was ecstatic about the idea.

"Thank you," she said, blinking to dispel the mist in her eyes. "Will Liston be there?"

"Yes. And that young Dr. Long from America, who's here to address the academy about anaesthesia. And Dr. Richley is bringing someone I want you to meet, a young Miss Nightingale. She shares many of your own ideas—about hygiene and the nature of disease, for example."

"She's a physician?"

"A nurse, yet a very unusual one. Like you, she seeks to raise the status of women in medicine, making nursing a vocation rather than a pastime for camp followers and vagrants."

"I should like very much to meet this Miss Nightingale."

"Perhaps you can recruit her to assist you at your clinic."

"Perhaps we can be partners," she said, gently correcting his assumption.

He smiled. "I do believe you women will someday change our civilized world." He rose to leave. "And so much the better. Well, have a good day. I'll be out at tea, so I'll see you at dinner."

After deciding on a gown of apricot silk, then asking Emmy, her new maid, to have it refreshed and ready by evening, Ravenna left Henley House to spend the morning, as she had the previous one, attempting to gain admittance at the mystery woman's home in Cheapside. She didn't spend an inordinate amount of time by the actual stoop, since she did not want to become another of the woman's tormentors, but Raven hoped that she would soon grow to trust her, as the woman trusted Garreth.

The visit, however, proved futile again. She was sent away by an elderly woman, most likely the grandmother.

Again Raven left a calling card, which was probably con signed to the dustbin.

Raven idled away the rest of the day ambling through St James's Park, then took tea alone in her room, writing her daily letter to Garreth.

As dinner approached, she felt the long-absent fluttering of her heart. She was more nervous than she cared to admit. Seeing Liston again would be painful, for he was becoming the toast of the medical community, a place he should have shared with her father. Surgery was becoming a safe, humane medical procedure, thanks to ether and to Liston's other recommendations. She tried to concentrate instead on the questions she would pose to Miss Nightingale.

The earl was at his most charming and jovial as he greeted their guests, all of whom were personal friends of his as well as her father's. Were Ravenna not so apprehensive about the evening, she would have wondered at the coincidence.

"Dr. Richley," she heard the earl say, then she turned toward the door in time to see the expression on Sandy's face when he first beheld Miss Nightingale.

She was a tall, buxom woman, and her curves announced to everyone present that she wore no corset. For that alone, Raven liked her immediately.

And it was clear to all who happened to be watching that the earl was charmed by his new guest.

"Miss Nightingale, may I show you my collection of medical treatises? Some of them date back to the Elizabethan era," the earl said, offering his arm. Then together they strolled down the hall to the library while Raven took his place greeting the guests. Her lack of confidence vanished at that moment, for all she could think of was the sparkle she saw in the earl's eyes.

Maybe he had found the blessing he so richly deserved. The earl escorted Miss Nightingale in to dinner. At the table, which boasted some of the finest medical minds of their times, she was vocal about the roles for women in the medical field. The Royal Academy would have dubbed such talk fairly treasonable as well as indecent and unchristian, but this was no ordinary gathering. Anyone whom Raven's father had chosen as a friend had to have an open mind.

Indeed, when dinner was over and custom would have had the ladies retire to the drawing room, the earl bade them stay and encouraged his guests to share memories of Sir Richmond. The stories had them laughing aloud, then shedding a few tears.

"I will never forget the time," Liston began, "when your father was so involved in his project in the laboratory that he quite forgot to eat, to bathe, to rest—except when he'd slump over his table, only to awaken several hours later, then start right up again where he'd left off. One night in a neighboring laboratory, someone's chemical reaction went awry and set the place on fire. We all escaped to safety until we realized that Richie was not among us. Several chaps—myself included—volunteered to dash back into the building and find him. So run we did, through the flames and clouds of smoke, until we burst through Richie's door. He was carefully pouring something from a flask into a chemist's tube, oblivious of the heat and acrid air. 'Come on, man,' I shouted. But he said irritably, 'Can you not leave me alone, Bobby? I told you yesterday that—' 'Come on, damn you,' I shouted—pardon me, ladies—then I yelled at him, 'Don't you *smell* anything?' Bewildered, your father looked at me, Ravenna, then sniffed at his beaker, and only then, when he couldn't smell his solution because of the smoke, he said, 'What have you done? There's smoke in this room! It will contaminate my proteins!' "

Finally, after a good laugh all around, Liston finished.

"We dragged the poor chap out of there, but he kept muttering, 'My proteins. You've ruined them!' "

When the laughter was dying away, Miss Nightingale asked, "What are proteins?"

"I'm not really sure," Liston replied, sobering up. "They are something Sir Richmond was working on as a student. He called them—what was it?—'constituents of living matter.' " Turning toward Ravenna, he asked, "Do you know what he meant, my dear?"

All eyes shifted toward her. She licked her lips, not wanting to seem like an idiot. "My father believed, as you said, Sir Robert, that living tissue consisted of various combinations of these things, these proteins. All human flesh, he said, from any person at all, had the same arrangements of proteins. Likewise, the flesh of all individuals of a certain animal species, say a horse, have the same arrangement of these proteins, which is quite distinct from any other species."

"That's quite fascinating, Lady Westbrook," a young man sitting opposite her interposed. "And did your father determine whether tissues from similar animals, for instance, a chicken and a duck, had similar arrangements of these—proteins . . . or whether dissimilar species, as say from a horse or a honeybee, possess quite varying arrangements?"

She looked at him thoughtfully. "I have no idea, sir," she said.

The young man persisted. "Do you perhaps have any of his notes, or journals on this subject?"

"I'm sorry."

"But might I call on you again, and have a look through—"

"Patience, sir," the earl interjected. Then he said to Ravenna, "You must excuse our young Mr. Darwin. Although he never knew your father, he is so much like him that I wanted you both to meet."

"Please forgive me," Mr. Darwin mumbled, looking down at his hands.

"Oh, do tell us, Darwin," Liston encouraged him. "What do you find so interesting in this—arrangement of proteins?"

Shy-eyed, and embarrassed to be addressing such an august group, Darwin began. "Well, sir, if—if the proteins of a duck and a chicken, say, are similar, it would be a way of determining—on a scientific level—that the two species were roughly related. Therefore, if one took samples of a monkey, for instance, and compared them to . . ." At this he trailed off.

"Go on," Liston encouraged him.

Mr. Darwin looked around the table at the eager faces.

"Yes, Mr. Darwin," Ravenna said, "go on."

He looked down at his lap again, then replied, "It's only a whim, not worth discussing."

"Many great discoveries begin with a whim. Please tell us," Raven encouraged him.

"In due time," the young man replied, his cheeks flushed.

Shortly afterward, the group retired to the music room, where the young wife of Lord Thus-and-So entertained them on the pianoforte. Although she and her husband were to have been the sole dinner guests that evening, they had been quite dwarfed by the rest of the company, and hence had remained mute throughout the meal. Ravenna could not even recall their names as the Lady's fingers began traveling across the keys.

Nevertheless, Lady Thus-and-So played something rich and passionate, proving that she had talent as well as taste. The piece was by an unpublished composer she'd met in Vienna—a Herr Schubert. He'd written the piece especially for her. As the woman's fingers caressed the keyboard, Raven's eyes rested idly on the earl and Miss Nightingale. He reminded her so much of Garreth that her mind imagined it was indeed her husband who was sitting in front and catercorner to her own chair.

As the deep, haunting melodies filled the room, she remembered Garreth's touch, his long fingers exciting her skin; his powerful, lush lips covering her own. The music covered her like her husband's body, enfolding her in its arms as his did.

"Oh Garreth," Ravenna whispered, so intoxicated by the music and her remembered love for him that she leaned back in her chair and allowed herself to go pleasantly mad.

"Ravenna," he said, and she gasped—for it was not the earl who approached her.

"Garreth . . ." she whispered, "you've come back to me."

"My darling," Garreth murmured as he took her hand and pulled her to her feet, escorting her to the front of the assemblage and into a sensual dance. His right hand scorched her back as it led her through macabre movements; their bodies were without substance and they danced on, heedless of the chairs and masses of human proteins who were in their way. With laughter in his eye, Garreth led her *through* them, through arms and elbows and even through the sound board of the pianoforte itself. She wondered then whether she had died and was rejoining Garreth on some fantastic level.

"If this is death," she whispered to him, "it is nothing to be feared."

Then she looked around, wondering whether her father's spirit would be among the guests, whether their laughter and fond memories of him had beckoned his spirit to join them.

Lady Thus-and-So finished the piece, paused for a moment, then began another. After several introductory chords, she opened her mouth and began to sing. The words were in German, not a sensual language like French, but her voice and the music were breathtaking. Raven regretted that she would never meet this Herr Schubert—who'd died unrecognized and in poverty, according to Lady Thus-and-So—for he had a poet's understanding of love, and of the inherent tragedy in daring to love.

She sang a cycle of sensuous love songs while Garreth and Raven danced on and on. Then Garreth himself began to sing, and his rich baritone filled the room. His voice wooed Ravenna; it was a musical representation of all that is beautiful in a man.

"I'll never leave you again," he promised her when he had finished singing, kissing her forehead, then the top of her head. "Nothing will ever stand between us again."

She looked into his face, hoping that he would tell her he'd been released, that the murder charge had been dropped. But suddenly the music stopped and Garreth's faced dissolved into a collage of pastels. "Garreth!" she screamed as a hand grasped her shoulder and pulled her from him.

"Ravenna," a voice said, and her eyes flew open.

Her husband in the flesh stood looking at her curiously. "Garreth!"

"No, my dear," a similar voice apologized. "How I wish I were."

"Are you all right, Lady Westbrook?" young Mr. Darwin asked anxiously. "You fainted, it seemed."

She tried to stand, but her father-in-law stayed her attempt.

"Sit for a moment," he encouraged her, and she obeyed while she thought over carefully what had just happened.

A relapse, she was certain. The ergot was still in her body, affecting her brain. Her father had often suffered such events, owing to the residual ether in his blood.

A sense of profound hopelessness filled her, as if she had no will to go on. This, too, was an aftereffect, and she would try to fight it, see it for what it was.

Yet this lapse in her sanity reminded her that Garreth was still not free, and this time it was up to her to rescue him. There was no time to waste for him, and for the others whose fate depended on her.

She would gain admittance at Cheapside on the morrow if she had to make her bed along the street while she waited.

Thirty-eight

A cold wind whipped the hem of Raven's cloak, sending puffs of frigid air up her legs. Peg was overdue, and Raven paced and stamped her feet as she waited outside the boardinghouse door for the girl's return. Like a mother who had bought her daughter a cherished gift, Ravenna excitedly held in her hand the package she would give Peg—inside was a fur-lined cloak.

No more would Peg leave home with rags around her shoulders.

Soon she and her family would come to live at Riverside. Peg would be Ravenna's laboratory of one, as her father would say. If Raven could cure the girl, there might be hope for her half brothers and their wives.

But Peg did not return, and as the afternoon sky darkened and the air turned from chilly to unseasonably cold, Raven sat on the stoop, feeling discouraged and at sea. What had she thought to gain from this interview? Even if the woman admitted her, she was only a tiny step closer to Garreth. The woman, after all, had no power of her own. And Garreth seemed so removed, so far away.

Overhead, stars became visible one by one as night fell. All around Ravenna, the fires of the homeless appeared one by one as well, scattered all along the street like the stars above them. She hardly had the strength to get up and find her way home, and yet she wondered again how the people who were lighting those fires would survive the entire night out in this cold. Perhaps she would stay with them, as her father had on many occasions, lest she forget their plight.

And among them, how many Garreths existed from day to day, how many earls of Henley without an estate? Surely excellent people were born daily in the slums, only to rot like perfect fruit overlooked by the harvester.

With her legs pulled high up against her chest, Ravenna rested her head upon her knees as she waited. She would see Peg's mother, or she would starve and freeze in trying.

The lamplighters had come and gone even to this unimportant place when the door behind her cracked open. She swung her head around at the noise, then jumped to her feet.

A small nose was poking around the door.

"Peg," she called out. "Oh, Peg, you're safe inside."

The door closed, but she pressed her hand against it, just hard enough to prevent its closure.

"Peg," she repeated. "Oh, please, Peg, let me in."

Slowly, the door swung open, and Peg, dressed in her well-worn frock, curtsied then said, "Mum says for you to come in."

Smiling with relief, Raven crossed the splintered threshold.

The hallway and stairs ascending to the upper rooms were dark and dour—like Harlixton, she mused. She wondered where the tenants were, or whether they'd all been scared away.

The sitting room she was ushered into was surprisingly neat and cheerful. There was no fire in the hearth, which made the room seem hardly warmer than the outdoors, yet the absence of smoke gave the room a clean smell, and the walls were white, without the usual sooty film. Crisp white doilies graced the several chairs, and the tables and other furnishings were of highly polished hard wood—gifts from

Garreth, no doubt, since no one in Cheapside could afford such elegance.

"Mum asks if you'll take tea, ma'am," Peg said, curtsying again.

"Might I see her?" Raven asked hopefully.

"Oh, no, ma'am. Mum be sickly."

With her mind suddenly so weary of everything the vicar had touched and polluted, Raven was quiet for a moment. Then she asked, "Peg, has she been ill long?"

Peg bit her lip, then answered, "Only since that man did come 'ere." Then it was as if something broke in the child, for she began to weep.

"What man?" Ravenna asked, then motioned for the girl to approach.

"The tall one, ma'am. He beat her something terrible."

"Which tall one? Cholly Makepiece?"

"I d'not know his name, ma'am. He hasn't come 'round in a se'nnight."

Handing Peg the package, Raven said, "This is for you."

Peg's eyes grew wide with a Christmas-like anticipation. "For me, ma'am?" Then opening it, she squealed, "Oh, ma'am, 'tis heavenly."

"It's just like mine," Raven said, pointing. "You see, Peg, as Garreth's wife, I am related to you in some technical way. You are my—why, I'm not quite sure."

"You mean we're cousins or such-like."

"Perhaps. Think of me as your aunt." She wasn't sure how much the girl knew about her parentage. "Aunt Ravenna."

"It has a pretty sound to it. Aunt Ravenna," she said, trying it out on her tongue. "Thanks ever so much, ma'am."

"Aunt."

"Peg," a weak voice called from another room. "Offer our guest some tea."

Rising to her feet, Peg walked back into the hall, then

Raven called, "Ma'am, I simply must speak to you. Garreth's life depends on it."

After a moment of silence Raven heard, "Please don't bother me. I offered you a cup of tea against the cold. But kindly leave me alone."

"Mum," Peg called. " 'Tis Aunt Ravenna come calling. She brought me the warmest cloak you did ever see!"

"Give it back, sweet love," the voice called.

Raven had no desire to shout, so she simply walked in the direction of the voice.

"I won't hear of it," Raven called, then opened the next door off the hall. It reminded her of her search for Lady Philippa, though this time there were only two doors to choose from.

Again a thin figure huddled on the bed, and as Ravenna approached, her hand went to her face in horror.

The face that stared back at her was pathetic, like a victim of war, or an oft-beaten dog. Deep bruises encircled both eyes, there was a gash down her cheek, and her arm was in a makeshift sling. There were marks up and down the other arm as well. She would never have recognized this creature as the pretty chatelaine who had met Garreth at the door.

Biting her finger like a strap stuck between a patient's teeth, Ravenna said, "Cholly did this to you."

"No, ma'am," the woman said.

"Then who?"

"No, ma'am," she repeated.

Raven studied her eyes, the dilated pupils, the sallowness where there should have been white. Jaundice, not unlike what ailed poor Charles.

"I'm here to help you," Raven said. "Garreth's father—his real father, that is—will take you to Henley on Thames, where you can have your own cottage, raise your daughter in clean air. But you must help me."

"No, ma'am," the woman said again, and Raven looked

even closer at her eyes, fearing that madness was already setting in.

"What is your name?"

"Ursula, ma'am, Did Peg offer you some tea?"

"Yes, and—"

"Has she brought it, then? Peg," she called out, and the girl rushed immediately into the room, as if she'd been standing at the keyhole.

"Mum?"

"Tea, girl. And be quick about it."

"Yes, Mum," she said, then curtsied to Ravenna and turned on her heels to leave.

"Ursula, you must think back carefully," Raven stated with a touch of command. "Tell me what happened on the night the vicar was killed."

"He done it—Garreth."

"But it was an accident."

"He made me do it, drag the body over to the park. He's evil, I tell you."

"Ursula," Raven said, chiding her like a child, "you know that isn't true. Garreth says he killed the vicar in self-defense, that the elder man would have killed him."

" 'Tisn't true. 'Tis Garreth what killed the old man, a kind gen'leman 'e was too."

"Ursula," Raven repeated, this time with sternness in her voice. "Do you know the penalty for lying to a court? You are found guilty of a thing called perjury, and you go to jail. And unless you say what really happened that night, Garreth may hang."

A tremor passed through the woman's body. There was still sanity left.

" 'E's rich enough," she replied, shrugging. "Let 'im buy 'is way out."

"But you don't understand, Ursula. The people of Reading want vengeance. They know nothing of Garreth's innocence. Only you do."

Ursula looked down at her hands, then turned them over and back several times. Ravenna had seen the same gesture in babies who were first discovering their fingers.

"I didn't see nothing," Ursula said.

"Oh, but you did, Ursula. Even you admitted that you helped Garreth drag the body to the Upper Moor Fields. The court will consider you an accomplice unless you show that both of you were in danger when Garreth killed the Reverend Pembroke."

Peg appeared in the doorway, balancing a tea tray. "Mum," she cried, "you mustn't let them take you away!"

"I'm not goin' no place," she reassured her daughter, then motioned for the girl to serve the tea.

They all sipped acrid tea in silence; there was no milk or sugar. Raven stared at Ursula, while the woman did her best to ignore her, stealing only furtive glances now and then to confirm that her guest hadn't looked away.

Finally Raven rose and approached her. "You have been physically abused. There is evidence all over your body. If I might examine you—"

"No. Don't you go and touch me now."

Jumping back, Ravenna said, "Please forgive me. I mean you no harm."

"I said I'm all right."

"But you're not. You've been severely beaten, and you require medical treatment. I can help you."

"Is that so?"

"And you must no longer fear Cholly."

"Oh no? And do you not fear him?"

"I used to. Now I fear nothing and no one."

With that, Ursula leaned back against the thin pillow and grunted her assent to an examination.

After studying her, Ravenna was utterly convinced that the woman suffered the vicar's malady. And that soon her daughter would be an orphan.

Ravenna looked through her medical bag, finally finding a packet of *jen shen*.

"Please open your mouth. This is medicine."

Eyeing it suspiciously, Ursula mumbled, "It don't look like medicine."

"But it will make you feel better, and right away," she assured her, placing a pinch of the powdered root under her tongue.

Ursula grimaced at the strange taste permeating her saliva, but her eyes grew wide as she said, "I feel a tingle-like. Ooh, it do feel strange, Peg, like being soused."

Grabbing a scrap of paper and a nib from her bag, Ravenna asked, "Can you read, Peg?

The girl smiled. "Yes, ma'am," she said proudly.

Scratching out Madame Liu's name and address, Ravenna said, "This lady will give you more. I've written the name. Tell her you're my niece."

"Oh, ma'am," Peg replied, blushing with pleasure while her mother's cheeks grew red, but for a different reason.

"You needn't regret the past, Ursula. Come, live with us. You're part of Garreth's family, regardless of how you joined it. And Peg—Garreth can help her. Get her away from all this."

"Can you make her better, then?"

So she knows.

Swallowing hard, Ravenna said, "I'll try."

Then Ursula told her of Peg's headaches, her dizzy spells, the pains in her joints.

"I promise to help," Ravenna said. "But you must help us."

Ursula hung her head ashamedly. "Oh, ma'am, I do love Garreth as if he were my own kin. Mind you, there was never anything sinful between us, so you'll not have to forgive your husband on that account. He offered—as a gentleman, mind—to get us out of here, a cottage in the country, he said. A dozen times I refused him. 'How would it look?' I said. He's a good, dear man, and I'd never hurt 'im. But Cholly—he said that if I don't—"

The door to the parlor burst open, and a voice boomed at them, "What lies are ya tellin' 'bout me, Ursula?"

They all turned to look at the enormous, rain-splattered figure standing with arms akimbo inside the door.

"Cholly," Ursula whispered, cowering against the stained wall that served as her bedboard.

"Well, ain't this a purty sight?" he sneered. "My lady the countess! An' how do it feel to be a widow?"

"Cholly, what are you saying?" Ravenna had meant to shout this, but her voice was strangled into a harsh whisper. "Is he—"

"Oh, he be still alive," Cholly said, guffawing like a bear. "But ye'd do well to dust off yer black veil."

Instinctively, she rushed toward the door, wondering all the while how she could protect Peg and her mother from their unwanted guest.

"Oh, yer not goin' anywhere," he said, standing in her path, then pushing her back in the room.

"Ravenna's done nothing," Ursula cried.

At that, Cholly tilted his head back and laughed like a demon at a witch's burning.

"I do 'ave a debt to settle wit' 'er," he said. "And this time, no one's gonna be around to save your purty little neck."

Thirty-nine

Suddenly *Ravenna* was in prison, with her jailer an angry, vengeful man who felt religious zeal about righting the wrong she'd inflicted upon him.

"D'you know what it be like in them prisons, yer countess-ship?" Cholly sneered, using his mock title for her.

"I can only imagine with creatures like you in residence."

"Hey, now," he warned, pointing a blackened callused finger at Ravenna. "One more like that, an' I'll show you what it means t' 'ave a real man b'tween them purty legs."

"Then you would add rape to your many crimes. The Crown takes a dim view of repeat offenders, Cholly."

"And I'm sure ye'd like to see me swingin' from a yard-arm."

"No, Cholly, I wouldn't."

He stared at her with something approaching thoughtfulness. "Them be purty words, but I'm sure the old duke'll 'ave 'is say."

"Not if I assure the *earl* that you'll leave me and my family alone."

"Like ye left my family alone? Like ye left me alone when I did what I saw fit to my own kin?"

"That was different, and you know it. You abused your daughter."

"And that brother-in-law of your'n? Did 'e not abuse you? Old Cholly tried to warn ye—'Watch who ye do talk to,' I said, but you kept flirtin' with 'im, battin' them purty eyes at 'im while yer husband had 'is back turned."

His words took her by surprise. "So Charles sought to hire you—not to warn you off."

"Aye, yer countess-ship. 'Twas his idea all along. I wanted nothing to do with ye, 'cept scare ye a bit. I'd no desire to return to that rats' nest ye sent me to. But he said he'd sack me if I didn't do as he said."

"Don't tell me you didn't enjoy—hurting me."

"Oh, aye, it give me great pleasure. But now who's to pay? Old Cholly, that's who, not that rich brother-in-law of yourn who 'as the magistrates in 'is pocket."

"Cholly, Charles is sick. He didn't know what he was doing."

"Oh-ho," he said, rubbing his enormous thigh with a proportionately enormous spate of fingers. "The gentry can do what manner of abuse they likes, while us poor folk get sent to them dungeons. That fancy hostel where his countship be takin' 'is holiday ain't nothing like what I lived in at Bourne End."

"Cholly, will you forgive me?" Raven asked with as much genuineness as she could muster, and indeed she was sincere in her request. She should not have meddled in his affairs.

"Forgive ye?" He guffawed again. "That's not 'ow it do work. There ain't no forgiveness for the likes o' me."

Ravenna offered her hand, even though she was repulsed at the thought of his touching her. "I forgive you, Cholly. Just let me go. Leave Peg and Ursula and my family in peace. Let Ursula testify, and I'll see that no charges are brought against you. Garreth has never done anything to you. I am the one who wronged you, not my family."

This comment gave him pause. Finally he said, "You remind me o' my own Daisy. She's a good girl, even though she disgraced me."

"She was in love, Cholly. She gave you a grandson. It's only the Church and the laws of man that condemn it."

"Well, what d'you know?" he cried. "Ye're an 'eretic as well as a witch and a shrew. In America, they burn the likes of you."

"It's what my father taught me," she said, doubting he could possibly understand. "That we must follow our own conscience when doing something of great importance."

He slammed his hand on his thigh again. "Enough, woman. I'm sick o' your fancy words. Shut yer trap while I sees what's goin' on out there."

As he left the sitting room, he called out, "Don't ye be goin' nowhere," then he laughed crudely and locked the door behind him.

At last, Ravenna was alone in the makeshift prison cell. Her aloneness was refreshing, like the solitude she had felt in her cottage in Taplow after enduring the cramped intrusiveness of life with her father.

As remarkable an observation as this was, Cholly reminded her a lot of her father in his last days. She wondered yet again why the male of their species, even an ill-bred lout like Cholly, was so complex. It was no wonder to her that a woman did not write Shakespeare's plays. Only a man could create Macbeth or Iago or Lear with his curses.

Her solitude gave her a moment to study the contents of the room. Here and there she saw Garreth's hand. On the wall was a map of London dating back to 1720. The writing was almost microscopic, but to her delight she saw that a lot of the things on the map still existed, including a crude rendering of the row of houses in which she now was imprisoned. On the left was a dashed line that said "New Road to Kensington," and she laughed. It was the road upon which they had entered London, but it was hardly new, having earned a century's worth of ruts and holes by several generations of carriages. The palace was sketched in but was labeled BUCKINGHAM HOUSE. London, Westminster, and Southwark were all represented, and there were angels trumpeting at the four corners of the map. She recalled with amusement those antique maps on which the cartographer drew as much as he knew, then put dragons and malevolent forces around the edges.

Those mythical figures were a favorite image in her father's lessons to her. "You see that dragon?" he'd say, pointing at the medieval world map mounted on the wall of his study. "That figure was drawn by an ignorant man. It is a symbol of *ignorance*. Far better for him to have drawn *nothing*"—and he'd throw out his hands dramatically—"than to have come to an ignorant conclusion." Then he'd point to Ravenna and say, "See that you keep your mouth *shut* until you can speak from a place of knowledge. A conclusion drawn without facts is like that monster on the map. It signifies *nothing*."

It was a lesson she had just learned again several times— at Harlixton Hall.

Suddenly she heard a scream. Peg unlocked the door and ran into the room.

"Ravenna, help me!" she cried. "Cholly's gone mad again."

Jumping up, Ravenna rushed into the hall with the trembling girl, then saw a pot fly out of Ursula's open door and crash against the wall.

"Stop, Cholly!" Raven commanded, then saw that he had thrown other things against the walls, while poor Ursula, her nerves already as tight as strings tuned to the breaking point, cowered on her bed.

Then the tightly tuned string inside Ravenna snapped.

"Cholly," she demanded, feeling a newfound rage spreading through her blood. "Stop it! Get out of here and leave us alone."

But he did not stop. He was having some sort of fit.

"You'll pay!" he roared. "All of you. I'll teach you to toy with Cholly Makepiece!"

"Ravenna," Peg whispered urgently. "Can you give him something? He's going batty."

"Shh," Raven whispered, but she was thinking the same thing herself. Yet how to do it? Certainly, he wouldn't pause for a drink of ale, if there was any in this female dwelling, and it would take a while for a drug to have any effect.

Help me, Father, she thought in spite of herself, for she had vowed to lay him to rest. She tried conjuring up his face, thinking as he would think.

The dragons from the map flashed through her mind. Dragons . . . monsters . . . serpents. The serpent in the garden. Snakes. *Think, Ravenna, think.* It seemed insane, but she recalled her father toying with the idea of administering medicines the way snakes administer venom, through small punctures made in the skin. *Hypo-epidermic,* he'd called it, but he'd abandoned the concept in favor of inhaling medicines in vapor form.

She had to do something fast.

"Ravenna!" Ursula cried as Cholly turned on the woman, throwing himself on the bed and tearing at her already tattered gown.

"Run and get my medical bag," Ravenna ordered Peg while she did her best to distract Cholly, grabbing on to his stinking, threadbare coat and trying to pull him off the bed.

"Get away. Yer as pesky as a gnat," he complained, then turned and punched Ravenna on the chin. The force of the blow threw her backward, and she bit down, tasting blood as her upper teeth sank into her tongue.

Peg ran back into the room on trembling legs and handed her the bag.

It was a wild, perhaps insane idea, which carried risk to her as much as it turned her stomach. Pawing through the bag, she found some atropine, medicinal when taken in minute amounts but paralyzing in large doses.

Mustering up as much saliva as she could, Ravenna

chewed up a pinch of atropine and decided where to strike. The chest would have been preferable, but she could hardly ask her target to strip. A bare wrist beckoned her, and she reasoned that a snake bite even on the wrist quickly had the desired effect. Slowly she walked toward Cholly, focusing only on his wrist, remembering Dr. Wo's instruction to become one with one's opponent, like one's teacher. However, as she approached him, she heard a buzzing in her own ears. She hadn't thought this out properly, for the cut on her tongue was sending the atropine rapidly into her own bloodstream, up to her brain.

She had hardly a moment to strike before she herself would be overcome.

The sensation was sickening; her head began to pound. Her target was only inches away, but suddenly he seemed across the room. She had lost her perception of depth.

Think, Ravenna. Remember how it was when you were drugged. She tried to recall how she'd learned to remain conscious while under the influence of those other poisons.

But the last time she'd had her father's image to help her; this drug did not produce hallucinations, only seizures and paralysis.

Pitching herself forward, she fell on Cholly's wrist as if it were a life-saving piece of wood and she was about to drown in the Thames.

" 'Ere, what's this?" he cried angrily as she bit into him. He flailed his arm, but to the horror of both of them, she could not let go. Her jaw was utterly frozen into his flesh.

"Get off!" he roared, flopping one way then another, hitting her over the head like a persistent dog who had sunk its teeth into him.

Her head was reeling, but with all her remaining consciousness she focused on biting him, on sending the atropine into the cut rather than down her own throat.

Finally a sound blow to her temple sent her spinning away from him, but she took a piece of flesh with her.

"You witch!" Cholly screamed. "What 'ave you done?" And he looked at the tear in his dirty wrist.

Sickened, she spat, trying to purge her mouth of the human and herbal debris. But Cholly, of course, took this for some further insult and picked her up by the fabric of her dress.

"I've had enough of you," he growled. "If I 'ave to swing by my neck, at least I'll die knowing I killed you first."

"No!" Peg screamed.

Cholly's head snapped her way and said, "Another word and I kill yer mother, and you, too."

With a child's tears bursting out of her eyes, Peg ran over to her mother's bed, then jumped in beside her. Together the two huddled in terror.

Seeing that he had subdued them all for a moment, Cholly sat down in the single chair in the room and took a few calming breaths. His wrist was bleeding badly, making the wound look much worse than it was. And of course, with all that exposed flesh, Raven imagined him to be in quite a bit of pain.

She had her own troubles, for she found her limbs quite out of her control, as if they had all been broken and encased in splints. Her head was pounding from the blows and the atropine, and her heart—her poor heart—was fluttering as it tried to function with the invading venom sabotaging every attempt.

"Well, yer countess-ship," Cholly said finally. "You've 'ad this coming for a long time." Rising unsteadily to his feet, he limped toward her. "Would you like for them to watch, or do ye wish to be alone with me, all private-like?"

"You're a beast," Ursula spat out.

"Another word from you, and you're next—and *this* time Peg'll watch the whole thing."

"No—" Ursula protested.

"Not another word!" Cholly warned.

"Leave them alone!" Peg cried, then jumped up and foolishly ran toward him.

"Peg!" her mother screamed, leaping to her feet as well. Both mother and daughter attacked him then, biting and clawing.

"Get out of my house," Ursula demanded, and raised her arms as if to push Cholly toward the door.

"You just never learn, do ye?" He shook his head, then grabbed Ursula by her gown and threw her roughly to the floor. The back of her head hit the floor first, and they all heard a sickening snap. Ursula's head flopped to one side, and her tongue fell out of her mouth.

"Mum!" Peg screeched, then ran over to the lifeless body on the floor. "Oh, Mum," she wailed, tugging at her mother's arm as if to waken her.

"Peg . . ." Raven murmured, then Cholly grabbed her by the hair and pulled her to her feet.

Her knees buckled, and down she went again.

" 'Ere now, no tricks." He tried to get her to stand, and failed again. "All right, yer bloody countess-ship," he said, then swung her clumsily into his arms and walked out into the narrow hall.

Where are the tenants? Raven thought sleepily, remembering the set of keys at Ursula's waist so long ago.

There was no one about. Not even the grandmother appeared.

There was a daybed of sorts in the sitting room, and Cholly walked unsteadily to that room, dumping Raven on the cushions, then fumbling with the buttons of his breeches. She could tell by his jerky manner that the atropine was having an effect on him, not quickly or powerfully as it had on her—since the capillaries of the tongue work more quickly than the vessels in the wrist—but enough to make his hands shake. If she could just resist him for several more minutes, until the drug became more effective . . .

But it was difficult to focus on anything; her mind was jumping from one topic to another. Part of her was celebrating the success of her experiment—hypo-epidermic transmission of medicine had worked. Perhaps in a controlled experiment, with animals and a more refined mode of delivery . . . a lancet, perhaps, with some sort of trough in it. Her mind wandered to the details of such a device. Would it work? Would this establish for *her* a place in medical history?

She smiled an idiot's smile, finding she could focus only on the lancet and not on the big brute who was struggling with his buttons.

"You witch, you'll pay for this," he growled. "You put some sort o' spell on me, and you'll pay."

But her mind was flying across oceans. In this form, the atropine apparently *was* like ergot, for she saw many images—the native Americans, then the uncharted wilderness, where finally she saw those monsters with their foul breath.

One monster was very real, and its breath was foul as it leapt upon her, rubbing its thick, stubbled skin against hers until she felt raw.

She tried to speak, but gave up immediately. She couldn't get her jaw to open, not the least bit.

She thought, instead, of herself delivering a paper on the hypo-epidermic lancet, while the crowd of physicians jumped to their feet, hailing the daughter of Sir Richmond Marisse.

The burning feeling spread to her breasts as the monster ripped at her dress and rubbed his chin against her defenseless flesh, ripping farther down until he could strip her to her shift.

The applause in her ears was deafening. In the blink of her mental eye, she had composed her speech, telling the circumstances under which she had come up with her idea, how the idea had worked on herself as well as her adversary.

But her skin remained sane enough to register the cold, and she huddled her arms against her chest, shivering.

"Not so fast, wench," a voice sneered, and her arms were pinned to her sides. She was like a specimen on the table, and she struggled to get back to the lectern to continue her speech.

Something was stinging her from head to belly, and she limply registered that the monster was rubbing his beard everywhere, hectoring her skin.

She tried to swat him away like an insect, but she couldn't move.

A heavy weight settled between her thighs; it reminded her vaguely of her husband's weight, and she struggled to open her eyes.

"Grrth," she mumbled, but she saw only the monster from the map lying clumsily on top of her. *What is he doing?* her mind queried as he tore at her skirts, exposing more skin to the chilly air.

The applause was still deafening as she tried to move her legs. A knee against her thigh held her still.

"Stop struggling, b-b-b—" the voice stuttered, then she heard, "G-God damn you." The monster lifted his hand and struck himself on the temple. That seemed to correct something in his mind, and he said, "That's b-b-better. You b-b-bitch, I'm going to show you what's it's like to lie with a-a real man. Maybe you can 'ave the child yer 'usband'll never g-g-give ye."

A bleeding hand touched her again; more ripping; more cold. She focused on the applause, the doctors cheering. A large mass was pressing into her body, hands still fumbling over her, her legs unable to move, *get away, get away.*

"Here now, why so sh-sh-shy?" the voice mumbled while clumsy fingers tugged at her legs. "Old Cholly'll . . ."

"Father," she murmured, her eyes blurring. "Let go . . . Father." In a moment of madness, it seemed as if her father were attacking her, trying to destroy her. And in another

moment, something coalesced in her brain. Her obsession
with her father had itself become a monster, raping her
mind as surely as this ill-bred lout was raping her body.
Cholly was merely a symbol, an incarnation of something
that had been preying on her long before she'd ever heard
of him or his daughter.

"Let me go!" she croaked, speaking to all the monsters
who held her in thrall. "Let me go!" she gasped. "I want
my husband—get away from me . . ."

Abruptly, the monster was pulled away, and he grunted
as he was thrown against the wall.

Then two bodies were whirling across the floor, merging
into a blur of arms and legs and groans from effort.

"God damn you," a voice raged, and she heard slugs and
punches and the sounds of teeth cracking.

"I'll kill 'er," the monster roared. "She's a witch." An
arm snaked out and grabbed her hair, tugging her into the
fray.

"Stand aside!" another voice commanded, and a different
hand grabbed her, throwing her out of the whirlwind. She
felt like a piece of flotsam spinning out of a hurricane.

Suddenly there was a loud *boom,* like a cannon on the
wharf. The monster lunged for her, but then his eyes rolled
upward and he collapsed into her body. Blood from a gaping neck wound sprayed her arms and shoulders and ran
down her chest as she fell on her back.

The monster's weight was pulled off her once again, then
its body dumped on the floor beside her.

Ravenna saw a dust cloud in the room, smelled gunpow-
der. The Earl of Henley was poised in the doorway, a smok-
ing pistol in his hand.

And standing over her was Garreth, her beloved Garreth,
a look of both horror and joy on his face.

"Grrth," she murmured.

"Don't try to talk. You're safe now."

It was the third and final time her husband would rescue

her, and as he hoisted her into his arms and carried her to the waiting coach, Ravenna knew they were finally going home.

Book V

Riverside, Henley on Thames

Forty

"I could sleep forever," Ravenna mused, snuggling into the sleeve of Garreth's holland nightshirt.

"I feel as though I have just awakened from a long, cursed sleep," he countered affectionately, "and now I have a lifetime of catching up to do."

His arm tightened around her shoulders, and she felt the oceanic contentment an infant must feel while held in its father's embrace. In Garreth's arms, she wanted to put off all adult responsibility, all goals and aspirations, and just be held by this excellent man, to breathe in his fragrances, feel the textures of his skin and hair, melt and merge into him.

The young Queen Victoria herself had pardoned Garreth, and ordered his immediate release from prison. It seemed she had once had a brief crush on Sandy, until duty bound her to marry Albert. They remained friends, and though the magistrates would not honor Sandy's appeal, the Queen had opened her heart and listened.

When Garreth arrived at Henley House in London, he had gone insane when he'd learned of Raven's whereabouts. But his intention to rage at her vanished when he saw first-hand the danger she was in.

The pistol had been Sandy's idea, as protection against any undesirables along the way.

But he had never anticipated using it.

When Ravenna explained to Garreth the menace Cholly had been during her residence at Harlixton, he'd cried, "Ravenna, why didn't you tell me? I should have had the man locked up again."

"But there was nothing provable," she said. "And the last thing I wanted was to have him madder at me than he already was. As it turned out, he also had Pembroke's syndrome." That was her own recasting of the curse, to separate it from the Harlixton name. "It seems Cholly and your stepfather visited the same wenches in the city."

"Ghastly business," Garreth said, shaking his head. "God must favor us, to have given us this second chance."

"Yes. He must, for how often can the sins of the fathers be eluded by the children?"

"How often indeed."

"And we have eluded them, haven't we?" she said, not realizing she had spoken aloud until Garreth said, idly stroking her hair with his long fingers, "What, my darling?"

Looking into his eyes, she said, "Our fathers—their unquiet spirits. We've finally put them to rest. With Cholly's death, I felt somehow I could bury my father as well—at least, the broken, repulsive thing he became in his last days."

Turning his body so he could fully face her, Garreth cupped her face with his hands. Closing her eyes, she felt his lips, moist and sweet, capture hers in an affectionate kiss. Instantly, the heat of desire spread through her limbs like a flame through a dry field. She wanted him with every cell and fiber in her body. Her mouth opened as his lips, his teeth, his tongue, merged with hers. There were so many textures to enjoy—the smooth, firm teeth, the moist flesh of his inner cheek, the warmth of his breath.

Ravenna's hands grabbed at his shirt. Obliging her, he pulled it up and off his body, then repeated the quick gesture with her woolly nightgown.

Under the counterpane their bodies pressed and entwined. She understood then the sensuality of wrestling, leg against leg, arms reaching out and clasping other arms. She wanted Garreth to enter her at once, but he took his time, using his hands like lucifers, igniting small fires on every inch of body.

Releasing her mouth, he kissed both her cheeks, then her forehead, then behind her ears, entwining his fingers in her heavy mane of hair, then laughing as he had trouble releasing himself.

"I warned you," she teased him, sitting up.

"I know," he quipped, pulling the strands of hair playfully out to their full length and creating black wings before letting the tresses drop around her shoulders.

Their play had a calming effect, and they both sat up in bed, their heads bent together as they watched their four sets of fingers explore each other, twining and entwining, holding and releasing.

"I can't believe you're here with me," Garreth said. "That I'm here, in this place, in this bed."

"Nor can I." For the first time in many months, she was lying in her own bed, not on some guest's mattress.

They were both home at last.

Growing sober, Garreth began. "Say you'll never leave me."

"I'll never leave you."

"Say you'll love me forever."

"I'll love your forever."

He grinned at her. "Well, that's all I want out of life. It's your turn."

Sharing his mischievous look, she said, "Say you'll give me a houseful of children."

Laughing, he promised, "I'll give you a houseful of children! A dozen, at least."

"At least."

"And it will give me infinite pleasure to do so."

"I know."

She slouched into a beckoning position and opened her arms to him.

Looking down at her, he said, "My God, but you are beautiful."

Taking him in her arms as he put his full weight upon her, covering her body with a counterpane of flesh and bone and love, she said, "Promise me you'll still say that when my belly is great with our child and my legs are enormous and my breasts are swollen and my veins are bright blue and my—"

"Shh," he chided her. "I shall love you and I shall think you beautiful when you are as fat as a bear, when you are sick, when you are old and parched, when your hair has become white and your teeth have fallen out and your hands shake with the palsy. Even then I shall think you beautiful."

"Even then?" she whispered.

"Even then," he repeated. "For you shall be surrounded by the dozen strong men and women to whom you gave life, and they, too, will think you beautiful, even as you breathe your last breath."

They both grew silent again, for the image of Garreth's mother was present in the room. By learning who he was and the story of his birth, Garreth was also free to love Lady Philippa, for she had spared him from the curse that had plagued his half brothers and their families.

"Garreth," Ravenna said. "Let's go to your mother—Justine says that she is holding on, and she even has her lucid days now that she has rejoined the family and has her rooms among the others. It was the isolation as much as her condition that was driving her insane."

Garreth made a fist of frustration with his right hand. "If only she would leave that wretched place, come to live with us here."

"I know," she said grimly. "But Harlixton is her home. It keeps her alive as much as the medications I send her. Let us go to her ourselves."

"Very well," he said. "Let's go to her—with you carrying her grandchild in your body—and ask for her blessing."

To give her assent, Ravenna pulled his mouth toward hers and kissed him with all the love she was feeling. Using her hands like cotton cloths, she rubbed his back, the sides of his body, his slim hips. Opening her thighs, she coaxed her body until she was perfectly under him, ready for him, longing for him.

Come to me, give me a child.

Then the swollen male part of him was probing, opening her, entering her. She gasped afresh at the wonder of their joining, their hips locked in a perfect embrace, their bodies moving in a seamless dance.

Tension was building in her body. She wanted him deeper, into the center of her, never to part from her. The sweat was beading on his brow as he clung to her, his movements becoming frantic as he was swept up by the forces that neither of them could control. They were climbing and falling at the same time, soaring off a high cliff, then crashing headlong into a roiling sea.

The forces inside them were almost too strong to bear, as if they would both split at the seams. She held on tightly to his back, then grabbed at his thick dark hair, crying, panting, feeling weak and powerful, and every contradictory sensation in the human spectrum.

The tension grew and grew in her until she was fire and water, liquid heat, until all of her life was focused on a center, painful, ecstatic, unbearable, bursting. Then it broke in her and she shook, her legs jumping as if the nerves had been cut. Liquid pleasure soaked her like a high tide, and she cried out again, arching her back and pulling Garreth deeper inside her.

Then he cried out as his own body shook, and she smiled, for in that moment of ecstasy, he was giving to her ecstasy as well. His body jerked and spasmed as he gave to her, totally out of control as she slowly grew lucid, and she could watch him shuddering, several steps ahead of him in their descent toward earth. This was his moment of creation, the moment that would make him immortal.

His body quieted as he lay on her, still joined with her as they collected their thoughts. Together they rested as their bodies separated of their own volition. But Garreth was still inside her, the best part of him, the essence of him.

"How do you feel?" he asked, stroking her hair, careful not to get his fingers entangled in the now hopelessly knotted mass.

"I feel the way every woman feels after she has conceived a child with the man she loves."

"And how is that?"

"Content, complete. Blessed." She squeezed his hand. "How do you feel?"

"The same."

He turned her face and kissed it again, but this time with the control of a man who has rallied his senses and feels only great affection.

"If it's a girl, shall we call her Philippa?" she asked.

"Or Richmond if it's a boy?"

Both of them pondered these options.

"No," Garreth said finally. "Let's begin again, with new names. And may our children escape the burdens of the past."

Forty-one

It is often said that a woman gets moody and unfathomable during pregnancy, to her husband's dismay.

In the Henley household, the opposite was true. When Ravenna's condition was confirmed, she immediately went into a nonstop euphoria, while poor Garreth brooded around the house, snapping at the servants, arguing with his wife about things he had no concern for.

Frequently, he reduced her to tears with his irrational outbursts, then failed to recognize them as bordering on madness. He accused *her* instead of being overly emotional. She found herself having to tiptoe around him, never quite sure whether a gesture or remark would send him into a fit of temper. As the months progressed and her body took on the shapelessness she had waited so long for, she found herself spending more and more time with her father-in-law, who was himself suffering from a recent rejection.

"But Sandy," she said to him one lovely August afternoon, "Miss Nightingale has a calling. She is young and passionate. Certainly a man can understand the importance of following one's destiny."

Patting her hand, he said, "I know. I know too well. For when I was young, I left the person who loved me most in the world."

"You see, you must understand, then."

"And yet," he sighed, "it was the biggest mistake of my life. I never followed my vocation, and I lost my family as a result, causing so many people—including you—a great deal of suffering."

"What was it you wanted to be? And what stood in your way?"

They were walking along the Thames, which bordered Sandy's property and gave the big house its name. The flora along the shore was held in strictest check by the earl's gardeners and hence they had a pleasant view of the river.

"I am embarrassed to say it," the earl began, "but I wanted to be—"

"Well, well," a voice interrupted them from behind.

They both turned their heads to see Garreth.

"My boy," the earl began with pleasure, then paused to study the enigmatic look on Garreth's face.

"Garreth?" Ravenna added, also perplexed.

"I see that you are not following your doctor's orders, but instead wandering far afield, like the last time."

"Garreth," she teased him, "there are no such orders, except from you. And you're being unfair."

"Oh, unfair, is it? What's fair and what is real are often two different things. I suggest you get back to your room at once."

"I will not," she said defiantly, for this was not the Garreth she had married, but some mood of his.

"You see what a bad influence you are on her, Father. She has become quite unreasonable."

The earl laughed, but there was no mirth in Garreth's face. If his behavior hadn't been so preposterous, Ravenna would have obeyed him at once.

"My husband is not himself," she quipped. "It is the result of his . . . delicate condition."

"Really, Garreth, I should take a tonic if I were you," the earl laughed. "Perhaps Ravenna can suggest—"

"Enough!" Garreth roared, then—incredibly—he grabbed his father by the lapels of his coat and held him menacingly. "You will not speak to me in that fashion. And you will not turn my wife against me. You, who have caused me so much grief."

"This is enough indeed," the earl retorted. "You will release me at once," he ordered, but still with some humor in his tone, for he could not possibly fear his own son.

Garreth held on harder, and there was a predatory malice in his eyes.

"Garreth," Raven said, touching his arm. "Has something happened? What's wrong?"

"Get back to the house," Garreth spat out at her, clutching Sandy's coat so hard, she feared the material would rip in two.

Sandy was similarly alarmed. They had accepted Garreth's moods, but this violence was uncharacteristic even for him.

"I want you . . ." Garreth said through clenched teeth, "to leave my wife alone. You already ruined the other important woman in my life. I would not have you ruin this one—and especially the child she carries."

Ravenna looked at Sandy incredulously, but the humor had left his face. His eyes had grown cold. He nodded with some private understanding, then stated, "Very well, Garreth. How shall we get this behind us?"

"Father—" she protested.

"No, Ravenna," Sandy interrupted her. "Garreth has something he needs to settle with me. I, uh, ruined his mother, after all, made his early years and young manhood a living hell, caused him to—to kill his stepfather, then brood over it for years."

Garreth pulled again on Sandy's coat so that the older man was struggling to keep his feet on the ground.

"Why didn't you come for us?" Garreth demanded. "If

you knew—why didn't you come? Why make her live with that—that despicable man?"

"I have no good answer for you," Sandy said, "except that I wanted to save her from scandal. Think of it, son—a vicar's wife who was impure when she came to her marriage bed, with—"

"Impure?" Garreth exploded. "You dare speak to me of that?"

"Son," Sandy said with great control and reason in his voice. "Those are not my words. To me, your mother was . . ." Then his voice wavered. "I . . . never stopped loving her. And I, too, suffered for what I did."

"Suffered? Ha! In what way did you suffer?"

"Garreth," Ravenna pleaded, but he turned to her and demanded, "Get back to the house. This is between us, Ravenna."

During that momentary distraction, Sandy broke free of Garreth's grasp but did not seek to leave. Instead he approached Ravenna as if she were an intruder, and said, "Please leave. This is between my son and me. It is not for your eyes."

"I won't leave you, Father."

Angrily Garreth turned toward her, as if tempted to strike her.

"Leave us," he warned, then raised his hand.

She felt an irrational wave of fear, since she had been injured so many times in the course of loving him. She needed to protect the child growing inside her, and she turned away, clasping her belly.

The air crackled with the force of something unstarted, like sweltering summer heat before the relief of a downpour. Someone was going to be hurt. Sensing this, and sensing, too, that Garreth was not in his right mind, Sandy said, "Stop it. She's done nothing to you." Then, as if to direct Garreth's rage and bring it out in the open, Sandy took two quick strides, grasped Garreth by the back of his coat, and threw him sideways to the ground.

"If you must fight, Garreth, fight me. I'm the one who's guilty, not the women who love you."

Stunned at his father's strength, Garreth sat on the ground, his knees up, his weight supported by his hands outstretched behind him. There was a moment of silent staring, in which they both wondered what would happen next.

Then Garreth jumped up, and with a growl, he launched himself at his father, his fingers curled like claws.

But Sandy was quicker, and while Garreth went for the jugular, Sandy raised his clenched fist and smashed Garreth in the jaw. As the son staggered backward, the father quickly stripped to the waist, pulling off coat and cravat and shirt and throwing them to the ground.

Taking his cue, the son did likewise, tearing off his own clothing, then tossing them far from his feet.

"Leave us, Ravenna," Garreth said again, and when she opened her mouth to protest, he roared, *"Now."*

Then both men promptly forgot about her as they faced each other. Backing up out of the immediate clearing but dawdling so she could watch, Raven marveled at the intense passion between them. As they'd stripped off their clothing, they seemed like two lovers preparing to couple. She blushed at the thought, and commanded her mind to think no farther in that direction. Yet this was something that transcended civilized morality. As they circled each other, the sweat already beading on Sandy's brow, the two opponents were well matched. Despite the difference in their ages, their bodies and stature were similar. As much as she feared for their safety, she was also fascinated. There it was again, another manifestation of the complex male spirit, the demons that periodically needed release.

She wondered how therapeutic it would have been had her father beaten senseless the viscount who'd maimed him. In that regard, her father's injury was a double affront, for not only had he been damaged but he'd lost his ability to exact vengeance. He'd lost his manhood as well as his hand.

As she watched, tears spilled down her cheeks, her own woman's way of seeking release. Garreth was circling his father again, looking for an opening, not so sure anymore that he could win an easy victory.

Sandy had his fists up in a defensive posture, his eyes pinned on Garreth's hands. Garreth leapt forward and struck, but Sandy raised his left arm like a shield and the blow hit harmlessly on the contracted muscle. Sandy used the next instant to punch Garreth on the nose. Raven bit back her scream as blood trickled from the nostril. But the blow seemed to clear something in Garreth's head; he looked at Sandy with a moment's composure.

The father, using some kind of male wisdom, punched his son again, this time on the right cheek, which made Garreth's head snap.

Grunting in anger, Garreth curled his fingers again and lunged at his father, this time striking a perfect blow to the lower jaw. Apparently Sandy bit down, for when he turned his head, Raven saw blood burst out of his mouth.

"Stop it!" she cried, but neither man took heed of her words, or even her presence.

Seeing each other's blood, however, subdued them, and each aimed their next blows at sturdier stuff—shoulders and pectoral muscles and arms.

The air was filled with their grunts and their panting, their groans as a blow hit its mark, and again Ravenna thought of lovemaking, of the intensity of focusing only on one's partner. They were still equally matched, though their power was equally fading. Neither man was used to such brawling.

Sandy hit Garreth squarely on the collarbone, then Garreth hit lower, between the ribs. This seemed to knock the wind out of the older man, and he staggered backward, leaning over as he struggled to catch his breath.

"Father," Garreth gasped, "are you all right?"

Still panting, Sandy averted his eyes and chest, refusing to show weakness and struggling to prepare himself against any further assault.

"Stop it, Garreth!" Ravenna screamed, but as Garreth approached his father curiously, Sandy straightened up and socked Garreth with surprising strength, catching his son on the left cheek.

Blood flowed out of the torn flesh. Garreth put his hand up to assess the damage.

Raven could tell, somehow, that Sandy was appalled, but he hid it well, moving in for the next assault. Garreth raised his fist and smashed Sandy in the mouth, opening up the cut on his lip. This time Sandy delayed in responding, and Garreth hit him again in the face, bruising his cheek. Sandy's jaw fell slack. It was Garreth who now seemed restored, preparing for his next attack.

But Sandy's body had lost its tension, and he didn't make a move except for the involuntary heaving of his chest. He looked his son up and down several times, and despite the pain that had stretched his face taut, there was a complex mixture of emotions registering on his face—respect, pride, relief, and finally, love. Ravenna could tell that he was feeling very close to his son, as she'd been told combatants often feel toward one another after a battle.

"My son," Sandy said, then found the strength to laugh with pleasure.

Garreth continued to stare back, not quite sure how to respond, but together he and his wife watched as Sandy laughed, then looked spent, then finally wept, unashamedly.

"I will always love your mother," Sandy said. "Always. I feel the same hurt that you do." Then he opened his arms in a gesture of love, beckoning Garreth.

This was a moment Raven felt should be shared only by father and son, and at last she retreated. Before they disappeared from sight, she turned once more. They were both sitting on the ground now, arms around each other.

As she walked back to the house, she inhaled the marvelously fresh air, and she sensed that the two men she loved most in the world were feeling the same freshness in the atmosphere.

It was proving to be a glorious summer day, and Ravenna delighted in the fact that their child would be born during the long, warm days of the year. No dark winter morning, no dreary *uht* time, when the unquiet spirits of the dead were abroad, putting curses on the newly born.

She had counted the weeks; only three or four to term. If born at that moment, the child would probably survive. *Life is wonderful,* she thought to herself, rubbing her enormous middle.

She was feeling comfortably fatigued and decided she would bring a chair out to the garden and rest among the well-tended shrubs and flowers.

Boswell came running down the path at surprising speed, waving his arm toward her.

"My lady," he said, breathing heavily, "there is an urgent message from Harlixton Hall. A coach is waiting to take you, Lord Westbrook, and Lord Henley there at once."

"What's wrong?" she asked, anxiety causing her muscles to contract around the baby.

"It's Lady Harlixton, my lady. The man—a Mr. Travers . . ."

"Yes, John Travers."

"He says that she is dying, but that she is quite conscious and is asking for you—all of you."

Ravenna bit her lip. They had never gone to see her, for she'd denied their entreaties, as much as she could understand them.

Looking confusedly back from where she'd come, she needed to make a quick decision. She could not run as swift as Boswell could, yet she feared an interruption of the moment between father and son.

The two men saved her the decision, for they appeared out of the wooded area and in plain, though distant, view.

"Garreth!" she called at the top of her lungs. "Father! Come quickly!" Then she waved for them to come.

Possibly thinking it was the baby, they both broke into a strong sprint, with Sandy lagging only seconds behind.

"Ravenna," Garreth shouted. "Are you all right?"

Racing to her side, he grasped her arm.

"I'm fine."

"I apologize, my dear, for upsetting you," Sandy said as he caught up.

"I'm fine, Father. But Lady Philippa . . ." She paused, fearing to go on.

"She's dead?" Garreth whispered.

"Not yet. She is dying, John Travers said, but her mind has cleared. Enough to ask for us." She looked at Sandy intently. "All of us."

Again there was an enigmatic look on Sandy's face, of impending sorrow—

But anticipation as well, and even joy.

Forty-two

The shortest route from Riverside to Harlixton was the path along the Thames. The two properties, though in different counties, adjoined at their back fields, and the distance from house to house was scarcely two miles.

Were this a different day with a different purpose, and were Lady Ravenna Westbrook in a different physical circumstance, she and her company would have made the journey on foot. John Travers, however, awaited them in a coach, and it was hardly the time for a stroll.

Though impatient to get going, Sandy and Garreth cleaned off their blood and dirt and put on fresh clothes before they left. Raven, too, changed her clothes, selecting a maize-colored day dress with matching ribbon around an Empire waist. She still cared not a whit for style, but noted as she checked the mirror that she would have looked quite fashionable in her mother's time.

Quickly she prepared her medical bag for their visit, adding fresh herbs from her garden for the younger Pembrokes.

As she turned to leave, Garreth entered through the adjoining door, his eyes alight with a sort of spiritual frenzy. This was the day that would forever change his life, and he knew it.

"We must hurry," he said, and nodding, Raven grasped her leather bag with both hands, only to have it wrenched away and swung up under his arm.

"I'm quite fit, Garreth."

"No, you're not," he countered. "I would forbid you to come, except that . . . except that I know how much this means to you."

She touched his sleeve. "It means a lot to all of us, particularly Sandy."

John Travers was waiting for them atop the coach, while Sandy paced a small circuit on the drive.

"We must hurry," Sandy said, sounding just like Garreth, and he, too, had a frenzy in his eyes.

"Mistress Ravenna," John Travers called out when he saw her, jumping off his driver's seat to greet her.

"John, how good to see you again!" she cried, and they embraced as best they could.

"And here you are, about to be a mum," he exclaimed, clearly embarrassed by having made physical contact with her obvious condition.

"It's all right, John," she said, hugging him a bit longer than he would have liked. "I'm not a china figure. I won't break."

"Yes, mistress, that is, my lady," he said, feeling even more awkward. "It only be that, well . . ." He looked away, and she saw that he was about to weep.

"Don't worry about me," she soothed him. "I'll be fine. But tell us about Lady Philippa. Has she suddenly taken a turn? Why are we being summoned now?"

" 'Tis the lady herself what sent for you. ''Tis the end now,' she said, 'I can feel it. Soon I'll be able to hold all the grandchildren in my arms. Bring Garreth and Ravenna to me. And Sandy . . .' Beggin' his lordship's pardon," he added, bowing his head so that Raven could see the balding pate. " 'That we may together bless the little-un that is to come.' "

Ravenna had three men to help her into the coach, and she feared there would be another brawl over who would have the privilege of doing so.

Finally, they all participated, each escorting a part of her—hand, shoulder, elbow—up the single stair.

"My dear, will you be quite safe?" Sandy asked anxiously as she leaned back into the velvet seat. "With all the bumps and dips in the road . . ."

"I hope I will be all right," she said as the coach got under way. "In truth, I would not recommend this journey for a woman so near her time."

"What are you saying?" Garreth asked in alarm. "Are you at risk? Will the baby be—"

"We shall survive this," Ravenna said. "For I must go. I love your mother, too."

By coach, the trip to Harlixton would last several hours. Ravenna feigned calm, though in truth, she became worried when she first felt the gentle tightening just under the place where her waist used to be. She breathed rhythmically, hoping the feeling would go away.

It did, but inwardly she dreaded its return.

"We are not far from the Harlixton land now," Garreth commented after an hour's travel. "Father, did you grow up knowing Mother? You were neighbors, after all."

Sandy smiled. "I knew your mother before she knew me. I was fourteen when I first set eyes on her, having lived most of my young life in London before my father inherited Riverside. Philippa was a mere twelve, and at the time, there seemed to be a vast difference in our ages. I first saw her in the village of Taplow during an extremely harsh winter. She was part of a detail of gentlewomen going from cottage to cottage inquiring if anyone needed extra blankets, food, shoes, that sort of thing. My mother was also part of the detail, and I had come to the village to see whether she needed any additional supplies. I am sorry to admit that most of the ladies were cold and discouraged and longed to get away from the reality of the poor. Your mother, the youngest present, took charge of the group, encouraging them, reminding them that there were children without adequate clothing and warmth, and weren't they lucky that their own sons and daughters were safe and snug in their homes. I'll never forget her rallying speech, for she seemed a mother even then. I vowed then and there that I would someday marry her."

"How very much like my wife she must have been," Garreth said, taking Raven's hand and squeezing it.

"Yes, very much so," Sandy agreed. "As you see, we both have the same excellent taste in women."

Ravenna smiled, even though her stomach tightened again, this time with moderate pain in her lower back. Her heart started beating faster. She had delivered hundreds of babies in all kinds of conditions, but she did not relish the prospect of giving birth at Harlixton Hall, whose ghosts still roamed the upper floors.

"Ravenna, are you all right?" Garreth asked, touching her cheek with his free hand. "You looked quite peaked for a moment."

Truth and deception warred within her mind for a moment. Finally she said, "I'm not quite sure, but"—she licked her lips—"I think my time has come."

"Then we must turn back," Sandy replied, preparing to strike the roof of the coach.

"No," she said firmly. "We mustn't. This may be our only chance to see Lady Philippa. The lucid speech John recounted to me suggests that the end is indeed near, as she herself has sensed, that her wits have rallied one last time. And besides, the baby may not arrive for hours yet."

"But what if we're on the road? How shall we manage?" Garreth said in alarm.

Sandy tried to hide his own fear with a smile. "We shall be guided by the physician in our midst. Come on, man, we mustn't wilt in the face of this." Turning to Raven, he said, "I heard stories from the servants about how you performed a cesarean section on the smith's daughter, and that you quelled the pain with tiny needles placed in her forehead."

Raven's body shuddered at the memory. "Some other time . . . I will tell you about it."

"Of course, of course. It was silly of me to bring it up. And yet, I stand in awe of you. Had you had any prior training?"

Again she shuddered, remembering. "Only observations and some experience with general surgery. It was audacity, and the lack of an alternative for the poor girl, that gave me the courage."

"Ravenna," Garreth said, clutching her hand as if he were the one in labor, "what if you need such surgery? Should I mount one of the carriage horses and ride for the doctor?"

Another tightening caught her, and she sat stock-still for a moment.

When it was over, she answered, "If there is an emergency. But I would not have you leave me now."

Sandy rapped on the roof of the coach, then leaned out the window and shouted to Travers to hurry, explaining the situation. In only several heartbeats, it seemed, the coach was accelerating, the bumps and jolts intensifying.

Garreth had a stricken look on his face. "Is it very bad?" he asked.

Ravenna laughed, then patted his hand. "I am about to experience what every mother since the beginning of time has endured. Even yours and mine."

In truth, she was frightened of the pain, but she would not show her fear to the two men, who were growing paler by the moment.

They all sat in awkward silence, each with their concerns. Another tightening came, this time lasting a little longer. Ravenna tried to keep the pain from registering on her face.

"I wish we could sprout wings and fly to our destination," Sandy said, shifting restlessly in his seat.

Garreth said, "I, for one, have no wish to see our child born at Harlixton Hall."

"Nor I," Raven said. "But I guess the baby would have it otherwise."

The tightening eased, and again, for several silent moments, she tried to ignore what was happening to her.

"So the last time you saw Lady Philippa was when Garreth was a baby?" she asked.

Sandy nodded. "Can you forgive me, son? You were right to confront me. I should not have left your mother to that beast."

"I forgive you, Father. I only have to assume that it was also my mother's wish that she not involve your two families in a scandal."

"That would be like her. I hope that your children will inherit a kinder world to live in."

"When did Lord Harlixton die?" Raven asked. "I doubt she would have been at liberty to leave as long as he was alive."

"He died just after Charles was born."

"Ah," she said, "so by then it would have been too late. Perhaps she was aware somehow of what the vicar had done to her. And she wanted to spare you." She gritted her teeth as another tightening, this time more painful, commenced.

Sandy noticed the blanching of her cheeks and said, "Are you sure I shouldn't ride for the doctor? This coach can certainly be pulled by three horses. We'll be waiting for you at Harlixton when you arrive."

She was about to say that wasn't necessary, when she felt a tiny pop from somewhere deep in her body and a gush of water warmed her underclothes.

"Oh," she cried, jumping off the velvet seat.

"What is it?" Garreth asked, reaching out his arm to steady her.

"Are you all right?" Sandy chimed in.

"So far, yes," she said, for she felt no pain at that moment. "But by the time we get to Harlixton Hall, we may have a grandchild to place in Lady Philippa's arms."

Forty-three

"Travers!" Garreth yelled out the window, and John pulled the horses to a stop before any further instruction.

"I'm going for the doctor," Sandy insisted.

"If you must," Raven said, realizing she hadn't actually thought about this aspect of her pregnancy. She didn't trust Longacre and didn't want him near her body. For years she had heard about the native women who delivered themselves, and she'd naively hoped that she could be as they, allowing Nature to be her midwife.

Sandy leapt out of the coach, then after a quick transaction with Travers, the elder servant unharnessed one of the horses.

"Mind these aren't ridin' horses," Travers warned as Sandy mounted up bareback.

Although her father-in-law looked quite comfortable and in control, she called out, "Will you be safe? Without a saddle?"

Holding the horse's mane, he turned his mount around toward her and said, "I did this all the time in my youth. Just like your beloved savages." Then he winked and rode off, like some bold explorer of the New World.

The remaining trio watched him disappear around a turn in the road, all of them using this as a distraction from what lay ahead.

It was Ravenna who broke the silence. "John," she called up to him. "Might you have a blanket?"

"That I do, mistress," he said, relieved that he had an immediate task.

Another pain, this time much stronger, hit her like an inner slap. "Oh," she gasped.

"My darling," Garreth said anxiously. "Are you sure you're all right?"

She could not reply until the pain had peaked, then gradually subsided.

"It may not be long," she said, catching her breath. "I need to get out of this coach, walk around."

"Walk around?" Garreth cried.

"Like the savages." She grinned, feeling wonderful now that the pain had vanished.

Flinging open the door, she jumped to the ground, doing a little dance to show him how fit she was. She noticed once again how clean the air was. The sun was kind and warm. It was a perfect day to be born, and it seemed appropriate somehow to give birth to their child out of doors, away from human society, which had caused them such pain.

How lucky, too, that he would born in the light of day, long after the unquiet spirits of the dark *uht* time had gone.

She surveyed the area, then decided on the spot.

"See those trees? she said, pointing. "In there. That's where our child will take his first breath."

"Are you serious?" Garreth gasped, then said, "Yes, I can see that you are. Here among the beasts and vermin, the future Earl of Henley is to be born."

She laughed at his panicked frown. "This is Berkshire, hardly darkest Africa. And vermin live in cities, far away from this natural place."

John Travers, meanwhile, was beside himself with embarrassment. He looked steadily away from them, trying—like a good servant—to seem invisible.

Garreth jumped out of the coach after his wife, then said, "Can you walk that far?"

"Of course I—" Then another pain hit her, this time with a wallop. She bent over and would have lost her balance were it not for Garreth's strong arms grabbing her and holding her upright.

"I've got you," he soothed.

She tried to breathe as all her native advisers had counseled her. But in the face of such a pain, she found it difficult to concentrate.

When it was over, she said, quite humbled, "We must hurry. I may not be able to walk much longer."

"I have a better solution," Garreth said, then lifted her in his arms, supporting her, her medical bag, and the blanket as he headed in the direction she had pointed.

"It's a wonderful day to be born," she said, allowing herself the luxury of resting against his broad shoulder. "I only hope we can get to Harlixton before . . ." She left the words unspoken.

"Shh, don't think of that now. At least Sandy will get here ahead of us. There will be time for them alone together."

She lifted her head an inch. "And you, Garreth? Don't you want to see her?"

"I'm not sure," he answered truthfully. "Although my mother is someone I must come to terms with, and lay to rest."

Another pain hit Ravenna, tearing at her body like an inner earthquake. She screamed, trying to stay in control and finding herself quite overwhelmed. The contorted face of every woman she had ever delivered flashed before her eyes, and she truly marveled at how they'd pulled through.

"Oh, Gar—" she tried, but could not finish.

"I'm here," he reassured her, seeming calm and in control though she could feel his heart beating rapidly as she lay against his chest.

They walked into a bower of trees, whose lush leaves provided as much privacy as thick velvet bedcurtains. When they were well out of sight of the coach, Garreth said "Here. It looks level and free of twigs and stones." He set her down, then immediately spread out the blanket.

Using the brief respite before the next pain, Ravenna stripped off her petticoat, stockings, and underclothing and set them on one corner of the blanket.

"You're soaking wet!" Garreth cried.

Smiling, she began, "Birth is a messy—" Then the next pain cut her off and she fell to the ground, barely making it to an edge of the blanket. Again Garreth was at her side, holding her around the shoulders as she groaned and clutched at her belly.

The pain peaked like a hot brand between the hips, and she clutched Garreth so hard, her nails dug into his flesh.

"Lie down, Ravenna," he whispered, but she did not move, only shake her head because she could not respond in words.

Then the agony eased, and she was herself again.

"What a difference between theory and practice!" she managed to joke.

"Lie down, Ravenna."

"No," she insisted. "I want to do as the native women. Let me sit up against you. Here, I need your support, like this."

Then she got into a sitting position, feet flat on the ground, legs bent up into tepees, and asked him to get behind her, so that he became as a chair for her to lean against. They became two seated figures, his body matching and enveloping hers. When the next pain came, each arm clutched frantically around one of his knees while his body steadied and supported her. All the while, he murmured comforting words to her.

Gradually she lost touch with the lovely day, the bright

sun, the perfect warm air, and focused only on the pains, which struck and receded with the regularity of the tide.

But through it all, Garreth was there, his body sheltering hers, his words soothing her like a balm.

Between each pain, she closed her eyes and rested limply against his large frame, her arms draped over his knees, her head resting against a thigh. They had experienced ecstasy together, and now they would experience this, the culmination of their love.

The pains soon came closer together, so that she had less time to collapse, less time after each one to put it out of her mind.

Then, to her horror, each contraction waned but the pain persisted.

"Oh, Garreth," Ravenna wailed. "Something must be wrong. It hurts so much."

She felt the tension in his body, saw his fists clenching and unclenching.

"I feel so useless," he complained. "If only I could do something to help you."

"You are helping," she whispered, leaning back into his chest, "I could not do this without you."

When the pain returned, she screamed, full, open-mouthed, without restraint. She wanted to scream, wanted to think only of herself and what she had to do. Her mind flashed to a dream she had had in her youth, of being splayed out on the ground with each limb tied to a stallion. At the downstroke of an executioner's hand, the horses would gallop off in four directions and rip her apart. Yet in the dream, she had held on, had clung to the ropes and kept the horses back. During her struggle, she had screamed, and out of her mouth came fire of pure gold.

"Good God, Ravenna," Garreth cried, but she could not tell him that she was holding on and in control.

The pain subsided—for a moment, at least. Ravenna's mind cleared and she felt great relief, not unlike the heavy, spent feeling after lovemaking. She turned her head back to see her husband, loving him more than she thought possible.

Garreth's face was blanched and drawn.

"It will happen very soon now," she said.

"But what about the doctor?" he asked, horrified.

"Nature is our doctor, it seems."

"What shall I do?" he asked. "Should I—"

"Stay with me, as you are," she reassured him. "When it's time to help, I'll tell you."

But in fact, she was not sure how they would proceed. She was terrified of the thought of his body separating from hers, even to face her and assist in the birth.

"To think," he said, "that every mother has had to endure this to give life to her child."

"Yes, think of it," she said with awe in her voice. "It is no wonder that God spared the favored sex from this burden."

"But this is your work. To help women endure it. Forgive me for ever expecting you to abandon it on my account."

"For you I would give up—" Then another pain racked her body, but instead of screaming, she dug her heels into the ground and pressed. Something inside, some force or demon, demanded release, and she found herself helping it, pushing it out, pushing, clenching her teeth and helping. She had witnessed this in countless other women, and yet she was just as overwhelmed as they were.

"Gar . . . reth," she managed to whisper. "I . . . I need your . . ."

"Yes, my darling, I'll help. I only wish I knew what to do."

Then the demon's grip loosened, and she relaxed. She wanted only to close her eyes and sleep, for a fog had settled over her brain. Yet she had to remain lucid. She needed to tell Garreth what to do.

"Help me . . . lean up against that tree," she said, and

he sprang to his feet, guiding her awkwardly backward until her spine rested against the coarse, hard birthing chair that Nature had provided. She lifted her skirts up and out of the way, wishing she could just toss them aside yet feeling modest even at a time like this. After all, John Travers awaited by the coach.

Garreth was kneeling next to her, looking even paler than several moments before. Ravenna smiled, for he was experiencing what fathers had felt since the beginning of time.

"Oh, Garreth, be brave. Other men have survived the births of their children."

"I could easier survive a battle with the French."

"Now, quickly," she urged him, for she felt the demon rallying again. "Help me. The baby is coming. I want you to help him into the world."

Garreth was breathing deep with apprehension, but she somehow explained to him what to look for, how to assist.

When the next wave came, she pushed, this time feeling more powerful, as if she herself were the demon. She thought of those monsters at the edge of the map, and she hoped her father was watching them from above.

Then again the demon subsided, and she opened her eyes, feeling excited, impatient to hold her baby in her arms.

"Not long now, my love," she said.

But Garreth had a worried look on his face, different from an expectant father's expression.

"Ravenna," he began cautiously.

"It takes a while," she reassured him.

"No, it's not that. It's . . . well, when you were pushing, I saw part of a foot."

Her heart jumped.

"Are you sure?"

He nodded, his face growing even paler. "What am I to do?"

"You're quite sure?" she repeated. "It wasn't a hand, or a bit of cord?"

"No. I'm sure I saw toes."

A footling breech, a dangerous situation for any newborn. She had attended only one such birth, and the baby had no survived.

Yet she had to hide her panic, for Garreth's sake. She explained to him the dangers, the precautions they had to take from then on. Again she talked rapidly, not certain how much time she had before the demon possessed her again.

"Take off your shirt," she said, "and as the baby emerges wrap it securely. You must keep it warm. It's the cold air on its skin that makes a baby take his first breath. He must not breathe until he is safely—oh . . ."

When the next pain came, she pushed with all her remaining strength. Her baby was in danger, she had to help him.

"I see the foot again," Garreth cried.

The demon was whipping her like a mongrel dog, but she gasped out her advice: "Wrap it . . . hold the foot, but don't pull . . . oh . . . oh . . ." And she pushed, pushed kept on pushing, *I have to help,* she thought over and over pushing and pushing, trying to imagine the body moving inching its way toward safety.

"I have it," Garreth said. "It's a perfect foot."

"Don't . . . pull . . ." she gasped.

"No," he said, "but he's moving. The baby's coming. I'm wrapping him up, it's all right, it's going to be fine."

The demon quieted but Ravenna kept on pushing, driven by a demon of the mind. *Help him, help him, help him live.*

"It's happening!" Garreth cried, and she felt as if she were splitting apart, and then came a blessed lightening "I've got the baby! Here it is! But—my God, what do I do now? It's not breathing!" he wailed, holding the wrapped bundle as if it would explode.

"The baby's safe," Raven said, recovering immediately and becoming a midwife again. "Give him to me."

Garreth thrust the bundle into her hands, relief awash on his face.

"There now," she said, wiping off the wrinkled face with the hem of her gown and clearing out the mouth with her finger. Two blue eyes stared at her in wonder, then closed tightly as the new little person let out a testy wail.

"My son," she said, leaning back into the tree as if it were Victoria's throne.

Garreth let out a sigh, then burst into laughter.

"She has her mother's beauty," he said, unwrapping their child only enough so that Raven could see for herself.

"Garreth," she said, already forgetting the pain and the danger they'd just been through. "Is a daughter really what you want? Are you not disappointed?"

"Ravenna, my love," he replied with amusement, "when one grows up in a household of four boys, one longs for the presence of a girl. Not only am I delighted, but my mother will have the daughter of her own flesh that she always longed for."

"Oh, Garreth," she said, her mind fully recovered now, "we must get to her in time."

Ravenna tried to rise but obviously could not. Her work as a midwife was not quite done.

"We'll make it in time," Garreth soothed her. "I sense somehow that she's waiting for us."

"There isn't much left to do," Ravenna said, showing Garreth how to hold the cord, then how to cut it with the clean knife she carried in her medical bag.

"You do this all the time?" he asked, struggling to get the blade through the chewy white tissue.

"Yes," she said, "and I always feel a bit sad about it."

"We must engage in arm wrestling sometime," he said, still working at his task. "I'll wager we're evenly matched."

"There's still more," she said, and instructed him through the final phase of the birth process.

"Whew," he sighed when he had finished, mopping hi brow with the back of his wrist.

For the first time, she noticed, really noticed, that Garrett was naked to the waist. Even in her condition she enjoyed the sight of him, noting the taut muscles coated with a fine mist of sweat even though the day was hardly hot. Garrett watched her eyes moving across his body, and he laughed again.

She was feeling carefree and light-headed, holding her baby and drifting into a strange, almost drugged sleep There was more to do, yet she couldn't concentrate. She forgot about Lady Philippa, about all that had happened and wanted only to rest.

She heard her name, yet she didn't respond, didn't care about responding.

"Ravenna," a faraway voice repeated, then she felt a distant hand shaking her shoulder. "Ravenna," the voice insisted. "Ravenna, something is wrong. You must help me."

Her eyes were closed, and she allowed the fresh air to wash over her. *Nothing is wrong. Everything's perfect.* Her arms relaxed, and a bundle of cloth dropped out of her hands.

"Ravenna!" a voice commanded, and a hand slapped her on the cheek. "Ravenna, what's happening? You have to rouse yourself. You're bleeding quite a bit. Don't you remember—Anne, and the woman in the village—the same thing, I think, is happening to you."

Something that was just said troubled her mind, but what was it? She forgot . . . her mind seemed like cotton wool, all airy nothingness.

"Ravenna, for God's sake!" the faraway voice said, then a bundle was thrust against her cheek. "It's the baby, Ravenna. You must rouse yourself for *her.*"

The bundle was warm and pliable and squirmed against her skin. Then it let out a howl that shocked her even in her stuporous state.

She could only whisper, she felt so tired, but she breathed, "Stand . . ."

"What?" Garreth replied quickly.

"St-stand."

"Stand? What do you mean?"

The bundle was removed from her cheek, and she demonstrated her wishes by trying to get up to her feet.

"St-stand," she repeated.

"Ravenna, what are you doing?" Garreth asked in a panic. "You mustn't stand up!"

"Must . . . stand," she murmured. "Stop the . . ."

She had pushed too hard, it seemed, before her body had been ready to expel the child. The subsequent bleeding was Nature's protest.

Using all her available strength in a single thrust, she pushed her weight into an unsteady upright position, then pitched forward. Garreth caught her, struggling to hold on to both her and the baby.

"I've got you," he said, then tried to sit her back down.

"No," she whispered. "Walk."

"Will that help? What about medicines?"

"Can't—can't remember. Help . . . me stand."

He nodded, then set the now-howling baby down on the blanket.

"Patience," he said to the baby, still holding Raven around the waist.

The baby's howling served like a siren in a dense fog. It kept Raven focused, motivated her. On shaky legs she placed one foot in front of the other. The exercise made her feel somewhat better, though she had already lost a lot of blood. She tried to recall Herr Doktor Grunewald's letter . . . what was his advice? She'd had the letter memorized . . . now she could not dredge up a single word.

She was on her own, without a mentor, guide, father, or any other higher power.

"My . . . bag," she murmured, and Garreth scooped it up in his arm.

"What do you need?" he asked.

"I . . . uh, can't . . . I'll . . . show you," she stuttered, still using the baby's cries as an anchor in a turbulent sea.

Her eyes refused to focus; her head was so heavy, she longed to take it off her neck and lay it on the ground, but she sorted slowly through the packets of herbs until she found the one she sought—trillium, the birthroot.

"Let me help," he urged.

"I . . ." But she couldn't explain what she needed.

Commanding her eyes to work, she put her trembling fingers into the packet and pulled out a pinch between her thumb and forefinger. Her fingers were hardly strong enough to stay together, and the powder fell into the dirt.

"Ravenna," Garreth said sternly. "Let me do it. I saw how you helped my mother."

With his steady hands, he took another pinch of the root, then pressed it between her upper gum and teeth. The taste was vile, and she retched, but Garreth pressed against her gum until he was sure the stuff would not be dislodged.

"Walk," she murmured, and with Garreth's arms around her they walked slowly toward the riverbank. The veil over her mind was getting no worse, and she felt hopeful, almost confident, that the bleeding would stop. Garreth held her so tightly, they proceeded like one slow-moving creature, their bodies molded one into the other. She was dimly aware of a great thirst, her throat was as dry as old leather, and she whispered, "Water," then nodded toward the Thames.

Garreth guided her to the water's edge, then sat her down like a rag doll. Scooping up water in his cupped hands, he held it to her lips. Tentatively she tasted it, shocked yet fortified by the cold. Then she drank more, slurping like a beast until her lips touched Garreth's strong hands.

Gently she kissed each palm, resting her head for a moment between the laced fingers.

"More," she said, feeling stronger, and Garreth scooped ɔ another draft of the chilly drink.

Over and over she asked for more until her eyes were ide and bright, and her stomach felt as it had when she'd ʰallenged her best school chum to a snow-eating contest.

"Oh," she groaned finally, holding her belly, "I'm freez-ɩg inside."

"But safe, I believe."

"Yes. I'm out of danger."

She became a midwife once again and assessed her ʰysical situation. The hemorrhage had stopped. As fate ʳould have it, she *had* saved the life of the "next woman."

That woman was herself.

"Oh, my darling, I was so afraid that . . ." Then Garreth ʳushed her against his chest.

"It's over," she said. "Let's rush to your mother's side. ʰow her little Alexandra."

Again Garreth swept her into his arms, then retraced their ʰeps.

Their daughter was waiting for them, wrapped snugly in ⱼr father's shirt, fast asleep.

Within a dense bush, they hid the birthing blanket and ᵥerything else connected with the birth. They would return ɩd bury the afterbirth, as the savages did, to repay Nature ɔr her gift to them.

"There's some tea left in the coach," Garreth said. "It ʰould refresh you."

"I'm fine now," she replied, holding the baby tightly ᵍainst her chest while Garreth carried her tightly against ɩs.

When Travers saw them, he jumped down off his perch ɩd ran to them, grinning and laughing.

"God has blessed us all," he said.

Forty-four

If ever there were heaven on earth, then Raven experi‐
enced it as the coach rushed willy-nilly toward its destina‐
tion. For even though they were in a race against tw‐
formidable opponents—time and death—inside the coach
she and Garreth and tiny Alexandra were enfolded in a so‐
wrap of laziness and loving.

Her precious daughter, not even an hour old, was nursing
contentedly at her breast, pulling at her with a strength an‐
vigor her father had never matched. Indeed, Raven marvele‐
at the newborn's determination, already holding he‐
mother's finger in a viselike grip.

Draped around her shoulders, Garreth's arm held her pro‐
tectively. They made a comfortable tableau, bodies inter‐
meshed, warmth and breath intermingling.

"Garreth," Ravenna said dreamily, "I have never bee‐
happier in my life."

She couldn't see his face, but she sensed that he wa‐
smiling.

"I have only one more wish," he said.

Turning her face upward, she saw the anxiousness etche‐
amid the happiness.

"I know," she said, finding his hand and squeezing it.

They had crossed the line between Buckinghamshire an‐
Berkshire, and were less than a half hour away. Travers wa‐
handicapped by the loss of one horse, but he was coaxing

he remaining three to run at an impressive speed. If she
hadn't felt so lazy and content, Ravenna would have bitten
her fingernails to the quick out of worry.

The weather continued to be perfect, with just the right
amount of heat and light and freshness in the air. When
she grew old and feeble, Ravenna would tell tales of this
day to her grandchildren—Alexandra's children—while Alexandra would undoubtedly throw up her hands and complain that Gran had told the story at least a hundred times.

Leaning heavily into Garreth's broad chest, she listened
to the strong beating of his heart, the *hush . . . hush* of his
breathing, and marveled at how much they both had gone
through to get to this moment. His mind was like an open
book to her now, the secrets of his heart fully revealed.

"Garreth," Ravenna said, and his arms tightened around
her. Still holding the baby, she turned her lips upward and
sought his in a calm, gentle kiss. The frantic frenzy of new
love seemed quite removed from her; they were old lovers
now, and their kiss was full of memories and shared experiences rather than awe and discovery.

Resting her cheek in the crook of his arm, she let him
stroke her hair, which, of course, was full of twigs and dirt
and wild curls.

"Beautiful," Garreth teased, pulling a leaf from above
her ear.

"If one is a jay in need of a nest."

She felt a cool breeze on her nipple, and saw the baby
had let go and fallen into a contented sleep. Straightening
up, she handed her to Garreth.

"She looks just like you," he said, admiring the tiny face,
whose lips were still nursing on their own at frequent intervals. "What if we save the name 'Alexander' for our
future son, and call this child 'Ravenna'?"

"God forbid," Ravenna said. "She is a child of the day.
Of sunshine and bright light. She'll be spared the darkness
that shrouded our lives, so I'll have no dark names—par-

ticularly my own! Perhaps, instead, we should call her 'Apollonia,' after the sun god."

Garreth wrinkled his nose. "Alexandra is best."

Carefully, Garreth tucked Alexandra into the velvet-lined box that Travers had given them as a temporary cradle. She just fit, and Raven wondered whether it reminded her of her former home. Then, with his arms free again, Garreth wrapped them around his wife so tightly, she could hardly breathe.

"What would I have done without you," he said.

Then he was kissing her like a lover who has almost lost his beloved, raking his hands through her hair then cupping the sides of her face. "I was so afraid . . . I might lose you," he choked. "That I would go back to the emptiness of the time before I met you." He held her face tightly between his hands.

"That time will never come back," she said firmly.

"Never. I promise you."

"Look," she said, pointing out the window of the coach. "We're here."

The coach made a sharp turn off the road and plunged through the Harlixton gates. Seeing the familiar wrought iron, Raven felt all the apprehension that her happiness had held at bay. Would they find Lady Philippa waiting for them, or a corpse?

"I wonder if Sandy returned with the doctor," she said, feeling already well removed from the birth she'd just experienced.

"Perhaps he used it as an excuse, so we could be alone."

"I did wonder why he rode off like that."

"Undoubtedly he wanted to have a better chance at seeing my mother alive, and he could tell her that we were on our way."

"Oh, Garreth," she said, taking his hand. "Can you imagine what it was like for them? It was as if you had been taken from me, and I had been forced to marry—Cholly Makepiece."

"Don't dwell on what cannot be changed," he said, though he was visibly shaken at the thought.

Their coach was accelerating, as was the bumpiness of the ride. John Travers obviously shared their impatience. If they arrived too late, he would blame himself. The horses were covered with sweat and lather, and Raven hoped Rex was still around, for he had a special way with tired animals.

They were approaching the classical fountain. One major turn in the road and they would see the big house.

"We're almost there," Ravenna said excitedly.

But they were traveling too fast to make the turn safely. And with the odd number of horses, they were listing to one side. John tried to slow down as they rounded the turn, but the horses had grown clumsy in their overheated condition. The lead horse, without his partner beside him to share the load, lost his footing.

"Oh, God!" Ravenna screamed, grabbing the baby's box as they lurched sideways, then back roughly, then rocked and shook until they came to a sloppy halt. The lead horse had managed to remain upright, but he was out of control, jerking and struggling with his harness.

"There, there now," John Travers soothed him, jumping down and freeing the horse, who continued to twitch and shiver. "Are you all right, mistress?" he shouted back.

"We are fine. Not a scratch. But will the horse be all right?" she called out the window.

"He'll be fit soon enough," John replied, "though I'm that sorry I can't take you to the door. I dare not force him to pull us any longer."

Picking up the sleeping Alexandra and cradling her in her arms, Ravenna felt a single moment of respite. After all, they were safe.

"Can you walk?" Garreth asked, and after she nodded, he pushed open the door and helped her to the ground.

"I only wish I could run," she said.

"You mustn't try, but I can. I'll send Frederick back with the gig."

"There's no need, Garreth. By the time the gig is prepared and sent to me, I'll be at the front door."

"But—"

"Run," she insisted. "Run to her. You must see your mother alive even if I don't. And . . ." Ravenna hesitated, hugging Alexandra one more time before handing her to Garreth. Although she longed for Philippa to cradle the baby in her own withered arms, Ravenna felt a new mother's instinct to keep her infant close.

Garreth secured Alexandra in the crook of his arm, then dashed off. "I love you!" he shouted as he sprinted toward the house. It was only after he had left her side that Ravenna realized how odd he would seem bursting through the front door naked to the waist and holding a newborn.

The roses were a riot of color on either side of the drive. Seeing them made Ravenna feel teary, since she was in the postpartum time, when everything is monstrously sentimental. She felt a strange kinship with them. The blossoms were the plants' offspring; like them, she had given birth.

She quickened her pace, feeling an urgent need to cradle her head against Philippa's chest, to tell her that she now knew what Philippa knew, that she, Ravenna, was now also a mother.

Please God . . .

Raven prayed that Garreth would get to his mother in time, so she could see and bless her granddaughter, who already carried the seeds of her own babies deep within her tiny body.

She broke into an uncomfortable trot, while her body cried out against it so soon after childbirth. She had lost a lot of blood, and was feeling faint—as on her first journey to Harlixton Hall—but she could heal tomorrow. Today, she was in a race against Death himself.

Please, please, stay alive, my lady, Ravenna prayed, forcing her tired chest to take in more air. *I'm coming to receive
your blessing, too.*

Her lungs and throat were already raw from the effort of
giving birth, and as she pushed air into them anyway, her
heart began fluttering. "Not *now,*" she said aloud, like an
angry governess. She would not slow down, but would trust
her heart to keep beating, as it always had in the past.

She was breathing heavily, resisting dizziness, when her
heart lost all its rhythm. She couldn't slow down, arguing
with herself that she had survived every other cardiac event
and would certainly live through this one.

She was halfway to the house, rubbing the center of her
chest, groaning in spite of herself, when she tripped over
a stone and crashed to the ground.

Garreth had disappeared through the front door. Yet perhaps he would dispatch the strongest footman to return and
carry her.

She rested her skinned cheek against the paving stones,
wanting only her soft bed, a fresh gown, clean sheets. She
couldn't run anymore.

Garreth reappeared through the door, and seeing her, he
bolted back down the drive, sprinting like a champion. She
had just time to admire his form, the sweat-moistened muscles, when he reached her and scooped her into his arms.

She expected a reprimand, but he said, "She's still alive.
And able to speak."

"Oh, thank God."

"She's quite lucid, in fact . . . the way I remember her
long ago." He turned around on his heel and dashed back
to the house. "Sandy is with her. And the love is still there
between them."

Wyngate and Frederick were waiting for them just inside
the door. The butler, always thoughtful, was holding a shirt
for Garreth and a long summer cloak for Ravenna.

"Thank you, Wyngate," Garreth called, grabbing the clothing with his teeth as he passed by.

"Lady Westbrook," Wyngate called out as they passed, "how good it is to see you again."

"Thank you, Wyngate, it is good to see you. And thank you for the cloak," she said. She had not relished the thought of her blood-soaked garment on public display.

"May I offer you my heartiest—"

But they were out of earshot as he finished giving her his felicitations on the birth of their daughter.

The furnishings were the same in the great hall—the suits of armor, the Turkish rugs, the massive sofa and chairs. Yet the mood in the house was fundamentally different—a cheeriness had somehow replaced the sense of doom.

"Ravenna!" a voice squealed, then she looked up and saw Justine waving from the top of the stairs.

"Justine!" she shouted happily as Garreth carried her up the stairs, an ironic replay of the first time he had done so—after her dramatic fall.

When they reached the second floor, she said, "Put me down, Garreth," but he dashed past Justine toward the end of the hall, where Lady Philippa had been installed in her old suite of rooms overlooking the Thames.

"I'll speak to you at tea, Ravenna!" Justine's voice called out from behind, though she was following them down the hall. "I'm with child, thanks to you!"

"Justine!" Raven shouted back in utter delight. Looking at Garreth, she asked, "Did you know?"

"No, of course not," he replied, panting. "But I've heard that Charles is slowly regaining his mind because of the things you've given him."

"Oh, I'm so glad."

"Can you cure him?"

She bit her lip. "I don't know. I'm giving them all things the native Indians use to treat infections—antimicrobial extracts of certain fungi, mushrooms, and the like. Peg seems

much improved by them. She may even live out a normal
life span, provided she never returns to the squalor of the
city."

"But Charles . . ."

"Garreth, he may never regain his full sanity—his is the
worst case I've seen. I will run more experiments, with
animals first."

"In your new clinic and laboratory?"

She nodded as Garreth reached his mother's door. "Yes,
my new laboratory. Now, please put me down."

This time he obliged her and set her on her feet. Justine
caught up with them and squeezed Ravenna's shoulder affectionately. The stillness of the hall was unnerving. Not a
sound came through the door. Had death silenced the room's
occupant?

Garreth draped the cloak around Ravenna's shoulders,
then quickly covered himself with the shirt.

Standing thus poised in front of the door in a full-length
cloak, her imposing husband at her side, Raven felt like the
monarch herself about to make a royal entrance.

Garreth opened the door. For a moment, they stood in
the frame, studying the interior of the room.

Lady Philippa was sitting in bed, propped up by several
enormous pillows. In her lap rested her granddaughter.
Sandy, her first and only love, was sitting next to her, one
leg draped casually over the edge of the bed. Together they
were admiring the new baby, displaying the relaxed intimacy of a couple who had spent a half-century together
and had a decade or two left.

"You see, my love, she has your beauty," Sandy said,
then he stroked Lady Philippa's mummified cheek as if she
were in the prime of her youth.

"But she has your firm jaw, your coloring," she replied
in a voice that sounded almost girlish.

Sandy bent over and kissed his lady's forehead. "She has

the best of you and the best of me, because Garreth is her father."

"And Ravenna her mother."

Raven's breath caught at those words, for Lady Philippa had not yet noticed her, and thus had spoken from her heart.

"Mother," Raven called unashamedly, and approached the bed.

The dying woman looked up. Her eyes were clear and free of madness.

"Daughter," she greeted her lovingly, raising her arm as high as she could, which was only several inches, in a gesture of welcome.

Sandy picked up the baby and cradled her in his arms as if he had done so for a pack of children. Ravenna sat down close to her mother-in-law on the other side of the bed, resting her head against the frail chest. Lady Philippa was all sticks and parchment; two femurs and a pelvic bone served as her lap, two empty sacks against a rib cage were her breasts. But at that moment, she was more beautiful to Raven than the Madonna.

Stroking Ravenna's hair with a trembling clawed stick that was once her arm, Lady Philippa whispered, "You will always be my daughter."

"And you will be my mother, always," Ravenna choked out.

A deeper voice from across the room called out, "Shall we proceed, my lord?"

Ravenna looked up and noticed a man of the cloth, a young man with goodness and zeal apparent on his face.

Sandy arose, carefully placed the baby in a maid's arms, then replied, "Yes." Reaching over and touching Ravenna's shoulder, he said, "I've waited a long time for this moment. Will you and Garreth serve as our witnesses?"

She was too startled to answer, but Garreth stepped forward and said, "Of course." Walking around the bed to

where Ravenna sat, he took her hands and gently lifted her
o her feet.

Sandy folded the counterpane back and started to pick
up his intended bride.

Lady Philippa surprised everyone by motioning him away
and standing up unaided, albeit on unsteady legs.

"My darling," Sandy protested, "you mustn't try—"

"But I must," she insisted. "I've waited for a long time,
oo."

She was dressed in a clean white robe with her white
hair well brushed and lying against her shoulders like a
wedding veil. She looked part-bride, part-angel.

Sandy took her hand with one of his, and with the other
he held her firmly around the waist.

The young vicar approached, motioning that Garreth and
Ravenna stand on either side of them.

"Come, everyone," he exclaimed, "gather 'round the
bride and groom. Marriage is a happy event, to be shared
with loved ones."

The spectators in the room had grown to include most
of the staff, Justine, Clarity, Heath, St. Clair, and even Charles, whose crimes against Ravenna had long since been forgiven. All of them moved toward the bed.

The vicar opened his book and began reciting the familiar
service:

*Dearly beloved, we are gathered together here in the
sight of God, and in the face of this company, to join this
man and this woman in holy Matrimony; which is an honorable state, instituted of God, signifying unto us the mys-
tical union . . .*

Although Garreth and Ravenna had been positioned on
either side of his parents, Garreth's arm snaked out behind
them and he pulled Ravenna to him. She squeezed his hand
as they settled directly behind the older couple. These were,
of course, the same marriage vows that they had spoken,
yet she was hearing them as if for the first time.

Alexander George, wilt thou have this woman to thy wedded wife . . . Sandy beamed at Philippa. *Wilt thou love her, comfort her, honor, and keep her, in sickness and in health; and forsaking all others, keep thee only unto her, so long as ye both shall live?*

I will, replied Sandy.

I will, whispered Garreth into Ravenna's ear, as if giving himself to her, fully, without impediment, for the first time.

Philippa Mary, wilt thou have this man to thy wedded husband, to live together after God's ordinance in the holy estate of Matrimony? Wilt thou love him, comfort him, honor, and keep him, in sickness and in health; and forsaking all others, keep only unto him, so long as ye both shall live?

I will, Lady Philippa said with a voice as strong as a maiden's.

I will, Ravena whispered to Garreth.

Who giveth this woman to be married to this man? the vicar asked.

There was an awkward moment, and a shuffling of feet. Then Garreth released his wife and stepped forward. Taking Lady Philippa's right hand, he said, "I do," and gave his mother to the man she loved.

The vicar motioned for the bride and groom to kneel. There was another awkward moment as a maid pulled a pillow from the bed and Sandy helped Lady Philippa to her knees.

I, Alexander George, take thee, Philippa Mary . . . the vicar said, leading Sandy through his vow.

I, Garreth Daniel, take thee, Ravenna, Garreth whispered when he returned to her side. Then he spoke no more, as they turned their full attention to Sandy.

I, Alexander George, take thee, Philippa Mary, to my wedded wife . . .

A loud sniffle broke the silence of the audience. Without looking, Ravenna could tell that it was poor, good-hearted Manda, who broke down with little provocation.

. . . to love and to cherish, till death do us part . . .

Then Philippa stated her vows, her eyes shining with the same joy that illuminated Sandy's.

"Is there a ring?" the young man whispered, looking toward the earl with some embarrassment.

Instinctively, Ravenna grasped her own ring and pulled it off her finger. But Sandy shook his head, then reached into his pocket and brought out an exquisite wedding band of gold, diamonds, and tiny rubies.

"I've waited so long," he murmured so that only his bride and Garreth and Ravenna could hear.

Lovingly, he slipped the ring upon Philippa's finger, which was all bone and knuckle, then held it in place with his own burly hand.

With this ring I thee wed, Sandy said before the vicar could prompt him.

Garreth took Ravenna's ring out of her hand and slipped it back on her finger. *With this ring, I thee wed,* he whispered, so that only she could hear.

With shaking fingers, Lady Philippa reached into the pocket of her gown and pulled out a simple gold band.

With this ring, I thee wed, she said in a clear voice, startling the young vicar as she struggled to guide it over Sandy's thick flesh.

"Let us pray," the vicar stated after Sandy had finally pushed the ring over his own knuckle.

They all repeated the Lord's Prayer, then the vicar joined the right hands of the newlyweds, raising them up for all to see.

Those whom God hath joined together, let no man put asunder, he concluded. Then addressing the congregation, he announced, "Honored guests, I present to you the Earl and Countess of Henley." Then more softly, "My lord, you may kiss your bride."

Taking Philippa in his arms with all the wonder of a young man, Sandy lowered his lips and kissed her. She clung to him, her eyes closed, her breathing heavy and ragged. But as the kiss deepened, she relaxed, her breathing becoming regular, her arms resting lightly around her husband's neck.

There was not a sound among the guests. Even the baby was quiet, sleeping contentedly in the maid's young arms. Sandy and his wife were locked in a private embrace. Perhaps all present had fallen under the same spell, but later many of them reported the same impossible event—that before their eyes, Lady Philippa began to transform. The lines in her face became smooth, her hair took on a brilliant shine, her arms seemed fleshed out and young again. The power of Sandy's love had produced a momentary miracle. Ravenna blinked her eyes and stared in disbelief, then could tell by the shuffling noises and wide eyes that everyone in the room was seeing the same thing.

Sandy's love was healing his lady. Sandy's love had made her beautiful again.

Then Lady Philippa's body grew very still. Again everyone watched as Philippa's arms fell limply from her husband's neck, her head sagging to one side.

"Dear God—" Sandy whispered, clutching Philippa's lifeless form to his chest.

Her head fell back, and they could see once more the mummy's face, the mask of death she'd worn for so many years.

His breath catching on a sob, Sandy lifted the frail body into his arms and placed it on the bed. Then he sat down heavily beside his bride, a dazed look on his face.

Garreth took Ravenna's hand and escorted her out of the room. Again they seemed like the Queen and consort leading a procession, for everyone else filed out behind them. Finally Dr. Longacre, who had presumably been summoned to attend Alexandra's birth, closed the door on the grieving widower. He gave Ravenna a brief scowl as he hurried toward the stairs.

When everyone had left, Garreth pulled his wife into his arms and crushed her lips with his own.

"I'm free, Ravenna," he murmured. "Free to love you . . . as much as he loved her."

Epilogue

Henley on Thames, April 1848

"Hold still, now, my lady," Mr. James Goodfellow, the portrait painter, called out as Ravenna struggled to keep Alexandra from sliding down her spine and on to the floor. "I've almost got it. Another moment, please."

"Mummy, I want to ride horsey," the little voice behind Raven's back complained. "This is no fun."

"We shall ride horsey in a minute," she soothed her daughter, somewhat miffed that Alexandra was not seeing this miraculous event in the same light as she did.

"But this is no fun!" Alexandra insisted. "Please, I want to come down." Then she tried more resolutely to wriggle from her mother's grasp.

"Do you have it yet, Mr. Goodfellow?" Ravenna asked anxiously.

"Hold still just another moment, my young lady," he said politely.

"I shan't!" Alexandra wailed.

"Here now, what's all this?" a deep voice called out as Garreth walked into the studio.

"Daddy!" Alexandra squealed, then pushed herself out of Ravenna's grasp and jumped to the floor, finding her feet with the agility of a cat and scampering into his outstretched arms.

With a good-natured frown, Ravenna said, "She does not want to ride upon her mother's back."

"No, Daddy," Alexandra piped up. "I want to ride on your back. Play horsey, Daddy! Please, Daddy, please?"

"Well, now, that depends upon Mr. Goodfellow."

"My Lord, I would prefer a more cooperative subject, but I have enough for today."

"Hurrah!" cried Alexandra as Garreth got down on all fours and shook his straight black hair like a gorgeous mane.

"Go away, Mummy," Alexandra called as she mounted her steed.

"Now Alexandra . . ." Garreth reproved her. "You must address your mother with courtesy. Apologize at once."

Alexandra glanced at her mother with the mutinous look Ravenna remembered so well in Charles. "All right . . . I'm sorry," the girl said quickly, then turned her face and said, "Go, Daddy. Go fast and faster!"

Ravenna smiled, feeling indulgent toward her headstrong almost-three-year-old, who was so convinced of her own charms.

"Have a good ride," she called. "Remember, you must be washed and dressed in an hour. Andrew and little Philippa are coming."

"Go away, Mummy," Alexandra commanded her.

"Alexandra . . ." Garreth warned.

"It's all right," Ravenna said. "I have to nurse the baby."

Alexandra considers herself the victor, Raven mused as she walked down the hall. After all, her rival had retreated. Her father was hers alone.

Little did she know that another prize of great value awaited her mother—four-month-old Garreth Daniel Gordon, II, heir apparent to the Viscount Westbrook, heir to the Earldom of Henley.

Walking to the nursery on the third floor, Ravenna marveled at how much like her own father Alexandra was prov-

ing to be, the stubbornness, the quick wit—the absolute
belief in her own rightness. When a new nursery maid
painted a solution of mustard on Alexandra's thumb to dis-
courage her from sucking, her little spitfire promptly licked
it off and continued her feast. The maid soon left of her
own accord, and Raven wished her father could have been
there to see his granddaughter prevail.

But little Garreth—he took after his much-missed grandmother. He was the essence of patience itself. When Alexandra would throw herself into his cradle, rocking with a
fury that threatened to split the bed in two, he'd always
remain calm, smiling as Ravenna pried his sister off him.

No harm done, Garreth would say with his dark, trusting
eyes. *I'm still here.*

Upon entering the sunny nursery, Ravenna smiled at the
new nursery maid, who jumped to her feet and curtsied.

"Is he awake?" Ravenna asked.

"No, ma'am, but he be sleeping lightly."

Knowing her lady's habits, the maid curtsied again, then
left the room.

Ravenna approached the cradle as if it were an altar, feeling the same awe as when she'd first held him in her arms.

The best of you and the best of me.

Like his sister, little Garreth was born in the full light
of the noonday sun, free of night spirits, free of the demons
that had plagued his parents, and that to her was more valu-
able than the titles he would inherit.

"Good afternoon, my dearest," she whispered, then stood
and admired him, asleep on his soft tummy, a kernel of the
man he would become.

When she could resist her son no longer, Ravenna carefully lifted the little body from his cot. He came up without
moving a muscle, his face still turned to the side, flat as a
scone as it is lifted off a baking sheet.

Holding him against her left shoulder, Raven kissed his

cheek, his tiny ears, the downy dark hair on his head. He stirred only enough to mold himself to her body.

Her rocker was set by the western windows, so she could watch the Thames while she nursed. Sometimes Garreth would join her, standing at her side and admiring the vigor with which his son attacked her.

"You're no match for this one either," Ravenna often teased her husband.

Settling herself in the rocker, she positioned little Garreth against her breast. Even half asleep, he knew what to do. Drawing the nipple into his mouth, he began to suckle using light, rapid lip movements, which abruptly changed to a slower, more regular pulsating rhythm as the milk began to flow.

These were some of the most sensual moments of Raven's life—feeling the prickly-tingly sensation of milk being drawn from her body; enjoying the feather touch of baby fingers as they explored her flesh, the hardy caress of newborn lips; listening to the unashamed, rhythmic, smacking sighs of infant ecstasy. Garreth's downy head rested perfectly in the crook of her arm; his clear baby skin was smooth as alabaster. At times, when he was fully awake, he'd stare into her eyes as he nursed, with a look full of worship and wonder and infinite trust. Perhaps that was what he saw reflected in her own eyes.

Their joining was as primal and profound as lovemaking. She loved little Garreth more than life itself—would die or kill for him. It was an awesome feeling, the raw, savage mother love stirring in her breast.

In a blink of time's eye, her son would be a man, feeling the same fierce passion for his own children. She had to savor these moments because they were so fleeting.

The door to the nursery opened, and the elder Garreth entered.

"Ah," he said, "it is so restful in here."

"Alexandra, I take it, has worn you out."

"Absolutely," he said, pretending to rub a sweat-suffused brow. "I sent her off with poor William for a game of hide and go seek in the garden."

"Alas, poor William."

"I reminded her that her cousins were due this afternoon, but she wrinkled her nose and said that Andrew was always falling down and hurting himself."

"Oh, Garreth," Ravenna sighed. "I fear he will not live to manhood. What apparently has worked for Charles has failed for his son. I wish I knew more, that we lived in a future time when such diseases could be cured by simple antimicrobials. My father theorized that—"

"No more of your father, my love. We have our own lives to live now, our own discoveries to make."

He placed his hand on her shoulder, and together they watched their future contentedly nursing in her arms.

"These past years have been so wonderful, like a miraculous dream." She looked up into Garreth's face and enjoyed once more the guise of a freed spirit. He could never again look like the grave, burdened man she married. Grinning, she added, "Even Sandy is determined to make up for all the lost years. He's casting another bid for Miss Nightingale. After all, now that your status as his heir has been assured, there is nothing standing in the way of his starting another family."

Garreth's face clouded for a moment. "Children? At his age?"

"And why not? He's in his prime as far as Nature is concerned."

"But . . would *you* mind, Ravenna? I mean, having another woman's children in your household?"

She laughed at the furrow in his brow. "Garreth, I recall your statement of delight at Alexandra's birth, and I will respond in kind: When one is an only child, as I was, one longs for a house full of children. And so I say: the more, the merrier! Perhaps Miss Nightingale and I can compare the sags in our bellies as the years pass."

"I should be honored to call her my stepmother, sags and all. But tell me, has she received Sandy even once yet? Does she not consider him an old goat?"

"I have no idea. She has come to address the Royal Academy. He'll be in London these several days attending the proceedings."

"The Royal Academy? By what right . . . did you contact your father's friends?"

"Not at all. It seems that Sandy took his degree in medicine at Cambridge."

"In medicine? Why did he not speak of it?"

"He tried, I recall, several times, when we first came to live with him, but he is embarrassed about it."

"Embarrassed?"

"Because I am the daughter of Sir Richmond Marisse. And while my father went on to become prominent in his field, Sandy returned to what he called his life of indolence."

Garreth scoffed. "It was hardly that. Funding schools, orphanages, and hospitals; championing reforms and human rights issues in the House of Lords—a life of indolence indeed! Though I wonder why he never became a surgeon, if that is what he wanted."

"Perhaps he will, for he is hardly in his dotage. He said that when he returned to find your mother married and miserable, something broke in him. Without the support of the woman he so loved, deprived of the son he had sired, he brooded for much of his young manhood."

Gently Garreth brought her hand to his lips and kissed the fingers, savoring each as if it were a delicate sweet.

"I can understand that. Without you, without our children, I could not go on."

"Now, after all that has happened, it seems he is ready to live fully once more, maybe even to love again."

"Miss Nightingale is a fool to refuse him, particularly since he can only further her cause."

"One of the reasons for his trip, besides seeing Miss Nightingale, of course, is to hire several aspiring young surgeons who may welcome his support in exchange for some tutoring. Someday he hopes to turn our clinic into a hospital for the entire county, where he and I can work together."

"Together, is it? And what shall I do? Serve as horse for our willful daughter?"

"Why, you can continue the work of the current Earl of Henley—funding schools, orphanages, and other hospitals."

"It is work I would most enjoy. But come now, there is work of another sort that I have in mind." Then he called out, "Maggie, please come and attend to Master Garreth."

The young redhead appeared from her room, curtsying and blushing since the presence of both lord and lady always overwhelmed her.

"Yes, my lord, right away, my lord," she said, lifting little Garreth out of his arms and cradling him in her own.

Taking Ravenna's hand, Garreth led her out of the room and down to their own suite.

"This is wicked in the middle of the day," she teased him. "I have work to do."

"What finer work is there than to . . . make another child."

She smiled broadly, for she could only agree with him on that issue.

She began to unbutton her bodice, but he said, "Here, let me do it. Let me be your young buck instead of your tired old bed partner."

"Tired? Old?" She laughed as he took her in his arms. "You will never grow old."

"Nor you," said Garreth. "I think your mother showed us that—that love can defeat any adversary, even the ravages of time."

Garreth pressed his lips to hers, sharing his breath, his warmth, the very essence of himself with her.

"Till death us do part," he whispered.

"And beyond," she said. "For even after we're gone, our children will remember . . . how much we loved each other."

PASSIONATE ROMANCE
FROM BETINA KRAHN!

HIDDEN FIRES   (0-8217-4953-6, $4.99

LOVE'S BRAZEN FIRE   (0-8217-5691-5, $5.99

MIDNIGHT MAGIC   (0-8217-4994-3, $4.99

PASSION'S RANSOM   (0-8217-5130-1, $5.99

REBEL PASSION   (0-8217-5526-9, $5.99

ROMANCE FROM JANELLE TAYLOR